A Preacher's
Passion

Also by Lutishia Lovely

Heaven Forbid
Reverend Feelgood
Heaven Right Here
Sex in the Sanctuary
Love Like Hallelujah

Published by Dafina Books

A Preacher's Passion

Lutishia Lovely

Kensington Publishing Corp.
http://www.kensingtonbooks.com

DAFINA BOOKS are published by

Kensington Publishing Corp.
119 West 40th Street
New York, NY 10018

All Kensington Titles, Imprints and Distributed Lines are
available at special quantity discounts for bulk purchases
for sales promotions, premiums, fund-raising, and educa-
tional or institutional use. Special book excerpts or cus-
tomized printings can also be created to fit specific
needs. For details, write or phone the office of the Kensington special sales manager: Kensington Publishing
Corp., 119 West 40th Street, New York, NY 10018, attn:
Special Sales Department, Phone: 1-800-221-2647.

Dafina and the Dafina logo Reg. U.S. Pat. & TM Off.

ISBN-13: 978-0-7582-2942-7
ISBN-10: 0-7582-2942-9

First trade paperback printing: January 2009
First mass market printing: January 2011

10 9 8 7 6 5 4 3 2 1

Printed in the United States of America

ACKNOWLEDGING MY READERS

It was more than five years ago when the idea for this series came to me. I had recently finished another project and was sitting in front of my computer, looking at a blank screen.

"What should I work on next?" I asked God.

"*Sex in the Sanctuary*—and it's a book, not a play," came the answer.

Spirit had clarified this because everything I'd written up to that point had been in theatrical form. The idea of writing a full-length novel hadn't crossed my mind. Until now.

The story line came quickly: Two best friends who happen to be pastors' wives, one marriage great, the other in trouble. My first thought: I loved it, both the title and the story—the whole of which I knew couldn't possibly be told in a single novel. My second thought: I couldn't possibly write it! I grew up in church, a preacher's kid. I know church folk, and I knew that to write the story in the way it was coming to me—with unchecked emotion and sexuality—would be controversial. A book that contains scriptures *and* explicit sex? In the same chapter, sometimes on the same page? Uh, no, I don't think so.

As I began typing, I immediately began censoring the character voices. The more I did this, however, the more I felt a pull to *not* do it. I needed to write the story the way I heard it, to let these characters, these voices, these scenes and situations live on the page. Once I got past the fear and embraced this authenticity, the stories flowed, the characters came alive. It wasn't hard to capture them, as many of the voices, situations, and circumstances on the pages were not uncommon to those I experienced or heard about during a lifetime of intimate, behind-the-scene involvement with many types of churches and church members: from Baptist to charismatic, west coast to east coast, fifty-member congregations to fifteen thousand–member mega-churches. So I wrote what flowed.

Once these stories were finished and published, that's where you, the reader, came in. You embraced these characters, recognized people you knew, and sometimes yourselves, on these pages. You wrote me and shared experiences and situations that mirrored some of those described in the story lines.

"Everybody's doing it, but nobody's talking about it," is a comment I hear and read often. That was my experience growing up in church, silence on all things sexual, and why I'd initially been uncomfortable writing about sex (both its blessing and its curse) and related topics of masturbation, adultery, homosexuality, molestation, etc. But research and various statistics underscored the need for us to be able to talk openly, honestly (and yes, explicitly) about sex within a religious setting; not within the church's four walls per se, but definitely within the pages of a novel! And many, many of you agree.

"Thanks for keeping it real," is another common comment. And now, I take this time to thank you. Thank you for embracing these characters and this series: *Sex in the Sanctuary, Love Like Hallelujah,* and now, *A Preacher's Passion.* Thank you for joining me in this interesting, nontraditional dialogue. Thank you for your opinionated e-mails and passionate responses to the work. Thank you for your encouraging words, especially the pastors' wives who have written. Your encouragement is especially rewarding, because y'all know the real deal. Thank you so much for reading each book and then eagerly looking forward to the next one. I always say this about the value of readers . . . we writers are nothing without you! So while these words seem highly inadequate, they are sincere, heartfelt, and uttered with *agape* love . . . thank you.

1

Is That You?

People say Passion was fast from the womb. That when she heard men talking, she'd make a motion in her mother's belly that felt like a tickle. When she heard women, her mother got gas. Even before Passion was born, she decided that men were to be loved; women, tolerated.

She had one real girlfriend growing up, Robin Cook. They got along like two peas in a pod from the moment they met at Martin Luther King Jr. Elementary School in Atlanta, Georgia. For one, they were big tomboys, bigger than most girls their age. For another, they both hated their female classmates and constantly baked up evil schemes to right some imagined wrong done to them. Whether it was putting cayenne pepper in a girl's food, glue on her seat, or beating somebody up at recess, they were always getting into trouble, and usually together. But Passion and her family moved from Georgia to California when she was fifteen years old. She hadn't seen Robin since.

Passion sat in her living room, flipping through an *Essence* magazine and watching the MLM channel, a new, progressive, Black-owned network that was finally giving BET some competition. A minister, Derrick Montgomery, was speaking at a convention hosted by a group called Total Truth. Passion decided he looked as good on TV as he did in person. *That man is fine forever,* she thought, as she turned up the volume.

Passion wasn't a member of Montgomery's church, Kingdom Citizens' Christian Center, but the church she belonged to, Logos Word Interdenominational, fellowshipped with KCCC often. Passion loved Pastor Montgomery's fiery style, not to mention the way his body blessed a designer suit. She could always expect a good word plus some men worth watching when she visited Kingdom Citizens, and was one of many who'd visualized Pastor Montgomery sans suit or wife. Either him or Darius Crenshaw, KCCC's hot minister of music whose latest hit, "Possible," had spent months at the top of both gospel and secular charts. Pastor Montgomery was fine, but Darius could sing, play several instruments, *and* looked like "thank you, Jesus." Add the fact that he was single, and as far as she knew, available, and he was the obvious choice.

For all her salacious wonderings, Passion couldn't see herself actually sleeping with Pastor Derrick or anybody else's husband. She admired Pastor Montgomery's wife, Vivian, who was good friends with her first lady, Carla Lee. Even after news broke that Pastor Montgomery had an older son from a previous relationship, a son he supposedly knew nothing about until two years ago, his and Vivian's marriage remained strong. Word had it that the boy was even living with them now and playing basketball at UCLA. No, Passion would never act out inappropriately with Pastor Derrick. Well, other than the lusting in her heart for which she was already guilty. She'd probably not send love notes or nude pics to Darius Crenshaw either. But he was definitely daydream material.

An hour after the television program went off, Passion pulled into her favorite strip mall. It housed an inexpensive clothing shop, video store, nail salon, Chinese food restaurant, and the reason for her trip, Gold's Pawn Shop. Passion loved this store. Pawning had kept her lights, gas, or phone on many times right after her divorce, when she'd been struggling to raise her newborn daughter. She'd pawn gold, diamonds, anything she could to make it to payday. She prided herself on the fact that she always bought back her stuff and in the process would sometimes find a couple bargains, enough to where she continued to make regular visits even after her finances improved.

She stepped inside the store. As she'd expected for the middle of the day, it was quiet. Lin, the Korean owner, was behind the counter, helping his one, lone customer.

"Hey, Lin," Passion said cheerfully.

"Hey, Passion," Lin said. "What you buy today? I got tennis bracelet you like—just came yesterday."

"How much you want for it?" Passion asked. "I might be interested if you give me a good deal."

"I give you very good deal," Lin said. He unlocked the showcase and pulled out a bracelet set with tiny diamonds, effectively shown off in a black, faux-velvet case.

"This is nice," Passion said. She put it on her arm, turned it this way and that.

The other shopper, a woman, looked at the bracelet as well.

"It's pretty, huh?" Passion said to her, being friendly. "You think it's worth two hundred dollars?" That's the deal Lin said he'd give to Passion, because "she good customer."

The woman didn't answer, just stared. Passion looked up and stared back. The face was familiar. Then it dawned on her.

"Robin? Robin Cook? Girl, is that you?"

Robin was shocked, her response subdued. "Passion Perkins?"

Both women were incredulous. It had been twenty years.

"What on earth are you doing in LA?" Passion exclaimed, stepping forward to grab her former best friend in a bear hug. As she did so, she felt something cold, hard, pressing against her stomach. She pulled back, looked down. "And why are you buying a gun?"

Robin looked at Passion, then down at the gun, almost as if she didn't know how it had gotten in her hand.

"I, well, uh, girl, it's good to see you!" Robin placed the gun on the counter and hugged Passion with fervor. This had been her best friend back in the day. She was genuinely glad to see her again, but still couldn't have a sistah all up in her business.

Passion didn't miss the fact that her question had been diverted. But this was Robin, her home-girl from the ATL!

"Oh my God, Robin, I swear I thought about you just today. Listen, we've got to grab something to eat and catch up; you got time?"

"Of course." Time was all Robin had had for the past eighteen months.

Both the gun and the tennis bracelet stayed at Gold's Pawn Shop as Passion and Robin headed for the Chinese food restaurant three doors down. They quickly ordered, paid for their food, and sat down.

"Passion Perkins, or is it something else now?"

"No, it's Perkins again. I've been divorced almost five years, got a little girl. What about you; are you married, divorced, kids? Are you living here or just visiting? Girl, I still can't believe I'm looking at you!"

"Me neither," Robin said, taking a large bite of her egg roll. "Um, this food is good."

"Good and greasy," Passion countered around a forkful of chicken fried rice. "Just the way I like it."

Passion and Robin were silent a moment, devouring their tasty dishes, and then Passion probed again. "So, Robin, tell me wuzzup?"

Robin smiled as Passion mimicked the voice of their teens. She felt she could maybe share a few things with an old friend.

"Well, for starters, I'm divorced, no kids." Robin filled Passion in on her ten years in Tampa, Florida, after leaving Atlanta, her turbulent marriage and its equally turbulent end, the split-second decision to stay in Los Angeles after visiting almost two years ago, and her current employment.

"You've been here two years?"

"Off and on." Robin didn't want to tell Passion or anyone else where she'd actually resided during most of her LA stay—in prison for identity theft and credit card fraud. "I took some time off to, uh, visit family . . . came back a couple months ago."

"Wow, girl, you must be rolling to be able to take off work like that." Even as Passion said this, her thoughts returned to the gun left lying on the pawn shop counter.

"Hardly," Robin replied. "But sometimes you gotta do what you gotta do."

Like shoot somebody? "So, where are you staying?" Passion asked.

"Downtown," was Robin's short reply.

Passion studied the face of her former running buddy. Twenty years was a long time; maybe she shouldn't expect the two girls-turned-women to be as close as they once were. Still, Passion didn't understand the guardedness she sensed in Robin's demeanor—eking out conversation as if words cost money.

After an awkward silence, Passion reached into her purse and pulled out her cell phone. "I stay over in Leimert Park. Let's hang out one day soon. What's your number?"

They exchanged phone numbers and then Passion rose to leave. "You coming?" she asked Robin.

"Uh, in a minute, girl," Robin said, looking up at the menu, prominently displayed along the restaurant's back wall. "I think I'm going to get me something to go."

Passion leaned over and hugged Robin. "Well, it was good seeing you, Robin. Take care, and let's talk soon, okay?"

"Okay."

Robin waited until Passion walked out the door, and then placed a take-out order. There was just one other purchase she needed to make before leaving the area.

Passion wasn't sure why, but she didn't leave the strip mall when she got in her car. Instead, she sat watching the door to the Chinese restaurant. A couple minutes later, Robin came out of the restaurant, looked around briefly, and headed back to the pawn shop. She looked around again before going inside.

Passion waited until she saw Lin unlock the gun case and hand something to Robin. "I knew she was going back to buy that gun," Passion said to herself as she started the car and left the parking lot. "What is going on with you, Robin Cook? What is *really* going on?"

2

In the Way

Robin sat on the sagging bed of her dingy motel room. It was almost midnight, and her workday began at seven A.M. Still, she sat there wide-eyed, watching reruns of *Good Times*, eating Cheetos dipped in peanut butter, and washing them down with malt liquor beer. This was her ritual almost every night. After spending eighteen months locked down, where every move was ordered and every moment scheduled, Robin fully appreciated being able to have lights and television on after nine P.M. The one good thing the motel had was cable TV. Watching reruns of J.J. badger Thelma or a preteen Janet Jackson cozy up to her TV mom, Willona, saved Robin's sanity, such as it was.

Robin finished the bag of Cheetos and, licking the cheese off the fingers of one hand, picked up the gun with the other. She palmed the simple, semiautomatic Cobra compact, satisfied with the comfortable fit. Eyeing a crude, hastily drawn picture on a piece of paper taped to the opposite wall, she aimed the unloaded gun and fired off five shots in quick succession. V-I-V-A-N, the misspelled name on the paper identifying the drawing's inspiration, was safe. Along with being on the anti-psychotic drug Peridol, Robin was near-sighted. She thought she'd hit the target perfectly, but had the gun been loaded, no one would have died. *Gonna get bullets as soon as I get my check on Friday,* Robin mused, as she shot Vivian a couple more times before tossing the gun carelessly on the floor beside her.

Robin stared at the drawing, mentally replaying the events from two years ago. How she'd come to LA to reclaim her man, Derrick Montgomery, and after a failed coup d'état of Vivian's domain, been tossed out of their church like a sack of potatoes by a burly security guard. She thought back farther, to the beginning: Lithonia, Georgia, and Pilgrims' Rest Baptist Church. That's where she and Derrick first met. She'd been his assistant with aspirations to be much more. But somebody named Vivian had gotten in the way. Robin's smile was sinister as she imagined the future according to her plan. If it worked, Miss High-and-Mighty wouldn't be in the way for long.

Robin stumbled into the bathroom, shook three Peridols into her hand, and swallowed them with the remaining beer. She turned out the lights, and after peering at the moonlight spilling through the torn, stained curtain, closed the window on the loud sounds of brass-based banda music drifting in along with the cool, autumn air.

As she waited for the drug to take effect, Robin thought about Passion and smiled as dim recollections of a happier time flitted across her mind. Her smile turned to a frown as one of the faces in her reverie became that of a young Vivian Montgomery. She flopped over on her stomach, letting the dulling effects of drugs and sleepiness overtake her.

Robin kept repeating something over and over, until her snoring blended with the muted Mexican music and a steady, rhythmic creaking sound from the couple's bed above her. *I'm gonna get her. I'm gonna get that prissy muthafucka. . . .*

3

Don't Pass Me By

Passion sang along with the Logos Word choir, clapping her fiery-red manicured hands to their up-tempo rendition of a timeless, gospel classic. "While on others Thou art calling . . . do not pass me by!" She swayed and head-bobbed as the altos and sopranos traded increasingly difficult riffs of "do not" and "pass me by," while the band held down a contemporary syncopation of drums, keyboard, guitar, and horns. Passion reared her head back and sang louder. "Savior, blessed Savior, hear—my—hum—ble—cry." She had been praying, believing, wanting, and needing for too long. Whenever Jesus got there, she didn't want Him to pass her by!

Into the congregation's praise-induced frenzy walked the pastor, first lady, and a contingency of associate ministers, church staff, and special guests. They entered from a side door near the pulpit. Dr. Stanley Lee walked directly to the podium. His wife and the church's copastor, Carla, the associate ministers, and assistants sat in the first of two rows of chairs on the pulpit's left side.

"One more time, church," Dr. Lee's voice boomed into the microphone. "Oh, oh, oh, Savior," he sang, his rich baritone rivaling the able-voiced lead singer. He joyfully led the congregation, walking from one side of the pulpit to the other, clapping his hands and raising them toward heaven. This was his world, his element. Stanley Lee felt more comfortable in the pulpit than anywhere else. An attractive six feet and two hundred pounds, with a smooth bald head and even white teeth, his look was a decidedly nice addition to the room.

"Yes!" Dr. Lee exclaimed as the song peaked to its flourishing end. "Hallelujah," he intoned, as the church members clapped and shouted in praise. "And it is God's promise," he continued, "that before you call Him, He will answer, and that while you are yet speaking, He will hear.

"Whatever you need, God's got it. Whatever you want, God's got it. He's on His way to meet your need right now. And He shall not pass you by!"

The band started up again with the keyboardist making a run that the guitarist slid in on, and the drummer's dreadlocks flying as high as his sticks. The saxophonist poured notes in between strings and keys and hallelujahs and glories. Passion closed her eyes, basking in the feeling of joy and the spirit of God's love.

"Excuse me," a deep, slightly gruff voice said as a hand lightly grasped her forearm. "May I sit beside you?"

Any word except *yes* fled from Passion's mind as

soon as she turned toward the voice. It came from a solid-looking chest that pushed against a light gray silk shirt and tailored black suit. She looked at the hand that lightly grasped her arm and noted square, thick fingers with manicured nails. Looking up, she found a face full of character, confidence, and pure animal magnetism. The man wasn't typically handsome. He had a flat face, big nose, thick lips, and black, beady eyes. But when the man unconsciously licked those lips, nodded, and smiled, Passion noted the beady eyes were surrounded by long, curly lashes, and the lips looked soft and inviting, probably capable of doing things better not pondered in church. All of these thoughts were processed in the seconds it took for Passion to nod, smile back, and move over so the manly stranger could sit at the end of the pew.

The choir finished their selection and Pastor Carla changed places with her husband, giving him a quick peck on the cheek as he gave her the microphone and walked to his seat. Pastor Carla continued to the podium.

"My goodness, that is a man of God," she said, pointing to her husband and shaking her head in appreciation. The congregation laughed, used to Pastor Carla's romantic overtures to her husband from the pulpit. It was part of what the members loved about them, that they fanned the flames of their decade-old marriage openly and often. Innocent touches, light kisses, a hug here or there, theirs was a marriage many members held as the standard for unions.

Passion was one of those members. Unlike her imaginings of Pastor Montgomery, she'd never entertained an untoward thought about Dr. Lee. *If I could have a marriage like theirs . . .* she thought. The commanding stranger fidgeted beside her. As was typical, it was a crowded Sunday morning. There had barely been enough room to fit him in on the second row. *Maybe God is answering my prayer right now. Maybe His answer is this manly mass of muscle sitting beside me. . . .*

Pastor Carla continued, congratulating the choir on a job well done and greeting the Sunday worshippers. She then asked the visitors to stand so they could be recognized. The man next to Passion stood, as did a dozen or so others. While they stood, Pastor Carla encouraged members near them to introduce themselves and make them feel welcome.

"Hi, I'm Passion," she said, once the man whose name she'd heard was Lavon turned to her. "Welcome to Logos Word."

"Lavon Chapman," he said, taking her hand in his large, strong one and looking intently into her eyes. "It's a pleasure to meet you . . . Passion." Lavon paused before he said her name, caressing each syllable before it oozed from his juicy lips.

"Yes," Passion said, feeling slightly discombobulated. "Passion Perkins. It's a pleasure to meet you too." She didn't know what it was about Lavon that was so sexy to her but after five years of celibacy, it could have been that he was male and breathing.

"Interesting name," he continued in a low voice, as the ushers prepared to lift an offering.

"It fits me," she replied, then immediately could have kicked herself for what sounded like a flirtatious answer. "I mean, my grandfather called me that because of how feisty I . . ." She felt the hole she was digging get deeper. "What I'm trying to say is—"

"It's a great name," Lavon countered smoothly, saving Passion from further explanation.

Passion breathed a sigh of relief as Carla returned the microphone to her husband and Dr. Lee began to preach. She enjoyed the sermon, not because she'd remember either chapter or verse later, but because it gave her more than an hour of ongoing interaction with Lavon. Dr. Lee was one of those preachers who liked to interact with his congregants. He constantly encouraged the crowd to "turn to your neighbor and say" whatever phrase he wanted repeated for emphasis. He also referenced scriptures throughout his sermon. Passion shared her Bible with Lavon and when he placed his hand under hers to help her hold it, she thought she might have to excuse herself from the sanctuary. Was it her, or was he gently massaging her hand? It may have been her imagination, but either way Passion was now acutely aware of how long it had been since she'd enjoyed a man's touch.

Lavon enjoyed the service—and the company as well. He'd always preferred thick women, ones who wouldn't blow away in a two-mile-an-hour wind. Passion was like that: shapely, big breasts, wide hips, pretty face, nice eyes, and dimples. He was always a sucker for those. He also had a feeling the woman could live up to her name; something hot seemed to smolder just beneath her Christian conservatism. She was friendly too, which was refreshing. Often when he met women he felt as if he had to peel off layers to get to the real person, that they were so busy trying to be "all that" that they never got to be "all themselves." He liked a woman who was comfortable in her own skin, not trying to be someone she wasn't. Passion seemed like that. So did the church's first lady.

Lavon and Passion stood and shared small talk when church was over, neither seeming to want to end their meeting.

After learning he was from out of town, Passion suggested they go for coffee.

"I just need to speak with the pastors before we leave," Lavon said. "I'm working with them."

"Oh, really?"

"Yes, I'm helping to direct and produce a DVD series."

"Well, you go on, I'll wait outside," Passion said. Dr. Lee and Pastor Carla were friendly and it was always crowded in their office area after church, but Passion never liked to feel she was trying to be all up in their faces. She and Carla had talked on occasion, and she'd even helped out with a local Sanctity of Sisterhood Summit hosted at their church. Passion felt that if she ever needed any-thing—advice, assistance, whatever—that she could go to Carla, but considered theirs an acquain-tance, not a friendship. And for Passion, that was just fine. At the end of the day Carla Lee was still a woman, merely tolerated.

"Hey, Passion," Lavon said, when he found her waiting just outside the church doors. "We've been invited to Dr. Lee's for their Sunday brunch."

Passion was taken aback. Going to the pastor's house was something reserved for the "in" crowd at Logos Word, a crowd she never thought she remotely belonged to. Pastors Stanley and Carla were her mentors, her spiritual covering. She didn't know how comfortable she'd feel trying to treat them like regular folk, sharing a meal and small talk as if they were, well, normal.

"Are they sure?" she asked, with brows raised.

Lavon laughed. "What, is there something about you they don't know?"

Passion realized how her question must have sounded. She laughed too. "No, it's just that I'm not that close to them outside church. I'm just surprised, that's all."

Thirty minutes later, Passion and Lavon joined Dr. Lee, Carla, a couple associate ministers and their wives around the Lees' large dining room table. Between helpings of scrumptious steak, potatoes and gravy, corn, green beans, and a tossed salad, Passion's knowledge grew about Mr. Lavon Chapman.

Lavon was from the Kansas City area, and was media director at Mount Zion Progressive Baptist Church in Overland Park, Kansas. That's how the Lees knew him. His pastor, King Brook, was one of Stanley Lee's good friends and a fellow member of the Total Truth Association. Pastor Brook had recommended Lavon for the project when he heard what the Lees wanted to accomplish before the Christmas holidays. With a highly successful weekly television show himself, letting go of his director was a selfless gesture.

The series Lavon had come to put together was entitled *Eight Keys to Victorious Kingdom Living*. Each tape would focus on a different "Kingdom

Key," based on the fruits of the Spirit mentioned in the book of Galatians. The DVDs would include an interactive tutorial as well as a workbook to use during the entire series. By the time the Lees, the associate ministers, and Lavon finished discussing it, Passion was ready to order her copies right then.

After a decadent dessert of apple cobbler à la mode topped with caramel syrup, the Lees' guests prepared to leave. Brunch had lasted two hours, leaving less than three hours for everyone to rest and prepare for the church's evening service that began promptly at seven o'clock.

"See you tonight?" Carla asked Lavon, after giving him a light hug and thanking him again for his input.

Lavon flashed a sheepish grin. "Well, Pastor, I'm going to play hooky tonight, if it's all right. I know you offered a driver, but I think it's best I rent a car, considering how long I'm going to be here."

"How long are you staying?" Passion asked, her heart dropping at the thought of this man walking out of her life as quickly as he'd walked in.

"Eight weeks," Lavon and Pastor Carla said together.

Carla smiled at Lavon. "So you need to get to a rental car agency? Let me get one of the ministers to take you." She then looked at Passion and added, "Unless you've already got a ride."

"Thanks, Pastor Carla, but yes, I'm set," Lavon answered, annoyed at the guilt that rose up. What was that about? He was thirty-five years old, a grown ass man. If he wanted to skip a church service and have a female congregant drive him to his hotel . . . that was his doggone business. Not that Carla had said anything, but her silence was loud.

She turned and hugged Passion. "Will I see *you* tonight?"

"Maybe," was Passion's noncommittal reply. As much as she'd enjoyed the meal and the camaraderie of her first lady, she was ready for some one-on-one time with Lavon. "Thanks again for the meal, Pastor Carla," she said, heading out the door. "That apple cobbler was ridiculous!"

Without waiting for a response, she headed down the steps, hearing Lavon's last good-byes echo behind her.

A short time later, Passion and Lavon sat in the restaurant located in the second-floor lobby of the Sheraton Hotel where Lavon was staying, sipping decaf coffees. Being comfortable with each other was immediate; Passion reminded Lavon of one of his sister's friends and Lavon had the same cocky self-assuredness of her brothers—without being cocky. And she was glad he wasn't her brother.

"So, you think I can survive two months in Cali?" Lavon asked. He'd admitted to Passion that LA wasn't one of his favorite cities—full of what he called "plastic people."

"I think you can survive anywhere," Passion replied. "But put your boxing gloves on the next time you come to church. You're going to have to fight the women off you."

Lavon nodded his head and smiled. He didn't doubt what Passion said was true. If Logos Word was anything like Mount Zion Progressive, there would be no shortage of willing women to keep him company during his stay. In fact, he felt the woman sitting across from him could be among them. While not totally disinterested, Lavon knew he was here on business, with only eight weeks to do the job. He didn't have time for drama and didn't want to start something he couldn't finish. Lavon had always been a very sexual man, but he felt that if push came to shove and his hand wasn't enough, he had a couple friends who could provide him with a casual hookup, outside the Logos Word membership. Plus, he had a new girlfriend back home, also a member of Mount Zion Progressive. Lavon intended to keep his mind on kingdom, not kitty business. When he said good-bye to Passion, it was in the lobby, not his room.

Passion felt she was walking on air as she headed to her car, drove through the streets of LA, and arrived at her home. She didn't want to get too excited, but she was already "in like" with her dinner date. Lavon Chapman was a catch. Granted, she hadn't even known him twenty-four hours, but he was nice, intelligent, sexy, and very active in church. The latter was important to Passion; she wanted a godly man. And she rather liked the idea that he wasn't a pretty boy, wasn't the fall-over-backward kind of fine but striking in his own way, powerful and commanding. Walking into her house she remembered the feel of his hand under hers as they held the Bible, and the strength of his hug as they parted in the restaurant. His chest was solid as a rock and his embrace made her feel safe and protected. Passion knew she was a big girl; it took a real man to make her feel vulnerable inside his arms. Lavon did that. In time, she hoped he'd do much more.

4

Always and Never

Carla lay looking at the ceiling. Stanley enjoyed a deep sleep beside her, worn out, he claimed, from the long day. She didn't doubt he was tired; she was too. Sundays were always long, filled with church service, cooking, family, and friends. But where Stanley was ready to pass out when he got home, Carla was ready for love. Lately, it seemed as if she was always ready, and Stanley never was.

She turned slightly and eyed Stanley's sleeping profile. He looked peaceful, serene. Carla wished she felt the same. She reached out and touched her husband. *You're a good man*, she thought as his chest rose and fell beneath her hand.

Carla turned over, restless. Her mind drifted back to when they first met. He was thirty-five and already a hotshot preacher with a reputation for eloquence. She was a twenty-five-year-old single mother, returning to church following the devastating breakup with her child's father. Their courtship was fast and furious with no premarital sex, at Stanley's insistence, before their marriage six months after meeting.

Unfortunately there hadn't been much sex afterward either. The touchy-feely affections shown in church didn't carry over at home. Stanley fulfilled what he referred to as his "marital duty" with a five- to ten-minute poke once a week, maybe. In the ten years they'd been married, he'd given her two kids but never an orgasm. Those she'd accomplished with the help of "Denzel," her nine-inch-long, three-inch-wide monster cock with vac-u-lock attachment vibrator—so described on the back of the box.

Stanley's soft snores mocked Carla's restless state. Still wide awake, she eased out of bed and went to her closet. She stood on a small stool, reached toward the back of the top shelf, and pulled out Big D, encased in a wine-red velvet bag. She tiptoed past Stanley and quietly opened the bedroom door. Stanley slept rather soundly, but Carla was always cautious. Having Stanley catch her masturbating was one of her greatest fears. But between that and committing adultery, it seemed the lesser sin.

Carla passed the children's rooms and went downstairs to the den. She lay on the couch and reached for the remote: CNN, Bravo, the Food Network, Disney. She stopped on the Oxygen channel and turned up the volume; loud enough to cover gasps and moans, but low enough to not wake the family. She began to idly stroke herself and before long, slid Big D inside her. She tried to picture the dildo's namesake actor, a thought that always stimulated her, even as it made her feel guilty. Thinking of Stanley did not arouse her, and thinking of anyone she knew personally made her uncomfortable. She justified her visualizations by borrowing from Denzel's profession and calling it acting.

Carla tried repeatedly to imagine the familiar face. But as she stroked herself, another one swam into her mind's eye instead. It was an instant turn-on and she climaxed quickly. The name of her imagined lover whispered from her lips: the man who'd come to assist the Lees in their ministry . . . "Lavon."

5

Distractions

Lavon, Stanley, and Derrick Montgomery sat enjoying lunch at the famous LA eatery, Roscoe's House of Chicken and Waffles. It was a rare weekday when neither Derrick or Stanley was out of town and their day wasn't filled with meetings. Cell phone and e-mail were their most common modes of communication; this casual, in-person sit-down was a welcomed change. Plus, it gave Derrick time to get to know Lavon better. He'd met him shortly after Lavon began working for his best friend. From what King had told him and Derrick had observed, Lavon Chapman was a top notch producer, director, and a good man.

"It's a wonder one of those Mount Zion sistahs hasn't snapped you up," Derrick said, after finishing off a perfectly cooked chicken wing.

"They're trying," Lavon replied jovially. "A brothah has to stay prayed up!"

Stanley slapped Lavon on the back good-naturedly. "That's the way to do it, man. Can't have any distractions while we're kingdom building."

Derrick cleared his throat. "Speak for yourself but, uh, I wouldn't exactly call either Vivian or Carla a distraction."

"You know what I mean." Stanley dug into his greens and macaroni and cheese with gusto.

"No, I don't," Derrick countered. "Wasn't for Vivian by my side, I don't think I could handle kingdom business."

"I tell you what," Lavon injected. "I think both of you are blessed men. The Word says that a man who finds a wife finds a good thing. One of these days, I'll try it again. Has to be right though; I don't want to go through another divorce."

Lavon continued to share his life before Mount Zion with Derrick and Stanley. How he'd married young, acted a fool, and been rightfully kicked to the curb after several affairs. He spoke of his time in the military, where he'd first become familiar with broadcast production, shared humor and sometimes horror stories from his time with various ministries, and talked about how happy he was to be working with his pastor, King Brook. He almost slipped and mentioned Janeé, the mother of Derrick's oldest son, Kelvin. Coincidentally, Lavon had met Janeé while working at a church in Minneapolis, before knowing either Derrick or King. When he found out the entwined history those three shared, he was shocked but not surprised. He'd been in church long enough that not too much raised his brow. He was always amazed, however, about how small the world was.

Turns out, the same person was on Derrick's

mind. "You know," he said to Stanley, "Lavon knows Kelvin's mother, Janeé."

"Really, how's that?" Stanley asked, already aware of Janeé's relevance to Derrick. Shortly after Derrick found out that he and his high school friend and former, occasional sexual partner shared a son, he informed his minister friends and later, his congregation.

Lavon gave him the two-minute version of his and Derrick's former friend with benefits connection.

"How is Kelvin?" Stanley asked Derrick when Lavon had finished.

"Great," Derrick said. "Just your typical eighteen-year-old—hardheaded, stubborn, has all the answers while Viv and I know nothing. . . ."

"I see the apple didn't fall too far from the tree," Stanley teased.

Derrick grinned. "Yeah, payback is a mutha."

The conversation gravitated back to church matters and the taping of Stanley and Carla's DVD series. As Stanley and Lavon enjoyed sweet potato pie, Derrick sipped black coffee, his mind half on the conversation at the table and half on his son. He hadn't been joking when he told his friends how stubborn and hardheaded Kelvin could be. Even now he and Vivian were at odds with him about attending church. Kelvin had spent his high school years with his stepfather's family, and had grown up in Germany before that. Until moving into his biological father's household, religion had never been a part of his life. Kelvin was a handsome, talented young man, attending UCLA on a full basketball scholarship. Scouts were already courting him, calling him the next LaBron James. Kelvin felt his life was fine, perfect. He didn't think he needed God.

Derrick couldn't deny that everything was flowing nicely for his biological offspring, that all of Kelvin's dreams were coming true. He couldn't be happier for his son's success. But when it came to church, there was no compromise: everybody living in Derrick's house would serve the Lord.

6

Indirect Connections

Kelvin leaned his lithe, six-foot-four frame against the futon. His girlfriend melted into him, her head resting on his shoulder. Eighteen-year-old Kelvin had had his first sexual experience at fourteen. In the naive mind of recently deflowered Princess Brook, also eighteen, Kelvin was her one and only, for life.

She lifted her head and kissed him tenderly. "I love you," she said with feeling.

"C'mon now," Kelvin said, rolling Princess off him and standing. "I told you 'bout that love talk. Brothah getting ready to get signed can't have no steady girlfriend hanging 'round." His sobering words were tempered by his grabbing Princess and hugging her against his hard, six-pack abs.

"Whatever," she answered, staring at both of them in the mirror. There was no doubt in her mind; Kelvin was *her* man. They looked perfect together: he a tall, cocoa specimen of perfection, she a caramel cutie with curves in all the right places. Princess had liked Kelvin from the moment they met, at her aunt Vivian's house just before they began their freshman year at UCLA. She and her parents had joined the Montgomerys for a casual pool party and while Princess had acted unimpressed, spending most of her time on the phone with her friends back home, Kelvin had invited a female friend from high school, the one the Montgomerys still thought was his girlfriend. Princess's mom thought she was in love with Rafael, a boy she'd dated during her senior year of high school, and of whom her parents approved. Rafael's parents had been members of her dad's church for years. The assumption on the part of both the Montgomerys and the Brookses worked to Princess's favor.

"Why you frowning?" she asked Kelvin, who'd plopped back on the futon.

"The Rev," he said sarcastically, referring to his dad. "Man keeps sweating me 'bout going to church. I told him that religious stuff was for sissies."

"What'd he say?" Princess asked, knowing she'd never dare say that to her minister father.

"Well, I didn't say it quite like that," Kelvin admitted. "But I told him me and God was cool and all and I didn't have to go to church to talk to Him. He didn't want to hear that, just kept jaw-jackin' 'bout everybody in his house serving God." Kelvin jumped off the futon and began flexing his rapidly developing muscles in front of the mirror. "Don't nobody tell me what to do."

"Me either," Princess echoed defiantly while watching her man preen.

Princess's cell phone rang. Kelvin grabbed it, looked at the number. "Oh, it's Moms. Let me say hello." He got ready to open her flip phone.

"Boy, give it here!" Princess frantically tried to grab the phone, which Kelvin easily kept out of reach.

The phone stopped ringing. Laughing, Kelvin handed her the phone. "Thought nobody told you what to do? Don't know why I'm such a big secret anyways, since I'm 'your man' and all."

Princess hadn't told Kelvin about his indirect connection to her father. She knew he needed to know, but the time had to be right. Now, everything was still too new, uncertain. "I told you, my parents don't want me to date," she said as an explanation. "They want me to focus on school."

Kelvin grabbed his crotch. "Yeah, well you're learning something all right."

Princess blushed as she hit redial. "Whatever." She put her finger to her lips when Tai answered.

"Hi, Mama."

"Hey, Princess. I just called you."

"I know. I was in the bathroom." Princess swatted at Kelvin's hand as he tweaked her nipple.

"Oh, okay. Quick question: have you talked to your aunt Viv the past couple days?"

"Uh-uh."

Tai paused. "What about you? Is everything all right?"

"I'm fine."

Kelvin nodded his head, making a silly face in the process. Princess laughed.

"What's funny?" Tai asked.

"Nothing, just this silly movie on TV."

"Just don't let that box interfere with the books, Princess."

"It's Saturday, Mama. Most of my homework is already done."

Tai and Princess talked a bit more, about school, Princess finding a part-time job, and her attending Kingdom Citizens' Christian Center. Claiming a heavy school load, Princess had gotten away with attending only a couple services so far. Truth was, she was enjoying the freedom of actually being able to sleep in on Sunday mornings, and not attending church at all.

Princess changed the subject. "You want me to try and reach Aunt Viv?"

"No," Tai said quickly. "I'll try her again later."

The conversation ended shortly after that. Princess and Kelvin left to hook up with friends and attend a party. Tai sat at home and tried to figure out why the news she'd heard recently bothered her so, and which part was the more worrisome: that Robin Cook had spent the past eighteen months in prison, or that she had just got out?

1

Love Struck

Hope Taylor and Stacy Gray stood outside their church, Kingdom Citizens' Christian Center, watching the masses enter. The September weather was gorgeous—sun shining, birds singing—and the people milling around were as beautiful as the day.

"That boy looks just like his father," Stacy said, as she watched Kelvin mosey slowly toward the church's entrance along with a couple of his college buddies, wearing baggy jeans and a big UCLA pullover. A gaggle of girls followed closely behind.

"Sure does," Hope agreed. "Doesn't seem like he shares his father's enthusiasm for church though. With that scowl on his face, you'd think he was attending a funeral instead of a Sunday service."

Stacy laughed. "What kid likes to go to church these days?"

Both Hope and Stacy watched Kelvin's frown turn into a smile as he noticed another group of girls crossing the street. One of them, pretty and petite, signaled for him to call her. Kelvin bobbed his head discreetly before heading into the church.

"Well, looks like church just got a little better for Pastor's son," Stacy said with a smile.

Hope nodded, but was distracted by the sight of her handsome husband, Cy Taylor, entering the church with one of the ministers. Love-filled eyes watched as he laughed at something the other man said. Hope turned and saw Stacy wearing a similar love-struck look as she eyed her boyfriend of almost two years, Darius Crenshaw. The smile disappeared when Bo Jenkins, Darius's business manager, walked over and spoke to him.

"Guess it's time to head inside," Hope said, waving at a few members as she talked.

Stacy didn't hear Hope. She was too busy shooting daggers into Bo's back.

"It doesn't look like you're feeling too much love for Bo," Hope said.

"None at all," Stacy admitted, crossing her arms in the process.

"Anything you want to talk about?" Hope asked.

"He's just in the way, that's all. Barely gives Darius room to breathe."

"He handles Darius's business, Stacy. Of course they're close." Hope didn't know whether to share just how close. She'd never forgotten what her cousin Frieda told her—about seeing Bo and Darius bumping booties in the guest room at a house party. But when it came to significant others, sharing information and/or advice could get tricky. Sometimes, women preferred not to know, or at least to act as if they didn't know. "Something's working," she said, choosing the good cop tactic. "Darius beat out Shabach at last year's Stellar Awards. And look at him now, at the top of the charts."

"He'd be there anyway," Stacy snapped back. "Probably farther if it weren't for Bo. I know we'd be farther along in *our* relationship . . . maybe even married." Her eyes narrowed as she continued. "Yeah, Bo sometimes acts like Darius's woman instead of his manager. But I'm the one holding that title. And if he don't know . . . he's getting ready to recognize."

"Don't do anything crazy, girl. God don't like ugly."

"Neither do I. That's why I can't stand Bo's tore up behind."

Hope laughed.

"You know," Stacy continued, "there are some skank haters in the church who've been spreading the rumor that Darius is gay. But that's just jealousy talking." She looked at Hope with a sly smile and lowered her voice. "I can assure you that Darius is one hundred percent masculine prime beef."

Bo knows all about Darius's "beef," Hope thought. "Hmm," is all she said.

"I know, Ms. Christian. I'm not supposed to be doing the thing before I get the ring. But the end justifies the means, right? I *will* be Mrs. Darius Crenshaw, Hope. I'm going to snag KCCC's most eligible bachelor, just like you snagged Cy."

"Cy snagged me," Hope corrected. "I wasn't on the chase. But I've been where you are now, ready to be married, have kids, the whole nine. I'm not trying to tell you how to live your life, Stacy, but don't rush God, okay? If Darius is meant to be your husband, can't nobody take him away from you. But if he isn't, nothing you do will make him stay."

"I'd better get inside," Stacy said, quickly ending a conversation she no longer wanted to hear. "The choir's probably already in the stand."

"I'll be praying for you guys," Hope said. "Give me a call next week, okay? Cy will be out of town. Maybe we can meet for lunch."

Darius would be out of town as well, on a regional tour with Bo. Stacy forced away the thought and pasted a smile on her lips. "That sounds good, Hope. I'll call you."

Hurrying toward the church entrance, Stacy replayed Hope's words about God and what was meant to be. Stacy hadn't meant it when she said she would meet with Hope, but maybe she would. She could use a friend, a confidante. For all her bravado, there were nagging doubts about the close friendship between her man and his manager. And Stacy desperately wanted to share the news that no one else yet knew. . . .

She was pregnant.

8

Kingdom Citizens

Princess tried not to, but she couldn't help sneaking peeks at Kelvin, who was sitting near the back of the church. She'd made excuses when he'd asked her to sit with him, opting to sit close to the front with some of her friends. She didn't want to create any suspicions with Uncle Derrick and Aunt Viv, suspicions that would undoubtedly get reported straight back to her mother. Tai was already uncomfortable with the fact that Kelvin and Princess attended the same college. But when asked about him, Princess had given what she hoped was an investigation-diverting answer: "He's all right, Mama, and I know he's Uncle Derrick's son. But he's so conceited. And he has too many hootchie mamas around him all the time." Then she'd said something about needing to call Rafael. Tai seemed satisfied with her answer because Kelvin had only come up casually since then, and only in conjunction with talk about his dad.

Princess was tempted to peep at Kelvin again

but at that very moment looked up to see Aunt Vivian smiling at her. "Good to see you," she mouthed. Princess waved and blew her a kiss. Shortly afterward, an usher handed Princess a note. It was from Vivian, inviting her to dinner. Princess groaned inwardly. She didn't think it was a good idea. Sitting in a congregation of thousands was one thing, but Princess thought if seen up close, her love for Kelvin would be written all over her face. And her aunt Viv was a very good reader. She signaled to Vivian that she would call her, and then tried to take her mind off Kelvin and put it on Jesus. But unless Jesus was Black, six-foot-four, and played basketball for UCLA, Princess's attempts were futile.

With devotion over and offering about to be lifted, Princess, Kelvin, Stacy, Bo, Hope, Cy, and the rest of the Kingdom Citizens' congregants got into the groove of "Possible," Darius's hit record on both the gospel and secular charts.

"This song is fire," Kelvin said, sitting upright and enjoying himself—while not flirting with females—for the first time all Sunday. "Possible" was one of the few straight R & B, non hip-hop songs that was in Kelvin's iPod.

"Yeah, the band is jamming," one of his friends agreed. He and the other boys bobbed their heads as the instruments played and the choir sang. One by one the congregants stood and clapped, both to the beat and the inspiring words Darius had penned:

"*Possible—whatever it is, without a doubt God can work it out, it's*

*Possible—you just need to believe and receive, give
    you everything you need,
Possible—forgiveness, healing, abundance yield-
    ing, miracles appearing,
Possible, yes it's possible. Nothing is impossible,
    everything is possible. . . ."*

Derrick and Vivian joined the others on their
feet as the entire sanctuary praised God. Had she
not been standing, she would not have noticed the
commotion at the back of the church—somebody
apparently being forcibly ushered out, from the
looks of the security guard's rigid back. Vivian hadn't
seen who it was, but was aware that because of
their inner city location, the occasional unruly vis-
itor was not uncommon—usually someone drunk
or on drugs.

Tai's recent phone call immediately popped
into her mind. *Robin? No way,* Vivian thought.
After what had happened two years ago and the
subsequent restraining order, there was no way
Robin would try and enter the church—not in full
view of a packed Sunday morning crowd. Any further thought on the matter was interrupted as the
choir bumped their praise up a notch and a full-
blown Holy Ghost party broke out amid the pews.
Soon, Vivian was doing her own praise dance. She
joined in with the choir: "Nothing is impossible,
everything is possible with God!"

Unfortunately, not everyone was smiling or in a
party mood.

"Let me go, you big-headed muthafucka, let me
go!" Robin hissed as she pushed away from Greg,

the church's head of security and faithful KCCC member for the past five years. He'd successfully forced Robin several yards away from the church's entrance.

"Please leave the premises quietly, ma'am," Greg calmly responded. He wanted to keep things as civil as possible because anybody with eyes could see this woman's behavior was growing increasingly erratic. Even now he was thanking God that just last week he'd viewed her photo and police report while updating security files in the church office. Otherwise, he may never have given the average-looking woman entering the building a second glance.

"Look, you ain't God," Robin continued, breathing heavily. "This is a free country. You can't keep people out of church!"

"I can't, but the law can. The church has a restraining order against you, Ms. Cook."

"I told you my name ain't Cook, my name is . . . it's, uh, Jackson. J-A-K-S-U-N, muthafucka." Robin ran the syllables of the word together rapidly, giving it a lyrical, almost poetic quality. She had no idea where that made-up name had come from, but it sounded as good as any. As angry as she was, it was a wonder any lie came to mind. The gun in her purse was almost burning a hole in it. She wanted to pull out her Cobra and smoke this human barricade, jam the barrel in his face and earn some respect.

The self-assured man continued to eye her quietly.

"What you lookin' at?" she growled, reaching inside her purse and fingering the gun softly. "I said Jack—sun, muthafucka! Now move, so I can go praise—"

"You're not going anywhere," Greg interrupted, snatching Robin's purse. His senses had gone on high alert the minute he saw her reach inside the raggedy bag. "You wouldn't happen to have anything dangerous in here, would you?" he asked. "Nothing to harm Pastor, Mrs. Montgomery, or anyone else, right?"

Robin's already bulging eyes grew bigger. "What are you talking about? Give me my purse!"

Greg's eyes narrowed. He squeezed the purse and felt the gun. While still watching Robin, he reached in and pulled it out. "Whoa, what have we here?" he said, asking the obvious. "You think God needs help defeating the devil or something? Were you bringing this gun to kill Satan, or blast the hell out of someone? Which is it?"

Robin lunged at Greg but was no match for six-foot-two and two-hundred-fifty pounds of "you can't have this." He quickly handcuffed her to a nearby car, not for his safety, but her own. He then scanned the contents of her purse, confirmed it was indeed Robin Cook from her Florida driver's license, and pulled out a bottle of pills from the bottom of her purse.

"This your medication?" he asked, reading the label.

Robin glared at him, silently pulling on the handcuffs. "Let me go," she whispered, the fight appearing to leave her. "I'll go, just take off these handcuffs and give me my shit!"

Greg emptied the bullets from Robin's gun and then placed it and the other contents back in her bag. He uncuffed her, grabbed her arm firmly, and demanded the location of her car. Robin was seething, but knew her ill-conceived plan needed to be revised. She pointed to her car and walked complacently by his side as he ushered her to the vehicle. Greg hovered closely as Robin opened her purse, retrieved the car keys, unlocked the door, and got inside. Greg closed her car door and motioned for Robin to roll down the window. Robin hesitated briefly before doing so.

"What?!" she asked angrily.

"Look, I don't like treating anybody forcefully; you're a child of God like the rest of us. But I think you need help, a doctor or something."

Robin got ready to roll up the window but Greg placed his hand on the glass. "I'm not saying you're crazy"—*like hell I'm not*, he thought—"but everybody can use a little help now and then, am I right?" He managed a slight smile and looked at Robin with compassion.

Something pricked at Robin's heart, almost caused her to believe this man meant her good. But the feeling lasted no more than a second. He was just another one of Vivian's puppets, somebody else kissing that heifa's ass.

I hate her, Robin thought. But she tried not to show this emotion as she sweetly asked the security guard for her bullets. "I live in a rough neighborhood," she reasoned. "I'm not going to shoot anybody. Now, can you give me my bullets back? I ain't got money to buy no more."

"I can't do that, Ms. Cook," Greg replied. "And if you don't have a license to carry that weapon and get stopped by the police, you can go to jail."

The word *jail* reverberated through every fiber of her being. As much as Robin hated anyone or anything, she hated thoughts of returning to that hellhole the most. Again, something connected to Vivian stood in the way of having what she wanted, what she deserved. Her dark mood quickly returned. "Get your hands off the glass, muthafucka," she snarled. "And let me go."

Greg released the window, which Robin promptly rolled up, even though the temperatures hovered around ninety degrees. She accelerated from the curb and away from KCCC without looking back.

Immediately Greg called an assistant who was posted inside the church. "Escort Pastor and Lady Viv directly to the executive suite as soon as service is over," he said in clipped tones. "No fellowshipping, no waiting, no exceptions."

9

Her Name Is Not Stella But . . .

Carla had been both anticipating and dreading this meeting ever since Stanley got called out of town and volunteered her to meet with Lavon regarding the Kingdom Keys DVD series. Carla tried to ignore her nervousness about their meeting in her home. The location had been arranged before Stanley got called away, so Lavon could see where he wanted to tape the series' intros. He'd thought that taping these greetings from the Lees' home would add a warm, personal touch. Stanley had thought it an excellent suggestion. But now he was gone and Carla was home alone. Her anxiety turned to something else when she opened the door.

"Come in, Lavon," Carla said, in what she hoped was a casual tone.

"Hey, Lady Cee," Lavon replied cordially. He had a habit of nicknaming the many ministers with whom he did business, especially when there was an easy camaraderie. He'd felt comfortable with Carla since "hi, my name is . . ."

"You hungry, thirsty?" Carla asked, as they walked through the foyer and into the Lees' massive formal living room, stylishly decorated in French country chic.

Lavon was about to say no when a tantalizing smell brushed past his nostrils. "I didn't think so, until I got a whiff of whatever's cooking right now."

Carla gave an understanding smile. It was a rare breed who could pass up her homemade meals. "That would be my baked pork chops," she said. "Go through those French doors to the patio; we can eat and talk out there."

Lavon had noticed Carla's ample cleavage as soon as she opened the door. He continued what he hoped was a discreet perusal of her shapely, plus-size figure from behind as she sashayed into the kitchen. She had on flat sandals and wore a floor-length jersey dress with a peek-a-boo slit to just above her knees. Thick, shapely calves teased him from behind the cut fabric. The jersey hugged Carla's big behind, an attribute that made Lavon's mouth water. He shook his head, trying to clear the sexual thoughts that quickly flooded his consciousness. He walked toward the French doors while taking in as much of the house as he could see—Dr. Lee's house, he silently reminded himself. As if to underscore the thought, he passed by five pairs of Lee eyes staring at him from a huge family painting mounted over the marble fireplace. "*Mrs. Carla Lee*," he muttered under his breath.

Carla hadn't missed a thing, had felt his eyes on

her all the way down the hall to the kitchen, and heard his footsteps when they finally crossed the living room's hardwood floor. The air fairly sizzled between Carla and Lavon every time they met. They both tried to ignore it, even as Carla's body made other plans. She knew Lavon was thinking similar thoughts and beyond these illicit contemplations, she didn't want to think of much else . . . her husband, for instance.

Carla brought iced tea to the table and within minutes returned with two steaming platters of down-home Southern cooking: baked pork chops smothered in gravy, cabbage stewed with apples and onions, buttery mashed potatoes, and thick, golden slices of corn bread made from scratch.

"Lord have mercy, woman!" Lavon exclaimed as she set down his plate. He eyed the delicious fare appreciatively, at a loss for words. "Lord have mercy," he murmured again, picking up his fork and diving in with relish.

Carla laughed at how Lavon was very clearly enjoying the meal. As she'd expected, he had a voracious appetite, and she didn't think it was limited to food. "Slow down there now," she said as Lavon cleaned half his plate in minutes. "Nobody's going to take it from you!"

"Not unless they want to get shot," he retorted. "Lady Cee, I haven't had food this good since my mama died. I didn't think women cooked like this anymore."

"Most women don't," Carla admitted. She took her hands and traced her ample figure. "And I guess I shouldn't either, at least not very often."

Lavon set down his fork, wiped his mouth with a

napkin, and took a drink of tea. "You're beautiful," he said simply, looking at Carla without blinking.

The simple statement caused Carla to catch her breath. There was such raw sexuality in his beady-eyed stare. While appearing totally respectful, Lavon had caused Carla to become wet with a single phrase and a solid glance.

"Thank you," she whispered, picking up her fork and trying to re-engage an appetite that was suddenly gone, replaced by a different kind of hunger. "You're not bad yourself," she added, not trusting herself to look up.

Carla battled with what was suddenly an overwhelming need for physical love. The night she'd fantasized about the man now at her table flashed into her mind. The angel on one shoulder reminded her how much she loved her husband, while the devil on the other asked how well he'd loved her back—and how long was she going to deny her desires. Carla picked up the pork chop bone, not aware that Lavon watched her. She gnawed off the meat the fork missed and licked the gravy from her fingers.

Lavon watched her tongue lick her fingers as if mesmerized. If the way she ate was any indication, this woman loved to abandon. He in that moment knew he was going to sleep with Carla Lee just as sure as he knew his name. It wasn't a question of if, but when. There was an unspoken conversation happening between them, one of which neither was totally aware. While Lavon was an admitted church ho in the past, he'd shied away from married women. For the last few years he'd pretty much toed the straight and narrow, until today. Now, all bets were off. He sensed Carla Lee was just like the smothered pork chop she'd just enjoyed—spicy, appetizing, and finger-licking good.

"Should we discuss the series' intro now or . . . after we eat?" Lavon asked slowly.

Carla felt warmth from her belly button to her G-spot. "Afterward," she breathed, visions of replacing her plastic penis with the real thing dancing in her head. The desire for Lavon was so unexpected and so strong, she didn't even have time to process it. She just reacted to its call.

Carla and Lavon finished their food quickly and got up from the table. Neither had to voice what they both knew was getting ready to happen. Any page in the Bible would have decried her actions, so Carla kept the mental book closed. She locked the front door and directed Lavon toward the stairs. "Straight down the hall and through the last door on your left," she said softly.

Carla admired Lavon's muscular legs as he climbed the stairs, tight buns encased in the slacks of a casual khaki summer suit. She walked to the kitchen, placed the dishes in the dishwasher, made sure all the stove's burners were off, and reached for the phone. There were a few calls to make that included three kids and a church assistant, to make sure she knew how much time she had without interruptions.

The moment felt surreal, as if it were happening to someone else. While always gregarious and earthy, she was a woman of control. But not now. Now, she was getting ready to do something she hadn't done in a decade ... have really, really good sex. Because there was no doubt in Carla's mind. Lavon would be real good.

Lavon felt a twinge of guilt at the thought of cavorting in Stanley Lee's bed. But to his pleasant surprise and Carla's measured sense of decency, he correctly guessed that what he stepped into was a guest room. Tastefully decorated in muted blues, grays, and tans, with contrasting black furniture, it was thankfully impersonal, with pictures of the ocean dressing two of the four walls. A mirrored closet ran the length of the wall directly across from the king-size bed. The faint, floral fragrance of lavender hung in the air, the only decidedly feminine effect in the entire room. The room was understated elegance, as was Carla's entire home. This fact had surprised him upon his first visit; he'd imagined Carla's home would be full of loud, vibrant colors, a bit of garishness thrown in just because. *Maybe in other rooms*, he mused, as he sat down on the bed and fingered the silk comforter. But he decided against asking for a grand tour. The last thing he needed was to get too comfortable in another man's house. He knew he'd already seen more than he should have, but also knew there was no going back from the decision. As he stood to take off his jacket, the door opened.

Carla slipped into the room, eyeing Lavon nervously. She'd changed into a loose-fitting, thigh-length house dress, with a zipper that ran from top to bottom. She wore nothing underneath. All of a sudden, she felt like a schoolgirl, about to "do it" in her mama's house before Mama returned home. Her stomach was all aflutter, her breath short and quick.

Lavon sensed her nervousness, and her excitement. "Come here," he commanded softly, yet in a tone that brooked no argument.

Though her legs could barely move, Carla managed to make her way around the bed and stand in front of Lavon. At five-foot-eight, she was just a couple inches shorter than him, and probably only thirty, forty pounds lighter. Still, his was a giant presence in front of her. He emanated power, exuded testosterone.

Lavon placed his hands on Carla's shoulders and began kneading them tenderly. He looked deeply into her eyes. "How long have you been planning to seduce me?" he asked simply.

"Ever since you stepped into our office," Carla replied honestly, quickly wiping the image of her husband, who had also been in the office, out of her mind.

"And how'd you know I'd comply?" Lavon asked, directing Carla to sit on the bed and massaging her feet and calves.

"I—I didn't," Carla gasped as Lavon placed a tender kiss on a point just behind her knee and continued a brief trail up part of her thigh.

"What would you have done if I'd said no," Lavon asked, standing to remove his shirt and pants.

Carla stared, mesmerized. A large bulge was noticeable even in his loose boxers. She swallowed once, and again. "I would have lost my mind," she said finally, her eyes slowly drifting from the bulge to his face.

"Well, you know," Lavon said, reaching for the clasp on the zipper of Carla's dress and slowly pulling it down, exposing Carla's satiny brown body in the process. "We can't have that. Because a mind . . . is . . . a terrible thing to waste," Lavon said, as he placed kisses at the valley of her size-D breasts, across her round stomach, and near her hips.

It had been less than ten minutes and Carla was already in a frenzy. Stanley never touched her this way, caressed her, licking the flesh and then blowing on the wetness. Lavon's skilled actions were driving her wild. "I can't wait," she panted. "It's been so long, too long. . . ."

Lavon was a gentleman who'd never think of keeping a woman waiting. He kissed Carla deeply, and then used his strong fingers and skilled tongue to pleasure every inch of her size-sixteen physique. When he basked in the glory of her private paradise, Carla grabbed a pillow to muffle her screams. It had been ten years, and the re-entry into oral pleasure was almost more than she could bear. She begged him not to stop, to go on forever. Tears streamed down her face as she experienced one release after another.

Carla thought Lavon's art of loving her couldn't get better. She was wrong. After his leisurely performed oral symphony, he prepared for the encore. Almost with sixth-sense accuracy, he lavished love on her, initiating positions that for the past decade, Carla had only experienced in her dreams. Lavon was thick and thorough, strong and gentle at the same time. For more than an hour, Lavon took Carla to the moon, carried her around the planets and stars, before bringing her gently back down to planet earth. Carla lay thoroughly satiated, totally satisfied, and absolutely convinced that she'd just found the man who would help her get her groove back for eight glorious weeks. And just as quickly Carla realized that eight weeks, after ten years, just might not be enough.

But it would have to be . . . wouldn't it?

10

Former Best Friends

Even Robin's sour mood couldn't dampen Passion's joy. It had been a week since she met Lavon Chapman and in that time, she'd come to believe more and more that he was someone special. They'd only been together that Sunday at the Lees', but had talked on the phone, albeit briefly, almost every day. He was always as warm and charming as the day they'd met.

"I don't want to move too fast," Passion said, as she reached for another slice of pizza. "I kinda want to wait until I'm married or at least engaged to, you know, do the do, but Lord that man turns me on!" Passion took a hefty bite of her meat lover's special, rearing back on her sofa and kicking up her heels as she chewed. "I mean, don't get me wrong, I pride myself on being a strong, Christian woman and all, and maintaining proper values, but . . . it's been five years, girl! And that man's body? Uh, uh, uh!"

"This pizza's good, huh?" Robin said distract-
edly, her untouched slice growing cold on the
plate.

"I'm not uh, uh, uh'ing about some meat and
cheese, sistah. It's about the . . . Robin? Have you
heard a word I've said?"

Passion had been talking a mile a minute from
the time Robin walked into her modest abode.
Normally she wouldn't be mentioning her desires
to anyone, but with their shared childhood history, she felt comfortable talking to Robin. An
added bonus was that Robin didn't go to Logos
Word, didn't know Lavon, and was therefore one
less woman she'd have to keep away from her
blessing. But now, as she munched on her third
slice of pizza, she studied her friend. Robin surely
wasn't the girl she'd known in Georgia, but who
was the same person after twenty years? Robin always seemed, well, she didn't want to say odd, but
a bit different. It hadn't bothered Passion in the
past and she was determined not to let it affect her
now. She was too busy floating on her own cloud
to want potential rain from another. Still, she felt it
her Christian duty to try and uplift her friend.

She put down the pizza, took a long drink of soda,
and leaned back against the back of the sofa.
"Okay, girl, what's wrong?"

"Nothing," Robin said much too quickly.

"Girl, please. I may not have seen you for twenty
years, but you're still Robin and I'm still Passion.
You've been in a mood since you walked in my
house, when after all these years I thought we'd be
having a ball reminiscing and everything. You

might have kept to yourself back in the day but around me, you were never the quiet type. Talk to me."

"I fell in love too," Robin said.

Passion leaned forward and picked up her half-eaten slice. Was that all? She should have known Robin's mood was about a man. "Is that what has you down? Man problems?"

Robin nodded.

"Well, girl, drop the dime and share the info. Are y'all fighting, did you break up, what?"

Robin couldn't think straight. A part of her wanted to share with Passion her story about Derrick but the other part was too paranoid to reveal any information. After all, Vivian may have been controlling Passion, just like she did all the others.

"C'mon, Robin. It's me you're talking to." Passion rested her hand on Robin's arm until Robin looked at her. *Something about her eyes isn't right,* Passion thought, even as she maintained the smile on her face.

"Well," Robin said. "I used to hang with this guy, years ago, and then a woman came between us. Now, I want him back. That's the short version."

"Are he and this woman married?"

"Yeah, but—"

"Wait a minute, Robin. It's a married man you're after?"

"Yeah, but he was mine!" Robin's eyes narrowed, her breathing became rapid. She'd forgotten to take her Peridol and talking about Derrick increased her anxiety. "Where's my damn pills?" she said to herself, as she ransacked her junk-filled bag.

"What pills?" Passion felt a moment of real concern for her friend.

Then, in an instant, Robin's behavior changed. She calmed down and closed her purse. "No, just, uh, pills I take for migraines." She held her forehead. "I'm having one now."

"Oh, hold on," Passion said, rising from the couch. "I've got some prescription strength Tylenol. Let me get them."

"It's okay," Robin said. She grabbed her purse, rose from the couch, and headed toward the door. "Sorry, girl, but I'm going to have to cancel on the movie. I'm not feeling well."

Passion hugged Robin, told her she'd pray for her, and watched Robin get in her automobile. The car was old, rusted, and rattled loudly when Robin started it up. A billow of smoke followed as she drove away from the curb. Passion watched the smoke swirl into the air and then disappear, much like her desire to reconnect with her former best friend.

‖

Too Late for Games

As much as she was glad to see Robin again, Passion was relieved the afternoon had ended quickly. She was beginning to think that twenty years was too long a gap to take up where two friends had left off. Something had changed about Robin, something more than her hair color and dress size. She'd looked downright crazed when digging for her pills. Passion wondered just what kind of drugs her friend was using.

She didn't ponder the question long. Looking at her watch, she noted the day was fairly young and her daughter Onyx was with Passion's parents. Her focus immediately turned to Lavon, and what he had planned for the evening. He'd been too busy to meet during the week; maybe he'd have some time tonight. Passion sat on the couch, opened her cell phone, and dialed the number already programmed into her speed dial.

"Hello?" a familiar, deep voice asked.

"Hey, Lavon, it's me."

There was a slight hesitation before Lavon said, "Hi, me."

It was Passion's turn to pause as she wondered just how many females were ringing Lavon's number. She knew she wasn't the only one. No matter; it was too early for her to be possessive and too late for games. "It's Passion," she said simply.

"Passion! Ms. Passion Perfected, how are you?"

"Better now," Passion said with a smile. "And better still if I can talk an extremely busy, multitalented director/producer into taking a break and grabbing a bite to eat later on."

"We might be able to arrange something like that." Lavon had dodged Passion all week while hanging with Carla almost twenty-four/seven. During the day, they planned and worked on Kingdom Keys. At night they'd worked on Carla's kitty and Lavon's snake. But Stanley had returned from out of town on Friday, bringing in a reality check along with his luggage. Lavon had said he wouldn't get involved with anyone from Logos Word and what had happened? Not only had he gotten involved, he'd dived headlong, literally, into the feline charms of the first lady.

The madness had to stop, and maybe this was the diversion to help that happen. "So where are we going, Passion Perfected? I've barely eaten all day."

Passion masked her giddiness and ignored her pizza-filled stomach. "Hey, why don't you come over to my place? It's probably been a while since you've had a home-cooked meal."

Lavon choked down a guffaw. That's all he'd eaten was home-cooked food, and some of the best that had ever passed his knowledgeable lips. He felt he'd gained ten pounds. Plus, he wagered cooking wasn't all Passion had on her mind, that maybe she wanted to try and live up to her name. Unfortunately for Passion, Carla had already taken care of that. The woman was insatiable.

"Oh, no. A beautiful lady like you," he said to appease, "needs to be wined, dined, and showed a good time. Let's get dressed up, go for dinner and dancing. What do you say?"

What could she say, except yes? Passion hadn't been romanced in years. "I know just the place," she said, mentally browsing her closet for the perfect outfit, and thanking her daughter's grandparents that they'd taken her for the weekend. "Should I pick you up around seven?"

"I've still got a few hours of work to do. Can we make it eight?"

"Eight sounds perfect. See you then."

Several hours later, Lavon and Passion sat contentedly in a booth at the Lobster, a well-known seafood restaurant in Santa Monica. Dinner was good, the conversation, pleasant. Passion learned that Lavon was divorced, with a teenaged daughter from a previous relationship. Along with this knowledge came the facts that he was the oldest of four children, he loved football, his musical tastes ranged from classical to blues, and while he'd enjoyed their upscale fare of jumbo lump crab cakes and marinated Chilean sea bass, his mouth virtually salivated over anything smothered or fried. His love of good, down home cooking was especially pleasing to Passion, who, as a former Georgia peach, could definitely throw down in the kitchen. She believed the popular saying that the way to a man's heart was through his stomach, and there was no doubt that his heart, and something a bit farther south, were Passion's ultimate destinations.

Throughout the more personal conversation, Passion listened for hints of another woman, a serious relationship in which Lavon was involved. She'd used a couple different approaches to direct the conversation toward relationships, mentioning her own divorce and joking about the potential discomfort of dating and then dismissing a church member. Lavon admitted leaving the church his ex-wife attended, but added nothing about his current romantic situation. As Passion and Lavon left the restaurant and drove down Lincoln Boulevard toward the Sheraton Hotel, it became clear that Passion was going to have to "go direct."

She waited until there was a comfortable lull in the conversation and then asked bluntly, "So, Lavon, are you presently in a relationship?"

"What do you mean by relationship?" Lavon countered.

What do I mean by relationship? What do you think I mean by relationship? Why do y'all do that, get stuck on stupid whenever the RCM words—relationship/commitment/marriage—come up? That must mean you are in a relationship and if you are, then why are you wining and dining women in LA?

This flurry of thoughts happened in the time it took Passion to take a deep breath and change "pissed off" to "patient." Controlling her chagrin, she calmly replied, "I mean, are you casually dating, in a long-term relationship, engaged, taken, or available?"

"Well," Lavon said slowly, gathering his thoughts. He had to be careful with his answer. On the one hand, he didn't want to get seriously involved with Passion, and on the other hand, he didn't want it to come off as if he were a two-timing jerk who turned up the heat on the West Coast while Midwestern home fires burned. He decided to simply tell the truth. "I am dating someone back home; she's also a member of Mount Zion. I wouldn't call it casual exactly, but we haven't become exclusive."

Passion listened quietly, nodding her head in an "I see" manner.

Lavon continued. "We've only been dating a few months and honestly, I think she's more eager to jump into something serious than I am. She's twenty-nine, never been married, no kids. She's ready to settle down with someone. I want that too, eventually, but needless to say with a teenager and a divorce already on my résumé, I'm in no big hurry."

Fading fast were Passion's hopes for a quick commitment, a firm foundation for something deep and lasting to occur in the eight weeks that Lavon would be in LA. Being a divorced parent herself, she understood where he was coming from, but after five years she was more than ready to get married again—the sooner, the better.

Passion pulled just beyond the hotel's foyer entrance, stopped the car and turned off the engine.

"Sure you're not up for a cup of coffee?" He'd declined her previous suggestion of a walk on the Santa Monica Promenade or checking out a jazz band she favored, but Passion wasn't ready for the evening to end.

Lavon was. "I'll have to take a raincheck," he said, grasping Passion's hand lightly before raising it to his lips for a kiss. "Thank you so much for the pleasure of your company. I enjoyed myself tonight."

"Me too," Passion said, her eyes fastened on the lips that had just touched her hand. "Has anybody told you that you have extremely sexy lips?"

More like how many have told me, is what Lavon thought. "Maybe once or twice," is what he said.

Passion leaned over and touched her lips lightly to Lavon's. His lips were thick and soft, just the way Passion liked them. But she restrained herself from appearing too eager. "May I have a real kiss?" she asked playfully.

Lavon wanted to say no, but how would that sound? *It's just a kiss,* he thought. And Passion was a pretty woman. He leaned toward her already tilted body and pressed his lips firmly against hers. Passion immediately opened her mouth, gently prodding his open with her tongue.

They French-kissed for a long moment before Lavon gently pulled back. He took in Passion's half-moon eyes and slightly parted lips, and knew she wanted him. Passion had shared with him that she was celibate, information he'd use to make sure their friendship never went past first base, the kissing stage. Because, fortunately or unfortunately for Passion, Carla had all of the other bases completely covered, even if he were trying to forget she was in the game.

"That was nice, very nice," Passion murmured when it became clear there would be no second helpings of the kiss appetizer.

"And *you* are nice, a chaste woman of God." Lavon opened the car door. "Thanks again, Passion," he said as he exited. "See you in church tomorrow."

Passion's celibate declaration now felt like TMI: too much information to have shared with this new friend. The word had slipped out while discussing life post-divorce. *It might work in my favor,* she thought as she watched Lavon walk into the lobby. *When I let him make love to me, he'll know it means something.* With that decision made, that she'd definitely let Lavon hit it when the time was right, she started the car and merged from the hotel's circular drive onto the busy boulevard.

As she turned on Century and headed toward Crenshaw, she dissected and rated her evening with Lavon. All in all, she thought it had been an excellent first date. Getting to know Lavon Chapman better had its pluses. But as with everything in life, there was also a downside. One, Lavon was only in town for seven more weeks; after that, he'd be almost two thousand miles away. Passion had never tried a long-distance relationship and wasn't sure she wanted to start one now. Two, while Lavon wasn't permanently attached, he wasn't actually free. Passion wondered about the woman in Kansas, how she looked, whether she had kids, how in love she was with Lavon. She speculated as to whether Lavon would relocate to LA, and what life was like in the Midwest. Passion had once considered relocating to a smaller city, especially when Onyx was born. She wasn't past moving for a man.

"Just go with the flow, girl," Passion said to herself as she pulled into her driveway and got out of her car. A smile crossed her face as she walked up the steps. She had an eligible bachelor interested in getting to know her better and she was definitely interested in knowing him better. This exciting new development in her life would suffice . . . for now.

12

Crazy LA Traffic

Robin sat in her car, staring dispassionately as the congregants of Kingdom Citizens' Christian Center emerged from the sanctuary. She'd left her motel room an hour before with three things: her Cobra handgun, a pack of Kool Menthol 100's, and a plan. She chain-smoked one cigarette after another as she watched the members of Kingdom Citizens bask in all of their fellowshipping glory. Robin pulled the baseball cap she wore farther down on her forehead, her eyes glued to the church's parking lot. Robin watched—and waited.

The scene inside KCCC's executive offices was not as festive as the one outside. In fact, Derrick was having a hard time holding on to his temper as he waited for a logical explanation as to why Kelvin had showed up for service just ten minutes before the benediction. Kelvin used oversleeping, lack of transportation, and LA traffic as excuses for why he and the friend who'd given him a ride had missed church. For Derrick, none of these reasons were good enough.

"You expect me to believe that an intelligent, capable young man such as yourself doesn't know how to set his alarm? The same young man who is up at six-thirty during the week, sometimes earlier, to lift weights and run sprints? What kind of fool do you take me for, Kelvin?"

Kelvin sat slouched on a leather loveseat, silent. The air fairly crackled with tension as Derrick awaited an answer. Finally Kelvin shrugged his shoulders and said, "I don't."

"You don't what?"

"I don't think you're a fool, Rev."

"So since that's not the problem, you're going to have to tell me what is. Because I thought that after our last conversation, when I said in no uncertain terms that attending church was not optional, that this matter was settled."

Kelvin sighed, not wanting to tell Derrick how he really felt, but not wanting to keep perpetrating a fraud either. Truth was, Kelvin didn't agree with Derrick's take on God, didn't feel the need for religion. Even though he'd found out Derrick was his biological father only two years ago, Kelvin felt a special bond with him, respected his success. He enjoyed staying with the Montgomerys and getting to know his half brother and sister, Derrick Jr. and Elisia. In fact the only real disagreement he and his father had had since he moved in was that he didn't like attending church. Kelvin hoped this fact wasn't a deal breaker, but if he was going to continue to live with the Montgomerys, he had to have the freedom to live as he pleased.

"Look, Rev, you know I respect you and all that, but I just don't believe—"

An urgent knock at the door interrupted Kelvin's reply. It was Vivian. "Honey, we've got to go. Your uncle Charles has had an accident. They don't know if he'll make it."

"Accident, what kind of accident?" Derrick asked, rising from his chair and grabbing his jacket at the same time. Charles Montgomery was Derrick's favorite uncle, and his father's brother. He was as close to him as he was to his own dad.

"Some freak happening. An electrical wire came loose and hit the water while he was taking a shower. He was electrocuted."

Derrick leaned back against his desk. "Oh God, no," he said quietly, as the gravity of the situation sank in. "Please help him, God. Please put Your arms around my uncle until I get there."

Derrick's assistant came into the office. He'd jumped into action as soon as Vivian had seen him on her way to Derrick and told him the news. "Just take it easy, Pastor," he said to Derrick in a low, calming voice. "Everything is going to be all right. I've made your plane reservations and a town car is waiting to take you two to the airport. I've already called Mother Moseley. She said don't worry; she'll take care of the kids until you get back."

Derrick had never valued Lionel's levelheaded efficiency more than this moment. His assistant's unruffled poise helped to calm Derrick's rattled nerves. "Thank you," he said. He turned to Kelvin.

"I'll deal with you later. Do me a favor and drive the Jag back to the house."

Kelvin nodded somberly, trying to respect the serious mood and hide his excitement at driving the luxury car. But Derrick saw it anyway. "Give the keys to Mother Moseley as soon as you get home. I want the car to stay parked while we're gone."

Kelvin's somber mood was no longer an act. "I can't drive it at all?" he asked, having pictured in an instant cruising various California boulevards with his friends. "Can I at least go get something to eat first?"

Derrick was too preoccupied to argue. "Have that car home in a couple hours."

"Sure, Rev," Kelvin said as he took the keys from on top of the desk and headed toward the door. Just before he opened it he turned. "I'm sorry about not making it to church on time today, and I hope everything turns out okay with your uncle."

Derrick walked over and hugged his son. Moments like this made him all too aware that tomorrow was not promised, and that one should always be satisfied that if the last words spoken ended up being your last words period, that they were ones you'd want to leave behind. He almost lost his composure then, not knowing what he'd do if he didn't reach his uncle in time. "I love you, son," he said.

"I love you too."

Derrick turned to Vivian, who'd gathered up his briefcase and a couple personal items from atop his desk. "You ready?"

Vivian nodded.

"Let's go."

*   *   *

Robin sat up as a black town car and a black Mercedes, both with tinted windows, hurriedly exited the church parking lot. The car turned in her direction and passed directly by her. She tried hard to peer through the dark glass, but she had left her prescription glasses at the motel. Staring at the car as it traveled away from her, she wondered if her target was inside, but quickly dismissed that possibility. A shiny, pearl-white Jaguar was the cage that would be carrying her prey. Robin watched as the town car took the on-ramp to the 10 freeway. Seeing that, she sat back and lit another cigarette. The Montgomerys lived in Beverly Hills and never took the freeway home, at least not on the two or three occasions that she'd followed them. No, her plan was still solid. She just had to bide her time.

Kelvin called Princess as soon as he stepped out of the executive suites. "Where you at?"

"What kind of greeting is that?" she replied.

"The kind that's gonna get you a ride in the Rev's Jag if you're still out front. He and Lady Vee had to bounce—an emergency situation. They're on their way to the airport and he gave me the keys to drive his car home."

"Ooh, for real? Where are we going? Hey, let's roll to Malibu, or maybe even Las Vegas!"

"Girl, are you out yo' mind? You know the Rev wasn't gonna leave without putting the car on lock. Old Ms. Moseley is already at the house waiting to confiscate the vehicle soon as I get there."

"Why you calling me then?"

"Where you at?!" Kelvin walked to the car, which was parked directly in front of the executive offices. "Come over here, to the buildings behind the church. And lose your entourage. It's just gonna be me and you today."

Kelvin showed his swagger by striking a pose of cool as he leaned against his father's car. Within minutes he spotted Princess walking toward him. There was a sway in her hips and a smile on her face as she headed to her man.

Kelvin frowned, turned, and got in the car. He started the engine and began backing out before Princess had barely gotten the door closed.

"What's your problem?" Princess asked, looking at Kelvin as if he'd lost his mind.

"You, that's what," he responded. "Walking over like you want me to tap that ass right here in the parking lot." Kelvin gave her a sideways glance as he smoothly and carefully navigated the Jaguar out of the lot. "Thought you wanted to keep us on the down low around the folks." *And around the other girls at this church who I'm trying to get with.*

"I do," Princess pouted.

"Why? I never understood what that was about, being all secretive and thangs. So Derrick knows your parents, so what? You're eighteen, grown. They think you're not gonna date nobody? Who knows, it might make them feel better that you're with their good friend's son."

Princess wondered how she could tell Kelvin that he was the last person her parents would want her dating.

"Lemme call the home front and tell Ms. Mother Moseley that a brothah's got plans."

After the call, Kelvin connected his iPod to the car's stereo system. An up-tempo original hip-hop beat, produced by one of his college friends, pulsated from the high-end system and reverberated off the soft, leather seats. Kelvin was so busy profiling and Princess was so deep in thought about what and what not to share with Kelvin that neither of them noticed the beat-up Dodge that began following them as soon as they left the church.

Robin drove, shoulders hunched, hands gripping the wheel. She kept one eye on the road and one eye on the white car weaving in and out of the heavy Sunday traffic. Fortunately Derrick wasn't in much of a hurry today; even in her hoopty, she was keeping up just fine.

Robin took a hand off the wheel long enough to take the gun from the passenger seat and place it in her lap. She thought of her plan, about what she had in mind for Vivian, and a sneer appeared on her face. There'd be no guard to stop her this time. Robin would jump out of her car and pop a cap in Vivian before their fancy garage door was halfway up. "It's been a long time," she said aloud. "But you're finally gonna get what's coming to you. And I'm gonna get what should have come to me a long time ago . . . Derrick."

The white Jaguar took a turn that Robin wasn't expecting. "This isn't the way to your house, muthafucka!" she screamed. She gripped the wheel with both hands again, speeding through traffic until there was only one car separating her car from Derrick's.

The unexpected turn befuddled and unnerved Robin. She shook her head, tried to clear its fuzziness. Wanting to be sure she was thinking straight, she'd taken three times the normal dosage of Peridol before she'd left the motel, an act she thought would make her feel good. Unfortunately, the opposite effect was happening. Robin felt foggier than ever. And she was even more delusional.

"Yeah, thought you could lose me, didn't you? Just like all those years ago, back in Georgia, I mean Florida, I mean . . . you know what I mean! You took my man, Vivian," Robin whined, pointing to the head on the passenger's side of the car. "Why you always got to come and take my man?"

Robin's maniacal mind merged memories of working with Derrick at his first church with those of the twenty-something mistress who enticed Robin's husband away from their ten-year marriage. "I told you I was gonna get you," she bellowed. "I told you that nobody took my man and got away with it." Her voice dropped to a raspy whisper. "Nobody, muthafucka . . ."

A totally different drama was unfolding inside Derrick Montgomery's Jaguar.

"Okay, so let me get this straight," Kelvin said. "Your dad used to roll with *my* mom before he married *your* mom?"

"Right."

"And then after your dad got married, he was *still* hittin' it with my mom?"

"Uh-huh."

"Damn. So then what happened?"

"Mama found out about it and my parents separated for a while."

"Real talk?"

"And . . ." Princess paused before revealing the extent of her and Kelvin's unique connection. "She was pregnant with me at the time."

"Naw . . . c'mon now!"

"Serious."

Kelvin changed lanes and merged into the freeway traffic, which was fairly light for a Sunday. He moved over into the fast lane and increased his speed.

"How you know all this?" he asked after a pause.

"Heard Mama talking about it with Aunt Viv. That's why I know they all would freak the bump out if they found out we were together."

"Damn girl, you almost my sister!" Kelvin shoved Princess playfully before placing a hand on her leg.

"Almost ain't is, nucka. And somebody's glad about that."

Kelvin squeezed Princess's thigh. "Somebody sure is."

Kelvin saw his exit and looked over his shoulder to change lanes. "Damn! What's that car doing?" Kelvin watched as an old, beat-up hoopty almost broadsided his father's spotless ride.

"What?"

"That car almost hit us," Kelvin said, suddenly exhibiting the frightened nervousness of an eighteen-year-old. "Let me get away from this fool!"

Instead of exiting the freeway, Kelvin merged back into traffic and accelerated. He looked in his rearview mirror. The rusted out hoopty had dropped farther behind him, still weaving in and out of traffic.

"That fool must be high," he said, relaxing with the distance building up between them. " 'Cause he's trippin'!"

Princess looked back and didn't see the car. She relaxed as well, taking her hand and placing it near Kelvin's crotch.

Robin grabbed the gun, her mind in a frenzy. "What, you tryin' to shake me? You tryin' to lose a muthafucka?" she yelled at the Jaguar. "I told you that I was gonna get your ass. I told you!" Robin pressed the gas pedal down as far as it would go, and zoomed around the slow-moving semi that had temporarily hidden her from view. Thinking she might lose them again, Robin stuck her left hand out the window and tried to aim the gun at the Jaguar. Being right-handed, trying to use her left one was a risky proposition; her shot hit the side mirror of an unfortunate SUV. Robin continued firing wildly, her car wobbling as she tried to aim, drive, and shoot.

"Dammit," Robin exclaimed, even as drivers around her reached for cell phones to dial 911.

Kelvin and Princess were oblivious to the crisis they thought they'd outrun. Kelvin slowed down, tilted his body into a mean lean, kept one hand on the steering wheel and placed the other one back on Princess's leg.

"Where are we going? I'm hungry," Princess asked.

"Um, me too," Kelvin replied with a mischievous grin.

"Shut up," Princess said playfully, batting Kelvin's hand away from her breast.

The hip-hop track that had been bouncing off the car's interior came to an end, replaced by the sounds of horns honking. Both Kelvin and Princess looked around, finally realizing that LA traffic was crazier than usual. Cars were speeding around them, or pulling over. Kelvin looked in the rearview mirror and saw the reason why.

"Is that a gun?" Kelvin shouted.

"What? Where?" Princess screamed back at him, looking around.

At the exact moment Princess screamed, Robin's wheels locked. Panicked, she dropped the gun and grabbed the wheel with both hands, unsuccessfully trying to regain control. The gun skidded off the asphalt, under several cars, and would later be recovered by the LAPD. The Dodge skidded in the opposite direction, clipping the back end of a pickup truck and doing a one-eighty before flipping over twice and coming to rest upside down in the freeway's center lane. Miraculously, the SUV with the shot-out mirror and the rear bumper of the pickup truck were the only cars affected by Robin's erratic actions. The only cars except the one now resting, tires still spinning, on its hood.

Kelvin's leg shook so badly he could hardly press the gas pedal and get the Jaguar to the side of the highway. Once he pulled over, he put the car in park, turned off the ignition, and sat with his forehead pressed to the steering wheel. His heart raced, as did his thoughts as he tried to come to grips with what he'd just witnessed.

Princess stared straight ahead, motionless as a statue. Time seemed to stand still as the surreal scene of the grizzly accident repeated itself in both their minds. Within minutes, the sound of sirens cut through the hazy silence, shaking both Kelvin and Princess out of their trancelike states.

"That was some crazy shit," Kelvin said, his voice barely above a whisper.

"I saw it, but I can't believe it," Princess whispered back. "What was wrong with that person?"

"I don't know," Kelvin answered, while wondering if he'd really seen a gun when he looked in the mirror.

"Did you really see a gun?" Princess asked, reading his mind. "Maybe it was some gang stuff going on."

"I don't know what it was," Kelvin responded, finally calm enough to restart the engine. "But I just thank God we weren't any closer. It could have been us flipped upside down."

"Yes," Princess whispered. "Thank God." She looked back to see an ambulance, fire truck, and several police cars surrounding the overturned car.

Kelvin watched as well, and saw firemen and medical personnel looking into the windows of the badly battered vehicle. "Man, whoever that is will be lucky to get out of there alive."

Princess looked back one more time as Kelvin steered the car onto the highway. "No," she said before forcing herself to turn away from the tragic scene. "Whoever's in that car is dead."

Several people looked on as firemen used their equipment to pry open the smashed door on the driver's side. A medic stooped next to the body dangling upside down, held in place by a durable seatbelt. Careful of the broken glass and large drops of blood, he grabbed the accident victim's arm. Holding his fingers against the victim's wrist, he waited a moment, repositioned his fingers and waited another moment. Then he turned and gave a curt nod to the fire chief standing behind him. "I think I feel a pulse."

13

Project Darius

Stacy lay quiet and content in Darius's arms. He was always good, but had been especially attentive in tonight's lovemaking, giving Stacy several orgasms before enjoying a sustained one of his own. But as usual, it wasn't long before he jumped up and headed to the shower.

Stacy's afterglow turned to an after "no." After two years, she was tired of feeling like, like . . . *How do I feel?* Stacy wondered. It was hard to describe in words, in several words even. Darius would be totally into her one moment, and then totally disconnected the next—like now. She didn't feel as if she were a *part* of him, as if she were really *with* him. A part of her always felt as if she were on the outside of Darius's life looking in. She'd stewed on her situation ever since having lunch with Hope the month before—about the best way to handle getting what she wanted. Summer had given way to October and while she hoped the answer to the dilemma was in her womb, she wasn't one hundred percent sure. She'd told Hope about the baby but hadn't told its father. The timing, and his mood, had to be perfect.

Stacy got out of bed and walked into the kitchen. She leaned against the counter, slowly sipped a glass of water, and thought of why she and Darius couldn't seem to take their relationship to the next level, why after two years things seemed to be at a standstill. In every instance his manager, Bo Jenkins, was either the "stand" or the "still." He was why she could never spend the night at Darius's house—because roommates Bo and Darius had agreed to not have overnight guests. What kind of joke was that? Grown men splitting the rent telling each other who can do what? Why she could never go out of town with Darius—Bo always made it seem that while he was indispensable, she would only be in the way. And what was worse, Darius listened. What kind of business manager tells a client how to run his personal life? Stacy knew Bo had discouraged Darius from getting married as well, saying a wedding at this point in time would diminish Darius's largely female fan base. At the root of every issue she had with Darius was one thing and one thing only: Bo.

Stacy stomped into the bedroom. Darius sat on the bed, having just put on his shoes. She stopped directly in front of him, her unwashed punanny inches from his face.

"We've got a problem, Darius," she said, hands on hips. "And his name is Bo."

Darius kept his look neutral, masking surprise. Bo is exactly who Darius had been thinking of when Stacy walked in, and all while he showered and dressed. He stood up and brushed past her. "What now?"

Stacy ignored the chagrin in Darius's voice. This wasn't the first time that Bo being an issue had come up—so what. Obviously Darius didn't understand just how much his business manager worked her nerves.

"This is what," she said, sweeping her hand in a head to toe motion. "You being dressed, going home. Why can't you spend the night at my house? Two years, and I can count the times you've spent the night. Bo, right?"

Tonight especially, the reason was Bo. He'd told Darius that there would be a surprise waiting for him when he returned home. But Stacy didn't need to know that. "I told you," he said, walking over to Stacy and using a hug to try and diffuse the situation. "I like to sleep in my own bed."

Stacy pulled out of his embrace. "What's so wrong with mine? It's good enough for fucking, but not for sleep?"

"Stacy, don't use such crass words."

"Crass? Hmph. Crass, my ass, Darius, I want real answers."

"Well, you're not going to get them tonight, not with that tone of voice and not in that mood." Darius decided to meet Stacy's indignation with some of his own. That's what he usually did to take the wind out of Bo's sails. The move worked just as well on Stacy.

"Look," she said, following Darius into the living room, where he retrieved his keys and travel pouch. "I don't want to have an attitude with you, I really don't. But you know where I'm at with us.

It's been two years; we're both in our thirties. How long are we going to date?

"I want to really feel like you're my man, Darius, not just when you're in my house, or at the church. I want to be with you, really *be* with you: travel, hang out on the daily, wake up next to you, fix you breakfast." She walked over to where Darius was standing by the front door. "Is that too much to ask?"

Actually, yes, is what Darius thought. "Of course not," is what he said.

"So act like it then," Stacy said with a pout in her voice as she pulled Darius into an embrace. "Stay with me, if not tonight, the next time you come over. Or let me stay at your house, and come with you on one of your upcoming tour dates."

"Okay," Darius said, looking at his watch over Stacy's shoulder.

"You mean it?" Stacy asked, releasing him. "You'll stay? I can come?"

"I will stay and we'll see about you attending an out of town concert."

"See, baby, was that so hard? I want us to be together forever. It's you, Darius, that's all I want."

Darius gave Stacy a quick kiss on the lips and was out the door. Somebody else wanted only him too, and Darius didn't want to keep him waiting.

The smell of scented candles greeted Darius as he turned the knob and entered the condo he shared with his personal assistant/business manager and lover of three years, Bo Jenkins. Darius smiled. He and Bo had gone through a lot, and when Stacy arrived on the scene it almost caused their breakup. But love had prevailed; Bo now understood that Stacy was a necessary accessory to Darius's heterosexual persona. His and Bo's relationship was stronger than ever, and that Bo had been willing to accept Stacy, keeping Darius's best interest at heart, made Darius love him all the more.

"Hey, you," Darius said as he walked into a living room shimmering with more than a dozen white candles. A bottle of champagne chilled in a bucket, and the sultry sounds of Joss Stone added to the ambiance.

"Hey, back," Bo answered. He gave Darius a quick hug and peck on the lips, ignoring the "just showered" smell with which he'd become familiar. That drove him crazy when Darius first started seeing Stacy—Darius coming home smelling like Dove or Ivory or some shit neither Bo nor Darius would be caught dead buying. He'd finally purchased Darius a travel bag, a supply of their preferred soap, Calvin Klein's Obsession, and explained to Darius before a date with Stacy: "so yo' ass can smell the same going and coming."

"What's all this?" Darius asked. "My birthday is still weeks away."

Instead of answering the question, Bo asked his own. "Don't you want to get comfortable? I've got a few things to share with you and I'm sure you've, uh, already had quite a night."

Darius couldn't lie. "Sometimes that girl acts like a nymphomaniac. It's like she—"

"OMG, TMI, keep those details TYS." Bo had adopted his best diva pose as he delivered this line, finishing with a "tsk, tsk, tsk" and sashaying over to the bottle of champagne. "I don't know about you, but I could use some bubbly."

Darius laughed. "I'm sorry, baby. It's just that you're my best friend in the world. It's hard not to share everything with you."

This had the desired effect, as complimenting Bo always did. "Go on in there and take those clothes off, boy," Bo said with a grin. "And don't worry, double-oh-eight will give you a break tonight."

After a quick change into cashmere sweats, Darius joined Bo on the couch. "What's TYS?" he asked, taking the champagne flute Bo held out to him.

"To—yo'—self," Bo said, punctuating every word. He lifted his glass. "Cheers."

They spent several moments in companionable silence, enjoying the champagne. Two flutes later, Bo decided he did want to hear what had happened with Stacy, and Darius obliged him. Bo couldn't have been happier that Stacy was harping on Darius about Bo always being around, and that she kept bugging Darius for them to get engaged. Watching Darius's reactions to her pleas had helped Bo change his strategy. He'd become the patient, noncomplaining (well, not much anyway), empathizing partner, the one always there with a shoulder to lean on, and an ear to hear. Bo figured that the more Stacy showed her ass, and the less he did, the faster Darius would realize which one of them he truly wanted.

Bo walked into the kitchen and came back with

a snack tray of mini sandwiches and a pile of colorful root vegetable chips.

"Thank you, baby," Darius exclaimed. "I was just sitting here trying to remember the last time I ate."

Bo set the tray down and headed toward the bedroom. "Did that skank ho fuck you senseless and leave your stomach empty?" he asked over his shoulder.

Darius laughed. "Something like that. And, Bo, I've told you. Stop calling her that. It's not right—disrespectful to women in general and Stacy in particular. Bo, do you hear me?"

"Sorry," Bo mumbled, with as much sincerity as there was pork in a kosher butcher shop.

Darius finished a salami and turkey combo with melted provolone cheese in three bites. "She can't cook like you anyway," he said when Bo returned to the room. "These are so good. What did you do, zap them in the microwave?"

"No, baby, only the best for you. Those are oven baked, and I got the rolls from this kosher bakery in Fairfax. They're made fresh every day."

Darius reached for another sandwich, this one a savory roast beef paired with roasted red and pepperoncini peppers, arugula, and Cabrales blue cheese. The savory combo burst upon his palette with the first bite. He enjoyed the flavors, his eyes closed as he slowly chewed.

Bo fairly preened with satisfaction. "I knew you'd like that one; it's my favorite."

Darius finished the first and immediately took a second bite. "Mine too," he said around a mouthful of beef.

The CD player switched from Joss Stone to *Whitney Houston's Greatest Hits*. With "You Give Good Love" playing in the background, it seemed to Bo the perfect time to give Darius his surprise. He casually handed Darius a luxuriously wrapped packet, held together with a golden seal.

"What's this?"

"Open it and find out."

Darius opened the packet and pulled out the contents. On top was a brochure with pictures of châteaus, a river, and nightlife scenes. Opening it, Darius saw they were pictures of Quebec, Canada.

"What's this?" Darius repeated. "You going somewhere?"

"Not without you," Bo said as he snuggled closer to Darius. Darius had told Bo months ago about wanting to visit Quebec, Canada, after seeing a television documentary on the province. Bo had begun planning a holiday trip shortly after that conversation. Quebec was one of three cities in Canada that performed and recognized same-sex marriages, a subject Bo and Darius had also casually discussed.

Darius opened the second brochure. It was a flight itinerary, outlining a trip to take place over the Thanksgiving holidays. "First class! That's what I'm talking about. Baby knows how a brother likes to roll!" Darius leaned over and gave Bo a quick kiss before continuing to examine the packet's contents. Along with the brochure on Quebec and travel itinerary was a brochure of the luxury hotel for their weeklong visit: the Fairmont Le Manoir Richelieu, and various brochures on skiing and other entertainment options. Darius was overwhelmed at the obvious care and careful planning it had taken for Bo to put this together, and that he'd done it all for him. Few were the times Darius could remember feeling so loved and cherished. He stared deeply into Bo's eyes before enfolding him in a long, gentle embrace. It was all he could do to express his gratitude; it was enough.

After several moments, Bo whispered, "Isn't there one more envelope in the packet?"

Darius went through the brochures and found a small envelope he'd overlooked. It was heavier than the other envelopes, with obviously something besides paper inside. It was a small key. He raised his brow in a questioning gesture.

"That," Bo said, pointing to the key, "holds the final part of your birthday present. But for that you'll have to wait until your actual birthday, when we're in Quebec."

"Bo! That's too far away."

"Only a few weeks; they'll fly by."

"Give me a hint."

Bo thought for a moment. "Well, considering how 'Possible' is heating up the charts, let's hope it goes double platinum."

Darius knew Bo had intentionally confused him. "You're not going to tell me, are you?"

Bo arose from the couch and pulled Darius up with him. They headed toward the bedroom. "No," Bo said, as he rubbed his hand across Darius's cashmere-covered behind. "But it will be worth the wait."

* * *

Stacy tossed and turned, unable to sleep. Her thoughts were in turmoil, and all about Darius. She felt she needed to make a move, make something happen, and soon. She felt for sure that if the relationship did not move forward, it would begin to go backward. In a way, it already had, with Darius spending more time performing out of town, which meant away from her.

But was it the right time to tell him about the baby? For some reason she continued to hesitate. The timing just didn't feel right. At times she'd even questioned if what she'd done was the correct move, or whether it would backfire. She lay on her back remembering how the idea had come about.

It was a night much like this one, when she couldn't sleep. Belatedly, she'd remembered that she hadn't taken her birth control pills that day. She'd traipsed into the bathroom and retrieved them from the medicine cabinet. She popped one in her mouth and was reaching for her water glass when she stopped midmove, the pill on her tongue. Slowly, she turned toward the mirror, opened her mouth, and lifted the tiny white pill off her tongue.

That's it, she thought, taking the pill and dropping it purposefully into the toilet. She'd then taken her birth control pill dispenser and dropped it in the trash.

"Mrs. Crenshaw," she'd said aloud, referring to herself by Darius's last name as she eyed herself in the mirror, "it's time to start Project Darius Jr."

The rest hadn't been difficult. Darius didn't always wear a condom, and didn't worry about pregnancy because he knew Stacy was on the pill. They both had a healthy sexual appetite. Before Stacy had time to think it through, much less change her mind, she was pregnant. Darius was getting ready to be a father, and if her plan succeeded, Stacy would soon be his wife.

14

Marital Obligations

Carla Lee's world was upside down, and Lavon Chapman was the man who'd flipped it. She'd only known him four weeks. It felt like a lifetime. The first week they'd become intimate had been glorious. Stanley was out of town and the kids busy with school. Carla and Lavon had screwed like teenagers, every position, everywhere. But after that week, things had gotten tricky. Stanley came home, and because of his dedication to the Kingdom Keys series and the short time they had to produce it, had cancelled his remaining out of town engagements for the length of Lavon's visit. Lavon and Carla still saw each other almost all day every day, but Stanley was there as well.

Stanley's return didn't totally stop the lovers from their trysts. Citing engagements with Vivian or one of the other members of Ladies First, an organization for pastors' wives, Carla met Lavon at the Sheraton and enjoyed stolen hours of mind-boggling ecstasy. Lavon's unparalleled oral expertise was like crack cocaine; the more she had, the more she wanted. She kept telling herself that this good sex was blowing her mind because of how long she'd gone without it. She rationalized that the affair was only eight weeks out of a lifetime marriage. November would come and Lavon would be gone, leaving her with wonderful memories and a va-jay-jay that tingled every time she imagined his face or heard his name.

"Lavon," she whispered.

"What'd you say?" Stanley asked, coming into the kitchen.

Carla had been so deep in thought she hadn't heard her husband, or realized she'd said her lover's name out loud.

"Did you say Lavon?"

"Did I?" Carla asked, busying herself by grabbing fixings for a salad she hadn't planned to prepare—anything to keep her hands busy. "I may have; I'm trying to organize a 'to do' list in my mind and getting copies of my SOS tapes to him is one on the list."

"Speaking of, how'd your meeting go?"

"Hmm?"

"Your meeting?"

"What meeting, Stan?"

Stan stopped from getting a soda out of the refrigerator and looked at Carla. "Didn't you tell me you had a meeting today with Ladies First? Planning for the next Sanctity of Sisterhood mini-conference?"

"Oh, that meeting." Carla had momentarily forgotten which lie she'd used for her afternoon delight at the Sheraton. "No, Bo, that got cancelled so I met with someone else instead."

"Who?"

She didn't miss a beat. "Oh, you don't know her, she's not a pastor's wife. Just a sistah who needs prayer, and a friend."

Carla wasn't in the habit of lying to Stanley; their marriage had been above board for a decade. But she hadn't always been saved, and back in the day, she could lie like a rug, look you straight in the eye and tell you the sky was red with so much conviction you'd almost believe her. In the last three weeks, Carla had found the art like riding a bicycle—a skill that came back with practice.

Stanley came behind Carla and put his hands on her shoulders. "Have I told you lately how special you are?" The contact was brief, rote, reminding Carla what she had to look forward to once Lavon was gone. But she hadn't missed the sincerity in her husband's voice. He cared for her, loved her in his own way.

A wave of guilt washed over Carla. What was she doing? Here was a man who'd married a single mother, adopted her daughter as his own, gave her two sons, supported the family financially and in every other way for ten years, and never once gave her cause to suspect he was unfaithful. And how was she thanking him? By screwing the man Stanley had brought in to take their ministry, their successful, fruitful ministry, to a higher level. This is why for the past month Carla had refused to really think about what she was doing; it didn't feel good. She knew she had to end things with Lavon.

"I love you, Bo," she said, with a catch in her voice, as she turned and hugged her husband tightly.

Stanley noticed the emotion behind the words. He held Carla at arm's length, searching her face for answers. "Are you all right?"

"Yes, just emotional I guess, that time of the month."

"Oh, I see. So that's why you haven't been bugging me to fulfill my marital obligations, huh?"

It was true. Since Lavon had arrived in LA, Carla hadn't had sex with her husband, nor wanted to. The weekly intimacy that she usually initiated had fallen by the wayside, along with the validity of her marriage vows. "I know you're busy," she said as a reason.

"And I know how much that aspect of marriage means to you. Maybe this weekend?" he suggested.

"Whenever you want, Stanley," Carla said, falling short of the enthusiasm she'd hoped her voice would convey.

Carla's cell phone rang. She picked it up off the counter and checked the ID: Lavon. Seeing his name immediately made her wet, something the man standing in front of her seemed unable to do. Guilt clinched her heart again. Yes, she had to end her affair with Lavon, and she had to end it now.

Stanley gave Carla a peck on the cheek and walked out of the kitchen as she flipped up her phone to answer it. "Hello?"

"Hey curvy Carla, how's my bowl of honey doing today?" Lavon's voice was low and sexy, the voice that so expertly whispered sweet somethings in Carla's ear at the point of climax.

She closed her eyes, willing herself to tap down the joy that bubbled over in spite of her resolve. "I'm glad you called," she said in businesslike fashion. "There are some things I need to discuss with you. Are you free for lunch tomorrow?"

"Oh, Stanley's there. Yeah, baby, tomorrow's fine. Say, noon, in my room? I'll order in lunch and uh, tailor-make your dessert."

Carla almost moaned aloud. She'd tasted his desserts, had had seconds and thirds. Of all the diets she'd ever gone on, she knew this one would be the hardest. "Yes," she said after a pause, "the coffee shop will be fine."

Silence on the other end. And then, "What's going on? Did something happen?"

At the same time Carla's resolve was weakening, Stanley walked back into the kitchen, with boys Shay and Winston in tow. She had to get off the phone. "That sounds good, sistah. See you tomorrow."

Minutes later Carla sat at the dining room table, laughing loudly and eating heartily with the men in her life—the only ones who rightly belonged there. Brianna's cheerleading practice would be ending soon and they'd all be home, one happy family. Carla intended to keep it that way.

That Friday night, Stanley kept his word about making love to Carla. After they'd showered, separately, Stanley crawled into bed and on top of Carla. He kissed, or a better description might be pecked at her mouth, his tongue darting in and out like a roach looking for a getaway in a suddenly bright room. Carla tried to slow the pace, taking her tongue and slowly, lovingly, tracing the outline of Stanley's mouth, her body grinding against his in a sensuous motion. "Let me on top," she whispered, as she grasped the back of his head to deepen the kiss.

She then grabbed his buttocks, kneading them in a circular motion, slipping her fingers down its crevice. While this was a tactic Lavon thoroughly enjoyed, the act obviously made Stanley uncomfortable. He shifted his body, reached between his legs, grabbed his shaft and pushed it roughly inside Carla. The familiar, decade-old dance ensued: *pump, pump, pause, pump-pump-pump-pump shift, pump, pump, pause, kiss one nipple, kiss the other, pump, pump, pump, pump, ahhhhhhhhhhh.* And then it was over—for Stanley.

Carla sighed, even as her eyes welled up with tears. Just as quickly she tamped down the emotions. She would not feel sorry for herself. God was good and she was blessed with a godly man, a wonderful father for her children, a beautiful home, and a nice life. So what she didn't have the intimacy she desired. It was a small price to pay for what she'd been given. *When Stan met you, you were a single mother in a roach-infested apartment . . . remember that!* "Yes, remember that," Carla whispered as she slid softly out of the bed so as not to awaken her husband. *Remember that,* she thought, as she went to the closet and reached for "Denzel." And she tried to remember, tried to ignore her feelings, tried to embrace the passion for the man who years ago had embraced her. But as she found physical release, with the help of her "monster cock," it was Lavon, not Stanley, who she remembered, the one who in that moment she knew she could not forget.

15

Just a Little More

Passion smiled as she waited for Lavon to answer his phone. Her ex had just picked up Onyx, who would be spending the next two days with him, his wife, and their recently born son. And Lavon had finally agreed to come over to her place for a home-cooked meal. In the past few weeks, she'd mostly talked with him at church, and aside from a midweek lunch date, hadn't enjoyed any one-on-one time. She'd tried to be patient, reminding herself that he had been brought in for a time-sensitive project. Still, she wanted more to happen faster, and was glad she was finally going to see him in what she hoped would become an intimate setting. Lavon would only be in town a few more weeks. Whatever was going to happen needed to happen now. The thought of what could happen later on that night caused her to giggle.

"What's so funny?" Lavon said as he answered his phone.

"Hey, Lavon! Oh, nothing. Just a silly thought I had."

"I'm glad you're in a good mood." He was welcoming this feeling because the coffee he'd had a couple days before had left a bad taste in his mouth. Or more like the news that had come with the coffee, that Carla wanted to chill things out. Hopefully Passion would help him honor her wishes. "Uh, yeah, what's up?"

"Oh, I just wanted to make sure you liked strawberries . . . before I made dessert."

"Strawberries are cool," he responded, remembering the last thighs from which he'd licked whipped cream. But those thighs belonged to someone else, were married to someone else. "Yeah, strawberries are fine. See you later."

A few hours later, Lavon sat on Passion's couch, pleasantly full from a dinner of baked chicken with mashed potatoes and gravy. Georgia women could sure throw down in the cooking department, although if it were a contest between Carla and Passion, Carla would win. Lavon shook his head to interrupt the thought; he had to try and stop thinking about *Pastor, Mrs.* Carla Lee.

"I wish they'd come back," Passion said, referring to the R & B group Boys II Men, whose concert DVD was playing on her television. "They're one of my favorite groups."

She handed Lavon a saucer of strawberry swirl cake, topped with a sugar glaze and thankfully, no whipped cream.

Lavon could only imagine where Passion would have wanted eating whipped cream to lead and he was determined that Carla would be the only member at Logos Word he screwed. "This is good," he said. "I don't think I've ever had strawberry cake."

"My grandmother's recipe," Passion said, delighted her dessert was a hit. "Oh, and I've got some whipped cream if you'd like."

"No, no, no, that's okay," Lavon responded a little too forcefully. "I mean, I wouldn't want to cover up this perfection with cream."

They finished dessert and Passion took their plates to the kitchen. When she came back, she cozied up on the couch next to Lavon, rocking gently as Boys II Men sang about making love. "I'll make love to you; like you want me to . . ."

Passion's mind raced as she sat next to Lavon. On the one hand, she was physically turned on by him and wanted to take their intimacy farther than the few kisses they'd shared so far. On the other hand, however, she'd been celibate five years for a reason: She wanted to "live holy," as her mother would say, and be married the next time she made love. But it felt so good snuggling up next to this man. *Just a little farther,* she thought as she leaned her head on Lavon's shoulder and placed his hand in hers.

Lavon shifted his body and placed his arm around Passion. His middle finger drew lazy circles on her upper arm as his other hand stroked her thigh. Passion felt a tug in her lower belly as feathery sensations stoked a dormant fire. She raised her head and placed a light kiss on Lavon's cheek.

As "Water Runs Dry" flowed into "On Bended Knee," the conversation lessened and the kisses intensified. Lavon nipped and traced Passion's full lips with his tongue. His hand moved from stroking her arm to stroking her nipple, its hardened presence protruding under the knit top and silk teddy she wore. The friction caused Passion to gasp, granting Lavon's tongue full access to her mouth, her own tongue swirling around his, her hands traveling the length of his muscled arm. *Just a little more . . .*

Lavon was a highly sexual man. Despite his pledges to the contrary, his hand was soon inside Passion's loose knit top and under the teddy. He kneaded her mounds of flesh as he trailed his tongue from her cheek to her neck, planting kisses along the way. Before Passion could decry his mouth leaving hers, his lips fastened onto her nipple, his tongue creating tingles from her breasts to her buttocks.

Passion moaned aloud. Her mind screamed stop even as she parted her legs to grant access to the hand pushing its way between them. Lavon rubbed the fabric covering her treasure while Passion pressed his hand harder against her. Her body demanded more, begged for intimate contact. The clothes were in the way.

"We'll be more comfortable in my bedroom," she whispered. They kissed again, and this time it was Passion's fingers that went on a treasure hunt. Her eyelids briefly fluttered open when she felt Lavon's large, hard manhood pulsating underneath his light wool slacks. Her body reacted to the possibilities of what this massive piece of muscle could do inside her. "Lavon, I want this," she whispered, squeezing it gently. "I want this so much."

Her words wound their way through the lust-induced fog inside Lavon's brain. This wasn't Carla, this was Passion, and he was not going to have sex with her. He stopped abruptly and covered Passion's breasts with her teddy before sitting up.

"I'm sorry," he said, his voice gruff, his breathing heavy. "I got carried away."

"I know, me too," she said. She sat up and away from Lavon even as her body screamed its protest at the sudden end to his physical contact.

"Maybe I'd better go," Lavon said.

"No, don't," Passion responded quickly. She placed a hand on his arm before he could rise, and turned once again to face him. She was suddenly nervous and self-conscious.

"I . . ." Passion stopped, sighed, and began again. "I am very attracted to you, Lavon. It's been a long time since I've felt this way about anyone."

"You're celibate, and I—"

"Yes, it's been several years since I've had sex, but it's not just your physical presence I enjoy." Passion forced herself to not look at the outline of his still hardened penis resting almost midway down his thigh. "It's your sense of humor, our conversations. I like being around you."

"I enjoy you as well," Lavon admitted. "But the truth is, I'm only here for a few more weeks. I am involved with someone else. It wouldn't be right for me to sleep with you."

That's right, Passion remembered. *The lucky woman back in Kansas.* His words caused an ache in Passion's heart and caused her feelings for him to deepen. They were the words of a good man, an honorable man. She wanted him more than ever . . . when the time was right. She prayed that one day the time would be right. Her still throbbing body wished the time were now.

"Can I cook you breakfast in the morning?" she asked.

Lavon looked over quickly, his expression quizzical. "Aren't you listening to me, Passion? I can't do this with you." He rose to leave.

She rose with him. "I know you can't, and as much as I want to make love with you, I know I can't either. But it's been so long since I've been held by a man, slept next to a man. It's a lot to ask, but could you maybe just do that? Spend the night and let me fix you breakfast in the morning?"

"I don't know if that's a good idea, Passion," Lavon said. "I'm not sure I could keep myself . . . away from you."

"Then maybe for a little while, until I fall asleep?" Passion knew she was begging, but she didn't care. Her longing for male closeness was stronger than her pride.

Lavon looked at the beautiful woman standing before him, size 40-DD breasts barely concealed by a knit top and satiny teddy, wide hips filling out print lounge pants. He watched as Passion nervously moistened her lush mouth with her tongue and smoothed back her black, shoulder-length hair. Lavon hadn't had sex all week. He was horny, his manhood ached for release. Release stood in front of him, begging him to spend the night.

"Where's your bedroom?" he asked.

Just a little more, she thought as she reached for Lavon's hand to show him the way.

16

Save Her from Herself

Lavon arrived back at his hotel Sunday morning with just enough time to shower and change for church. Fortunately the series production had found its rhythm and the taping was going smoothly. It was a good thing he didn't have to think too much. Between his unreleased sexual tension and Passion's soft, pliant body that periodically bumped up against him during the night, Lavon had hardly gotten any sleep. He hadn't gotten any breakfast, either, after deciding he needed a cold shower more. He'd eased out of Passion's bed at seven-thirty, leaving a note and her house five minutes later.

A blinking message light on the phone greeted Lavon as soon as he opened the door. Seeing it, Lavon remembered he'd turned off his cell phone the night before, just as he'd arrived at Passion's house. He hoped there were no emergencies.

He decided to listen to the hotel messages first.

There were two; one from last night and one from a half hour before. Both were from Carla.

First message: *"Hey, Lavon, Carla. Stanley wants to invite you over for dinner tonight to discuss the completion of Kingdom Keys. Dinner's at seven. If you can make it, give us a call or just come by."*

Second message: *"Ahem, good morning, Brother Chapman. I'm assuming you didn't get the messages from yesterday, either here or on your cell. Anyway, we'd like to invite you over for an early Sunday dinner, around five thirty. No need to call back, we'll see you in church."* There was a long pause before Carla hung up the phone.

"Well, Chap," Lavon said, undressing as he walked toward the shower, "you've gone and done it now."

Less than ten hours after leaving Passion's bed, he sat at the Lees' dining room table. Carla looked lovely in her perfectly coiffed braids pulled up and away from her face, a form-fitting dress that showed off her curvaceous body to perfection, and a pair of low-heeled mules. As she walked from the dining room to the kitchen, Lavon discreetly studied her backside. Carla had the best ass he'd ever seen, bar none. It was large, hard, and as round as a basketball. After his sexless night with Passion, he wanted Carla more than ever.

Carla stood in the kitchen feeling the same way. Women's intuition told her that Lavon had been with someone the night before, and as unfair and unjustified as it was, a wave of jealousy consumed her. She was married and had absolutely no rights to Lavon, but that didn't stop her from being envious of the woman who'd enjoyed his illustrious charm and lovemaking skills. Her earlier resolve disappeared as fast as her Sunday chicken and dumplings. Carla had watched how much Lavon enjoyed the meal, and she wanted to be sopped up just like the sauce on his plate.

Carla brought out a moist, lemon-frosted pound cake made from scratch. She was surprised to see Stanley rising from his seat, reaching for his suit jacket.

"Where are you going?" she asked.

"Derrick just called, and I think he could use some support. He's doing much better since losing his uncle, but I want to say a prayer with him, in person." Stanley put on his jacket and reached for his briefcase. "On the way to his house, I'll drop off the kids for the church musical and probably be back around eight. I figured that until I get back you two could discuss SOS and which promotions would be best to put at the end of these DVDs."

"You probably should be here, baby," Carla replied, mentally begging him to come back and help save her from herself. "You know best how you want the DVDs to look."

"But you know me," Stanley said, coming around the table to plant a kiss on her lips. "And nobody makes me look as good as you do. I trust your judgment in watching the tapes for the best footage. It will give us a leg up on our work tomorrow. And like I said, I'll be back in a few hours."

Lavon didn't trust himself alone with Carla and quickly sought to get out of the situation. "I'm not sure I have all the DVDs," he said as he walked with

Stanley toward the door. "It would probably be best to do this tomorrow, Doc."

"Well, let Carla check out whatever you have; we don't have time to waste." With that, Stanley called to his three children, who were all on program to sing with the youth choir. "Y'all ready to go?" Brianna, Shay, and Winston came bounding down the stairs with a chorus of "yeahs" and "uh-huhs."

Stanley looked the epitome of the perfect father as he held the door open for his children. He blew his wife a kiss. "See you soon."

Lavon and Carla stood still a full two minutes after Stanley left, both silently trying to talk themselves out of the inevitable. And then they were in each other's arms.

"I missed you," Carla said as she led Lavon to the guest bedroom.

"Me too," Lavon responded, his hand on Carla's generous backside. "And I'm getting ready to show you how much."

17

Dirty Laundry

"It's me, girl, open the door," Kelvin said impatiently, banging on Princess's door at one o'clock in the morning.

Princess rubbed sleep from her eyes as she undid the latch to her dorm room. "Kelvin, what are you doing here? You trying to get me in trouble?"

"I'm in enough trouble for the both of us," he said, pushing his way into the room and dumping a large, stuffed backpack on the floor. "I left the Rev's."

"You what?"

"Left, got kicked out, however you want to look at it. Me and the Rev had words or whatever. I told him I wasn't going to church, and he told me that it was either that or get out. So I got out."

"And you came here? Kelvin, you can't stay here—"

"Oh, I'm your man but you gonna throw me out too? Is that how you roll?"

"No, but—"

"But what? Look, whatever, I'm only here to crash for the night. This weekend, me and you are moving into our own place."

Princess was sure she was dreaming. All she'd ever wanted was for Kelvin to be her man only, and now here he was saying he wanted them to live together? It was more than she could have prayed for. Once they were living in the same house there would be no way for him to be with anyone else; all the other girls would have to back the bump up. Yes, she knew about the other girls. She'd just kept believing they didn't mean anything, that they threw themselves at Kelvin because he was an athlete, but that she was the one who really mattered in his life. Now, here was the proof. He was at her place, saying he wanted them to live together. It didn't matter the reason. The bottom line: he was here and Princess thanked her lucky stars that her roommate, Joni, was spending the night in her boyfriend's room.

Princess pulled Kelvin toward her and sat down on the bed. "We can't get our own place, Kel. Where are we gonna get the money?"

"Don't worry about that; I've already got the hookup. A friend of my dad's is, let's say, 'sponsoring' me. He's a huge basketball fan and wants me to be able to focus on that and school, and not worry about money."

"You talked to this man tonight?"

"I talk to him all the time. He's like a play uncle who I've known since I was thirteen. I've been kicking around the idea of an apartment for a while, since even before attending church got to be such a big deal. He feels the same way I do, that I shouldn't have religion forced down my throat. And he's got hella bank and friends in real estate. For him it's no big deal, but for us . . ."

"I'm surprised you don't wanna hook up with your boys and make this a party pad."

"Oh, it's gonna be that; it's definitely gonna be party central, baby, but not with a bunch of hardheads. Plus, the place can't be in the name of anybody on the team. The rules are strict about us college ballers not getting paid. So Geoff's gonna pay the year's rent in advance and we'll put the condo in your name." He reached over and hugged Princess. "It's gonna be our own hot spot, baby, just you and me."

Our own spot. Princess didn't mind rooming with Joni but setting up house would definitely have its advantages. A part of her was already relishing the freedom, but another part was hearing her parents' voices, already knowing how upset they'd be if they ever found out she'd moved off campus, was sexually active, who she was sexually active with . . . and not necessarily in that order.

"So what's it gonna be, we down or what?" Kelvin's countenance was serious as he awaited an answer.

Princess pondered her answer. If she said no, the question might not come again. Girls were waiting in line to hook up with Kelvin. But if she said yes, that was a different kind of weight. She didn't want to imagine the consequences of her parents finding out, and with her mother's nosy intuition, combined with Aunt Viv's regular phone calls and dinner invites, it wasn't "if" the truth about her living situation would ever come to light, but "when."

"So what's it gonna be?" Kelvin asked again. "'Cause if you ain't down, I need to keep moving. Geoff's already got a place for me to look at, and since he knows the owner, I might be able to move in tomorrow. But we gotta handle the paperwork ASAP, feel me?"

Princess took a deep breath and with one word turned the page of her life to a new chapter. "Yes," she said softly, and then with more confidence. "Yes, Kel, I'll do it." Princess cut the parental umbilical cord in that moment: *I'm grown and can do what I want. I'm not Mama and Daddy's little Princess anymore. The quicker everybody realizes that, the better.*

"I'm sorry to hear that, Viv," Tai said sincerely. "But the boy is grown, and he comes from a very different background. I know it's Derrick's house and all but—"

"You're preaching to the choir," Vivian interrupted. "Me and Derrick have very different views on this. I mean, the boy just came to live with us six months ago. He's never attended church regularly. My idea was to slowly incorporate church into his lifestyle. But Derrick wouldn't budge. Stubborn, manly ego; that's all this is about."

"So where is he?"

"Kelvin? He got an apartment. Janeé finally shared that much with us after we failed to hear from Kelvin all weekend. She said he was fine, that he wasn't mad at Derrick, and that he would be in touch with us."

"Sounds like his mother is okay with him living on his own."

"Actually, I think she's relieved he's no longer living with us. Don't get me wrong, I think she wanted Derrick and Kelvin to get to know one another better, and to develop some sort of relationship. But I don't think she was ever totally comfortable with the idea of his living here. She never said anything; it's just the feeling I got."

"Hmm. So he's staying in an apartment all by himself?"

"No, Janeé said it's him and a friend from his poli-sci class, somebody he knows from high school."

"Hmph."

"I'm just gonna pray for him, Tai, that's all I can do. He's a good kid, and we're going to miss him being around. Especially D2, he's really proud to have Kelvin as his older brother. I plan to invite him and his new roommate to Sunday dinner when he calls, and I'll ask Princess to come too."

"How do they get along—Princess and Kelvin?"

"Okay, I guess, but aside from the time y'all were here, they've only been over once at the same time. Kelvin had some girl with him and Princess had a cell phone glued to her ear. She still call herself in love with Rafael?"

"I guess so. El isn't at church much since he started college at KU. But last time we spoke, he talked about seeing Princess over the holidays. I guess it could be worse. At least I know who she's seeing and at least if they're screwing—which I think they are 'cause they're all googoo-eyed over each other—it's only a few times a year."

Tai sighed, thinking how she'd been just a little older than Princess when she got pregnant with Michael, her oldest child. "I definitely need to have a talk with her when she comes home for Thanksgiving because, trust, I'm not ready to be a grandmother."

"I'm 'bout to pull over and give you the business . . . . ooh baby, can I get a witness . . ." The sounds of T-Pain oozed out of the speakers as about twenty partygoers grooved to the beat. Princess melded into Kelvin, her hands around his waist, his hands gripping her backside. Couples bumped and ground around the room, while others smoked blunts and/or drank the Vodka-laced punch Princess and Joni had prepared.

"Here," Joni said, giving Princess a partially smoked joint.

Princess took a hit and passed the joint to Kelvin. "Naw, I'm good," Kelvin said, continuing to dance. Princess passed the joint over to Joni's boyfriend, Brandon, who had attended school with Kelvin in Santa Barbara. He and Joni were now roommates with Kelvin and Princess and as Kelvin had predicted, their place was party central.

Aside from the creative story she'd had to invent for her mother, Princess and Kelvin's moving in together two weeks ago had gone quite smoothly. Kelvin's uncle-friend, Geoff, had provided a nice, roomy, furnished, two-bedroom condo less than two miles from the UCLA campus, and had covered rent and utilities for the rest of the school year. A week later, Brandon and Joni suggested they all become roommates, and agreed to provide food, transportation, and recreational necessities for Kelvin and Princess in exchange for the second bedroom. So far it was a perfect arrangement for these best friends.

It also helped Princess with the story she told Tai: that Joni's family owned the condo and Joni had asked Princess to become her roommate. She'd rationalized the move for her mother saying the room and board monies her scholarship provided could now be used for study aids, field trips, and to supplement the small check she received from her part-time job. Princess told her mother she wanted to be independent, that she liked having found a way to save her parents some money. When Tai asked Princess about the secrecy of the move and her, the mother, finding out about it because of a disconnected phone number, Princess simply said she'd been too busy moving to call home, a story that Tai told Princess she didn't believe for one minute.

"You think I was born yesterday," Tai had said when Princess used a loaded schedule as the reason she hadn't told Tai about the move. "What's his name, Princess?"

"Who?" Princess had asked innocently.

"Are you telling me it's just you and Joni in the apartment—there are no guys staying with you? Remember, I was your age when I got pregnant with Michael. Things haven't changed that much since then."

"Well, uh, Joni's boyfriend comes over a lot. His name is Brandon."

"And what about you? You expect me to believe

you're so in love with Rafael that you're not talking to anybody, not attracted to any of the fine boys on that big campus, not even a little?"

Princess laughed. "Well, I do kinda like this one boy."

"And are you kinda having sex with this boy?"

"Mom!"

"Princess, it's been a while since we've talked about it but I want you to remember the things I've told you about abstinence and safe sex. I believed you when you said you hadn't slept with Rafael, but that conversation was a year ago."

"But, Mom—"

"Let me finish. You're a grown woman, full of life, hormones raging, wanting to spread your wings and try new things. I understand that. I was a lot like you at your age. I know what it's like to be so in love you're willing to do anything for the man. And believe me, whoever this dude is will ask you to do anything, and everything. All I'm saying is don't be stupid, don't give yourself to just anybody and whatever you do, don't mess around and get pregnant. Don't get me wrong—you know how much I love your brother, and how much I love King. I don't regret my life. But who knows what would have happened and how my life would be different if I hadn't had a child at such a young age?

"You're smart, beautiful, and have so much to offer the world. I just want you to be smart when it comes to men, baby, okay? Wait for the man who is willing to give you his name, or at least as much as he's getting from you . . . your whole heart."

That's right, I'm giving my baby everything, Princess thought as she walked toward her and Kelvin's bedroom. The party was winding down; only six or seven people remained. Just as well. The smoke, drink, and grinding against Kelvin all night had made her hot for her man. She was going to give it to him every way he wanted.

Princess neared the laundry room, which was adjacent to the kitchen. She'd almost passed it when she heard a sound. She almost ignored it, but then she heard it again and stopped. A bumping sound, and as she walked to the door and placed her ear against it, a low moan. Princess jerked the door open. The sight that greeted her was Kelvin's smooth chocolate ass with a pair of café au lait legs clutched tightly just above it.

"Kelvin! What the fuck is going on?"

The scene was obvious, but Kelvin still used one of the most popular answers given when caught in the wrong: "Nothing." Then under his breath, "Damn."

Meanwhile, Fawn, the woman who'd been moaning as Kelvin pounded her, pulled down her minidress and tried to scurry past Princess.

Princess grabbed Fawn's weave. "How you gonna come up in my house and fuck my man?!" Princess pulled on the weave, tried to knock Fawn to the ground.

Fawn struck back, grabbing Princess's halter top. "If he's your man, why is he with me? Let me go, tramp!"

Princess ignored the perky 32A's that had popped out of her halter. A tussle ensued, the two women rolling on the floor of the small hallway.

"A fight, y'all," someone yelled from the living room.

Kelvin grabbed Princess and Brandon grabbed Fawn, pulling her toward the door. "Party's over for you, *mami*," he said before opening the door and pushing her out, tossing her purse to the ground beside her. "And don't think your boy ain't gonna hear about you creepin'."

Whatever comment Fawn had was swallowed up by the sound of the slamming door.

"You were fuckin' her, I saw you!" Princess screamed. She and Kelvin were in their bedroom and Princess was livid. "How could you do this, Kelvin? And in our own house, *my* house. This place is in *my* name."

"I wasn't, we were just messing around!"

"Yeah, I saw your messing around."

Kelvin was embarrassed that he'd gotten caught, knew he was taking a big chance by making out with Fawn in the laundry room. But that had been part of the excitement, the illicitness of it all. Plus Fawn was so fine. She'd been coming on to him all night, had been after him ever since she started dating his teammate. Fawn always told Kelvin that the only reason she was with Tyson was because she couldn't be with him. Tonight she'd proved that she wasn't just talk, and even Princess being upset didn't dampen his desire for finishing what he and Fawn had started.

Princess continued to vent. "Kelvin. You're not gonna make me a fool. You either want to be with these hos or you want to be with me!"

"Oh, you got ultimatums? It's like that now?"

Princess sat on the bed, tears beginning to flow silently down her face.

"Look," Kelvin said, going to sit beside her. "I'm

sorry; I shouldn't have disrespected you like that. That girl don't mean nothing to me. I'm just high and shit and, well, I'm sorry, baby. Forgive me?" He tried to put his arm around Princess.

"Don't," Princess hissed. "Don't even think about touching me right now. You need to go wash that girl's stank off your dick."

"I told you we didn't—"

"Oh, so you had your pants down 'cause you were getting ready to do laundry? Whatever, Kelvin, I'm not sleeping with you. Now are you going to move to the couch, or am I?"

18

Bi the Way

"You still haven't told him?" Hope asked. "He's the father, Stacy. He has a right to know."

"And he will know, just as soon as the time is right."

"Why are you waiting?"

Stacy shrugged.

"Because you're not sure," Hope answered softly. "Because as much as you want it to, you're not convinced that this baby will make the difference you hope it will."

Stacy's eyes welled with tears as she nodded yes.

Hope looked at her still-skinny friend. She was carrying the baby well. It might be another two months before she started showing. She didn't want to judge what Stacy had done, but the moment Stacy had confided in her, the pregnancy became Hope's business. She wasn't going to be dishonest in how she felt about the situation.

"Is it Bo?" Hope questioned, wanting to talk about the pink elephant that was always in the room where Darius and Stacy were concerned. Hope felt it might be time to tell Stacy what she knew. She prayed for guidance. "You know, if there's smoke, there's usually fire. What would you do if, you know, there is truth to the rumors about him and Darius?"

"There's no truth to them," Stacy shot back. "And even if there is, it will all be over once I give Darius the one thing Bo can't." She patted her stomach for the confirmation her voice didn't quite convey.

"I hope you're right," Hope answered.

"I don't believe it anyway," Stacy said, trying to convince herself yet again. "Gay men don't screw women the way Darius does me."

"But he might be bi, Stacy. I never told you this but Frieda—"

Stacy held up her hand. "I don't want to hear it, Hope. Whatever Frieda thinks she knows is probably nothing I·haven't already heard. Darius loves me; I know he'll do the right thing when he hears about his child."

Even though both Stacy and Hope had lost their appetites, they took a moment and tried to enjoy the delicious Thai dishes before them.

Stacy barely touched her food. Hope's life fascinated her; the only woman Stacy knew who had actually gotten who she wanted. Cy had been one of LA's most eligible bachelors, and definitely KCCC's prize, until Hope came along. Now Darius occupied that spot. And Stacy wanted to do what Hope had done . . . get her man.

"I know some might not agree with what I did," Stacy continued. "I know you probably think I should have waited on God, like you did. But what happened to you doesn't happen everyday, Hope. The Cinderella story comes along maybe once in a lifetime."

"Yes, I wish you'd trusted God," Hope agreed. "But it's not my place to judge you."

"I appreciate that, Hope, I really do," Stacy said, her eyes once again filling with tears. "And can you do one more thing? Can you pray for me?"

Later that evening, Stacy watched the doorknob turn as Darius unlocked it with the key Stacy had given him months before. Tuesdays had unofficially become their night, the one night when Darius was almost always free. She tried to see him two to three times a week but if he only had one night to spare, Tuesdays was it.

Stacy had taken time with a simple yet hopefully delicious dinner, and Darius's reaction did not disappoint. "Baby," he said, taking her in his arms and kissing her soundly. "Something smells delicious."

Stacy relished his kiss before responding. "Nothing too fancy; just some oven-baked barbeque chicken, baked potatoes, and a salad."

Darius plopped down on the couch. "Well, I'm starved." He leaned his head on the back of the couch as the familiar sounds of cooking—cabinets opening and closing, pot lids being lifted and replaced—along with those of the smooth jazz radio station filled the air. *Those are two things they have in common*, Darius thought, remembering the many nights he listened contentedly while Bo prepared a delicious meal. *Cooking and me.*

A frown crossed his face as thoughts of Bo and

Stacy occupied his mind. Thanksgiving was weeks away; he had to tell Stacy about his plans to be out of town. Knowing how upset she'd be once she learned these plans included Bo, Darius had decided to tell her it was business, a record promotion his label had sprung on him at the last minute. He hoped a trip to Big Bear for Christmas would make his Thanksgiving no-show a bit more palatable.

Soon the sound of clanging pots and pans was replaced by the tinkling of forks hitting plates and barbeque sauce being licked off fingers.

"This is good," Darius said, reaching for another piece of chicken and placing more salad on his plate. "Sweet and spicy, just how I like it."

"Hmm," Stacy answered. "And the chicken is good too."

Darius laughed. He really did like Stacy. Sometimes he wondered how he could have met two people so different yet so perfect for him in their own way. Stacy gave him a feminine touch, and an accepted look in the eyes of the public, and Bo gave him, well, Bo gave him everything else. Darius was so excited about spending the holiday with his lover. He knew he might as well bite the bullet and deliver the news to Stacy.

"I've got some news to tell you," he began, leaning back in his chair and wiping his mouth with a napkin. "And you're not going to like it."

Stacy leaned back in her chair as well. "Okay, where are you going and why can't I go with you?"

Darius laughed. "Has Dionne Warwick been by here, girl? You probably know where I'm going."

"I didn't need the psychic network for that one." Stacy got up from the table and began clearing away dishes. Darius joined her.

"There are only two things that work my nerves about us: your busy travel schedule and the amount of time you spend with Bo."

"Aw, hell. Well, I guess I'd better not tell you the second part of the news then."

"Don't tell me he's going with you. Why can't I go? Last year I couldn't go to your grandmother's, and the whacked reason you gave for not inviting me? That she wasn't very sociable to couples who weren't married. And now this?"

"He's my business manager, baby. And it's not just him: one of the label execs, his assistant, and a promotions manager are also going. All this travel isn't as glamorous as it sounds. Interviews and signings all day, and playing crowded, smoky clubs at night."

"Yeah," Stacy said sarcastically. "Sounds horrible, like surgery even."

"Well, not that bad." Darius came up behind Stacy as she placed dishes in the dishwasher. He licked the outside of her ear, one of her sensitive spots.

"Stop," Stacy said, only half serious. "You want dessert? I made chocolate cookies with pecans."

"Yes, Stacy Gray, I want dessert. Only thing is . . . you're all the chocolate I need and I have my own nuts."

Stacy laughed. "You're silly." Darius continued his oral assault, gliding his tongue down her ear, nibbling her neck, and placing love bites on her shoulders. All the while he performed a slow grind as she stood entrapped between him and the kitchen sink.

Stacy grabbed a plate of cookies and Darius's hand. "In case we get hungry later," she said.

Once in her bedroom, the seduction continued. Darius eased Stacy out of her pants and planted whispery kisses along her inner thighs. He continued the trail across her slim hips, around her navel, along each breast and finally a deep, thorough plundering of her mouth.

"Darius, baby," she whispered between kisses. "I want to go on this trip with you. I miss you too much when you're away. I promise not to be a bother. I can hang out in your hotel room and then come to the concerts at night."

With three in the bed, it might get rather crowded. "Next time, love. I promise, the next full concert we do out of town, you can come with me." *Oh, God, why did I just promise that? Bo's gonna have my ass!*

"I guess that will have to be okay," Stacy said, beginning her own oral orientation of Darius's body. She tugged at each of his nipples until they hardened, then stopped suddenly. "When is this trip?"

"Thanksgiving," Darius muttered.

Stacy stopped foreplay and sat up. "You're joking, right?"

"No, baby, it's a holiday promotion. You know Shabach's been working overtime since he lost out to me at the Stellars. I'm number one in gospel right now and he can't stand it. I gotta keep up the momentum, Stacy."

"I understand that. Shabach's been all over the place: radio, TV, Internet. But they won't understand you bringing your girlfriend along on a *holiday*?"

"They specifically discussed no one bringing significant others. They want us to be focused. We're hitting like, five, six cities in seven days. . . . They want us to—"

"You're going to be gone a week? Through your birthday too?"

"I know, baby, it sucks, big time. Which is why I've planned something special to make it up to you."

Stacy was in full pout mode: lips out, arms crossed. "What?"

"This." Darius rolled over and took an envelope from the nightstand; the envelope idea inspired by Bo's Canadian trip gift to him two weeks earlier.

"What's this?" Stacy's response matched Darius's to Bo's exactly when Bo had sprung their Thanksgiving vacation on him.

"Open it and find out." Exactly what Bo had said. The similarities would have been almost laughable if they weren't so scary.

Inside the linen, gold emblem-sealed envelope was a brochure, and on the cover a beautiful scene of a snow-covered mountain, transposed above another scene of a roaring fireplace in a cozy suite. Across the top of the brochure, the calligraphed words: "Big Bear."

"We're going to Big Bear?" Stacy asked.

"No, I thought I'd give the trip to my mother

but wanted to see how you liked the brochure," Darius responded sarcastically. His smile lessened the bite however, as did his hand drawing lazy figure eights across Stacy's thigh.

Stacy slapped him playfully with the pamphlet. "Smart butt." She pulled out the remaining contents of the envelope and found brochures on skiing, hot air balloon rides, a business card for a limousine service, and a paper Christmas tree.

Stacy yelped. "Christmas! We're spending Christmas together! Okay, you exasperating man," she said, rolling on top of Darius and wrestling him playfully. "You've just made up for me having to eat turkey with the crazy Grays.

"You know I've lived in California my whole life and never gone to Big Bear? And I've only seen snow once, when we visited one of my uncles who lived in Indiana. Hope and Cy went to Big Bear last year. She said it was beautiful. I really admire them," Stacy continued as she scanned the various brochures. "Hope and Cy. They have the type of relationship I wish, well, never mind."

"You wish we had, is that what you were going to say?"

"Yes, it is. I love you, Darius. I want to spend my life with you. Is that wrong?"

"No, Stacy, it's not wrong. I love you too. And I like Hope and Cy," he said, the businessman in him instantly thinking of ways he could network with the church's most prosperous multimillionaire. "Maybe we can have dinner with them sometime, rub shoulders with somebody who has it all."

"Okay, baby," she said. "I'll set something up the next time I talk with Hope."

"Well, I've got something up right now," Darius countered as he took Stacy's hand and wrapped it around his hardened shaft. "Can we do something about that?"

"Mm," Stacy purred as she straddled him. "I definitely think we can."

19

Take Care

Lavon felt horrible. He'd avoided Passion for two weeks, hiding behind the production of the Kingdom Keys series. But she deserved better. He only hoped she would forgive him after he told her what she needed to know.

Passion's bright smile as he entered the hotel lobby's coffee shop tugged at Lavon's heart. He liked to think of himself as a decent man, as one who had put his player days behind him. He knew Passion was ready to trade in her celibate status for sex with him, but it couldn't happen. What he had with Carla wasn't over. It would make life simpler for him to have the feelings and attraction for Passion that he had for Carla, but this was not the case. He felt that this conversation would at least set one thing right.

"Hey, Perfected Passion," he said, kissing Passion lightly on the cheek before sitting down.

"Hey, yourself," Passion responded. She'd hoped for a steamier greeting, but it was the middle of the day in a coffee shop after all. She was using her lunch hour to meet with Lavon; he'd said it was the only time he had. "I've missed you."

Lavon forced himself not to squirm. "With only a few weeks until I return home, the schedule is crazy."

"How's it going, the production? I'm really enjoying Pastor's sermons, can already see how this series could be one for every believer's library."

"Oh, definitely. Dr. Lee can preach *and* teach. That's one of the things that makes production difficult—hard to find where to cut anything out. But I think everyone will be pleased with the final result."

They took a moment as the waiter came over. Passion ordered a turkey sandwich, Lavon, black coffee.

"C'mon now, big man like you has to keep up his energy. You sure you're not hungry? My treat . . ." Passion lifted her eyebrows suggestively while a smile kept the atmosphere light.

"I had a big breakfast," was Lavon's reply. That his breakfast had included Carla assuaging all of his appetites was the tidbit left unsaid. He turned the conversation to the reason he'd agreed to meet with her.

"Passion, I'm here to ask for your forgiveness," he began sincerely. "I've taken this friendship farther than it ever should have gone."

Passion's heart sank. "Lavon, we're both adults. I think what's happening here is what we both want."

"That's just it, Passion. Nothing is happening here. I mean, nothing *else* can happen here, between us. I feel that I took advantage of you by acting like a free man, when I'm really not."

When Lavon had agreed to lunch, this is not what Passion had expected. Not this conversation—in fact, not much conversation at all. She'd held out hope that lunch would be ordered through room service, with a dessert that wasn't on the menu.

"Is this about your girl back in Kansas?" Passion was surprised at the hurt she felt, even as Lavon's honesty impressed her. "Y'all been talking?"

Lavon spoke a simple truth. "My heart is elsewhere, Passion. And you're a good woman. It's not fair to keep going down this road. I overstepped my bounds by spending the night with you. The liberties I took were inappropriate, even though we didn't have sex."

Passion remembered Lavon's hands under her nightgown, rubbing and massaging her bare skin before he'd rolled over and away from her to the other side of the bed.

"I understand," she said. But she didn't, not really. Being celibate and righteous didn't feel good at the moment. She regretted passing up the opportunity for a torrid night of love, one that may have led to a future with Lavon. But maybe it wasn't too late. . . .

"I envy the woman in Kansas," she continued truthfully. "I wish it were me. But I appreciate your being a man and coming correct like this before my heart really got twisted."

"Any man will thank his lucky stars to get a woman like you, Passion. I mean that. Another day, another time, who knows what may have happened. But the situation is what it is. I'm sorry."

Passion reached for Lavon's hand. "Don't apologize, Lavon. We can't always control our feelings, or our heart. And as much as I want you, I'm willing to respect your decision."

Even as she said these words, Passion envisioned a lifetime with the man in front of her. She didn't want to totally close the door. "But does this mean we can't be friends?"

"That won't be difficult for you? I don't want to play with your feelings."

"I'm a big girl. Let me handle my heart, okay?"

Lavon looked at his watch. It was time to head to the church for an afternoon of production. "Let's just play it by ear, Passion. At least I'll see you at church, right?"

As kindly as they'd been spoken, Lavon's words felt like a dismissal. Passion stood, as did Lavon.

"Of course, I'll see you at Logos. Take care of yourself," she said, giving him a hug. She left the coffee shop without looking back.

20

Everything Except . . .

Carla only half listened as Brianna went on and on about cheerleading. She loved her children immensely, and was especially close to her only daughter. Which is why she felt guilty at the relief she felt when they picked up Brianna's friend and the two teenagers fell into their own private conversation.

Truthfully, Carla's lack of interest in her children wasn't the only thing making her feel guilty; it was the lack of interest in her husband and the ministry. She knew it was also wrong, but Carla felt truly alive for the first time in years. It wasn't just the sex, which was mind blowing, it was how Lavon made her feel: young and playful, desirable and valued. Even as she thought this she could hear Stanley's voice in her ear, full of respect, admiration, and compliments. But it wasn't the same. Stanley always seemed to come from an intellectual standpoint, where Lavon came from his heart.

His magnetism was palpable, his appetite matched her own. Both she and Lavon knew they were playing with fire, felt their feelings for each other deepening. But neither was willing to give up what they had . . . each other.

Carla wanted desperately to talk with someone about what was going on—but who? She thought of her sister and just as quickly dismissed the thought. Carla had always been the wild child while her sister, Marlyne, was the goody two-shoes. Marlyne had probably not even looked at another man since being married, much less thought of being with one intimately. Of course, talking to anyone at her church was out of the question. She thought about Vivian, Tai, or one of the other women in Ladies First, the organization comprised of female ministers' and preachers' wives. Maybe Tai . . .

Carla dropped the girls off at the mall and told them she'd be back in a couple hours. She then drove down the street to a coffee shop, ordered a vanilla latte and some courage, and took out her cell phone. After a few pleasantries about their churches, children, and the SOS conference, Carla changed the subject.

"Well, girl, I need to tell you the real reason I called. I'm dealing with something and need an ear to hear, if you know what I'm saying. I know you can keep a confidence so . . ." Carla took a deep breath and dove in. "Tai, I'm seeing somebody."

Tai remained silent as she digested what she'd heard. As soon as Carla had mentioned a "real reason for calling," Tai had thought *affair*. She'd immediately assumed Stanley was the one cheating . . . but Carla?

"I—I didn't plan for it to happen," Carla said into the silence. "I know it's wrong. . . ."

"How long have you and Stanley been having problems?"

"About ten years. No, that's not fair; we're not having problems, I'm having them."

Carla gave Tai a brief rundown of her decade-old marriage, making sure she gave Stanley the props he deserved. Carla also made sure Tai understood that she didn't blame Stanley for her dissatisfaction in the marriage, that it was her issues, and her desires that were at fault.

"What are you going to do?" Tai asked.

"I don't know. I know what I should do, what is the right thing to do. We tried to end it a while back but we couldn't. Tai, it isn't just sexual. I think I might be falling in love with this man."

"Who is he, a member of your church?"

"No, thank God." Carla dared not say more than that. It was already hard enough not to mention Tai's church member's name.

"Well, Carla, I can't say your situation is one in which I can directly relate. Unfortunately, my experience is on the other side. I may have looked here or there, but King has been the only man for me since I was fifteen.

"I guess at the end of the day, the answer to your dilemma is in the question. Is what you want worth more than what you have?"

It was an excellent question. Carla had a lot:

good man, nice home, wonderful family, and thriving ministry. The only thing missing from the picture perfect life was the part Lavon had helped her uncover. She had everything anyone would ever want in life, except herself.

21

Mira

"How is she, Doctor?"

"Better, she's doing better. But she still has quite a journey ahead of her. The burns are healing nicely and the swelling from all the surgery is going down. This one's a trooper, I'll give her that. Not many would have survived such a horrific car accident, one that required being pried from a flipped-over car by the jaws of life."

The nurse, Beth, walked around to the other side of the bed and changed the patient's IV. It wasn't protocol, but she'd become personally vested in this patient's success. It was such an unusual story—a veritable Jane Doe with no identity, no family, no friends. The hospital staff had named her Mira, short for miracle, because that's what she was. The patient cheated death with every heartbeat, defied the odds with every breath.

"Did you hear that, Mira?" the nurse asked. "You're doing better."

The patient, who had been partially comatose during her stay, stirred slightly. Her eyes moved but did not open.

The nurse smiled. Mira had heard.

22

First Instincts

Vivian lay on her poolside chaise, relishing some quiet time alone. The Montgomery clan's schedule had been jam-packed since summer. Vivian looked forward to the holidays when both their family and the ministry adopted a decidedly light schedule.

Checking her watch, she saw there was another hour before her daughter, Elisia, came home from school. Derrick Jr. would be at least two hours. Their father was out of town and Vivian had no appointments. She was footloose and fancy free and although there was a myriad of things on her to-do list, doing absolutely nothing felt like the best possible choice.

The Montgomery backyard landscape provided a beautiful and quiet retreat. Tricolored bird-of-paradise mixed with pink camellias, blush red peonies, lavender crocus, and blue Japanese anemones to provide a symphony of color, nicely contrasted against the lush green grass. Along with the state-of-the-art barbeque grill, pool, and hot tub, a luscious waterfall from the mouth of a majestic lion head added to the aquatic tranquility. Vivian viewed the layout through partially closed eyes, her racing mind staving off the nap she desired.

She'd just turned on her side for a more comfortable sleeping position when the phone rang. It was her best friend, Tai.

"Hey, girl," she said with a smile in her voice.

"Hey, back," Tai responded. "What's shakin', bacon?"

"Would you believe nothing? And that I'd have it no other way?"

"No, I can't see you doing nothing. But life's been crazy, huh, girl?"

"That's an understatement."

Tai and Vivian usually talked at least once a week, but the women hadn't shared an in-depth conversation since right after Derrick's uncle died. That's where Tai decided to start. "How's Derrick doing?"

"He's okay. One day at a time," Vivian answered, sitting up and sliding into her sandals. She headed inside for a glass of sparkling water. "At least, he acts like he's doing okay, though honestly, I'm not sure if he's really processed it yet. His schedule has kept him busy and right now, that might be a blessing."

"King and I are praying for you guys. How are you holding up?"

"You know I loved Uncle Charlie," Vivian said. "We didn't get to see him much these past couple years; that too is a burden on Derrick. Thank God we got there in time to say good-bye. Now I'm choosing to remember the good times, to celebrate his life. His home-going celebration was standing room only." Vivian shared some of the details of the three-hour long tribute given to Derrick's father's brother. "We've all got to go," she concluded. "Let's hope all of our lives can be celebrated the way his was."

"Speaking of life," Vivian segued, "thanks for talking up somebody who's better left forgotten."

"Who?"

"Robin Cook."

"Girl, stop! You saw her?"

"It's old news now, happened more than a month ago. Uncle Charlie's passing made me forget about it." Vivian filled Tai in on Robin's attempt to get into the church, and how their head security man, Greg, found a gun in Robin's purse after denying her entry.

"A gun?" Tai repeated incredulously. "I don't like this, Viv. Sounds like that woman has serious mental problems. I've felt funny ever since I heard she'd been in jail."

"Crazy what a small world it is, that one of your members would know Robin."

"They knew her mother actually, but yeah, we've got probably a couple dozen members with Georgia roots. But things happen for a reason. I don't have to tell you to take care of yourself."

Vivian agreed. "Fortunately, I've got help with that. Greg has put the security force on high alert. We even put a picture of her in the foyer's bulletin area asking anyone who sees her to contact security immediately."

"That's a good idea."

"Hey, I believe in exposing the devil. No sense trying to keep this on the DL."

Vivian and Tai discussed other topics before getting around to the holidays.

"I guess you guys will do the usual over at Mama Max's, right?" Vivian asked, referring to Tai's beloved mother-in-law. "And with both Michael and Princess home from college—"

"That will be an interesting homecoming," Tai interrupted. "There are a few things I have to talk to Princess about, not the least of which is whoever she's screwing in California. I don't know why kids think we're stuck on stupid. Something is going on with her and I need to know what."

"Her moving out of the dorm without telling you can't be easy to deal with," Vivian said, knowing at least part of what was on Tai's mind. "That has got to be one of the biggest challenges of parenting . . . letting go. And when kids turn eighteen, like it or not, you've got to do that. Trust that you've taught her right from wrong, a love for God, and the ability to make good decisions. And then more than trusting her, you've got to trust God."

"Easy for you to say. Elisia is what, eleven?"

"Not so easy. Remember we're dealing with an eighteen-year-old too, one who flew the coop shortly before Princess. And believe me, it's affecting Derrick more than he is letting on that his son decided to move out of the house." Suddenly, it pricked Vivian's consciousness that Kelvin and Princess had moved at about the same time. She made a mental note to do some investigating, even as she chose not to say anything to Tai about her thoughts. There was no love lost between Tai and Kelvin's mother; best to not give Tai any ammunition for suspicions or reason to trip out.

Instead she changed the subject. "We've invited Lavon and the Lees over for dinner next week. Derrick is really impressed with him and his broadcast production knowledge. Sounds like the series he's producing for Stan and Carla is going to be excellent."

The minute Vivian mentioned Lavon, followed by Stan and Carla, Tai's intuition perked up. *Lavon . . . Carla . . . could Lavon be the man . . . ?* Tai couldn't fathom the two of them together. Lavon couldn't hold a candle to suave Stanley in the looks department. Besides, she knew Lavon was seeing a Mount Zion member. No, it couldn't be Lavon.

The conversation soon ended, but their thoughts did not. Vivian hoped there was nothing to the subtle anxiety she'd felt at both Kelvin and Princess being on their own, while Tai hoped she was right about Lavon and Carla being a total mismatch. In time, both ladies would find out that one's first instinct was usually the right one.

23

An Expert at Everything

Stanley, Carla, Lavon, and a few others sat around the church's conference room table. They'd spent the afternoon viewing Lavon's work on the Kingdom Keys series in preparation for the last segment taping, scheduled for the upcoming Sunday's service. The excitement in the room was palpable. Everyone loved how the work had been produced and believed the series would be successful, both spiritually and financially.

In the almost two months since Lavon had worked with Logos Word Ministries, seven of the eight series topics had been taped: joy, peace, patience, kindness/gentleness, goodness, faithfulness, and discipline, referred to in the Galatians scriptural passage as self-control. Stanley would speak on the last and what he felt most important topic on Sunday . . . love.

"If everyone could truly understand and practice this unconditional love God talks about, we'd have heaven right here, right now. There's a reason why Jesus stated it as the greatest commandment—loving God with all your heart and your neighbor as yourself."

Carla looked down, not trusting her face to keep a neutral expression. She wondered how Stanley would feel about the unconditional love she'd been sharing with the man sitting on the other side of the table.

"You're right about that, Pastor," Lavon agreed. "But sometimes it seems there's not enough love to go around."

Knowing those words were meant for her, Carla kept her eyes on Stanley.

"Oh there's enough," Stanley replied. "There's more than enough. We just have to open our hearts to it, get past our egos, insecurities, selfish motives, fears. The Spirit has shown me that if everyone could love unconditionally, there would be no need for other commandments or laws." Stanley shared a few of the scriptures his last presentation would contain, his excitement about the topic building with each recitation. "That's the answer," he said, gently squeezing Carla's hand as he concluded. "Love is all we need."

Carla squeezed back, her eyes welling with tears. That she loved Stanley was not in question; she knew she would always love him. But she was no longer *in* love with him, and the acknowledgment saddened her. She was in love with another man, and what she thought would be a simple, two-month tryst was now complicated with feelings, heartstrings, and a desire to keep the ecstasy she'd found. *But he'll be gone next week,* she thought as she disengaged her hand from Stanley's and glanced across the table at Lavon. *And then, just maybe, I can put my heart back into this marriage.*

Lavon watched Carla covertly. Sitting across the table from her, with her husband at the head of it, was agony. Three, maybe four more times together is all they had. His flight left for Kansas City on Monday morning and according to Carla, that would be the end of their relationship. But Lavon wasn't ready to let her go.

He consciously shifted his focus away from his lover's lips and back to what Dr. Lee was saying. And just in time, as Stanley was speaking to him.

"I really like what you're doing with the intro," Stanley was saying. "You've got the first lady looking good. Her personality provides a perfect beginning to each DVD. Let's take a look at her footage, Lavon."

Each DVD began with a shot of Carla, comfortably seated in the Lees' sitting room. In the background was a vase of flowers and wholesome photos of the Lee family. Dressed to perfection, Carla greeted the viewer with humor and warmth: *Hello, you incredibly blessed child of God. I'm Pastor Carla Lee and I'd like to welcome you to the Logos Word family, by way of this DVD series. You are getting ready to unlock the wealth that is inside you, the hope of glory that is the Christ within. You will be transformed, renewed, and released into the greatness you possess. My husband, Dr. Stanley Lee, is here to give you the keys, darling, the keys to vic-torious living. His is an eight-key combination to your liberation, based on the nine fruits of the Spirit found in Galatians Five, verses twenty-two and twenty-three. So far we've discussed the keys of joy, peace, patience. . . . Oh yes, saints, that one was a doozy,*

*wasn't it? Lord, give us patience right now! This DVD
presents key number five in the series. And now, let's
head over to Logos Word Interdenominational Church
and hear the Word of God from the man of God—Dr.
Stanley Lee.*

Lavon had directed the shot to then dissolve
into the church's interior, where either the choir
or a soloist performed a song relevant to the
evening's topic. Another creative segue led into
Stanley's teaching. At the end of the DVD, Pastors
Stanley and Carla sat together, back in the Lees'
sitting room, where they thanked the viewer for
watching. The DVD ended with information about
the series, the ministry, and an announcement
about the Sanctity of Sisterhood Summits, of
which Carla was a primary speaker.

Ironically, it was the taping of these intros that
had given Lavon and Carla the most access to each
other. That they were filmed in the Lees' home
justified Lavon's being there. Usually they oc-
curred when Stanley was handling a myriad of pas-
toral duties. Since trying and failing miserably to
end things a month ago, Lavon and Carla had
been together almost every day. Instead of waning,
their desire had increased. Adding to that was
their genuine like of each other, and the discovery
that they had more than sex in common. Their camaraderie was that of best friends.

Various accolades rang out around the table as
the last of the six previously taped intros concluded. Everyone agreed that the intro, which had
been Lavon's idea, added a hominess to the series
that nicely complemented Stanley's more conservative and serious demeanor.

"Too bad we can't keep you," Stanley said to Lavon as the meeting concluded. "You're definitely an expert at what you do."

God forgive her but Carla was thinking that very thing in that very moment: Lavon was definitely an expert . . . at everything.

24

A Different Set of Keys

Passion sat in the Sheraton parking lot staring at the entrance. Now that she was here, she wasn't sure her decision to visit Lavon unannounced had been the right one. But she reasoned it wasn't unannounced exactly: she'd left messages on both his cell and hotel phones that she had a gift to drop off. That she hadn't heard from him was attributed to his understandably busy schedule. But a man had to come home sometime.

Passion felt an indescribable urge to see Lavon, to perhaps be with him intimately before he left. Dr. Lee had been talking about keys to victorious living, but Lavon had a whole different set of keys, the kind that had unlocked her pussy's passion. That's the area she most wanted victory in right now, being with him before he left LA. She knew her heart might get broken in the process, but being with Lavon was worth the risk.

Since admitting his heart was elsewhere, Passion

and Lavon had only gone out once, for lunch, and rarely talked on the phone. Passion had nothing against his girlfriend in Kansas City. But Lavon was here; and if there was any chance at all that his heart could be relocated, and connected to hers, Passion was ready to try and help that happen.

Passion nervously fumbled with the package in her lap, a going-away gift she hoped Lavon would find appealing. She felt the sterling silver chain with a cross pendant was an appropriate friendship present—something nice enough to remember her by yet casual enough to not make him uncomfortable. The more she thought about it, the more she felt that visiting Lavon was the right thing. He was the type of man she'd waited for, for five, long, celibate years. If she had to be a bit assertive to not let a gift like him slip through her fingers, then so be it.

Taking a last look in the rearview mirror and a deep breath, Passion opened the car door. While doing so, a black Mercedes pulled up to the valet stand. Passion turned toward her car to push her automatic lock. When she turned back, she stopped suddenly, and watched her pastor, Carla Lee, casually dressed in a warm-up suit, walk into the Sheraton lobby.

What is Pastor doing here? Once the second of shock had passed, Passion chided herself for feeling uncomfortable at seeing Carla at Lavon's hotel. They were working on a project together and this was Lavon's last week in LA. It made perfect sense that there would be last minute details to go over and issues to discuss. But where was Dr.

Lee? Why wasn't he with them? *Ah, probably out of town,* Passion mused as she unlocked her car door and got back inside.

"Hmm, what are you going to do now, Ms. Perkins?" Passion asked herself as she placed the keys in the ignition. Her fingers beat a steady rhythm against the steering wheel as she pondered her options: whether to wait in the lobby, until Carla left, or maybe have a cup of coffee in the coffee shop. *They're probably meeting in the coffee shop,* she reasoned. *But why wouldn't they meet at the church?* She didn't know, but she decided to find out. She'd tell the truth when she saw them—that she'd stopped by to give Lavon a gift. She'd interrupt them briefly if they were meeting, then wait in the lobby until their meeting was over. It was already eight-thirty; surely the meeting wouldn't take too long.

Passion walked into the hotel lobby and looked around. It was a quiet Tuesday evening, with not much activity happening inside. A few people stood at the registration booth, a couple more at the concierge's station. The light sounds of a piano coming from the atrium could be heard amid the mingling of soft voices. Passion looked around the strategically placed sitting areas for Carla and Lavon. She did a quick walk around before heading toward the coffee shop on the other side of the lobby. There were no familiar faces inside.

Of course, the restaurant. Passion mounted the escalator for the restaurant located on the hotel's second floor. She clutched Lavon's gift against her chest, willing herself to remain calm. She couldn't figure out why she was nervous anyway. It was just her friend and her pastor, after all.

Passion entered the restaurant and looked around. For as quiet as the lobby was, the restaurant was fairly crowded. She craned her neck this way and that, looking over the crowd of people.

The hostess came back to her station. "Table for one?" she asked with a smile.

"No thank you, I'm just looking for someone."

"Please, come inside. Your party could be in one of the booths around the corner."

"I'll do that, thank you." Passion passed the hostess station and walked into the restaurant. The room was L-shaped, a small portion of the seating hidden by a wall. If Lavon and Carla were back there, Passion knew she'd have to change the explanation she'd prepared of simply happening upon their meeting. The only way one could find someone this far back in the room was to deliberately look for them. "That's what I'll tell them," she said to herself as she rounded the corner. "That I'm looking for Lavon."

As it turned out, she didn't have to say anything. Carla and Lavon were not in the restaurant. The last option, Passion decided, was that they were in a meeting room and in that case, she thought it better not to disturb them. She figured others might be at the meeting as well. To run into Carla with Lavon was one thing; to try and explain her actions to a group of Logos Word saints was another. She decided to return to her car, maybe deliver the gift another time.

That's what she thought as she walked to the parking lot but once she reached her car, that isn't what happened. Similar to when she'd waited for Robin to come out of the Chinese restaurant, something would not let Passion leave. Call it a hunch, an intuition, a sneaky suspicion, or just plain being nosy. But Passion wasn't ready to go home yet.

She hadn't been ready to leave then, but she was more than ready two hours later. Passion enjoyed a wide-open yawn as she stared at the hotel entrance. Had she missed Pastor Carla leaving? She was almost certain that wasn't the case, but since it was almost eleven at night, she was beginning to wonder.

"Girl, what are you doing?" Passion asked herself aloud. Disgusted with the fact that she'd wasted two hours in a hotel parking lot, scoping out the lobby like some love-crazed fool, Passion turned the key abruptly and put the car in gear. As she put the car in drive and straightened the wheels, she looked over at the lobby doors one last time. There, at the valet booth, casually waiting for her car was Passion's first lady talking to Passion's desire. Passion watched as Carla took a compact out of her purse, patted her braids and reapplied lipstick. Lavon said something in Carla's ear. Carla's head reared back with laughter. While not touching, there seemed to be an intimacy to their conversation, a familiarity with which they engaged each other. Passion tried to once again employ the fact that the two worked together as reason for everything, but something about that explanation didn't fit the situation. What would Lavon and Carla have to meet about, alone, this time of night?

Passion sat idling as a black Mercedes pulled up to the entrance, the door opened, and the valet motioned Carla over. Lavon tipped the driver as Carla got inside the vehicle. Lavon leaned his head into the car window briefly, and then watched Carla's Mercedes until it exited onto the boulevard, before going back inside the hotel.

Passion slowly pulled her car back into the parking space, trying to figure out what she'd just witnessed. She pulled out her cell phone and dialed Lavon's cell phone number. The call went straight to voice mail and the sexy sound of Lavon's voice: *"Hello, Lavon Chapman here, owner of LC Production Company. I'm either on the other line or . . ."* Disconnecting the call without leaving a message, she then dialed the hotel number. Once again, she reached an answering service. Passion tried a couple more times to reach Lavon, both on his cell phone and his hotel room, without success. After a few minutes it became clear that for whatever reason, he was not available—at least not to her. She wasn't going to hold her breath for Lavon to return her call. Her women's intuition had kicked in full throttle. She believed she'd just discovered where Lavon's heart was, and who else had been receiving his "key."

25

Innocent Preacher's Kid

Princess spewed cola across the freshly mopped kitchen floor. She hadn't been prepared for Joni's crazy comment about Fifty Cent looking like a quarter.

"You are a fool, Joni!" Princess said, laughing again as she reached for paper towels to clean up her mess.

"Or maybe even a dime," Joni continued, as she added a jar of salsa to the pot of melting cheese. "No, his head's too big to fit on a dime. Better bump it down to a nickel."

"No, fool, Kanye's the one with the big-ass head."

Kanye was one of Joni's favorite rappers. "That big-ass head can lay down on my pillow anytime! Girl, get a mop. The floor's gonna be sticky."

"No, it ain't."

"Yes, it is, and I just mopped that shit."

Princess rolled her eyes. "Whatever." She walked down the hall and came back with a damp towel.

"God, you're lazy!" Joni teased while expertly

cutting avocados for her guacamole dip. She prided herself in the fact her classmates raved about her cooking skills, skills she'd found were rare among her college classmates.

"Forget you, bitch." Princess laughed as she put the towel on the floor and then used her feet to wipe it across the dirty spots.

"Yeah, you're *my* bitch," Joni countered, then changed the subject suddenly. "Brandon and Kel bettah not be out fuckin' other girls. They're taking a long-ass time to run a couple errands and get some chips."

"True dat," Princess agreed. "I don't think so though. I think we finally got they asses trained!"

"Right!" Joni stirred the nacho sauce and nodded her head to the hip-hop music blasting from the living room. "Hey, make a batch of your margaritas."

"Ooh, bet, that sounds good." Princess walked to the pantry and pulled out the necessary ingredients. "We're gonna have fun tonight, Joni girl."

Anyone who knew the innocent preacher's kid who'd left Kansas four short months ago wouldn't recognize the young woman cursing, drinking, and swapping jokes with her best friend while mixing an expert batch of margaritas. But Princess felt she had never been happier, and that she knew exactly who she was—Kelvin Petersen's woman.

Her anger at finding him humping a college classmate in their laundry room had lasted exactly seventy-two hours. That's how long it was before Kelvin invited Princess to a private industry party for R & B crooner J. Holiday. Kelvin showered her with gifts: hooked her up in "hella Prada," KLS stilettos, and a Tyra-like weave. Once at the party, he'd held onto Princess like she was gold, and when they saw Fawn, the female culprit of their recent romantic upheaval, Kelvin walked past her like she wasn't even there. Princess's heart had swelled in that moment, and all was forgiven.

"Where's the smoke?" Princess asked.

"Go look in the room on Brandon's dresser. I asked him to roll us a blunt before they left."

Princess returned shortly with a lit marijuana cigarette. She inhaled deeply, inhaled again, and then passed the joint to Joni.

"Look at baby girl smoking like a pro." Joni took a hit of the joint and continued. "I remember when you first started smoking, coughing and stuff. Girl, you were a mess." Joni knew that before coming to UCLA, Princess had barely drunk alcohol, much less tried any illegal substance. She'd proven to be a fast learner though. Princess's virginity had not been the only innocence lost since leaving home. Joni hit the joint again before passing it to Princess.

Princess took another long drag. "This shit is good; I'm buzzing already," she gritted out while holding in the smoke. "You got this food situation under control? 'Cause I think I'm gonna shower and change for our little get together tonight."

"Yeah, I'm cool," Joni replied. "But hurry up 'cause you're still gonna make the salad. Don't think I forgot."

"Damn," Princess said, pouring a glass from the pitcher of margaritas and taking a sip. "I thought you would once you got high." She giggled and started dancing toward the bathroom. "Don't worry, girl, I'm good for it. One designer salad coming up as soon as I get my fine on."

Kelvin was "getting his fine on" too, taking a long shower after spending a nice hour with insatiable campus twins Brandy and Sandy, sisters he'd been enjoying regularly for the past four weeks.

"Y'all sho' know how to show a brothah a good time," he said after he'd emerged from the shower and began to towel off.

"Hmm, you're the good time," Brandy said, sidling up to Kelvin and rubbing his naked body with her own. "Too bad you can't stay longer. Looks like Princess has you on a leash."

"I try," Kelvin said modestly, responding to the compliment while ignoring the leash jab. Talk of his lovemaking skills was already common among the "KBs"—Kelvin's Beauties—a group of about a half dozen sexual partners of which Brandy and Sandy were members. The club rules were simple: One: keep your mouth shut. Two: if you must talk (Kelvin knew that some things were just too good to keep to oneself), do so only with other club members. And three: don't talk. In exchange, each girl received regular sex, preferred seating at UCLA basketball games, and occasional flings with Kelvin's teammates. If Princess ever found out about any of them, for any reason, they were ejected from the club.

Kelvin hit the lock button on his key chain and climbed into the shiny, black SUV. He attached a Bluetooth to his ear and hit his cell phone's speed dial button.

"About time," Brandon said as he answered Kelvin's call. "You're about to get us in a whole heap of trouble, boy."

"Never fear, the K-man's here," Kelvin answered. "We gots it all under control, son."

"Yeah, right. Just don't depend on me to keep covering you, dude. You're my friend and all that, but I don't like being a part of your cheating on Princess. It almost feels like I'm cheating on Joni just by helping you."

"Aw, dog, don't go getting all soft on me," Kelvin said with a sigh. "I'm handling my business. Besides, it ain't like I have a ring on my finger. Just stay with me, pad'na. Soon as I get this contract, everybody wins."

"Yeah, yeah, tell me anything. You're not even in the league yet and look at you. What are you gonna become once you get signed, K-ho?"

"More like, K-can't-ho-no-mo," Kelvin said with a laugh. "Once that multi-milly contract comes in, I gotta dock the dick. Can't have the baby-mama-drama and what not." Princess excluded, Kelvin prided himself on always using condoms.

He navigated his Jeep to the curb. "I'm here, dog, where you at?"

Brandon bounded out of the mall entrance and a short time later, he and Kelvin were back at the condo. The sounds of laughter greeted them as they opened the door.

"I see the party's already started," Brandon said as he leaned down and gave Joni a kiss. "Look at your eyes—you're high."

"Where's the chips?" Princess asked Kelvin as he slouched down on the couch beside her.

"Aw, damn," he replied. "Brandon forgot to stop by the store."

Princess pushed Kelvin off her. "Uh, hello? That's what y'all were supposedly going out to get. What happened?"

"Don't out the pout, mamacita. We had to take care of priorities." Kelvin nodded to Brandon, who pulled out a small packet of multicolored pills.

"You bad boys," Joni said. She reached for the pills but Brandon pulled back. "Gimme!"

"Not yet. We're gonna wait for the crew to arrive." Brandon threw the packet to Kelvin, grabbed the keys from the coffee table, and headed for the door. "What kind of chips do you want again?"

While Joni answered Brandon's question, Princess asked Kelvin, "What's this?"

"You know what this is, girl. Stop trippin'."

"Ecstasy?"

"Yeah, and that's what you're going to be experiencing later on tonight."

"I don't know, Kel. Blunts are cool and all, but I feel a little funny taking, you know, real drugs."

"You're gonna love the way they make you feel," Joni said, coming back into the living room. "You think I'd take anything that was really going to hurt me?"

"Yeah," Kelvin said. "And do you think I'd give my baby anything that would hurt her? This is just a little sumpin' to help make the night right." He rose from the couch and walked into the kitchen. "Oh yeah, you got the 'ritas crackin', fo' sho', fo' sho'." He poured a glass and walked into the dining room, where Princess and Joni had set up the food. "Man, hope Brandon hurries back with the chips. I'm hungry."

"And the wings, y'all forgot the hot wings." Princess came into the dining room. "It took all that time to find some drugs?"

"Girl, let your man handle his business. I'll go back out and get the wings."

"Never mind, I'll have them delivered. We probably need to add some stuff anyway the way folks keep calling and inviting themselves to our spot."

"That's because your spot," Kelvin said as he grabbed Princess from behind and placed a large hand on her cootchie, "is the right spot."

"Stop it," Princess cooed. But her actions reflected that she didn't mean what she said.

As the night progressed, amid the food, dance, ecstasy, blunts, and margaritas that flowed like water, Princess felt a high she wished would last forever. She was having the time of her life. And just when she thought things couldn't get better, her party became one for two and moved to her and Kelvin's bedroom. That's when her ecstasy went to another level, one of the Kelvin kind. For the first time, she experienced multiple orgasms, and thought Kelvin's libido would last all night. It almost did, and as the fingers of night waved to the morning, Princess curled her satiated body next to his and thought with conviction: *I'm gonna be with this man for the rest of my life.*

26

Happy Thanksgiving?

Passion smiled as she watched Onyx cuddle up against her grandfather. They were in deep discussion, Passion's father speaking to her daughter in a heartfelt tone, Onyx looking up with eyes of love. Passion could just about imagine the conversation, and in that moment Onyx confirmed what Passion thought was being said.

"Mama, Pawpaw says I'm the most beautifulest girl in the whole wide world," Onyx said proudly. "And he said he loved me this, no, this, no this much!" Onyx jumped off the couch and spread her little arms and legs as wide as they could go.

"Well, if Pawpaw says it, you know it's true," Passion replied, with a wink to her father. "You've got to be the most beautifulest."

"Mama," Onyx continued thoughtfully. "Is beautifulest a word?"

Both Passion and her father laughed, and she explained, "It's a special word Pawpaw made just for you. So if he says you're the most beautifulest, then you are!"

This answer seemed to satisfy Onyx because she nodded, hugged her grandfather, and skipped into the kitchen, where her grandmother was plating dessert.

"Thanks, Daddy," Passion said as she watched her daughter leave the room. "You always make her feel special, just like you did me when I was her age."

"I made you feel that way because you were . . . still are," he responded.

"Yeah, but I'm not your little girl anymore." Passion's voice broke unexpectedly. She covered it with a cough.

But not before her dad noticed. "You'll always be my little girl," he said gently. "And I'll always care about what's going on with you. Like how you're more quiet than usual, have been for the past few weeks."

Passion forced a smile before responding. "I'm fine, Daddy. Just overworked is all. You know we get the week off between Christmas and New Year's. I'll catch up on my rest then."

"I hate that you have to work so hard to support yourself and Onyx. Even with child support, it can't be easy out there. Maybe one day you'll find a nice fella there in your church. Everybody needs somebody."

The tears Passion had carried but refused to acknowledge the past two weeks threatened to erupt. But she wouldn't cry over Lavon. She wouldn't! She'd done good all day long, even as the holidays and her siblings all spending them with their individual families, made her single status that much more obvious. She'd focused on her blessings—having a mother and father still alive; her health and strength; and her daughter. She'd been sincere when she thanked God during the Thanksgiving dinner prayer. She had too much to be thankful for to feel sorry for herself.

"Mama!" she said, rising from her chair and heading to the kitchen. "Where's that good old sweet potato pie?"

Reminding herself of why she was thankful helped Passion make it through the rest of the afternoon. But when evening came, and her ex-husband picked up his daughter, Passion was left alone with nothing but her thoughts. She tried for the umpteenth time to reach Robin, only to find the number no longer in service. This was one of the rare times Passion wished for a female friend, somebody to share the feelings that were bottled up inside her, locked there since seeing Pastor Carla at Lavon's hotel.

Passion sighed as she pulled a container of vanilla ice cream from her freezer and scooped a generous amount next to a slice of warm pie. She walked into her bedroom, propped up her pillows, climbed into bed, and hit the remote. Unfortunately the scene that replayed in her head was louder than the one on the screen.

It had happened the Sunday following the week she'd seen Lavon with Pastor Carla. He hadn't returned her phone calls, but could not avoid her when she stepped in his path after Sunday morning services.

"You're a busy man, Lavon Chapman, too busy to return phone calls."

"I wasn't too busy. I just didn't want to talk to you, didn't know what more could be said and didn't want to continue feeding something that couldn't grow."

Lavon's blunt honesty surprised her. There was a pause before she answered. "Well," she said, trying to add levity, "why don't you tell me how you *really* feel?"

Lavon led her away from the crowd gathering just outside the church doors. "I told you, Passion. You're a good woman, but my heart is elsewhere. I couldn't see us being just friends knowing that the attraction ran deeper than that, that our relationship had already gone beyond friendship."

"Yeah, I know where your heart is . . . but isn't Dr. Lee's heart there too?"

Then it had been Lavon's turn to be surprised. He'd fixed an intent stare on Passion, yet remained silent.

"I saw her the other night, at your hotel."

Lavon had begun walking then, even farther away from the church. "When were you at my hotel?"

"Oh, so she was there on more than one night? Interesting."

"What is interesting is that you came to my hotel uninvited."

"The way I see it, unless your last name is Sheraton, that is not *your* hotel. But you're right, I did come even after you failed to return my calls. But I had a reason; I'd wanted to give you this."

Passion pulled the box from her purse. "It's a

going-away present for you, something to remember me by."

"Look, Passion—"

"There's no need to trip, okay? It ain't like it's Tiffany's or nothing. And yes, I definitely thought about taking it back after what I saw, but at the end of the day, the truth is, I already bought it and I want you to have it, even with what I now know."

"And what do you think you now know?"

"Oh please, Lavon. The first lady at your hotel at ten o'clock at night? C'mon now."

"Pastor Carla's a busy woman. She's also very involved in the Kingdom Keys tapings, as you well know. Don't make a mountain out of a molehill."

"Hmph, a mountain is probably *not* what you were climbing the other night, but you probably ended up breathing heavy nonetheless."

"Girl, you're trippin'."

"Yeah, whatever."

"It was an innocent meeting about the Kingdom Keys—"

"In your room?"

Lavon hesitated before answering. *Did she come in the hotel?* he wondered. *Look for us in the restaurant, the coffee shop? Damn, maybe she saw Carla coming out the elevator.*

"What the first lady does is none of my business," Passion continued before Lavon could respond. "That's between y'all and God. It's a moot point anyway since you're headed back to Kansas City next week. Right?"

"I'm headed there and then to Minneapolis for the holidays, to spend time with my daughter, visit other family."

They'd wrapped the conversation shortly afterward and went their separate ways. Lavon had called once, to thank her for the cross and chain. She'd called him once, and they'd exchanged e-mails. And then the truth hit Passion square in the face: it wasn't enough.

"I miss him," she said aloud, reaching over to her nightstand and picking up the phone. "I miss him, and we're both grown-ups." *Maybe he and Carla had a one-night stand. Maybe they didn't even have sex. Maybe he just performed a little licky, licky. Maybe she poured her heart out about a troubled marriage, or counseled him on how to have a successful one.*

Passion didn't believe for one minute the two had just talked, but those thoughts were pleasant ones as she waited for Lavon's voice mail. To her surprise, he answered.

"Hello?"

"Uh, hey, Lavon. You caught me—I mean, I was expecting your voice mail."

"Would you like me to hang up so you can leave a message?" There was a smile in his voice.

Passion was smiling too. "No silly . . . happy Thanksgiving."

"To you too. It was a pleasant one I hope."

"It was. I spent it with my parents and my daughter of course. She's with her dad now, hanging out with that side of the family tree."

"That's good. It's always good for a daughter to have a relationship with her father, no matter what."

"How's your daughter—Felicia, right?"

"Hey, you remembered. She's great. Seems like

she ages five years every time I see her. Yesterday a little girl, today a woman."

"I miss you, Lavon." The words flew out before Passion could catch them.

Silence. And then, "I hope God will bless you with the man you deserve, who will give you the love that you are so worthy of. "I'm sorry I hurt you, Passion. I know you were hoping for more than what exists between us."

"Yes, I wanted to be with you . . . still do. It's been five years, and I'd be lying if I said I didn't regret not taking the chance at a little loving when it was right here, hard and ready, in my bedroom."

Remembering Lavon's thick, juicy manhood made Passion squirm. She wished for the umpteenth time that she could redo the night he had spent at her house.

"I'd better go," Lavon said at last.

"All right then. Talk to you later."

Passion rolled out of bed and went to prepare another sweet potato pie à la mode. On the way back to the bedroom, she stopped by her DVD collection and picked out her Tyler Perry favorites. Tyler Perry was her preferred writer because his work always made her laugh, no matter what. She knew that seeing Madea—whether going to jail, reading a Black woman's diary, or having a family reunion—would make her feel better. What was the famous saying . . . ? It was better to have loved and lost than never to have loved at all.

Another thought came into Passion's mind as she watched Madea. Maybe that's what she should say about Lavon's good-bye: "hell to the no." With him leaving LA, whatever he had or didn't have with Pastor Carla was over. And since he'd been with her, he couldn't be too connected to the woman in Kansas City. And they'd just enjoyed a warm, easy-going conversation reminiscent of the ones they'd first shared.

The thought of a second chance with Lavon filled Passion's heart with joy. As she laughed at Madea's antics during their family get-together, she smiled even bigger thinking of a little reunion of her own.

"I had to call you," he whispered, as if his voice might be heard beyond her cell phone.

"I'm glad you did." She whispered too, even though she was alone in the family room. Sounds of laughter were heard from the floor above her— a house full of people she knew she needed to re-join. "But you're okay? Your day was good, turkey with all of the trimmings?"

"No, I'm definitely missing some trim but"— they both laughed—". . . as good as it could be without you. I miss you, Carla. I know I shouldn't, baby, but a brothah's feeling jealous because someone else is with you, and not me. And the thing is, I like Stanley, which makes me feel bad that I want you, but not bad enough to let you go. Am I alone in these feelings?"

"It's complicated, Lavon. I was with a lot of men before Stanley, and I've never felt the way I do now, with you. But it's not just about us; I've got a family, three kids, a ministry, a following. I've got women looking up to me as their example." Carla was already talking low but dropped her voice to a whisper. "My heart hasn't been whole since the day you left. I can barely sleep next to Stanley. When I think of others, there's no way I can be with you. But when I think of being true to who I really am, there's no way I can't."

"I've got some news for you."

"What's that?"

"I'm coming back to you, baby."

"You're going to come visit me, love?"

"Not visit, move. I'm not going to give you up, Carla. I've taken a job in LA."

I've taken a job in LA, taken a job in LA, not going to give you up, I love you. . . . A litany of Lavon's words had played in Carla's head since he'd said them a couple hours ago. She couldn't remember what her guests had said, or when they'd left. She knew her quiet demeanor was so un-Carla and hadn't gone unnoticed. But she hadn't trusted herself to speak much, because everything she'd wanted to say was about her heart, Lavon.

The litany continued as she prepared for bed. One moment she was excited. *Lavon is coming back!* The next, petrified: *Lavon is coming back?* He'd stayed in town a week past the time everyone else thought him gone, and they'd been together every day. To be on the safe side, they'd switched him to a hotel in Long Beach, far from where most Logos Word congregants resided and even farther from the church. Carla remembered their last night together: bittersweet, full of passion. *Okay, let me use another word here,* she thought, and replaced the emotion that was her church member's name with another, *rapturous ardor.* They'd made love with even more abandon than usual. Believing they wouldn't see each other again, at least any time soon, neither had held back. There'd been tears upon parting, from both of them.

Carla sighed as she eased into bed next to Stanley. She hoped he was asleep. He wasn't.

"You all right, Carla? You weren't yourself today, and people noticed."

"Oh yeah, I'm all right. Just got stuff on my mind is all."

Stanley rolled over and faced Carla, who was lying on her back. He touched her arm. "Want to tell me about it?"

A part of her wanted to tell him everything, to spill her heart and hope he understood. But that was a split second thought. For the first time in ten years, Carla had a secret her husband would never know.

"Oh, Stan, I want to but . . . it was something told to me in confidence."

In an uncharacteristic move, he pulled Carla toward him and held her close. "You had me scared for a moment," he said, nuzzling her cheek and neck. "I thought it was something about us that was bothering you, like maybe you'd found some young stud and were kicking me to the curb or something."

Carla's body tensed at this near truth. She tried to relax, but all she wanted was for Stanley to let her go so she could roll over and think about Lavon until she fell asleep. That's if she could sleep. She was so wound up from hearing Lavon's sexy voice on the phone that she was considering a late night rendevous with Denzel, which had remained in its red velvet sheath the entire time Lavon had been in LA. She gave an air kiss to Stanley and then attempted to roll over on her side.

Stanley didn't let her go. Instead, he raised up and partially straddled her, moving toward her lips for a kiss. She'd never been less turned on, but tried to summon up desire based on the true love she had for her husband. She closed her eyes and opened her mouth for Stanley's average French kiss. All the while his tongue made small circles within her mouth, Carla remembered Lavon, and how he plundered her with his tongue, especially in her nether lips. She moaned with the memory.

Stanley moaned too, rolling over and pulling down his shorts. He got on top of her, raised her nightgown and shifted her leg for better access. He kissed her again, briefly, before kneading her breast.

That's not dough, Stanley, she thought dispassionately as he almost tore her breast off. *But if it were, this bread would be set and ready to rise.* Carla giggled at the thought.

Stanley stopped. "What's funny?"

"Nothing."

Stanley raised up and looked at Carla until she opened her eyes. "What?"

"That's what I'm asking," he said. "What's going on with you? It's not just today you've been preoccupied. You've counseled women for years and I've never seen it affect you like this. Who is this woman?"

"Stanley, it's con—"

"We two are one; there is nothing that can't be shared between us."

"I'm sorry if I've been distant," Carla said in response. "I promise I'll do better." To further appease him, she added, "Maybe it's time for us to have a date. It's been a while since we've done that. Go to San Diego or Vegas or something, just the two of us. Would you like that?"

"I'd like this," Stanley said in response, rubbing the top of her mound with his hand.

Carla put her hand on top of his. "I'm tired, Stanley. Maybe tomorrow, okay?"

Stanley fell back on his side of the bed. Carla turned on her side, her back to his. They were each thinking the same thing—that in ten years, this was the first time Carla had ever turned Stanley down.

Darius and Bo enjoyed each other's caresses as they gazed at the fire, cocooned in the classic jazz guitar riffs of Wes Montgomery. The day, in fact their entire stay at Fairmont Le Manoir Richelieu, had been perfect, like a lover's dream. Their days had been filled with indoor golf, skiing, and cruises down the St. Lawrence River, the nights with clubbing, casinos, and impassioned lovemaking.

"Where are you going?" Darius asked, as Bo untwined himself from Darius and stood.

"I'll be right back," Bo whispered with a wink.

Darius heaved a love-filled sigh as he leaned deeper into the couch and watched the flames dance within the fireplace. Snow-covered mountains lit by a thousand stars were visible from their floor to ceiling windows, a glorious contrast to the heat palpitating inside the suite. A thin layer of newly fallen snow lay outside their balcony doors. A log crackled, broke, and sent sparks of fire flying. Darius rose, placed another log on the flames, and sat back down.

A smile snuck onto Darius's lips and refused to go away. For the first time in his life, he had everything he'd ever wanted: a lucrative record deal, hit single, and a wonderful lover. In this moment, Darius couldn't imagine his life differently, and especially without Bo in it. It had been over three beautiful years with this man; Darius knew that Bo was the love of his life.

"A penny for your thoughts, gorgeous," Bo said, as he walked back into the room with two flutes and an ice bucket.

"Oh, they're worth way more than that," Darius said, his voice low and husky.

"Hmm . . ." Bo popped the cork on the extravagant bottle of Krug, Clos du Mesnil and filled his and Darius's champagne flutes. He looked deeply into Darius's eyes a long moment before speaking, and was met by Darius's love-filled gaze.

"There are no words to say how much I love you," Bo began. "So I'll keep this simple. I love you more than life itself, baby, more than the very breath it takes to speak this truth. I can't see myself ever living without you." His voice almost broke and a single tear slowly slid from his eye down his left cheek and dropped from his chin.

Darius set down his glass and took both of Bo's hands in his. "I was just thinking that very thing before you came back," he whispered. "That I can't imagine life without you. Even though you're crazy, I'm crazy about you. You're my forever."

They raised and clinked their glasses. "To forever love," Bo said quietly.

"Yes, to forever love."

Before long, the bottle of champagne was empty. Both Darius and Bo enjoyed a pleasant buzz, their magical surroundings creating an enchanting atmosphere. They kissed lazily, passionately, as if they'd just met, as if they'd known each other several lifetimes.

Bo broke the kiss and reached behind him. "This is for you," he said simply.

"What is it?" Darius asked. He hurriedly unwrapped the medium-sized box only to find another box within it, and another one after that. His unwrapping became more frenzied with each opened box, until he reached the smallest one, about two by two inches. "What is it?" he repeated softly.

Bo leaned back against the sofa, crossed his arms and smiled.

In direct contrast to his previous frenzy, Darius slowly and carefully took the wrapping from the smallest package. A gold-plated container was inside.

"It's locked," Darius said as he tried to raise the lid.

Bo held up a thin, silver key. "Remember this, from the night I told you about this vacation? I knew you'd forget it."

"You're always looking out for me," Darius said softly. His eyes locked on Bo as he opened the lid.

Showcased brilliantly against the deep, chocolate velvet was a diamond-encrusted platinum wedding band. Custom designed along the lines of a Mo-kume puzzle ring, the two interlocking pieces were both platinum, one outlined with gold etching and the other holding a series of diamonds that to-taled two carats. Together, they resembled arms around shoulders, interlocking perfectly, fitting together completely, like Darius and Bo.

Darius was stunned into silence. He prided him-self on opulent jewelry, and had never seen any-thing so beautiful. "You can't afford this," he said, at last.

"No, now I can't afford anything *else*," Bo clari-fied. "As it is, yo' ass bettah have another hit and *soon*, or we'll find that sucka at Gold's Pawn Shop." Bo had never handled being serious for long, and once again used humor to ease his discomfort—and fear. Because giving Darius the ring was only part of what they would hopefully be celebrating.

"You nut," Darius replied. "It's beautiful. Thanks, baby."

"Not as beautiful as you," Bo said. "Here, let me," he added, once Darius had taken the ring out of the box. Bo quietly slipped it on his finger.

"Man, Wes is the baddest. Listen to that." Darius rose from the sofa and brought Bo with him. They slow danced to the serenading strings of Mont-gomery's "Oh, You Crazy Moon." Time stood still as they swayed to the beat, the plaintively sensual melody cascading around them.

The two stood motionless as the song ended, still holding each other close.

As the last notes of the guitar strings flitted

against the soothing snare and tinkling piano, Bo pulled back enough to look deep into Darius's eyes. "Lover, will you marry me?"

Darius's heart jumped in his chest. It was the last question he ever would have expected. Quickly replacing the shock were feelings of complete and total euphoria. "Yes," he said, thinking of nothing and no one but the present moment. He hugged Bo tightly. "Yes, you unbelievable, loveable nut. . . . You'll be mine forever."

"I mean, for real," Bo continued. "I've researched it all, made all the arrangements. Our getting married is legal in Canada. If you're ready, we can be one by this time tomorrow."

Darius was stunned. He loved Bo with all his heart, but a *real* marriage? For the first time since they'd talked that morning, he thought about Stacy. A tiny flaw surfaced in Darius's otherwise perfect moment.

"It can be just between us," Bo said, correctly reading Darius's thoughts. "She doesn't have to know. No one has to know. But we'll know; you'll know and I'll know. No matter what happens with"—he refused to bring her name into the moment—"anybody, we'll always be together."

Darius disengaged himself from Bo and walked to the fireplace. He absently stoked the flames before replacing the poker and walking to the balcony. He opened the French door and a cold burst of wintry air, along with a spattering of snowflakes, cascaded onto his face.

"It's beautiful out here," Darius said, taking a moment to breathe in the cold scent.

Bo came behind him with the wool throw from

the sofa. He wrapped it around Darius's shoulders. "You'll catch your death of cold out here," he scolded.

"Like I said, always taking care of me. . . ."

"And I always will."

"You're right, you always will . . . because my answer is yes. Let's do it."

Bo didn't trust himself to believe he'd heard what he thought he heard. "Let's do what?" he asked tentatively.

Darius wasn't sure he believed what he was saying either, but the words coming out seemed totally appropriate. "Let's get married."

Stacy feigned enjoyment as she sat with Hope, Cy, and one of Cy's associates at the Gibson Amphitheatre. The Thanksgiving concert featured contemporary jazz artists: Peter White, Kirk Whalum, Boney James, Dave Koz, and others. The music was excellence personified, the ambiance classy. At any other time, Stacy would have enjoyed the evening. Even her arranged "date," in another moment, would have been interesting. He seemed intelligent, clean-cut, and interested. But Stacy's heart was elsewhere. It was in Canada, somewhere around Quebec, with Darius Crenshaw.

All day long she'd tried to focus on why she should be thankful, including her and Darius's upcoming Big Bear Christmas vacation. But it still rankled her that she couldn't accompany Darius on his last-minute Thanksgiving promotional visit to Canada when she knew Bo had gone. When she'd called Darius to wish him a happy holiday, she'd heard female voices in the background. Darius had told her they were in a restaurant, enjoying a late breakfast. *Late because . . . ?* Had Darius and Bo enjoyed a foursome the night before? Or even worse, had they enjoyed each other?

Every now and then the gay rumors Stacy had heard about Darius would creep into her mind. She blocked them out, mostly. Darius and Bo seemed especially close, but aside from the beginning when he'd acted hesitant, Darius had proved to be an ardent and capable lover. Yes, he mainly liked it doggy-style but then, so did she. Was that a reason to make a person gay? *But he could be bi.* Stacy shook her head, hoping that, like an Etch A Sketch, the pictures forming there would disappear.

William, Stacy's date, noticed her agitation. "Hey, beautiful, can I get you another glass of juice?"

Stacy was glad for the distraction. "Yes, in fact, I'll go with you."

Once outside the auditorium, Stacy and William decided to sit at an outside table and eat a bite along with their drinks. In her zeal to forget about Darius and try and enjoy the evening, Stacy decided one glass of Pinot Noir wouldn't hurt the baby and after she'd had the first one, ordered a second.

"Looks like somebody's trying to get tipsy," William teased. "It's okay, beautiful. I'll buy a bottle if you'd like."

"I'm fine, even though I am trying to get my buzz on." *You really are a nice guy,* Stacy thought while smiling at him. *Too bad you're not Darius.*

"So, what's a fine girl like you doing single?" William asked.

Oh, here we go—the "why are you thirty and single" dialogue. Not! "I'm not really single," Stacy replied, after another sip, more like gulp, of wine. "It's just that my boyfriend had to go out of town on business."

"On a holiday?"

"He's in the music business."

"And he didn't take you with him? You ask me, that man's a fool."

Stacy stood, immediately feeling light-headed and a bit sick to her stomach. Her smart comment of "well I didn't ask you" got swallowed with the gulp of air she took to try and quell her nausea.

"You all right?" William asked, standing up and putting his arm around her.

"I will be," Stacy said. After a couple deep breaths the light-headedness disappeared and her stomach calmed. "Look, William, I've had a wonderful time, really. But I think I'm going to call a cab and go home."

"I wouldn't think of it," he countered. "I'll drive you."

"And I wouldn't think of your missing half of an excellent concert on my account," Stacy said. "Please, give Cy and Hope my best and tell Hope I'll call her tomorrow."

"At least let me wait with you until the cab arrives."

"Thanks for your concern but there's no need. I really am much better. I skipped our family's Thanksgiving gathering—guess my empty stomach doesn't appreciate red wine."

"Well, I hope to see you again." William leaned forward for a kiss.

Stacy turned her head and pressed her cheek against his pursed lips before spinning around and almost running away from her date. "Thanks again," she yelled, without looking back. She made it all the way to the side of the building, and away from prying eyes, before she threw up.

The ginger ale she'd purchased while waiting for the cab eased her stomach. Now, as the taxi idled in holiday traffic on the 101 freeway, Stacy regretted she'd left the concert. It was stupid of her to drink wine. But her need to drown out thoughts of Darius had also drowned out her common sense for a moment. She'd left a fabulous concert, great company, and a good man behind. And for what? So she could go home and be alone? Watch the umpteenth rerun of *A Charlie Brown Thanksgiving*?

"That was stupid," she mumbled under her breath. "He's in Canada, having a ball, and look at you."

"Excuse me?" the cab driver inquired.

"Nothing," Stacy answered, barely aware she'd spoken out loud. *Nothing*, she repeated inside her head. Because that's what she'd gotten out of ruining a perfectly good evening for someone who had not once cancelled a good time for her and who, even now, was undoubtedly in some five-star hotel, eating five-star food, enjoying champagne wishes and caviar dreams.

Once inside her apartment, Stacy determined to change her sour mood. Being involved with a celebrity was never easy. Time and time again

Tanya, Darius's sister, had told her to chill the bump out, to stop being paranoid and acting like all the other insecure women. Tanya was right.

Stacy reached for her phone and dialed Tanya's number. She'd avoided her friend since getting pregnant, but didn't want to be alone with her thoughts. After getting voice mail, she hung up without leaving a message and went into the kitchen to scrounge for food. Within minutes, she had a scoop of turkey salad between two slices of bread. She'd gotten through half of it, along with a helping of chips, when it happened again, a wave of nausea accompanied by dizziness.

Stacy walked into her bathroom, opened the medicine cabinet, and took out an antacid tablet. She thought she'd escaped morning sickness, but here she was nine weeks along and throwing up for the first time since she'd found out she was pregnant. Rubbing her stomach, she remembered that she wasn't alone after all. She had company, the kind that would hang around for at least eighteen years. The thought made her smile, made her feel better about her day. "Happy Thanksgiving, Darius Jr.," she said with a smile. "Mommy loves you."

Her room was quiet, except for the constant hum of various medical devices surrounding her bed. After more than a month, the ventilator had been removed; she was breathing on her own. Face and upper body bandaged, the heavily sedated patient was barely aware of her discomfort. The movement of her chest, and occasionally eyes, were the only signs of life, that and the continual blip on the EKG machine, the proof of a heart beating.

The door swung open as Beth entered, doing evening rounds. She kept up a steady monologue in a soft, southern accent as she went about her tasks—exchanging IVs, checking vitals.

"You may not think so now, Mira, but you have much to be thankful for today. No, you couldn't eat turkey, and no one came to visit, but just think of those who endured what you did and aren't alive now. You're our miracle, Mira, a living, breathing miracle."

The nurse continued with a regimen of detailed oral care. "Doctor says you're coming along just fine. Says he can't understand why you're not talking. Your throat is still quite parched, but it's healed enough for you to be able to converse. We've all been wondering about you—who you are, where your family is. So far the hospital hasn't turned up much. I think they wanted to wait until you could talk before they resorted to fingerprints or dental charts, stuff like that. Those blasted things are so expensive, and you without insurance and all. . . . Well, any that we know of anyway."

Slowly, the nurse removed one layer of bandages after another and began a tedious bathing process. "Oh my goodness, well look-a-here. The burned skin is peeling off. That's a good thing; the more that comes off on its own, the less they'll have to scrub. I won't lie to you, Mira, the rehab on burns is far from pretty, but doctor says you'll be ready to begin in another couple weeks or so, when you'll be well enough from your surgeries.

Then your healing can truly begin, Mira." The nurse smiled at the eyes that followed her so intently. She stopped rewrapping the bandages and took Mira's hand. "One of these days, before you know it, you'll have your life back. Well, not like it was before but who knows? Maybe even better. The Lord works in mysterious ways, that's what my mama always said. 'Course, growing up in the hills of West Virginia, it didn't take much to seem mysterious to us."

Beth finished rewrapping the bandages, lowered Mira's bed, fluffed the pillows, and straightened the bed linens. She hummed a cheery tune as she documented the charts, noted the time, and finished her report.

She headed for the door, then stopped and turned abruptly. "You know what I just thought of?" she said, laughing. "Now I hope you don't mind this but I sure did think of this line just now, from one of my favorite movies, *The Color Purple*. Remember when Miss Celie was leaving that mean ol' Mister, was going off with Shug to start a new life? Old mean Mister didn't think she had a chance, didn't think she could make it without him. You remind me of her, your spirit that is. A lot of us in this hospital didn't think you'd make it either, but you've got a will that won't quit. Remember what she said from the back of that car? That's what I want to say to you. You may be Black, and with all those bandages, you might look a little ugly. But you're here. By God, Mira, you're here!"

The nurse's laughter was genuine as she turned out the light and stuck her head back into the room. "Sleep well, Mira. Happy Thanksgiving."

Robin watched the door for a moment after the nurse left. She thought of how kind the woman was, even smiling a bit at her *Color Purple* reference. Like many, Robin had watched *TCP* a zillion times, could recite much of the dialogue before the actors said their lines.

"That's right," Robin whispered, her voice hoarse and raspy. Her eyes darted around the room wildly. "Y'all muthafuckas hear dat? Did y'all hear dat? I'm here."

27

Thicker than Water

"You ain't no competition, old man. Whatchu got, whatchu got?" Kelvin talked game as he faked to the left before turning to the right and scoring an easy layup under a bright December sun. Derrick followed him to the top of the key where play began again.

"You better be glad this isn't twenty years ago," Derrick said, hand-checking Kelvin as he bounced the ball between his legs and went for a fade-away jumper. The ball bounced off the rim, Derrick got the rebound and sank the ball for two.

"Okay, it's time to take care of business," Derrick said. Father and son went back and forth on the scoring until thirty sweaty minutes later they'd finished their game. "You didn't think you'd beat me, did you?" Kelvin laughed as he downed a pint of water.

"Not really," Derrick admitted, while toweling sweat from his body. "I need to hit the gym for oh, about the next year straight, then I *might* be able to win *one* game!"

"Maybe next lifetime," Kelvin said, in a tone so truthful the comment failed to be cocky.

Derrick laughed, shaking his head at the amazing similarities between himself and this young man he'd met just a little more than two years ago. Blood was indeed thicker than water because while Kelvin grew up in another country, in a totally different culture, he and Derrick shared characteristics in a way that was uncanny: the same walk, same crooked smile, and Kelvin's basketball braggadocio could have been taken from Derrick's high school "trash talk" book.

Basketball is what helped Derrick and Kelvin bond as they got to know each other. When Kelvin moved in the year before, his b-ball skills instantly made him an idol in the eyes of his half-brother, D2, and no one, especially his half-sister, Elisia, could resist his charm.

Even his stubbornness, or some would say *especially* his stubbornness, was a trait he inherited from his father. Looking back, Derrick was glad Vivian had stood her ground and made him call his son shortly before Thanksgiving and offer the olive branch. He knew he should have done so sooner, but also knew that as much alike as they were, a month or so of space had been good for both of them to calm down.

He'd never meant the confrontation that day to get out of hand, but after losing his uncle his emotions were already raw. It had not been a good time for Kelvin to raise his voice about what he was not going to do. In the end, Derrick realized he was in no position to try and change a boy who was almost a man when they met, and if there was ever any hope of being a real father, he needed to start out as a real friend.

"You still hoping to sign with the Lakers?" Derrick asked, once they'd reached their vehicles, parked side by side.

"Yeah, it would be nice to stay in LA," Kelvin answered. "Princess, I mean . . ."

Derrick's parental meter immediately kicked in but he worked to keep it casual. "Naw, naw, go on now. What about Princess?"

Kelvin didn't see any reason to keep hiding that he was seeing Derrick's minister friend's daughter. After all, the girl was grown. "Me and Princess been hangin' out for a minute."

"That so," Derrick responded lightly.

"Yeah."

"Her parents know about it?"

"No, I mean, I don't know. Maybe."

"Are y'all . . . is this a boyfriend-girlfriend thing? Look, son, I'm not trying to run your life but Princess is like a daughter to me."

"She's *like* your daughter but she's *not* your daughter. And I'm your son so it should be cool, right? What, you don't trust me with her?"

"Let's not get into an argument, Kelvin. But here's the deal. I've been where you're going. I know what it's like to be talented and a fly guy . . ."

Kelvin rolled his eyes.

"And have all the young ladies swinging on your jock. You're nineteen, single, and probably not monogamous. I just don't want Princess hurt, that's all."

"I don't want her hurt either, Rev. It's hard sometimes though. Women want to get all clingy and what not."

"I sure hope you two are not sexually active," Derrick said, although with Kelvin being his son he doubted that was true. "But if you are, just be honest with her, son. If you're playing the field, let her know she's not the only one on the team. And make sure you use protection. You are using protection, aren't you?"

Kelvin nodded. Since he was using protection with all the other girls, he felt he didn't really lie.

Derrick sighed. He'd just gotten back on track with Kelvin. He didn't want them to become estranged again. He didn't want to go behind his back either, and King had to know what was going on with his daughter. "I don't want to have to keep this from King," he said after a pause. "He's my best friend."

"Yeah, well, I guess it's cool. Princess always talks to her moms, so she probably already knows." Kelvin opened his car door. "Lil' D coming next time?"

"You know it. Your little brother was sorry he missed out today but Vivian made him keep his earlier commitment with his debate team. He'll probably be calling you later this week."

"All right then, thanks for the game."

"Yeah, right, more like thanks for letting you kick my butt!"

"Letting me? Oh, you let me, huh?"

"You don't think you can actually beat me, do you?"

Kelvin laughed. "See you later, Rev."

"Good-bye, son."

Derrick watched until Kelvin's Jeep turned out of the parking lot. His mind raced. How long had he and Princess been sleeping together? Did King and Tai know about it? There was only one way to find out. Derrick reached for his cell phone. He needed a sounding board for this unexpected situation and hoped Vivian was home.

"What?" Tai bellowed.

Vivian knew Tai would not be pleased but she had hoped her girlfriend would not go ballistic. "Okay, Tai, I know it's not my place to tell you to calm down but—"

"You're right, don't tell me to calm down because it's not going to happen. Not when you're telling me that Janeé's son, the woman who has plagued my life since high school, is having sex with my daughter. Oh, hell no, this is not going to happen. We're going to put an end to this, trust."

"He's Derrick's son too, you know."

"And that makes it right?"

"Of course not." When Tai was this upset, Vivian knew there was nothing she could say to make things better. Still, she tried. "I'm just trying to get you to focus on Kelvin, not his mother. You already suspected Princess was having sex—remember how different you felt she acted when she was home for Thanksgiving? You were upset, yes, but a little more resigned to it when you thought it was Rafael."

"I should have made her talk to me, open up. . . ."

"Like we did when we were eighteen?" Vivian's

voice softened. "Princess is at that stage in her life where she's trying her wings, testing her independence. We all wish we could think for our children, help them avoid the mistakes we made. But Princess knows right from wrong. I remember you telling me about the talks you two once shared. Now you've got to trust that she'll remember all you've said. And, Tai . . . you've got to remember that God knows what she's doing, even when you don't."

28

Grown Folk

"Mama! Daddy! What are y'all doing here?" Princess hoped, prayed she was dreaming. She closed her eyes, opened them again. No, parents were still here, in the middle of UCLA's campus. This was no dream. It was no joke either. That King Brook, one of the busiest ministers in the country, was here on her campus and not in some pulpit meant something serious was going on.

Tai vowed to keep a rein on her temper. "This is what happens when you stop taking your parents' calls," she said, forcing calm into her voice. "We need to talk."

"But I've got class—"

"This can't wait," King said firmly.

Princess performed the age-old defiant gesture of crossing her arms. "Look, if this is about me and Kelvin . . ."

"That is exactly what this is about," Tai said, her voice rising. "Now, don't make me go off right in the middle of this campus because I'd rather not but I'm not beyond it. Who do you think you are to not take my calls? Girl, I brought you into this world and I'll—"

"Tai," King interrupted, placing a hand on her forearm. He turned to his daughter. "Princess, your mother and I are very upset about what we've learned this week, not to mention you not returning our calls. We're here to get to the bottom of whatever's going on here, and we're not leaving until we do—understood? Now, let's go."

Princess balked, trying to figure out how she could keep them away from the condo. When confronted over the phone earlier in the week, she'd admitted that she and Kelvin were seeing each other. But she'd refused to answer any further questions and hadn't returned her parents' calls since that singular conversation. That, she belatedly deduced, was what had led to the bum rush she was now experiencing. *I should have just answered my phone!*

"Uh, why don't we just walk over to the food court," Princess suggested.

Tai was immediately suspicious. "Actually, Princess, I'd like to see your place. And I want to meet your roommate too. It will be good for us to know the person whose place you're sharing."

Telling her parents that the place was Joni's was the only way she could justify being able to afford living there. Hopefully that lie would remain intact. "Well, uh, she won't be home until tonight. She'll probably hang out with her boyfriend after class."

"That's okay. I'd still like to see where you live."

"So would I," King somberly agreed.

There was no logical reason for not going to her house. She knew her parents were already suspicious. She took the long way around to the parking lot, trying to remember what shape the house was in when she'd left that morning. Were there any blunts lying around, any alcohol on the counter? What if Kelvin was there? No, she remembered, he'd be at practice. But what about Brandon—what if he was there getting high this very moment? Princess sighed. It didn't matter. There was going to be drama no matter what.

If only I'd taken their calls, Princess anguished again. But how could she, knowing how Tai felt about her dating at all, much less dating Kelvin, the son of her father's former paramour. And what was her dad thinking? It probably wasn't as much about the fact that Kelvin was Janeé's son as it was that Princess was sexually active at all. When it came to King Brook, his daughter could have been dating Jesus and there still would have been a problem. She and her dad had never talked about boys and sex. In his mind, she was still "Daddy's little girl." At least that's what Princess imagined. It looked like she was about to find out what he was thinking, whether she wanted to or not. *Damn, damn, damn!*

The trio rode through the streets of LA, Princess giving directions, King navigating the rental car. Tai stared out the window. Conversation was limited, stilted. The beauty of the crisp December day went unnoticed. In what seemed like forever but was actually sixteen minutes, they pulled in front of Princess's condo.

"This is where you live?" Tai asked.

Princess nodded. "Yes."

"Hmm." Tai looked over Princess's head and met King's eyes. King shrugged. "Nice neighborhood," she added.

Please let everything be okay, Princess thought as she unlocked the door. The pungent scent of patchouli, not weed, greeted her. *Thank God.* Princess let out the breath she'd been holding. So far, so good.

"Wow," Tai said as she stepped through the foyer into the open, airy living room. "Joni's parents must have money!" Tai did a 360 turn, taking in the high ceilings, cherrywood floors, granite countertops, and luscious furniture. Except for the play station and video games scattered in front of the television and the lack of pictures and artwork on the walls, the place looked more like the home of a well-to-do couple than that of two college kids. *Wait a minute . . . video games?* Princess was never into the video game craze. Without asking, or the thought to ask, Tai walked down the hall.

Before Princess could stop her or at the very least carefully guide the "tour," King spoke. "Tai has her reasons for being so concerned about your dating Kelvin," he began. "There's more to this than you understand, but she, we, have your best interest at heart."

"I know, Daddy," Princess said, ready to dash after her mother.

King stayed her with a hand on her arm. "You *think* you know, baby," he continued. "But this is about more than your dating boys and being . . .

Well, it's hard for us to think of you as a woman doing . . . what women do."

Princess's embarrassment was surpassed only by her fear of where Tai was or what she was seeing. "Mama!" she said, heading toward her and Kelvin's bedroom.

She entered her room and stopped short, halted by the look on Tai's face and the tears in her eyes. Her mother was standing in front of the open walk-in closet, Princess's clothes on one side, what was clearly a man's wardrobe on the other.

"You're shacking up?" Tai asked softly. "The girl I sent to California to get her college degree to have a better chance at a better life is throwing it all away to play house? And then lying about it?"

"I told you I was seeing Kelvin—"

"Seeing, yes . . . living with, no."

King joined the ladies in the bedroom. "You're living with a man, Princess? I thought you shared this place with—what's her name, Tai?"

"Joni," said Princess and Tai simultaneously.

"I do," Princess continued.

Both King and Tai looked at Princess but remained silent.

Princess sighed and plopped down on her bed. "Our boyfriends live here too," she added after a lengthy pause. She made a circle on the floor with her foot and did not look at her parents.

"Well, I tell you what," King said in a tone used when no counterargument was expected. "This foolishness is going to stop, and it's going to stop now. Do you hear me, Princess?"

Princess continued making a circle on the floor with her foot.

King took a step toward his daughter, and then stopped. He clenched and unclenched his fists, wishing he knew Kelvin's whereabouts. "Do I need to have a talk with this young man?"

"No!"

"Well then, you'd better have a talk with him. And we want you out of this house and back in the dorm next week."

"But, Daddy—"

"No. No ifs, ands, or buts. You are here in California to get your education, not to get ruined by some nucka feeling his testosterone."

"What's gotten into you, Princess?" Tai asked. "You weren't yourself when you came home and this behavior is totally unlike you. What is going on?"

"I love him," Princess said softly.

"Love? Girl, you are eighteen years old. Eighteen! You don't know a thing about love; you've just gotten turned out by your first physical encounter. Trust me when I tell you the fairy dust will settle and you'll find out there's a lot more to relationships than screwing. And believe this too . . . you're not the only one."

"Oh, Mama, you're just saying that because of Janeé."

"What?" King and Tai cried simultaneously.

Princess felt the shift and went on the offensive. "Yes, I know all about your affair with Kelvin's mother, Daddy. That's really what this is all about. Y'all weren't so mad when I was dating Rafael, but now that you know I'm seeing Janeé's son, you're all upset. I like Janeé," Princess continued with a pointed look at her mother. "Maybe if you got to know her and her son, you'd like them too."

"No, you didn't go there," Tai answered, her tone low and dangerous. "You'd better check that attitude and remember who you're talking to. I don't care what you think you know about the problems your father and I have had in our marriage, but let me tell you this. When it comes to men and relationships, I've forgotten more than I hope you ever learn.

"You think you know so much because you've discovered your sexual side? An orgasm has given you wisdom all of a sudden? No child, all an orgasm will do is give you a baby. And that's exactly what is going to happen if the situation is as I think it is and y'all aren't using protection."

"Like how you and Daddy got Michael?" Princess said, referencing her older brother, who was conceived three months before her parents married.

"Oh my God, you want to die today," Tai whispered. She walked over to the bed, grabbed Princess and pulled her up by the arm. Princess's five-foot-four and 120 was no match for Tai's five-eight, 150. And neither of them were ready to handle the six-foot-four and 190 who walked into the room.

"Hey, what's going on here?" Kelvin asked. He stepped toward Princess and Tai.

"Careful, son," King said as he stepped up to his former lover's child. "I don't need much of a reason to jack you up right now."

"You can try," Kelvin said, all nineteen years of swagger in his voice.

"No, *you* can try not to land too hard when you fall," King retorted, forty-two years of swagger and experience standing toe to toe with his daughter's lover. Though only six feet, King was bulkier than Kelvin, not to mention angrier. He knew it would take only one good left hook to reduce Kelvin's extra inches to no effect.

King took a step closer to Kelvin, bringing them chest to chest. In that moment he snuck a glance, gauging the distance from his fist to Kelvin's jaw. Then he saw his daughter's face: eyes wide, mouth open. She looked petrified.

King stepped back. His and Kelvin's near fight had chilled Tai's anger. She released Princess's arm, held so tightly that a ring of red was left, which Princess rubbed gingerly.

"Kelvin," King said, taking deep breaths. "I shouldn't have stepped up to you in that way. We are all adults here."

"Barely," Tai interjected.

"And we need to be able to discuss this situation as adults."

"Mama, Daddy," Princess said, walking over to and putting her arm around Kelvin, "there is nothing to discuss. I love Kelvin and I'm staying with him. And I'm staying here."

Tai got ready to speak but Princess held up her hand. "Please," she continued. "I know you and Daddy are disappointed, and that you have your own ideas about how my life should go. I know I'm just eighteen. But I don't live under your roof anymore; I live on my own." She turned to Kelvin. "This is who I want." She turned back to her parents and said with resolve, "And this is what I want."

Tai turned and walked briskly out of the room, suddenly disgusted that she was standing by the bed that her daughter probably fornicated in every night. King, Kelvin, and Princess followed to find Tai standing in the living room, looking out the large picture window.

Everyone remained silent, digesting both the words and the weight of the moment. This was their little girl all grown up. And as much as they wanted to argue, both parents knew she was right. She wasn't under their roof anymore; she couldn't be forced to do what she didn't want to do.

"What about your schooling?" Tai asked, her back still to the room.

"My GPA is three point four this semester," Princess said proudly. "I'm not slacking off on school just because I'm in love. Getting my degree is very important to me."

King looked at his daughter a long moment. "Needless to say, Princess, I'm very disappointed in you. This isn't the journey I would have recommended. But you have a right to make your own choices. And your mother and I will make ours. You're on scholarship so we can't pull you out of school. But we're not going to support this lifestyle you've chosen in any way. We're cutting off the allowance we've been sending you and taking you off our insurance. If you want to be grown and on your own, you'll do it all the way."

"Have you guys really thought about what you're doing?" Tai asked, turning around. "You're both young. This is a time when you should be footloose and fancy free, a time when you should be focused on discovering yourself before you become exclusively committed to someone else. And that brings me to this question, Kelvin. Is Princess exclusive? Is she the only one you're seeing? Because if she isn't, and I doubt she is, then it also brings into play the dangers of HIV and AIDS, STDs, and pregnancy. And these are just the physical dangers. The mental and emotional pitfalls are even more dangerous.

"Well . . . ?" Tai repeated when Kelvin remained silent. "Is Princess the only woman you're sleeping with?"

Three sets of eyes looked on for the answer while Kelvin did the only thing he felt he could do—lie. "Yes, ma'am," he said softly. "Princess is my girl."

"But is she your only girl?" King prodded. "Never mind, you don't even have to answer that question. I know she isn't the only one." He turned to Princess. "And I hope you know you're not the only one, baby. This is what we're trying to save you from, the hurt that will happen when you can no longer ignore this fact."

"Man, you don't know me," Kelvin answered in defense. "No disrespect, but you don't know what I'm about."

King looked somberly at Kelvin. There was nothing more he and Tai could say, nothing that would change the situation. He walked over to his daughter. "Princess, I don't like what you're doing, but I still love you. Me and your mama will always love you. Remember that."

The front door opened and Brandon and Joni

entered the living room. Upon seeing the older Black couple, they stopped short. The two new-comers felt the chill immediately.

"Uh, hi, everybody," Joni said, recovering first and answering in her generally bubbly tone. She immediately saw the resemblance between Princess and her parents. "This must be your mom and dad. Hi," she continued, walking over with hand outstretched. "I'm Joni, and this is my boy-friend, Brandon."

King and Tai introduced themselves as they shook Brandon's and Joni's hands. "Nice to meet you," they all mumbled. Brandon made a hasty exit to his bedroom.

Joni tried for conversation. "That's a nice outfit, Mrs. Brook," she said. "How do you guys like California? Is this your first trip out here? Oh my good-ness, listen to me ramble. Are you guys staying for dinner or going out or—"

"We were just leaving," King replied.

"Oh, well." Joni began backing toward the hall to her and Brandon's bedroom. "Then I, uh, guess we'll hang out next time. Nice meeting you!" she said before almost running around the corner.

Tai walked over to Princess and hugged her tightly. She held back tears as she rubbed her hand across Princess's back, tears of remembrance, of how she was just a little older than Princess when she'd gotten pregnant with Michael. And how she too thought she knew everything when she'd made her choices.

"I love you, Princess," she said as she broke the embrace and stepped back from her daughter. "I'll be praying for you, for everyone. I wish I'd said more sooner, shared a bit more of my life. Maybe that would have affected a different outcome here, I don't know. It's too late for woulda, coulda, shouldas now." She whispered one last comment in her daughter's ear, then reached for her purse on the couch and headed toward the foyer.

King walked over and hugged his daughter. "Don't cut us out, Princess," he said. "Stay in touch with your mother, take her calls. No matter what happens, we're family. Nothing is more important than that."

King took a deep breath and walked over to Kelvin. "Don't hurt my daughter," he said simply, and exited the room.

Kelvin and Princess watched through the window as her parents got in their rental car and drove off. Princess slowly turned into the arms of her man. "You're not going to hurt me, are you, Kelvin?" she asked timidly, sounding very much like the little girl for whom her parents were mourning the loss.

"Naw, girl," Kelvin replied, hoping the scent of Fawn's perfume was not on his clothes. "I got you, baby," he said, pulling Princess into a tighter embrace. "I got you."

Princess held onto Kelvin as if he were a lifeline, so tight that she couldn't tell where his heartbeat began and hers ended. As Kelvin began to nibble on her ears, and caress her booty, her mother's parting words fluttered into her thoughts. *Baby, I just hope that since you're now embracing grown folk's pleasure, you are also ready to handle grown folk's pain.*

29

Be All Right

Lavon repositioned Carla and entered her from behind with one smooth stroke. He remained still for a moment before resuming the timeless dance of love. Carla moaned her appreciation, pressing her buttocks firmly against him, joining him in the dance.

"Did you miss me, baby?" he whispered in her ear. "Did you miss this?" A deep penetration accompanied each word. He reached around and grabbed her breast, gently massaging first one nipple, and then the other. "I'm going to give it to you real good, nice and slow, make up for the weeks I've been gone."

"Oh yes, baby, just like that, just like that!" Carla whispered. Lavon felt perfect inside her, putting her mind in a sex-induced daze.

After intense orgasms, both were quiet as they caught their breaths, marveling at the happiness they felt in each other's arms. Carla had barely been able to contain her excitement as she got her kids off to school and Stanley off to his weeklong revival engagement in Seattle, Washington. She probably shouldn't have, but she thanked God for the timing of Lavon's return matching Stanley's departure.

"Man, what have you done to me?" she asked, turning over and wiping a bead of sweat off Lavon's broad forehead. She wondered what it was about this average-looking man that did such above-average things to her mind, body, and soul.

"Well, if you have to ask," Lavon responded, "then I probably need to do it again."

"I'm serious," Carla said. She sat up against the bed's headboard and covered herself with the top sheet. "This moment is all I've thought about since you called. You were on my mind the entire time you were away. What are we going to do?"

Lavon sat up beside her. He took her hand in his. "I honestly don't know," he said, looking down at her hand and rubbing it gently. "I've never felt this way before, not with my baby's mother, not with my wife." He turned to look at Carla. "I have no right to you, to interfere in your marriage and family, yet . . ."

"I know," Carla said softly. "I've turned the situation over and over in my mind. I know we should stop seeing each other but . . . being with you has helped me become honest with myself. And the truth of the matter is, I haven't been happy with my life for a long time. Don't get me wrong; I love Stanley, my children, the church. But I've been using those things to fill a place in my heart that was empty until you came. I used the SOS ministry to try and fill the void in my heart and in my marriage.

"Stanley and I are good friends, and our marriage more like a business partnership. He makes the money, I take care of home and we co-run the ministry. I'd never want to hurt him, but I don't know if I can go back to life before you. I just don't know. . . ."

They were silent a moment, finding comfort in each other's embrace. Then Lavon kissed Carla's cheek, rolled out of bed, and put on his shorts. He stood over Carla a moment, taking in all that he loved about her, before turning away from her. "I have something to tell you."

Carla's heart jumped. *Is this it? Is he going to tell me it's over? Is this the last sex instead of the last supper?* Carla could barely get the word out. "What?"

Lavon turned and sat at the edge of the bed. "I slept with somebody else while I was here before, someone at your church. We didn't have actual sex, but we were intimate. It happened the week you told me it was over between us, that you couldn't see me anymore. Someone else was available, and I tried to forget about you by being with her."

"Passion Perkins," Carla said evenly.

Lavon's eyes widened. "How did you know?"

"Haven't you heard of a woman's radar? That and the funny way she's acted toward me lately. I've caught her staring at me with a strange look in her eyes. The first thing I thought was that you'd been with her or if you hadn't, she wanted you to."

"That's not all."

"Oh Lord, what else?"

"She knows about you, about us."

At this news, Carla got out of bed. She reached for her teddy and covered her nakedness. This was not a conversation to have in the nude. "You told her?"

"She saw us, one night when you came to the hotel. She saw you come in, waited, and saw us when I walked you out. I didn't deny you'd been at the hotel but I told her things weren't always as they appeared."

"And I bet she believed that as much as I believe in Santa Claus."

"She didn't make too big a deal out of it, said it was between us and God. But, Carla, I only spent the night once at her house. The moment you came back to me, I broke it off, told her my heart belonged to someone else."

Carla's eyes narrowed. Her stomach lurched. Not because Lavon had been with someone else; married women having affairs couldn't demand monogamy. No, her reaction was because she felt something coming around the corner, and its name was trouble. "We've got a problem."

Lavon sighed. "We've had a problem ever since I fell in love with a married woman."

"That's true," Carla agreed. "And a married woman fell in love with someone other than her husband. What are we going to do?"

"What do you want to do?"

"Honestly? I want to divorce Stanley and marry you. There, I said it."

"Spending my life with you would be my dream

come true. But what about your kids and the ministry?"

"My life is not my ministry; Logos Word will go on. But the kids . . . I don't know."

"And then there are the Sanctity of Sisterhood conferences," Lavon continued. "You're one of the primary speakers. What will women say about one of their leaders, their examples, getting a divorce?"

"They'll talk about me like a dog but I can't worry about that. People talked about Jesus and He knew no sin. And He, not me, should be their example." Carla went on, almost talking to herself. "That's part of the problem—putting preachers on pedestals, expecting us to be God. We are all sinners saved by grace. And if I ever fall off the throne somebody has put me on, I'll be the first one to ask for forgiveness.

"People are quick to judge. They see your glory, but don't know your story. I've sacrificed who I am for ten years, experienced the loneliness, tamped down my natural desires to be physically fulfilled. And I don't regret it. Stanley's a good man. He just doesn't understand intimacy and doesn't like sex." Tears welled up in Carla's eyes as she continued to talk. "I've asked him about it, begged at times for us to get counseling.

"But it doesn't matter. What's happening now, between you and me, isn't his fault. I should have pushed harder for me and him to get what you and I have now. But instead I focused on the kids, the church, and now . . ." Overcome with emotion, Carla couldn't go on.

"Hey, baby, there now, don't cry." Lavon pulled Carla into his arms. "It's gonna be all right. Everything's gonna be all right."

Carla desperately wanted to believe Lavon's words. But she was a wife, mother, and minister in love with another man. She wondered if anything in her world would ever be all right again.

30

Meetings

Lavon whistled as he walked down the boulevard near the home he'd found to rent in Studio City. He liked the ambiance of the area—cozy enough to elicit a small-town feel but large enough to maintain a city vibe. He especially liked being around the corner from Ventura Boulevard, a main road that featured shops, eateries, theaters, and other convenient businesses.

The surroundings, however, were not the reason for the song in Lavon's heart or the pep in his step. No, that reason was a woman named Carla Lee. Lavon changed from whistling to singing the lyrics that had rolled around in his head ever since Carla had left his bedroom, a song from one of his favorite artists and fellow Minnesotan, Prince: "Until the end of time, I'll be there for you; you own my heart and mind . . ." That, Lavon realized, was at the heart of the matter of his feelings for Carla—he adored her. And he'd do anything to make her happy, and to make her his.

Lavon pondered all this as he walked toward Bistro Garden, a quaint French cuisine restaurant he'd discovered shortly after moving into the area. He'd wanted Carla to join him for dinner but aside from having to get home to her children, she was paranoid about anyone seeing them. It was enough that Passion knew.

Lavon was just entering the restaurant when the loud, continuous blare of a car horn stopped him. *Carla!* A smile filled Lavon's face as he turned.

"Hey, you!" Passion said as she ran toward him. When she reached him, she enveloped him in a bear hug, excited, out of breath, and talking a mile a minute. "I thought that was you when I was stopped at the light and saw you walking and I was hoping, praying for that stupid light to change so I could get over here"—Passion stopped and took a deep breath—"and make sure it was really you."

She looked around. "Are you meeting someone? You looked like you were expecting somebody when you turned around."

"No!" Lavon said, trying to recover from the shock of seeing Passion. He thought that living in the Valley, a good forty-five minutes from her Leimert Park neighborhood, would ensure they never saw each other.

"My goodness, what are you doing here?"

Lavon cogitated on his answer. To lie was unwise, while the whole truth was unnecessary. He decided to stay somewhere in between. "I'm checking out a job possibility."

"Really? You're moving here?" Passion realized too late how excited she sounded. "I mean, that sounds great," she said a bit more demurely. Just then she remembered how she'd parked her car askew in the restaurant's valet zone and hit the flashers. She'd told the attendant she'd be right back.

"Oh, dang, I need to move my car. But can I join you for dinner?"

"Well . . ." Lavon cringed inwardly. How was it, he thought, that the woman he *always* wanted to be with could not be with him and the one he *never* wanted to see again always showed up?

"Well, what?" Passion said with a hint of impatience. "Dang, Lavon. It's just a meal. I asked to eat with you, not for you to eat me. Is there a problem?"

Yes . . . you, is what he thought. "I guess not," is what he said.

"Never mind," Passion said, her countenance changing along with her happy mood. "I don't have to beg anybody for company." She turned to leave.

"Wait a minute," Lavon said, tugging her arm gently. "Don't be like that. Go park your car while I get us a table. I'll explain over dinner."

Just over an hour later, Passion was headed back to her side of town. She unbuttoned the top button of her size-sixteen slacks, feeling the roiling of indigestion. She doubted the discomfort came from the French onion soup or the marinated chicken breast. She was almost positive her sour stomach had come from the conversation during dinner. Lavon, and more specifically his conversation, had made her sick!

Not at first. Things were delicious in the beginning as they'd conversed generally about the various goings-on since Thanksgiving, Lavon's potential new job, and how everyone at Logos Word anticipated the release of the *Eight Keys to Victorious Kingdom Living* DVD series at the first of the year. The camaraderie felt as it had when they first met, genuine and comfortable. It was one of the traits that attracted her to Lavon—he kept it real.

But talk of the Kingdom Keys series, and the subsequent talk about church in general and Logos Word in particular changed the vibe at the table. Passion found it odd that Lavon wasn't planning on attending their church, that he seemed vague about attending church at all. Her pastor immediately came to mind, and when Passion mentioned her, Lavon seemed vague:

"Pastor Carla, that's my girl!" Passion had exclaimed.

"She's okay, I guess," Lavon had responded without enthusiasm.

"She can really preach the Word," Passion had continued. "She has ministered to so many young women. I know I've been blessed from her testimonies."

"Uh, can you pass the rolls?"

And then he'd switched the subject to Kobe Bryant and the Lakers. Passion belched, rubbed her stomach, and undid another button. She didn't even like basketball!

Passion wondered about the mystery that was Lavon and his reappearance in LA. Her fingernails tapped on the steering wheel as she waited for the light to change. There was only one way to find out—actually two, and the first attempt had proved less than successful. "I think I'm due for a little ministerial counseling," Passion said firmly. "It's time for a little talk with Dr. Lee."

Passion tossed and turned throughout the night but by morning, she was resolved to get the answers she needed about the nature of Lavon and Carla's relationship. She went into work early and promptly at nine, left her cubicle and went to an empty conference room to make her call. Carla's assistant answered on the second ring.

"Thank you for calling Logos Word. Pastor Carla's office, may I help you?"

"Hi, Jill, it's Passion, Passion Perkins."

"Oh, hey, Passion. How are you?"

"I'm good. Yourself?"

"Fine. What can I do for you?"

"Well, this is really short notice but I was hoping to get an appointment with Pastor Carla. Is she going to be in the office today?"

"Yes, she is. Can I tell her what this is in reference to?"

"It's about something going on in my personal life. I would really like her counsel on the matter."

"I'm looking at her schedule just now and she might have an opening this afternoon. Where can I reach you?"

Passion gave her the number and hung up the phone. The ball was now in Pastor Carla's court. Passion wondered just how the first lady would bounce it.

She only had to wait an hour to find out. Jill called her cell phone and confirmed a two P.M. appointment at the church's executive offices.

31

Personal Matters

"I've never been one to run from problems," Carla said to Lavon, using her headset as she headed toward Culver City and Logos Word. "I'm sure you're the personal matter she wants to discuss."

"I wish I could be there with you," Lavon said, regretting for the umpteenth time he'd decided to eat out last night instead of ordering a pizza.

"Don't you think that would raise just a teeny bit of suspicion if you joined me for Ms. Perkins's counseling session?" Carla teased, trying to lighten the mood. "Besides, you have your hands full becoming the next hotshot producer at MLM Network."

"What if she asks about us?"

Carla sighed. "I don't think she'll do that. I think it will be worse. I think she'll ask my advice on how to get closer to you."

"That's easy . . . she just has to be you."

"You know . . . I like Passion. In a way, I see myself in her. I know what it's like to be a young, single mother, looking for love, companionship. And then she meets you, gets a taste of Lavon loving, and starts to imagine a life with you in it. Do I have the right, Lavon? Do I have the right to stand in the way of her happiness? I've got a man, I've got the life she longs for."

"First of all, you're not standing in her way. I'm a grown man, well able to make my own choices, and I choose you. Secondly, you might have the life she longs for but what about you? Do you have the life, and more importantly the love, that you need?"

"I do," Carla answered, feeling miserable and elated at the same time. "I'm talking to him."

Her comment warmed Lavon all over; he never loved Carla more than that moment. "Well, baby, that's all you need to remember. Everything else will take care of itself."

Their conversation ended just as Carla pulled into the church parking lot. She pulled her Mercedes into the reserved spot and went directly to her office.

"Passion!" she said as she rounded the corner of the outer office. She nodded to Jill and looked at her watch. "You're early," she added, walking over and giving Passion a hug.

"Sorry, Pastor. I thought it would take longer to get here. I couldn't believe how light the traffic was."

"It's okay, come on in." Carla turned to Jill. "Anything urgent?" she asked, pointing to a stack of phone messages.

"Nothing that can't wait until later. Oh, except the reminder about your SOS planning teleconference."

"Then hold my calls. Thanks, Jill."

Passion and Carla walked into Carla's offices and closed the door. The room reflected her bold tastes with pale lavender walls the perfect backdrop for the dramatic ethnic artwork and vibrantly upholstered armchairs done in patterns of red, yellow, purple, green, and blue. Carla pointed Passion toward one of the chairs and, after putting her briefcase and purse behind the desk, came back around to sit in the armchair next to her.

"Would you like something to drink? Coffee, soda, water?"

"No," Passion answered, nervously twisting the bracelet on her arm. "I'm fine."

Carla reached out and touched Passion's arm. "There's no need to be nervous, darlin'," she said sincerely. "There's nothing that can go on in your life that God can't handle." She rose up to put her right foot under her left thigh in the chair, a comfortable position that looked like two best friends talking. "Now, what's on your mind?"

Passion took a deep breath, wondering how to get into this potentially touchy subject. She looked Carla straight in the eye and decided to dive right in. "Lavon Chapman."

"Okay," Carla answered, proud of the straight face she kept. "What about him would you like to discuss?"

Passion gave Carla a brief rundown of her and Lavon's dating experience while he was in town for the Kingdom Keys series taping, and that while she'd told herself to keep it casual, she'd developed deep feelings for him.

"When he left in November," she continued, "I resigned myself to the fact it was over. I knew he was seeing a woman back in Kansas City. He openly admitted to me his heart was elsewhere. I have to give it to him, he's never led me on, never talked a game just to . . . you know . . . take advantage of me."

"But even though he's involved with this woman in Kansas City, you still have feelings for him?"

"That's the thing, Pastor. He isn't in Kansas anymore. He's here, checking out a position with the MLM Network. He's relocating to Los Angeles! Knowing that has brought all the feelings about him that I've tried to bury back to the surface."

"Have you told him this?"

"Lavon knows how I feel, and at one time, he was feeling me too, I *know* he was. That's why I didn't think things were all that serious with that other woman. You know I believe in the sanctity of sisterhood, Pastor Carla. I'm not one to go around trying to steal somebody else's man. But Lavon and I, while stopping short of sex, did become intimate. I thought there was a real chance at a relationship with him. But then, just like that, he changed. Said it was over, asked for forgiveness, and told me his heart was elsewhere. But, Pastor, I believe there can be something special between Lavon and me."

Carla remained calm on the outside but inside, her heart was in turmoil. She knew exactly how Passion felt about Lavon. It was the same way that she herself felt about him. And not just the physical aspect. Lavon treated a woman as if she were a precious jewel. If Passion experienced even a little of the love that Carla enjoyed, wanting more was only natural. There was only one problem: Carla wanted more of that love as well.

"How do you think I can help?" Carla asked softly.

"You can st—I mean . . ." Passion took a deep breath. "Pastor Carla, is there something going on with you and Lavon?"

Carla was as shocked to hear the question as Passion was to have blurted it out. But there it was, in the open. The proverbial elephant in the room had just raised its trunk and bellowed.

"Excuse me?"

"I'm sorry, Pastor. I know you're a married woman and I mean no disrespect. But one night . . . well . . . when Lavon was staying at the hotel, I went there to give him something and saw y'all together. It seemed rather, you know, not like it was business or whatever."

"What do you think it was, Passion?"

"I don't know; that's why I'm asking. What you do in your personal life is your business, unless it involves Lavon. Then"—Passion's tone changed and she again looked Carla directly in the eyes—"it becomes my business."

Carla shifted in her seat, trying to contain the immediate reaction that arose from Passion's statement. She understood Passion's anger, but Carla refused to be intimidated.

"I'm not sure I like your tone, Passion, nor your implication."

"All you have to do is deny that you're involved with him."

"No, all I have to do is stay Black and die."

Passion shot out of her chair. "Uh-huh, I *knew* it. You *are* seeing him. Married to a fine, upstanding man like Dr. Lee and sleeping with Lavon!"

Carla tried hard to hold the sistah-girl-neck-rollin'-hand-on-hip-get-straight-up-out-my-business persona at bay. She did not want the conversation to turn into a confrontation and get out of hand.

"Things are not always as they appear," Carla said after a pause.

"Did you two compare notes? Lavon said exactly the same thing."

"And no matter what my or any other woman's relationship is with Mr. Chapman, *your* only concern should be his relationship and feelings for you.

"Look, I can understand where you're coming from, Passion. I've been there—a single mother wanting companionship, looking for love. And Lavon Chapman seems like a fine man. But love is a two-way street. You both have to want the relationship for it to work out."

"Are you seeing him, Pastor Carla?"

"I won't dignify what you're implying with an answer. As for your seeing me at Lavon's hotel, a public place, well, I'm not going to explain, deny, or justify those actions either. I know what Lavon and I discussed . . . and God knows also."

"Yeah, but does Dr. Lee know? *That's* the question." Passion yanked her purse off the side table, totally convinced that Carla and Lavon were having an affair. She liked Pastor Carla, but respected and admired Dr. Lee. He didn't deserve to be mistreated.

Carla stood. "Dr. Lee is my business, Passion, not yours. But I want you to know I do understand where you're coming from, and I truly hope you find the love you're after. If you feel that's with Lavon, then go to him. Talk to him, tell him how you feel. If his is the love that's meant to be yours, it will happen. If not, then God's got someone even better for you."

Passion stared at Carla for a long moment. "You know, Dr. Lee talked about a scripture that says if you have aught with your brother, then go to him, and if that doesn't work, to the church. I came here, Pastor Carla, because I believe you're seeing Lavon, and if it weren't for you, he and I might have a chance at happiness. You didn't come right out and say you're seeing him, but you didn't deny it either. So I'm left to draw my own conclusions. If you are seeing Lavon, it's not right. And if I ever find out for sure it's true? I'm not going to keep quiet about it."

"Do whatever you need to," Carla responded, realizing the conversation was clearly at its end. She walked to the office door and opened it. "I'll be praying that everything works out for you."

Passion stopped and turned as she exited Carla's office. "And I'll be praying that what's done in darkness comes to light."

Carla and Jill watched as Passion strutted out the office, back straight, chin held high.

"Whoa, what was all that attitude about?" Jill asked, about to get an attitude of her own.

"It was about Passion being human," Carla responded quietly. "And about how at any given moment, we're all doing the very best we can. Continue to hold my calls, please."

"Sure, Pastor."

Carla walked back into her office, closed the door, and slumped down behind her desk. "Lord, Jesus, what am I going to do?" She prayed quietly, fervently, beseeching the throne of grace for strength to do what she knew was right. Therein lay the confusion: what looked right on the outside and what felt right on the inside were two different things.

Carla's eyes misted over as she reached for the phone. Tai answered on the second ring. "Carla? You all right?"

"No, but I'm gonna be."

"Why, what's up, sistah?"

"I think I'm getting ready to divorce my husband."

32

It's a Thin Line . . .

Stacy had only seen Darius sporadically since Thanksgiving. It was just as well. Delayed morning sickness was kicking her behind—rather morning, noon, and night sickness. Stacy had called in sick more in the past two weeks than she had in almost three years. People were speculating as to the reason on her job and from what Hope was hearing, at church as well. Stacy didn't care. Until she told Darius, which she planned to do during their Christmas Big Bear holiday, mum was the word on her condition.

Stacy turned off the boiling water, poured it over the peppermint tea bag, took the steaming mug into her living room, and sat on the couch to ponder her future. "Be careful what you pray for," her mother always said. Not only had she prayed, but Stacy had helped God along. One rash decision and a baby on the way . . . just like that.

Will Darius be as happy about this baby as I am? At three months, Stacy was barely showing. Still, with reality setting in, she wasn't as confident in her decision to force Darius's hand and make him commit, especially since he'd forgone spending the Thanksgiving holidays with her in favor of Bo. Stacy didn't want to believe the rumors about her man, but she could no longer out and out deny them. Maybe he was bi. After she had the baby, she hoped Bo would be "bye" instead.

What if his anger outweighs his desire to raise his child? What if my pregnancy pushes him away instead of bringing him closer? What if there is somebody else? Stacy sat upright as this last thought crossed her mind. What if there was somebody else in the picture besides Bo? What if there was another female in the mix? Stacy had spent so much time hating Darius and Bo's relationship she'd never seriously considered anybody else being the fly in her ointment.

"Forget waiting till Christmas," Stacy said aloud. "Darius needs to know about this baby now."

A short time later, Stacy sat in her car in front of Darius's condo. As strange as it seemed for a two-year romance, she'd never been inside his place, and had never understood Darius and Bo's crazy rule about not allowing overnight guests. His explanation about her loud lovemaking was as thin as the walls he used as the main excuse.

Stacy took a deep breath, opened the car door, got out, and walked toward Darius's house. She forced her nerves to still as she raised the large brass knocker. Her stomach was strangely calm, and for that she was grateful. The last thing she needed to deliver was a rug full of throw up along with her "you're about to be a daddy" news.

She waited and then knocked again. After several long moments, the door opened. She willed herself to look up, hoping to see Darius's sexy grin. Instead, it was Bo's sarcastic scowl that filled her view.

"Yes?" Bo asked, blocking the doorway.

Stacy decided on a friendly approach. She had the upper hand after all; she was carrying Darius's baby. "Hey, Bo," she said casually, as if she stopped by every day. "Darius here?"

Bo eyed her silently before turning and walking back into the lavishly appointed townhome. He left the door open. Stacy followed him inside. She almost gasped at the sight that greeted her. Darius's home was stunning.

"Your place is nice," she said sincerely, taking in the perfectly coordinated color scheme of brown blends: deep cocoa, tan, beige, and white with starkly contrasted navy accents. Rich artwork and platinum sconces gave the room a regal air, while a large bowl of jelly beans on the Leblon peroba and mahogany coffee table provided a bit of whimsy and casualness to the room. Stacy took in the expensively furnished surroundings in an instant, not missing the unidentifiable scent of something erotic and woodsy from a candle, oil burner, or something similar that permeated the room. "This is nice," she repeated again.

"Thanks," Bo said, looking at her with an expression that was hard to read. He turned abruptly and left the room. Stacy heard him open a door. "We've got company," he said, before conversation continued in a low tone Stacy couldn't hear. Instead of worrying what craziness Bo was spouting, she took the opportunity to check out more of the home, taking in a picture-perfect dining room and portions of a stainless steel kitchen. Her tennis shoes made little noise on the Caribbean walnut floors.

Stacy walked over to the upright piano in a corner of the living room and looked at the photos that crowded its top: pictures of Darius and Bo, Darius and his sister Tanya, their parents, Bo's family (at least that's who Stacy assumed they were), a family portrait of the Montgomerys, and a modern artist's rendering of a Black Jesus Christ. There was no picture of Stacy. Before she could digest that unsettling fact, a voice spoke from behind her.

"This is a surprise."

Stacy turned, her heart racing. "I know. I had to see you."

"I see."

Stacy noticed Bo standing a few feet away, arms crossed in a proprietary manner. Stacy copped an attitude. Bo was Darius's roommate, but Darius was her man. "Uh, can we go to your room, Darius?"

Bo's attitude changed suddenly. "That's okay, I was just leaving." He looked from Stacy to Darius before turning on his heel and going back down the hallway. Within minutes, he passed back by the living room on the way to the front door. "See y'all later," he called out before the door closed.

An uncomfortable silence ensued; then Darius remembered his manners. "You want something to drink?"

"That's cool," Stacy answered. "Something light . . . water, whatever."

"I have some iced coffee," he replied, heading to the kitchen.

The thought of acidy coffee made Stacy's stomach churn. She followed him. "Maybe some juice—apple or cranberry if you have any."

"Apple juice it is," he replied, pulling two crystal goblets from the custom cabinets and pouring a sparkling cider. He handed her a glass and leaned against the counter. "Cheers."

Stacy raised her glass in answer and took a tentative sip. The apple juice was soothing to her palate. *Behave,* she whispered silently to her and Darius's child. He or she seemed to listen.

Darius gently took Stacy's arm and led her back into the living room. They sat on the couch, silently sipping the apple juice.

Stacy spoke first. "Nice place."

"I know you're getting ready to go off on why I never invite you over, but I told you, Stacy. Bo and I don't entertain our female company at the house. It gets too complicated."

"It's okay, Darius. I like having you in my house." Stacy didn't want to argue, especially not tonight. She had come to deliver some complicated news, news that would make not being invited as a house guest fail miserably by comparison. Besides, she didn't feel comfortable in Darius's surroundings. Admittedly the decor was exquisite but for Stacy it was too polished, too perfect.

"Wow, Darius, I like your ring," she said, noticing the unique ring on Darius's finger as he reached for his goblet. "Let me see."

Darius held out his hand. Stacy took it in hers

and examined the uniquely designed jewelry. "What kind of ring is this?"

Oh, just my wedding ring. "A little something I picked up in Canada."

"It's nice, different. I've never seen one like that before."

"Thank you."

Another uncomfortable silence ensued. Stacy took another sip of apple juice, then leaned back against the sofa and tried to get comfortable. Her jittery nerves caused her stomach to churn again. Or maybe it was the apple juice. She set the half-empty goblet on a coaster. A million different thoughts raced through her head—serious, witty, sarcastic, somber—different ways to tell this man she'd loved for years that she was carrying his child. For all the words that raced through her mind, none seemed willing to come out of her mouth.

"I assume there's a reason you came over," Darius said. He turned more fully toward her. "You want to tell me what it is?"

"Yes, Darius, I very much want to tell you why I'm here." Stacy took a deep breath. "I'm pregnant."

Later Stacy would swear the earth stood still in that moment. For what seemed an eternity there was no noise or movement. Darius didn't blink or breathe. His goblet-filled hand remained poised halfway to his mouth. Stacy didn't move either, and after a few tense seconds, dropped her eyes.

"You . . . what?" he asked, hoping he'd heard incorrectly.

Stacy sat up on the couch. "I'm pregnant, Darius. We're having a baby."

Darius jumped up. "We? What's this *we* business? You told me you were on the pill, Stacy. How are you going to come here and tell me you're pregnant?"

"Accidents happen, I guess."

"Accidentally on purpose?" Darius asked. "Did you plan this, Stacy? Either you lied that you were on the pill or you stopped taking them. Which is it?"

"The pill isn't one hundred percent, Darius!"

"I can't believe this bullshit! How long have you been planning this, working on this little *project*?"

Stacy wavered between being hurt and angry. Her emotions were roiling. Once again she found it hard to form a coherent sentence. "I . . . Darius . . . this—I mean no, it just happened. Things *happen,* Darius." She said the last line more forcibly than the others, a touch of indignation adding to her strength.

"This is fucked up," Darius replied. "Just wait until—" Bo's handsome, smiling face swam into Darius's consciousness. The face that held the lips he'd kissed so tenderly moments before Stacy's arrival. *Bo was right. He warned me about her. And now look . . .*

Darius tried to calm the raging fury inside him. "Bo warned me about you," he said in a deceptively calm voice. "But I didn't listen. He called you a conniving bitch and I defended you—"

It was Stacy's turn to jump up. "Bitch! You . . . defended me? I don't need you to defend me from that peanut head, chapped lip—"

"Defended you," Darius bellowed, "because I *thought* you were a good woman. I *thought* you were different from the other females out there, thought you were *special.*" Darius's voice lowered but remained caustic. "But Bo was right and I was wrong. You're nothing special. You're just like all the rest of the she-hunters out there trying to trap their prey. And you think you've trapped me, don't you? Well, think again, Stacy!"

The intense emotion of the moment caught up with Stacy in an instant. Light-headed, she stumbled toward the door. She had never been one for tears, and growing up in a house full of boys had toughened her skin from a young age. But hurt, anger, and fluctuating hormones were threatening a boohoo. She was determined Darius would not see her cry.

Stacy leaned against the foyer wall, willing the tears to dry up and her head to stop spinning.

Darius was beside her in an instant. "I'm sorry, Stacy."

"Move, Darius." Stacy made a move toward the door and almost fainted.

"No, I'm not letting you leave like this. Come sit down."

Stacy didn't have the strength to fight him and allowed Darius to lead her back into the living room. His movements guided her to lie down on the couch.

"Just relax. I'll be back."

Darius returned with a cool washcloth and a glass of ginger ale. "Maybe this will make you feel better," he said, guiding the glass to her lips. "You're trembling."

"I—I'll be fine, Darius," Stacy said, patting her face with the cloth. "The last thing I need is pity. You've made it clear how you feel and—"

"Have you eaten today? Maybe you need something in your stomach, maybe that's why you felt faint."

He was right; Stacy hadn't eaten all day. Whenever she'd tried, she'd get nauseous.

"Will you try and eat something?" Darius asked.

Stacy nodded yes.

Darius went into the kitchen and pulled out the vegetable stew Bo had made for dinner that evening. He didn't miss the irony of serving his pregnant girlfriend his husband's soup. As if thoughts conjured him up, Darius's cell phone rang.

"Hey," Darius said, his voice low.

"She gone?"

Darius sighed. "No."

Silence on the other end. And then, "What's wrong?"

Darius could barely wrap his head around Stacy's news, much less think of a way to tell Bo. As it was, he knew his already dramatic friend would go off. "We'll talk when you get here."

"Well, when will that be? I don't think you want me to come back with her there. But then again, I guess we can all engage in a friendly game of Scrabble, or with her ignorant ass it'll probably be more like babble."

"You're a fool, man." A slight smile scampered across Darius's face as he listened to Bo. The need to have his friend close almost overwhelmed him. Things would be okay again once Bo got home.

They always were. "You might want to go to the mall, maybe a movie or something. I'll call you when the coast is clear."

A sound of exasperation escaped Bo's lips. "I'll tell you now, I don't like feeling homeless when I have a home. You need to pluck black-eyed Susie off the couch and send her ass packin'. Your baby wants to finish what we started before being so rudely interrupted."

"I'll call you soon." Darius's voice dropped to a whisper. "And, Bo? I love you."

When Darius carried the tray of soup, crackers, and a fresh ginger ale into the living room, Stacy looked better. She stood at the window, straight-backed, dry-eyed, looking once again like the boy-ish cutie he'd grown to care about. And for the first time he noticed the bump under her over-sized T-shirt.

"Ah, you're up," he said. "Then come into the dining room."

Stacy followed him into the dining room but didn't sit down. "Maybe I'd better go, Darius. I said what I came here to say, maybe we should just let this news settle before we talk again."

"You might as well eat, Stacy."

Stacy eyed Darius a moment before walking over to the table and sitting down. She had to admit that the aroma rising from the soup bowl was heavenly and for one of the first times since the morning sickness began, her stomach growled.

"Somebody's hungry," Darius said, without humor, but also without sarcasm.

Not knowing how to take his comment, Stacy didn't respond. Instead, she took a few tentative sips of the soup before digging in with gusto. The soup seemed to coat her stomach with calm and tranquility, the way her mama's used to do.

"I never knew my father," Darius said, interrupting Stacy's thoughts. "And my relationship with my mother is, let's say, interesting. I haven't seen her for almost five years."

Stacy remembered that Darius's grandmother had raised him while Tanya, who was actually Darius's half-sister, had been raised by her birth father. But Tanya and Darius had known each other all their lives and were close from the beginning. Stacy reminded Darius that she knew this. He'd forgotten he'd told her.

"Yeah, when I was younger, I used to dream of finding my father, of us hanging out, you know, playing ball, going fishing, doing the male bonding thing. I gave up that dream a long time ago."

His reminiscing continued while Stacy ate. With each spoonful, she felt stronger. Once finished, she took a moment to collect her thoughts and promised herself to stay calm. "Darius, I can't say I'm sorry to be carrying your child. I'm sorry you feel the way you do about it. But I'm going to have this baby. And I hope he or she can know its father."

Darius sat back heavily in the chair. He looked at Stacy a long moment. "This is a lot to digest, Stacy. I mean, this is probably the worst possible time for me to . . . What I mean is, I've got a lot going on, as you well know. Between the upcoming tour, the ministry, Shabach hatin' on a brothah, and the record company pushing for another album . . . And now to bring a baby in the middle of all this? I'd be lying if I said I was happy. I'm very upset about it actually, extremely upset. That said"—Darius got up from the table and stood looking out the dining room window—"I guess I wouldn't really want you to have an abortion—"

"I'm having this baby, Darius."

"I heard you the first time, Stacy." Darius turned to her. "Look, let's not argue anymore, what's done is done and somehow I have to, no, *we* have to deal with it. This doesn't change how I feel about anything else though—marriage, that whole situation. But I will be there to help take care of my child. You are sure this baby is mine, right?"

"Oh my God." Stacy got up from the table, stalked into the living room, grabbed her purse from the couch, and headed toward the foyer.

Darius followed her once again but didn't try to stop her as she opened the door. "It's not romantic, but it's reality. I want a DNA test. And if the baby's mine, I'll take care of it."

Stacy paused, just outside the Crenshaw/Jenkins residence. She never knew that one could feel as she did in that moment, able to totally hate and absolutely love the same person at the same time. As Stacy looked into the eyes of the love of her life and the father of her child, she said the only three words that seemed appropriate: "Go to hell."

33

I Am Not Okay

"Amen." Vivian, Carla, and Tai said together as Vivian ended the prayer that opened their conference call. "Now," Vivian said. "Which do we want to discuss first, the logistics or summit topics?"

"Logistics is easier," Tai suggested. "Everything we need for the conference is at the hotel."

"I've been online for a couple extracurricular activities to include in the handouts," Vivian said. "Perhaps we can look into group tickets to the Cirque du Soleil or a Broadway-type show."

"Actually," Tai said, "there's usually a great, old-school act performing somewhere. It might be fun to get our groove on with the Temptations or the Whispers. I think I heard Anita Baker was going to tour also."

Vivian laughed. "Everyone knows you love oldies, Tai, but how's it going to look for us to have R and B acts officially on our Sanctity of Sisterhood itinerary?"

"It's gonna look like we have good musical taste,

that's how it's gonna look," Tai quickly countered. "Where in the Bible does it say Christians can't listen to R and B? Girl, please. David Ruffin's voice on 'My Girl' is so anointed I can hear that song and almost start speaking in tongues."

"You are a mess," Vivian said, and Tai laughed. "Carla," Vivian continued. "You're awfully quiet. What do you think, should Christians listen to secular music? Carla?"

"I'm sorry, y'all," Carla answered. "My mind isn't really into this right now."

"I've felt you were unusually quiet since we all got on the phone," Vivian responded. "Are you okay?"

There was a pause before Carla sighed. "No, Vivian, I am not okay."

"Well, is it something you want to talk about? We're here for you, sistah. SOS business can wait."

"Actually this may involve SOS," Carla continued. "Or at least my participation in it. I've already confided in Tai about this, Viv, and since I'm ninety percent sure I'm about to move forward, it's time to tell you too."

"Tell me what?"

"I want to divorce Stanley."

There was complete silence on the phone as Vivian absorbed this news. She'd had absolutely no inkling there were problems in the Lee marriage and, after recovering from the shock of Carla's statement, told her so. "Where are y'all receiving counseling?" she asked.

"We're not. In fact, Stanley doesn't know about this yet."

"Don't you think he should?" Vivian asked softly.

"And are you sure he doesn't already? If you two are having problems, surely he knows you're unhappy."

"We've had this particular problem since we got married," Carla explained. "Stanley doesn't like sex."

"Oh, girl, I can't imagine a man who doesn't—"

"Well, imagine it, Vivian," Carla interrupted. "Stanley could care less about sexual intercourse. I don't know whether he just has a low libido or has such an adverse view of intimacy because of his strict, biblical upbringing, but he and I have never enjoyed a satisfying sex life."

Carla gave Vivian a brief snapshot of the Lees' love life for the past decade. "I've tried to get us into counseling," she continued. "But he refuses to go, says there's nothing wrong with our sex life and that he believes we do it more than most Christian couples."

"I wonder what happened to him?" Tai mused aloud.

"Believe me, I've tried to find out. I even tried to talk to his mother about it one time but you would have thought I cursed when I said the word 'sex.' She squinted her eyes, scrunched her nose up as if I'd farted, and told me that was a topic to be discussed only with one's husband and only in the bedroom. That's why I think it could be something psychological, something in what he was taught as a child that prevents him from relaxing and actually enjoying physical intimacy."

Vivian didn't know what to say. She and Derrick enjoyed a very satisfying sex life. But was not being physically intimate a good enough reason to end a marriage?

"You need to tell Stanley you're contemplating divorce," she said after a moment. "Perhaps knowing this will be the push needed to get him to seek counseling. I'm sure I don't need to say this but . . . you've got to try and save your marriage, Carla. You've got children and a ministry to think about. As a pastor's wife, and a pastor yourself, this decision is not just about you."

"This decision is all about me," Carla angrily retorted. "I've been living a lie for ten years and I'm not willing to die unhappy. I know this won't be easy," she continued in a calmer, softer voice. "I know it will be hard on the kids, that the ministry will suffer. But how can anything around me continue to thrive when my soul is dying?

"Do you ever wonder why I'm always so loud and boisterous? Why I laugh so hard and praise so much? It's because I'm afraid not to, afraid that if I don't, the frustration will seep through. It's not that I'm faking. I am loud and I do love God. But I've also developed a public persona that is 'first lady' acceptable. We're not supposed to have problems—especially sexual ones. Everybody sees my smile, but no one knows my sorrow. And I'm tired of denying myself."

Vivian sat up in her chair as a thought hit her like a punch in the gut. She tried to ignore it, but the feeling lingered. Her intuition was never wrong. "Carla . . . is there someone else? Have you developed feelings for another man?"

"I've done more than that," Carla admitted

quickly, ready to talk about it. "Tai already knows, Vivian. I'm having an affair."

Well, no wonder... "How long has this been going on?" Vivian asked. "Never mind, that's not my business. But as your sister in Christ I must speak my heart. First of all, do you love Stanley?"

"Of course I love him; I'm just not *in* love with him."

"I've heard that before but honestly, I've never understood that line. Love is love—in, out, up, down, around, through, or any other way—at least that's the way it should be with unconditional love, the kind in which we're supposed to operate. Does Stanley love you?"

"Yes."

"Then please hear this unsolicited advice. You and Stanley must seek counseling immediately. And, Carla, you have to be honest with him. Tell him about the affair and tell him why. Nothing can come between a couple faster than a secret. Get everything out in the open. And then let God work."

There was a long silence before Carla spoke. "What do you think, Tai?"

"You already know what I think about you and— you and this other man."

"You might as well say it. It's Lavon Chapman, Vivian."

"Oh, Lord." Vivian cringed. *Looks like he produced and directed more than a DVD series.* "This could get ugly."

Tai began again. "It was only a couple years ago that I was contemplating divorce. It's not an easy decision to make, and the only ones to make it are you and Stan. No one else. You're the ones who made the vows, so you're the ones who should decide to break them. Man might offer support but in the end, God is the supreme counselor. So most of all, you should listen to Him. But I'm your sister. You'll have my support no matter what happens."

"I appreciate that, Tai, and your words as well, Vivian. I know what looks to be the right thing to do, but my relationship with Lavon has awakened a part of me that has been asleep a long time, especially where true intimacy is concerned. There were parts of me I'd forgotten, parts that were buried under 'pastor's wife' and 'mama.' But Carla Danielle Ellison Lee is back; she's found herself. And she doesn't want to give herself up again."

"And she doesn't have to," Vivian responded. "She just has to introduce herself to Stanley Lee, her whole self. Maybe if he truly understands it's all of you or nothing, he'll be ready to do what it takes to change things. I know of an excellent therapist who counseled a couple from our ministry a couple years ago. The details were different but the problem was of a sexual nature. They're still together and stronger than ever. If you'd like, I'll give you his number.

"I'm sure this isn't an isolated situation, Carla. We'd probably be shocked at how many Christian couples are battling sexual issues. That's one of the reasons I don't feel led to ask you to withdraw from the SOS ministry, not just yet. Eventually, we'll have to take this before Ladies First, but I think your current pain may be another woman's gain, as God works everything out for His glory."

"And what if the counseling doesn't work, and

Stanley and I end up divorcing. Can God get glory out of that?"

It was a fair question, and Vivian paused before speaking. "God can do anything, Carla," she said finally. "But fail."

34

O Lord, My Strength

Later that evening, Carla waited in the sitting area of the master suite and watched time. She'd been doing it for the past thirty minutes, watching the hands of the curio floor clock inch forward as the pendulum swung back and forth. She watched time tick from life as she knew it to only God knew what. Tai and Vivian had spent the remainder of their conference call praying for Carla. Something must have happened, because by the time they'd hung up, she'd made the decision to talk to her husband, to try and work things out.

While she intended to have a forthright discussion with Stanley, she decided not to divulge the affair, at least for now. If all went well, she thought, she could end the affair with Lavon, she and Stanley could get counseling, Stanley would fall in love with the real Carla, the Lees would start having X-rated sex, their marriage would get back on track, and everybody would live happily ever after.

Vivian maintained her "truth is the light" stance while Tai was optimistic that Carla could get away with not telling Stanley about Lavon. "I'm sure I don't know about all of King's indiscretions," she'd stated matter-of-factly. "And the ones I did know about, trust, did not feel good. So I say if you don't have to . . . why tell? Why cause all that hurt if it can be avoided?"

Carla reached for her Bible and began reading from the page on which it opened, Psalm 18:

> *I will love thee, O Lord, my strength. The Lord is my rock, and my fortress, and my deliverer; my God and my strength, in whom I will trust . . .*

The bedroom door opened slowly. "Carla?" Stanley inquired.

Carla took a deep breath. "Hey, babe," she said, without turning around.

"Oh, you're in the Word," he said, noting the Bible as he walked over and kissed her forehead. "I wondered why the house was so quiet. Kids in bed?"

"Bri is probably on her phone and if I know the boys, they're playing videos even though they know it's bedtime. Are you hungry?" Carla asked, rising to go downstairs. Now that the time for the inevitable conversation was here, Carla questioned whether this particular night time was the right time. She was at the door before Stanley answered.

"No, I'm good. I had dinner at the church."

"Oh, okay."

They shared the day's trivialities while Stanley undressed and prepared for bed. Carla's watching his nightly ritual was bittersweet. Stanley was a good man, a solid man; there were definitely things about him she'd miss. *Miss? Wait a minute, what am I thinking? I'm not leaving Stanley, I'm staying with Stanley. Being with Lavon isn't worth all I'll lose.* She began reciting the Bible verses silently: *The Lord is my rock . . .*

"Carla?"

"Huh?"

"I was trying to tell you about the meeting tonight but you're a thousand miles away. Want to share?"

Stanley got ready to get into bed.

"Baby, can you come over here for a moment? Actually, there is something I want to discuss with you."

"Sure, babe, but can you make it quick? It's been a long day."

It's been an even longer ten years. "I'll try not to be long, Stanley, but this can't wait."

"What is it? Something with the kids? Please don't tell me it involves Brianna—"

"No, Stanley, the kids are fine. This is about . . . about us."

Stanley hesitated before plopping into the armchair opposite Carla. He rubbed his eyes wearily and leaned forward, his fingers steepled under his chin. "I'm listening."

Carla leaned forward as well. "Stanley," she began, "I love you very much, love the life and family we've created. But for a very long time now, a big part of me has been absent from this life. Every now and then I've tried to tell you about her, but I've never been successful."

Stanley leaned back in the armchair and kept listening.

"Baby, I'm talking about true and complete intimacy. It's a part of myself I've never been able to totally express with you."

Stanley sighed. "Is this about sex again? Carla, why does this keep being an issue for us? I thought we'd finally gotten to the point where we understood each other. And now, here you go again."

"I *don't* understand you, Stanley, and you don't understand me."

Stanley rose from the chair and headed to the bed. "I understand you're a nymphomaniac, Carla," he said with a bit of a chuckle. "Now come on, baby, I'm tired. Let's go to sleep."

Carla didn't move. His was the response she'd experienced for ten years—discounting her feelings, not taking her sexual needs seriously. Before, she'd always excused him because he had characteristics that were so good in other areas that mattered: loyal, good father, great minister, provider. She couldn't pretend anymore; it wasn't enough.

She walked over to her side of the bed but didn't get in. "This is serious, Stanley. I've asked you before and you've always refused. But I want us to seek counseling to find out why you have such low, actually no interest in sex. It's not just the physical aspect in itself, but the deeper level of intimacy between a man and woman that is reached as a result of that aspect."

Stanley yawned and pulled back the covers.

"And now it's to the point where if we don't get help, I don't want to continue in this marriage."

These words stopped Stanley in his tracks. "What did you say?"

"I'm saying that this situation is serious, that I've allowed a big part of me to be ignored in order to make our union work. I don't want to hide her anymore. I want to share her with you."

"So what are you saying, that because I'm not a nympho, a sex fiend, a freak, you want to divorce me?"

"I'm saying I can't keep going the way we are, with me having to pleasure myself to reach orgasm."

"Pleasure your—masturbation? In the name of God, woman, you've brought that unclean spirit into this house?"

"Unclean? Stanley, you can't be serious."

"The Bible says—"

"Don't go pulpit on me, Stanley Lee. I'm your wife, not a church member. I know what the Bible says—that the marriage bed is undefiled."

"Well, I sure hope you haven't been performing your little, how should I say it, finger exercises, where I lay my head at night."

"Oh, I've got something much better than my fingers to work with," Carla retorted, anger quickly replacing her calm facade.

"So that's what this is all about," Stanley exploded. "You're committing adultery? Is that it, Carla? Have you returned to your roots of being a whore?"

"You'd better believe it, baby," Carla retorted, his scathing remark about her promiscuous past cutting to the core, slicing through "Christlike" and "calm" with one verbal slash.

"You want to meet him?" she asked as she stomped to the closet and yanked open the door. She paused, chest heaving, staring Stanley down.

Stanley looked anxiously at the closet door. "What the . . ."

Carla walked inside and came out with a red velvet bag. She pulled out the monster cock, nine inches of anatomically correct rubber. "This can do much better than my fingers, Stanley," she said, advancing toward him and waving the unruly member like a fencing sword. "Meet Denzel, my other man!"

"Get that thing away from me, Carla," Stanley said, backing up to the bed and falling onto it.

Carla advanced menacingly, the dildo waving back and forth as though it were alive. "Scared of him?" she asked, crawling onto the bed.

Stanley dodged her and scooted to the other side. He jumped off the bed and pointed angrily at the penis. "Have you had that gangly pornographic *member* inside you, Carla, inside your vagina?"

"Oh, yes," Carla said, throwing the penis on the bed long enough to step out of her lounging robe. She was naked underneath. She picked the penis up. "Want to see how it works?" She spread her legs and poised the dildo between her thighs.

"The blood of Jesus," Stanley hissed. He began speaking in tongues, binding the devil and loosing his wife from her Satanic, sinful spell. "I mean it, put that thing away!" he yelled. He walked over and jerked the dildo out of Carla's hand, then flung it across the room as if it were poison. "Denzel" bounced off the wall and fell into a potted plant.

Carla and Stanley stood in the middle of their master suite, both breathing heavily and staring at the pot as if they half expected the dildo to bounce back out the container and walk over toward them.

"I think you're right about counseling," Stanley said, still looking at the potted plant. Then he looked at Carla. "But I'm not the one who needs it."

The dancing dildo had cooled Carla's burst of anger. At the end of the day, she didn't care what reason was used to get Stanley to a therapist, as long as he went. "Maybe it is me," she readily agreed. "But why don't we both go so we can make sure. I don't want to fight with you, Stanley. So much of our life is good."

She sat on the bed and covered herself. "All I'm saying is I want to be able to take our intimate time to another level. We've been married ten years, Stanley. Don't you ever want to do something different, add a little spark, a little spice to our lovemaking?"

"Obviously not."

"That's what I need to understand, baby. What happened to cause you to be so disinterested in this particular gift from God?"

"God made sex for one thing: procreation. We have been fruitful and we've multiplied. I'm almost fifty years old. I actually think at this time in our lives we should be having less sex, not more."

"You're five years from fifty, Stanley, and you act like that's old. My parents are in their sixties and still going strong."

Instead of responding, Stanley climbed into bed, pulled up the cover, and rolled away from Carla.

Carla scooted over to him and placed her arm across his midsection. "Is that what it is, Stanley? Is it something about how your parents felt about sex, what you were taught? Is sex a sin to you, even in the marriage bed? Were you . . . molested?"

"No!" Stanley said, throwing the covers off and turning to face Carla. "So now you think I'm a pervert too? What is it with you and sex? Is that why you want it so much? Were *you* molested?"

Carla was taken aback at the force of Stanley's anger. She'd never considered molestation before; the question came from nowhere. But now that it was out . . . just maybe . . .

"No, I wasn't molested," she answered. "When I lost my virginity at barely fifteen, I was a willing participant, looking for love in all the wrong places. I love you, Stanley, no matter what. And if something happened to you that turned you off from sex, baby, it's something that can be fixed—"

"I don't need fixing," Stanley said, flinging the covers aside and getting out of bed. "I need sleep . . . and peace. I'm going to the guest bedroom."

Carla watched him as he stomped out the door. "Oh my," she sighed, as into her mind came images of her lover and the things he had done to her—in the same bed where her prudish husband was soon to lay his head. *There I go again,* she thought sadly. No matter that her thoughts that evening had begun on Stanley. They'd ended where they always did . . . on Lavon.

"I will love thee, O Lord, my strength . . ." she began for a third time.

35

I'm Right Here

Lavon was trying to move on, as Carla had requested, yet again. "I have to deny myself," she'd told him, "and put God and my family first." It was proving to be the hardest move he'd ever made.

Against his better judgment, and at another of Carla's suggestions, he'd reconnected with Passion. Unlike the hard road away from Carla, the road to Passion had been relatively easy. A couple of e-mails and a phone call saying he was an available man melted the iciness he first encountered. He should have been grateful. Passion was a good woman. She just wasn't Carla.

He wasn't surprised to see her number on the caller ID when his phone rang.

"Hey, Lavon, check this out. I've got two tickets to the sold out concert to see Lauryn Hill!"

"Lauryn Hill? I didn't even know she was still performing."

"Only rarely. It's a benefit to raise money and

awareness about the civil war in Darfur. Speech from Arrested Development, Ziggy Marley and some other groups are performing too. It's at a small venue so the tickets sold quickly. It should be pretty cool."

"You surprise me, Passion. I never took you for the conscious type."

Hopefully you'll get a chance to learn that there are many sides to me, Lavon. "Is that a yes?"

"That's a yes," he responded, her enthusiasm making him smile in spite of himself.

"Perfect," Passion said. "I'll pick you up." She felt if things went her way, she'd drop him back off in the morning.

"Let's meet at the concert," Lavon suggested, not wanting Passion to know where he lived. Finally giving her his home number was enough. He didn't want her to get carried away. He knew Passion had high hopes for their future. But he intended this journey to be a conservative one: no intimate house visits and no sex until he was totally over the first lady.

Several hours later, Lavon and Passion were among the throng of satisfied music lovers leaving the concert hall.

"That was one of the best concerts I've ever attended," Passion gushed. "But the footage they showed of what is going on in Africa . . . that's just wrong."

"I always say no matter how jacked up America is, it's still the best country in the world," Lavon responded.

"And the richest, which is why we should be taking the troops out of Iraq and sending them to

Darfur, where some mess is really going down. Stop fighting that senseless war."

Lavon was surprised at Passion's passion. "That film really got to you, huh?"

"I'm sorry. I just hate to see such injustice in the world."

Lavon and Passion continued their discussion as they walked toward the parking lot, even as other thoughts crowded into Lavon's consciousness. "Where are you parked, Car—uh, Passion." *Shoot,* he thought, immediately realizing his error.

Passion ignored what Lavon almost said. "I'm on the lower level. What about you?"

"I'm up top. But I'll walk you to your car."

"It's still early. Why don't we go grab a bite somewhere."

"Another time, maybe? It's been a long week. I'm wiped."

"Okay," Passion said, not trying to hide her disappointment. "Another time."

Lavon walked Passion to her car, gave her a quick peck on the cheek before heading to his.

Passion sat idling on Ventura Boulevard, warring with what to do. She wasn't ready for the evening to end, and had sat for five minutes, cell phone in hand, wanting to call Lavon and change his mind. Common sense won out. *I don't want to come off desperate.* She put on her blinker to ease back into traffic and checked her side mirror just as Lavon's car went by. Without thinking twice, she pulled out two cars behind him, hot on his trail. Maybe it was time for a house call after all.

After a couple lights, Passion's foot eased off the gas pedal. *What am I doing?* Was it a good idea to

surprise Lavon at home? No, she reasoned, that
might be relationship suicide. *I'll just see where he
lives and keep going; and then wait until I get invited
over.*

Several turns and ten minutes later, Lavon
turned off Ventura Boulevard and onto a side
street. Passion slowed so Lavon wouldn't see her
car and eased to the corner just as Lavon parked
his car a few houses down. She turned off her
headlights and put her car in park, ready to drive
home as soon as she saw exactly where he lived.

Lavon sat in his car, not looking forward to
going into his empty house. He'd promised himself he wouldn't, but he couldn't help it. He had to
hear Carla's voice before going to bed.

"Hey, baby," he said when Carla answered on
the first ring. "I had to call you. I want to see you so
badly."

"Then turn around," Carla responded. "I'm right
here."

Lavon's head jerked around. There on the
street behind him was Carla in her black Mercedes
sedan. Lavon hopped out of the car, walked
quickly to Carla's door, opened it, pulled her out
and twirled her in his arms. He put her down and
kissed her under the streetlight. They embraced
for a long moment.

"Baby, my sweet honey pot, what are you doing
here? Is this a dream? I've been thinking about
you all night."

"I know I shouldn't have come but I had a meeting over this way and when I saw your exit, I just
had to come by, see how you're doing. I don't trust

myself to stay more than five minutes, which is probably five minutes too long."

"I'll be good," Lavon said. And he meant it. He wouldn't try and seduce her; just seeing her was enough. "You're a sight for sore eyes, girl. Let's have dinner, in a public place, just to catch up. More than anything, I miss our friendship, Carla. I miss you!"

"I miss you too, Lavon. Maybe one cup of coffee wouldn't be so bad, in a public place. Just let me use your restroom first."

They held hands and smiled like teenagers as they walked into Lavon's house.

Passion's hand shook as she viewed the last of the pictures she'd taken with her cell phone camera. The images were far away and dark, but she believed if blown up, there would be no mistaking hotshot producer Lavon Chapman and Logos Word Pastor Carla Lee laughing, kissing, and embracing.

Passion made a U-turn and headed toward the 405 freeway. What she saw had made her numb. She didn't know what to do. Lavon had said he was a free man. Why couldn't Carla stay her married ass away from him! *But maybe he called her.* Maybe he initiated the meeting. Passion didn't know where to direct her anger, but she had enough "pissed off" for the both of them.

Her thoughts were jumbled, going a mile a minute. Should she confront Carla again? Confront Lavon? Should she turn back around and confront them now, together, at Lavon's house? Should she take the pictures to Dr. Lee and expose his adulterous wife?

Passion didn't know what to do and so decided, at least for the night, to do nothing. Instead, she pulled into a Louisiana Fried Chicken and ordered a three piece, a two piece, three sides and two slices of 7-Up cake. She called her parents and told them she was on her way to get Onyx. Lavon might be busy, but her daughter always had time for her. For tonight, she'd let the unconditional love of a child sustain her.

36

Why You Trippin'?

"It's nice, huh, baby?" Kelvin said, as he and Princess strolled down the avenue in Westwood. The Christmas lights twinkled against the pavement made damp by the earlier rain.

"It's okay," Princess replied. "But nothing like the Plaza."

"The Plaza?"

"Yeah, it's this place back home where they outline every single building in lights, for blocks and blocks. Our family used to go there sometimes for the lighting ceremony on Thanksgiving night. We'd park our car and find the perfect spot to watch the sky light up. Then we'd go for ice cream, and watch Mama and Daddy look all googoo-eyed at each other. That's if it was one of their good years."

"And if it was one of their bad ones?"

"Then Daddy would be replaced by Mama Max, who was even more fun because she'd always buy us big tins of popcorn to take home: cheese, caramel, and cinnamon. That was mainly when we were little though. We didn't go this year..." Princess's voice trailed off.

"You know you miss your moms. You should call her."

"But I'm not because whenever I do, she tries to get all up in my business." Princess sulked. "Gets on my nerves."

Kelvin remained silent as they got in the car, buckled up, and started for home.

"Have you told her about the invite yet?"

"Not exactly. I told her I was spending the holidays with Joni's family."

Princess was beyond excited at Kelvin's mother's invitation to join their family in Germany for the Christmas holidays, all expenses paid. Of course she'd said yes. While her choice to stay with Kelvin despite her parents' objections had brought her closer to him, their relationship was still a rocky road to navigate. Princess kept hearing rumors about other women, and Brandy and Sandy, known on campus as the twin tramps, always smirked at her when they walked by. When Princess asked Kelvin about it, he'd delivered his standard "you my girl, why you trippin'?" line.

Unfortunately, she also had a growing dependency on drugs and alcohol, and a lifestyle vastly different from the one she'd left in Kansas. Recently, after a night of ecstasy and vodka, she and Joni agreed to swap boyfriends. That was after Brandon and Kelvin had convinced them to kiss and fondle each other. Whenever a niggling voice entered her conscience and reminded her of the girl she once was, she popped another pill, lit another blunt, or poured another glass. Then she'd look at Kelvin and remember what a lucky girl she was. She had the BMOC: big man on campus. What more could she ask for?

"You've got your passport, right?"

"Uh-huh."

"Why are you sounding all scared and stuff?"

" 'Cause, I've never been out of the country before." *And I've never spent Christmas without Mama, Daddy, Michael, Timothy, Tabitha, Grandma, Grandpa . . .*

"You're gonna love Germany," Kelvin said. "*Es ist ein schönes land.*" His comment on the country's beauty was lost on his girlfriend. "Princess, what's wrong? Why are you crying?"

"I'm not crying."

"What, it's raining in the car, on your face?"

This comment elicited a smile.

"What's wrong with my baby?"

"I don't know. I've been feeling yucky lately. Maybe my period's coming."

"Well, in that case," Kelvin said, leaning over and kissing her after he'd parked in front of their condo, "we'd better get inside and get busy! Brandon probably copped some of the good stuff for us."

"I don't feel like getting high," Princess said as they walked up the steps.

Kelvin embraced her from behind, with a hand on her crotch. "Well, do you feel like me going low?"

"Stop it, silly boy."

"Yeah, and you love every inch of me."

"Yeah, whatever," Princess responded. But she couldn't disagree.

37

Trauma Drama

"Her name is Robin Cook. Last known address: Fremont Avenue in Tampa, Florida. Last residential address, that is. She got out of prison here six months ago after serving a year and a half for identity theft and credit card fraud. Before that, there was a restraining order placed against her by"—the administrator looked down at his notepad—"Kingdom Citizens' Christian Center and a Mrs. Vivian Montgomery, the wife of some big-time preacher. That's how her prints came up.

"There was nothing found regarding family, friends, either in Florida or here. Outside of the criminal information, it's almost like Ms. Cook didn't exist."

"After that accident, it's amazing she exists now," the doctor answered. "She's had reconstructive surgery due to the extensive cuts and burns on her face and several operations to repair damage to internal organs. But in another month or so we can get her over to the psych unit, find out her mental status. She insists on being called Mira, and rarely talks. She denies it, but I'm almost certain she should be taking some type of medication."

"Do you think she has some type of amnesia as a result of the accident, and that's why she didn't know her name?" Beth asked.

"There could be any number of explanations. That's why the sooner we get her fixed up and over to the psych ward, the sooner she can get better and go home. Maybe get a new, healthy outlook to go with her new face, huh?"

"I sure hope so," Beth said. "She doesn't talk much, but there's a lot of pain in her eyes. I hope there's some family somewhere who can help her recover. The plastic surgeon did great work but with the neck burns, the scarring . . . it's still going to be a big adjustment for her."

A short time later, Beth walked into Robin's room. Because of the relationship Beth had developed with the patient, she'd asked the doctor if she could be the one to speak to Robin, and though unorthodox, he'd agreed.

"Mira," she said, walking over and sitting gently on the bed. She took Robin's hand. "I've got good news for you."

Robin stared hard at Beth but said nothing.

"We found out who you are . . . your real identity. Your name is Robin Cook." The nurse said the name slowly, enunciating carefully, as if she were talking to a child, someone hard of hearing, or for whom English was not her first language.

Robin was none of these things. *I know my name, muthafucka. . . . I just didn't want y'all's asses know-*

ing. She masked her true feelings. "Robin?" she whispered innocently.

A huge grin spread across Beth's face. "Yes! Robin Cook. You remember?"

Robin frowned. "I like Mira."

Beth was relieved Robin knew who she was. Maybe her head trauma wasn't as extensive as she'd feared. "You just keep on healing like you are, sweet pea, and I'll call you anything you want."

"Mira," Robin whispered again.

"Okay, Mira." Beth got up from the bed and reached for the chart. "Let's take your vitals. It's almost time for dinner."

While her mind voiced its discontent, Robin played it cool on the outside. The nurse had treated her well, taken special care of her. Robin had decided early on that Beth was all right, for a woman, and that a friend might come in handy at this point since she had none. She had no plans to reconnect with anyone who knew her from before. No, she planned to leave Robin Cook behind in the hospital and reenter LA in general and Kingdom Citizens' Christian Center in particular . . . as Mira . . . Mira Monroe.

38

Happy Birthday, Jesus

Princess's smile was bittersweet as she watched the small Petersen children gather around the *Weihnachtsman*, the German version of Santa Claus, and receive their Christmas Eve gifts. Almost one hundred Petersens, in-laws and friends, had gathered for their annual holiday reunion at the Inter-Continental Berchtesgaden Resort in Berchtesgaden, Hintereck, Germany. The five-star establishment offered every luxury and, nestled in the Bavarian Alps, included breathtaking surroundings. Kelvin's was a fairly close-knit clan and Princess enjoyed seeing him interact with them, speaking fluent German effortlessly. Besides Princess, Janeé, and Janeé's mother, Nancy, representing for the African-Americans of the world, a spattering of other cultures, including Asia, the Middle East, and various European nations, were all part of the reunion. Their multicultured children offered a clear vision of the world to come.

Everyone had made Princess feel welcome since her and Kelvin's arrival two days before, so much so that she could almost forget the ache in her heart at missing her own family's Christmas traditions . . . almost, but not quite.

Kelvin and Princess slept in late the next morning, then enjoyed a delicious brunch that included vegetable omelets, smoked pork, potatoes, cucumber salad, pancakes with brandied raisins, apple and plum compote, and bread dumplings. Afterward, there was more gift giving, skiing, games, and fun discussions around the large, wood-burning fireplace. The day ended with a formal dinner and dancing.

"Are you having fun?" Janeé asked Princess as she sat down and took off her heels. "I know one thing, my feet are about to rebel against all this partying. If you haven't figured it out already, the Petersen celebration goes nonstop."

Princess smiled but said nothing.

Janeé stopped rubbing her foot and looked at Princess. "I'm sure you miss your family, this being your first holiday away from them."

"Yeah, I miss my family, but everyone here's been great . . . so nice."

"Princess, are you sure everything's all right? My boy isn't mistreating you, is he?"

"No, ma'am," Princess responded. "I'm just, I don't know. I haven't been feeling myself lately."

"You're not pregnant, are you?" Janeé teased. "'Cause as cute as you and Kelvin's kids will be, I'm not ready for the grandma label just yet."

Princess fixed Janeé with a worried look.

"Ohmigod, I hope not," she said slowly, reason dawning for why she hadn't yet got her period. "I can't get pregnant if I'm on the pill, right?"

"A woman can get pregnant anytime she's sexually active," Janeé said. "Have you missed your period? Felt sick? Tired?"

Princess hadn't felt sick, but her period hadn't come yet and she'd been lethargic since before the trip.

"No, I'm not pregnant," Princess said firmly, trying to convince herself and her body of this fact. "I think I'm just still jet-lagged."

"That's probably it," Janeé agreed.

Suddenly, Princess missed her mother immensely. "What time is it in America?" she asked Janeé.

Janeé looked at her watch. "In Kansas, just a little past eight A.M."

Princess stood. "I think I'm going to go call my family."

"I think that's a good idea."

A few moments later, Princess heard a familiar voice.

"Merry *Christ*-mas!" Tai said cheerfully in her standard Christmas greeting that emphasized Jesus' name.

Her voice brought tears to Princess's eyes. She closed her eyes, swallowed. "Hi, Mama."

"Princess." Pause. "I was praying to hear from you. We've tried for days to reach you."

"My phone doesn't get reception here, where I'm at."

Tai paused. "Where are you?"

"Germany," Princess said softly.

"That's what I figured. When I couldn't reach you on your cell, or at the number you'd left for Joni, I figured you'd lied about your plans. Then Mama Max told me Miss Nancy had left town for their family reunion in Germany.

"Why did you lie to us, Princess? I know we're not too close right now but your dad and I have been really worried about you."

"I know, Mama. But I didn't tell you because I'm spending this time with Kelvin's mom and I know you don't like her."

"How I feel about her has nothing to do with you. No matter what happens, you're my daughter, Princess. What if something happened to you?"

Princess started to cry.

"Princess, what's wrong?"

"Nothing, I just miss everybody."

"We miss you too. The holiday isn't the same without you. I'm sure Michael will be more than happy to not have to share the fruitcake though."

Princess smiled at the reference to her and her big brother's age-old fights over who would eat the most of the one cake no one else in the family liked.

"You guys are ahead of us, right? Christmas is just about over, in Europe?"

"Kinda . . . it's almost night here, around five o'clock."

"Did you enjoy your day, baby? Are you happy being where you want to be?"

"It was all right," she answered. She gave Tai a brief rundown of what her day had entailed.

"I guess there were no church services or any-thing, huh? Still, I hope you told Jesus happy birth-day, remembered the reason for the season."

Honestly, the baby in a manger wasn't the child she'd been thinking about. "Is Daddy up yet?"

"No, but I'll get him for you."

"That's okay; I'll call back later."

"I know he wants to wish you a Merry Christmas, Princess. Give me the number where you're at."

Princess gave her mother the information, they shared "I love yous," and she hung up the phone. Silent tears ran down her face as she sat in her room, thousands of miles from home, alone. *Or maybe not alone. I can't be pregnant!* Having gotten on the pill the same week she lost her virginity, Princess had never given pregnancy a second thought. On this she agreed with Kelvin—now was not the time to have a child. She laughed at who she called "igno-hos," women who slept around with professional athletes in hopes of getting preg-nant and securing a nice support check for eigh-teen years. She hoped the laugh wasn't now on her.

Princess curled up in the middle of the king-sized bed, feeling like the scared, vulnerable, eighteen-year-old she was, not the got-it-going-on, worldly woman she wanted so desperately to be. She re-membered her mother's words about grown folk's pleasure coming with grown folk's pain, and prayed she wasn't getting ready to experience the latter. Her mother had told her more than once that in the Brook household, abortion was not an option. "The giving and taking of life is God's business," she'd said—her "I brought you in, I'll take you out" position not withstanding.

"Please, God, don't let me be pregnant," Princess pleaded. She begged God for mercy as she tossed and turned. And then right before drifting off to sleep, she whispered, "Happy birthday, Jesus."

39

What Child Is This

"What child is this who laid to rest, on Mary's lap is sleeping. Who angels greet with anthems sweet, while shepherd's watch are keeping . . ."

The Kingdom Citizens' Christian Center's Christmas day early morning service was a congregation favorite, filled with music, communion, and the timeless good tidings, great joy message of Jesus' birth. As usual, the sanctuary was filled to capacity, the parishioners in colorful shades of reds, greens, and winter whites. The matrons of the church sported a variety of lively hats. Mother Moseley was especially proud of her red velvet number: a twenty-inch-wide dipped brim, with ornament-adorned wreath and battery-operated flashing Christmas lights around the hat's crown. The Montgomerys were a picture-perfect first family as they sat together on the raised platform—Vivian and Elisia in matching red dresses, Darius and Darius Jr. in identical forest green suits.

KCCC's two-thousand plus congregation came alive as the choir, band, and a perfectly pitched raspy alto soloist belted Darius's contemporary, R & B tinged arrangement of this century old holiday classic:

> *"This, yes this is Christ the King, whom shepherds guard and angels sing; Haste, haste, to bring Him laud, the Babe, the Son of Mary."*

Stacy sang with fervor from her seat near the back of the church. Even though she'd taken a leave of absence, she still felt as much a part of the choir as she would in the first row of the soprano section. She'd given the director no explanation for taking a break, though if not for the cut of her A-line dress, the reason would be obvious.

Stacy placed a hand on her rounding stomach. *What child is this? Darius Crenshaw Jr., or Dara, if it's a girl.* Love swelled within her as she watched her baby's father expertly lead the band while playing intricate riffs on the keyboard. He was some kind of fine in his black silk suit and red shirt, her caramel-colored lover with close-cropped black hair, shadow goatee, and body fit forever.

Looking back, Stacy was glad she'd called Darius the day after their fight. They'd both calmed down and were able to discuss the situation rationally. She assured Darius the child she carried was his, but agreed to take a DNA test to prove its paternity. Her friend and his sister Tanya had been great—joyfully receiving the news of becoming a first-time aunt. Hers was the first truly happy reaction. Stacy's mother was disappointed but resigned to the situation while her brothers had asked if they needed to "persuade" the father to do the right thing. Darius hadn't given his staunch Pentecostal grandmother the news.

But soon everybody would know about baby on board. Which was why Stacy hoped Darius would be open to the solution she felt would make the situation look more sanctified than scandalous. She planned to broach the idea when they reached Big Bear.

At four in the afternoon, the magic began. That's when the limo picked her up at the apartment, with Darius inside. He greeted her with a flute of sparkling apple-grape juice, while he enjoyed champagne. The ride to Big Bear was long but pleasant, filled with companionable silences. Stacy felt Darius was sometimes too quiet, but she was so happy to have this time with him she didn't want to pry, or do anything to ruin the best vacation of her life.

They arrived at Big Bear just as a slight flurry began to fall, and after settling into the rustic cabin Darius had reserved, ate a light dinner at a nearby restaurant. Stacy enjoyed the walk back to their place as snowflakes fell, but the California native was glad to return to their cozy room. Darius built a roaring fire, the perfect complement to the hot chocolate with marshmallows she fixed for them both.

"This is so perfect. Thanks, baby," Stacy said as she handed him a mug and cuddled next to him under a furry throw.

"I'm glad you like it," Darius said. "I like it too."

"You know, Darius, I've been thinking."

"Uh-oh."

Stacy laughed. "What, that's a problem?"

"There's always trouble when a woman gets to thinking."

"Oh, really?"

Darius tickled her. "Really."

"You know you're the more ticklish of the two of us," Stacy said, putting her mug down and reaching for his sides.

They wrestled playfully before it turned into a kiss. Their passion continued a moment before Stacy gently pulled back.

"Darius, I want to run something past you and I want you to hear me out before you get upset. Okay?"

"You mean more than about your being pregnant?"

Stacy sat up and away from Darius.

"Sorry, baby, that came out wrong. Come here, Stacy, come over here." He pulled her back into an embrace and after a few seconds Stacy once again relaxed into him.

"That's better. Now, what do you want to share with me? And if it's something that might upset me, why even get into it? We just got here so let's not have a fight on the first day."

"I don't want to fight at all," Stacy countered. "I'll just say what's on my mind and you can agree or not, your choice."

"Okay, shoot."

Could it really be this easy? Shoot, just like that? Stacy decided to go for it. "Let's get married."

"Oh, no," Darius yelled, feigning a heart attack. "You went straight for the jugular, woman."

"We're both twenty-one plus, no need for games."

"You're right about that, which is why I have to tell you that under no circumstances will you and me tie the knot."

"But what about—"

"Wait a minute, let me finish. That doesn't mean that we can't successfully raise a child together. After paternity is established, and don't trip, I believe it's mine, but after the tests come back, I will immediately set up a trust fund for the baby and have an attorney work out a fair child support arrangement. I'll buy a home for you, take care of you financially. I want to be an active, constant presence in the child's life. But, Stacy, I don't want to rush into a marriage just because a baby's on the way. A baby does not a marriage make, you know that."

"I know, but sitting in church today got me thinking . . . about all the gossip, what people will say. Yeah, single women have babies all the time but that still doesn't stop tongues from wagging. Another Black baby born out of wedlock—I was hoping ours wouldn't be a part of that statistic."

"Would you rather it was part of the divorced parent stat?"

Stacy was silent. She'd wanted to become Mrs. Crenshaw for a long time and wasn't ready to give up on believing it could happen.

"I'm going to make an appointment with Sistah Vivian," Stacy continued.

"Why?"

"So she can hear about the baby from me and

not through the gossip mill. And so I can get her counsel on how to handle it."

"And maybe so Pastor Derrick will talk me into doing the right thing?"

Stacy smiled. "If he can."

40

Christmas Just Ain't Christmas . . .

Darius stood abruptly. "I'll be back."

"What? Please don't go away mad, Darius. I'm not going to try and get Pastor Derrick or Sistah Vivian to change your mind, promise."

"It's not that. I think I left my cell at the restaurant and need to go back before they close."

"Left your . . . Darius, it's almost eleven o'clock. They're probably closed already."

"It's right up the way. I won't be long."

And before she could formulate an argument, Darius grabbed his coat and was gone.

Around the corner from his and Stacy's cabin, Darius knocked at another cabin's door. The door opened quickly.

"Get in here, lover boy," Bo purred. "What took you so long?"

"I forgot to put the phone in my pocket when we went to dinner. I just felt it vibrate a few minutes ago. And she's been on me like my own skin. I couldn't call you."

Darius and Bo shared a kiss and before long, Bo had his hands down the back of Darius's trousers.

"No, Bo, I've got to get back. I told Stacy I left my phone at the restaurant." He kissed Bo again. "I knew I shouldn't have agreed to let you come here. Knowing you're so close is driving me crazy."

"Good. Then you know how I feel, knowing my spouse is cheating on me. I wish I could quit you," he drawled, mimicking Jake Gyllenhaal's character in one of their favorite movies, *Brokeback Mountain*.

"You nut," Darius said, hugging him tightly. "You know she's just—"

"A decoy," they both said together.

"Yes, I know," Bo continued. "And I'm never going to like it, but if that's what it takes for you to be Mr. Gospel Success and have us still be to-gether . . . I'll do anything to be with you, you know that. Okay, lover, out you go. Maybe you can come back later, after she's asleep."

"I'll try. If not, I'll get away tomorrow."

"How?"

"Knowing you're waiting for me, I'll find a way."

Minutes later, Darius was back inside with Stacy.

"Did you find your phone?"

"Uh, yeah, they had it."

Stacy had called the restaurant immediately after Darius left and got the answering machine. She saw no need to mention this, however, reason-ing that maybe the employees didn't answer the phone after hours.

"Well, I'm glad you're back," she said instead. She lay on the bed in a provocative position, the silky fabric from her new, red, sheer nightie shim-mering against her sienna skin.

Darius stripped down to his boxers and climbed into bed. He pulled Stacy into an embrace. Stacy placed her leg over his and nuzzled his neck.

"Baby, I want to do like Keith Sweat and love you down, but it's been a crazy long day for your boy. Can we kiss, cuddle, and call it a night? I promise I'll make it up to you tomorrow."

Stacy wasn't too disappointed. Pregnancy had calmed her usually roaring libido, and she'd stayed out late with Hope's cousin, Frieda, the night before. "Okay Dee," she said, scooching up against him and yawning. "I know you're a man who keeps his promises."

Darius feigned sleep, waiting for Stacy to stop squirming. Almost an hour went by before he felt hers was deep, even breathing.

"Stacy?" he whispered, and then again, "Stacy," a little louder.

When he got no response, he waited another ten minutes and then eased out of bed. He tiptoed into the bathroom and without turning on lights, opened the closet to put on the sweat suit, socks, and shoes he'd placed there earlier, specifically for this getaway. Once in the living room, he quietly took his cell phone and the room keys off the coffee table, put on his coat, and crept out into the dark, cold night.

Bo's door opened before Darius knocked. "How'd you know I was out here?"

"I keep telling you we're soul connected. I know everything you do, where you go, what you're thinking."

"Oh, is that right?" Darius asked as he walked

over to the lit fireplace and took off his coat. "What am I thinking now?"

Bo embraced Darius from behind. "You're thinking about what a good idea it was that I came up here."

Darius turned and returned Bo's hug. "You're absolutely right."

41

Dreams and Nightmares

Where the hell did he go? Stacy paced from the living room to the bedroom, looking out the front window each time she passed by. Darius had acted strangely all evening. Secretive, that's how he'd been acting. When he went back for his cell phone she was convinced he already possessed, her suspicion intensified. And when he begged off lovemaking, her suspicion turned to belief. Something was up.

Her first thought, of course, was the presence of another woman. But that didn't make sense. Why would he invite someone else on their vacation? It was too bold, too ridiculous to even consider. But still, not impossible. And who would that someone else be? *Bo.*

"He wouldn't dare," she reasoned aloud. "He wouldn't bring anyone, especially him, up here right under my nose!"

That thought gave her peace for a moment. But after almost an hour of waiting, she couldn't take it any more. Stacy replaced her lingerie with fleece sweats and tennis shoes. When she couldn't find the cabin keys, she simply left the door unlocked and walked out into the night.

The frosty night air cut through Stacy's leather coat. She wrapped it tighter around her, wishing she had a hat, scarf, and gloves. She stood outside the cabin and looked around. It was dark and eerily beautiful, a lone streetlight and stars her only illumination. Snow covered the ground like a blanket and crunched underneath Stacy's feet. The sound caused her to look down. There, in the snow, was one big shoe print, then another, and another. Stacy followed the trail as best she could in the darkness.

The trail led to the front of a cabin just around the corner from where she and Darius stayed. Stacy stopped and stared at the wood siding, as if to do so long enough would enable her to see through it. But was she prepared to see what was on the other side?

Stacy eased up to the front window and peeked through the small pane of glass. The living room was pitch black. She walked around to another window. A dim light glowed, from candles she guessed, but tightly shut blinds prevented her from seeing inside. She turned and leaned her back against the cabin, pondering her next move even as she shivered from the cold. "That's it," she mumbled under her breath. "I'm not about to sneak around here like a *Cheaters* episode. I'll cuss him out tomorrow and then take my ass home!"

Just as Stacy walked by the front porch, the door opened.

"Yeah, I'll be there, just try to get away around noon," a voice whispered.

"Okay, baby, sleep well," she heard Darius say.

"Ain't nobody going to sleep!" Stacy shouted as she ran up on the porch. The door slammed quickly. "Who's in there, Darius? I swear to God I will wake up every soul on this mountain unless you get whoever's in there to open the door."

Darius was too stunned to speak.

Stacy started pounding on the door. "Open up, dammit, open this flippin' door now!"

Darius grabbed Stacy's arms and tried to pull her away from the cabin.

Stacy wrestled away from him and started banging on the cabin window. "I'll break this window if you don't bring your ass out here!"

"Here's my ass, bitch," Bo said indignantly, flinging the door open. "Now, what are you going to do about it?"

Stacy felt she could show him better than she could tell him. Before anyone could blink, 130 pounds of "I'm not the one" flew into Bo's chest. Bo went down with Stacy on top of him.

"Faggot!" she yelled, as she pummeled his face.

"Faggot?" Bo replied, swinging wildly. "You skank ass—"

"Stop!" Darius said. He lifted Stacy off Bo, even as Stacy's arms and legs kept flailing.

"Don't—touch—me," Stacy choked out, once she caught her breath. "I heard the rumors, saw the signs, but I didn't want to believe it. I didn't want to believe that you, a fine, upstanding, *Christian* man were a homosexual. Gospel's darling. Ha! Won't your fans, especially all those adoring matrons ready to bake you pies and fry you chicken just so they can say you ate their food, be surprised to find out where your mouth has been."

"Stacy, wait a minute," Darius said. "You're jumping to conclusions. Come in and let's talk."

"Come in?" Stacy asked in an incredulous tone, her teeth chattering. "Have you lost your mind? Well, get ready. You're about to lose a lot more than that!"

With that, Stacy stumbled back to her cabin. She was too angry to cry. What was supposed to be her dream vacation had turned into a nightmare. It was true. Darius and Bo were lovers.

A violent surge welled up inside her and before she knew it, Stacy was throwing any and everything not nailed down. She hurled a vase of flowers across the room, watching glass shatter and water splash as crystal met wood. She threw pillows, candles, sent a stack of magazines flying off the coffee table. She walked into the bedroom, tore into Darius's well-organized suitcase of designer duds and flung them every which way. She thought of cutting them up or setting them on fire but couldn't find any scissors, and the once roaring fire was now warm gray ash. Thoroughly exhausted, Stacy fell across the bed. The tears that moments earlier she'd been too angry to cry now flowed in abundance. They kept her company as she fell asleep. Darius did not come back.

Stacy awoke early the next morning to the sound of birds cheerfully chirping and sunshine streaming through the wooden shutters. The blissful setting couldn't be farther from her reality. She could tell her eyes were puffy from the effort it took to open them. As she sat up on an elbow, last night's nightmare flooded her mind: Darius, Bo, and the truth she'd always known and could no longer deny.

Stacy lay back and stared at the ceiling. She thought back to Hope's surprised reaction when she first mentioned her feelings for Darius. Hope recovered quickly and changed her facial expression. But Stacy had caught the look, seen the doubt. She'd seen it and ignored it, just like all the other signs, all the other times. But now there was something she couldn't ignore, being four months pregnant with Darius's baby. As if she needed further confirmation, she felt a fluttering in her stomach for the very first time. The tears began again.

But not for long. Now that she'd finally acknowledged what she already knew in her heart, Stacy had to plan her future—one without Darius. She'd go home, regroup, and put her life back together again. She didn't know what life after Darius would look like, but she intended to find out.

"Punk faggot," she spat out as she flung back the covers and stomped into the bathroom. That's when it hit her; Bo's MO. *This is just what he wants.* She went over the events of the past year and a pattern clearly emerged. Bo had been trying to get Stacy out of Darius's life ever since she entered it because he knew how much it aggravated her. He had made it a point to let her know when he and Darius were traveling together, called often when Darius was at her house, and frequently answered Darius's phone in his nauseating business drone: "DC Productions, Bo Jenkins speaking."

She thought about Thanksgiving and the sudden "holiday promotional tour" Bo had "arranged." Just like the dawn giving way to full sunshine, Stacy's revelation gained light with each passing moment. By the time she flushed, toilet paper wasn't the only thing that went down the drain. So did Bo's near sabotage of her and Darius's relationship.

He thinks I'm going to leave, and that's exactly what he wants me to do, Stacy thought as she held a hot washcloth over her puffy, tear-swollen eyes. *He thinks his love for Darius is stronger than mine, that his willpower is greater than mine.* "Well, you've met your match, Bo Punk-Ass Jenkins," Stacy said to the walls. "I'm not going anywhere!"

She turned out the bathroom light and glanced out toward the living room. She jumped in shock. Darius was back.

"Oh, you decided to leave your booty buddy?"

Darius sprung up from the couch. "Look, Stacy, I'm not going to be ridiculed by you—"

"Don't you dare give me attitude!" Stacy didn't back down an inch. "You won't be ridiculed, Darius? Well, what about me? What about your son? It looks like the joke will be on us. And that's still not enough for you to leave that asshole."

Darius had argued with Bo all night; he had no fight left for Stacy. "You're right—I'm gay, Stacy. Or at least I thought I was . . . until I met you. Now, I guess I'm bi. I love you . . . and I love Bo."

"Hmm. I guess you can call your next Gospel CD *Blessings Bi Darius,* and then you can call the secular counterpart, *Booty Bi Darius.* This is going to change your image a tad, don't you think?"

Darius inched closer to Stacy. "No, because you

are *not* going to put my business in the street. I've worked too hard to get where I am. Shabach thought he could keep the king of gospel crown, and I finally have that. I'll be damned if I let anyone or anything knock me off my perch. Do you understand me?"

Stacy laughed as she walked over and sat on the couch. "That sounds precariously close to a threat, *Christian.*"

In two long strides, Darius stood over Stacy. "That's a promise, *saint.*"

Stacy leaned back on the couch. "You might as well back the bump up—you don't scare me. I've got a cousin in prison now for *voluntary* manslaughter, nucka, and a quartet of brothers just waiting to jump your ass. Touch me and you'll get a beat down before you can sing do-re-mi. Now . . . do *you* understand *me?*"

Darius turned away and tried to get a hold of his anger. He was seething! Who did she think she was, talking to him like he was some punk? Well, she was going to find out!

He took a deep breath before speaking again. When he did, he'd borrowed some of Stacy's feigned serenity. It did neither one of them any good to turn gangsta. "What do you want to do?" he asked quietly. "I'm sure you don't want to stick around, so let's just part as friends, get our attorneys together when the paternity test comes back, and set up joint custody." He walked over to his cell phone. "I'll call the limo to come pick you up."

"You'd like that, wouldn't you? For me to walk out of your life nice and quiet, a perfect present with a *Bo* on top. But we've got a child on the way. I'm not going anywhere, Darius, and have not changed my mind from what I suggested last night. Only now, it's a demand. I want a legitimate father for this child. I want him or her to experience a two-parent family. I want to be looked upon with respect as the wife of my baby's father. And I want all of these things now."

Stacy's comments literally backed Darius up against the wall, where he now stood with legs and arms crossed. "You can't be serious."

"I'm very serious."

"But I've already told you—I love Bo."

Stacy squirmed a bit. "That presents a problem. He's got to go."

Just then the door to the cabin swung open. "I'm not going no damn where."

Stacy hadn't noticed that the front door was slightly ajar. But Bo's entrance, no matter how ill-timed or dramatic, no longer surprised her. "We'll see about that."

"Yeah, we'll see, ho."

Stacy jumped up. "No you didn't! I told you—"

"Bo, please," Darius pleaded.

"Oh, my bad. I said ho but I meant to say rake. Or I could have said shovel, ax, any kind of *farm tool* will do to describe your country ass."

"I might be country but at least I'm not queen. They call you Bo, but they should call you Burning for all that flame you're bringing in the room."

"Rugrat rake."

"Booty buddy."

"Stop it! Both of you just shut up. You're acting like you're two-year-olds. This is ridiculous."

All three of them stood in the center of the living room, waiting to pounce on the other's barb.

Finally Darius walked into the dining room. "Can we all just . . . sit down for a minute and talk rationally?"

If the situation hadn't called for crying, Stacy would have guffawed. *Rationally? He's asking me, his pregnant girlfriend, to sit down with his homosexual lover and have a rational conversation?*

Bo brushed past her and walked into the dining room. "Y'all got any alcohol?" he asked with attitude. " 'Cause I think I need a dranky drank!"

Stacy watched Bo follow Darius into the kitchen, as if he belonged there. In that moment, she saw just how crazy the situation really was. But what could she do? Leave and give Bo exactly what he wanted? Or stay, and get what she felt was hers?

"What am I doing?" she asked herself softly. Just then she felt the flutter of her baby again. *Securing your future,* she thought, her hand on her stomach. "Bring me some apple juice, Darius. And pop a bag of that popcorn. Might as well act like we're *at* the movies," she continued under her breath. "Because it sure as hell feels like I'm *in* one."

42

What You Pray For

"I can't believe I'm actually sitting here," Stacy said honestly. "Bo, it's no secret I don't like you, but Darius is right, we're all adults. Maybe getting this out in the open between us is a good thing, especially since Darius and I are about to become parents."

She turned to face him fully. "Don't you want what's best for this child, Darius's child? Don't you want us to be happy?"

Bo downed his third straight shot of Courvoisier. "I want what Darius wants. And the only way *that* man is going to be happy is with *this* man in the picture." Bo's voice softened as he turned to Darius. "Tell her, baby."

Oh, God, help me not to puke. Stacy slowly turned to Darius. "Tell me what?"

"Tell you why you'll never get married," Bo slurred.

"Bo, I think you've had enough," Darius warned.

"Sitting here while my husband talks to his baby mama." Bo belched. "Sheeet."

"That's what he calls you, his husband?" Stacy asked.

"Uh, no," Darius quickly interjected. "Bo's drunk."

"See my ring?" Bo asked, daintily holding his hand, palm down, for Stacy to observe.

"That's the same ring as . . . okay, Darius . . . I can't take much more."

"It's just a promise thing we did with each other," Darius explained. He looked at Bo sternly.

Bo lowered the glass. He knew when Darius meant business. This was one of those times. Bo had gone too far. "Don't worry, Spacy, I mean, Stacy. It's nothing. We just wanted to wear something alike."

Stacy looked pointedly at Darius. "Well, I want to wear something alike too, like a wedding ring."

Now it was Bo's turn to give Darius a stern look.

"Stacy, why can't we just take care of the baby together?" Darius asked.

"Because I am an integral, visible member of Kingdom Citizens' Christian Center, not to mention a woman worthy of your doing the right thing. I can't understand why you wouldn't want to create a stable family for your son." She glanced over at Bo. "Well, semistable anyway."

Darius sighed, reached for the liquor, changed his mind, and sat back in the chair. He looked at Stacy a long moment. "Bo stays," he said, finally.

"Where's he staying? Not with us."

"We'll work it out," Darius said.

Bo dropped his head in his hands. Then he

grabbed the liquor bottle and got up from the table. "Come over when you're done, Darius." He looked at Stacy. "Spacy . . . it's been real, and it's been fun, but it hasn't been real fun. Later."

Darius looked at his watch. "You okay?" he asked with genuine concern. "It's almost eleven o'clock. Are you hungry?"

Was he for real? Stacy wondered. In light of what happened, how could he sit there and calmly ask if she wanted food?

"Darius, I've just had it confirmed that you're bisexual and what's worse, that that shit isn't enough to make me leave. You won't leave Bo, even for the baby I'm carrying, and he's too sorry to consider leaving you alone. Do you seriously think I have an appetite?"

"You didn't just find out," Darius said softly.

"What?"

"You already knew. Women are like that. Y'all know these things. Now honestly, you want me to believe we've been together two years and you never suspected anything with me and Bo? You thought I was straight all this time?"

Stacy shook her head no.

"And yet you kept coming after me . . . and you stayed."

"Because in spite of everything, I love you. Yes, I've heard the rumors, I just ignored them. I didn't want to think you could love a man more than you love me. I don't mind your keeping Bo as your business manager—"

"He's more than that, Stacy . . ."

"He doesn't have to be."

"Yes . . . he does."

Stacy and Darius stared each other down for an eternity.

"I can give you everything," Darius continued. "Like I said, I'll take care of you and my son, buy whatever you need, whatever you want. You'll have the life you've always dreamed of. Because of my success, our child will have the best. Bo is a part of insuring that that success continues."

"It can't be in my face," she said finally. "You have to keep that shit on the DL, like you've been doing. And since everything is in the open now, I want to be a part of your life, your whole life, on the road and everything."

Suddenly Stacy felt as if she'd fought a ten-round match and lost. Everything hurt: her head and her heart. She dragged herself from the table. "I'm going to take a shower."

"I've been thinking," Darius began as soon as she emerged from the tub and began toweling off. "I know how the three of us could be together."

"I'm not living with Bo Jenkins, Darius!"

"Not with, baby, next-door to."

"What?"

"Do you think Cy knows about any duplexes for sale? Bo could live on one side, and you could live on the other."

"You're out of your ever-loving mind."

"This could work so much better if you'd stop hating Bo. He's a good person when you get to know him."

"I don't want to get to know him."

"Bo stays, Stacy. And if you're determined to stay as well, we all need to get along. I'll tell Bo the same thing. He has to respect you as . . . the mother of my child."

"And as your wife. I will not be a part of this, this charade, without being legal. You will marry me, Darius. And you'll spend the night in my house, in my bed. I don't want to know when you're . . . with him."

"Do you think Cy can find us a duplex?"

"Do you think you can find me a ring?"

Darius heaved a heavy sigh. "I guess so."

"You'll marry me?"

Darius nodded.

"Then I'll call Hope and ask for Cy's help in finding us (she almost choked on the word) a place."

"Good. I'll go over and tell Bo."

Stacy sat motionless for minutes after Darius left. No one would believe what she'd just agreed to. She didn't believe it herself. She'd just gotten what she wanted, what she'd prayed for. Darius Crenshaw, minister of music, king of gospel extraordinaire, had just agreed to marry her. But the reality wasn't as she'd imagined. In fact now was the saddest moment of her life.

43

Not My Business

Was it just over a week ago that she'd taken the pictures? It was, and as she spread out the profession-
ally enhanced glossies over her coffee table,
Passion was no closer to deciding how to use them
than the night they were shot. The pictures could
not have turned out more perfect: Lavon twirling
Pastor Carla around, their heads thrown back
laughing, him grabbing her hand, them kissing. It
was as if they'd purposely posed for the ammunition that could secure the demise of their relationship. The film development company had done
amazing work enlarging, lightening, and then
cropping the faraway shots. Pastor Carla and
Lavon's faces were clearly visible. Now the only
question was . . . what would Passion do with them?

Passion slowly picked up and studied each picture. A myriad of emotions played across her heart
as she did so. She'd thought that for a first lady
Pastor Carla was cool, until finding out about her
cheating ways. Passion knew firsthand how hard it

was to turn away from Lavon's animal magnetism and manly charm. But what about Dr. Lee? He was a distinguished man of God with more eloquence than Lavon would ever possess. What could Lavon possibly have that Dr. Lee didn't? Passion threw the last picture she was viewing back down on the coffee table. Dr. Lee was a good man. What Carla was doing to him wasn't right!

And then there was Lavon. Is a man who'd have an affair one worth having? And would exposing him and Carla drive a permanent wedge between him and Passion?

She reached for her phone.

"Hey, Passion."

"Hey, Lavon. How are you?"

"Busy, what's up?"

"I was calling you about the message I left a couple days ago, the one inviting you to bring in the New Year with me and Logos Word down at the Paladium. Shabach is headlining."

"Uh, yeah, got that message. Sorry I haven't gotten back to you but you know, Passion, it's just so crazy right now, I can't commit to anything. I heard about Shabach, but Pastor Derrick has invited me to their services with Darius and Company. Plus the network is having a New Year's bash so . . . I think I'd better stay flexible."

"I can understand flexible, but you want to go solo?"

No, I want to go with Carla. But he couldn't. He hadn't seen the first lady since they shared coffee, an outing that lasted about thirty minutes, when she was in the valley. "I just think it best I not make firm plans."

"Oh, okay."

There was an awkward silence as Passion hoped Lavon would show interest by asking her out—it was usually the other way around—and Lavon hoped Passion would end the call. In the end they both spoke at once.

"Well, I gotta go—"

"Look, do you think—"

"I have another call coming in," Lavon lied. "If I don't see you beforehand, happy New Year."

Lavon pushed away from his desk and rocked back in his executive chair. Why couldn't he feel about Passion the way he did for Carla? He reasoned it would be so much easier if he wanted the woman who was available. He should have followed his first thought and left Passion alone. She wanted more than he could give right now, he'd be better off with someone who just wanted to get their freak on, no strings attached. He'd met a woman recently who might be that person. After the New Year, he'd break things off with Passion once and for all.

Passion hung up the phone, clear about one thing: Lavon wasn't hers and never would be. He was in love with Carla Lee. She wasn't sure if she would stay at Logos Word, knowing what she knew, but as of today, Lavon Chapman was no longer her business.

Picking up her purse, Passion walked to her daughter's bedroom. "Come on, baby, time for Mama to go shopping for her New Year's Eve outfit."

"And mine too?" Onyx asked.

Passion smiled. "Yours too."

Acknowledging the truth about Lavon brought Passion a melancholy relief. At least she wouldn't continue putting her energies toward a lost cause. Lavon wasn't the only good man in Los Angeles. Passion was a strong, capable woman who still believed God would answer her prayer for a mate. She'd dress to impress on December 31, enjoy the festivities of Logos Word and, if she had to, hug and say happy New Year to herself!

44

Happy New Year

Two days later, Passion stood at the mirror, pleased with what she saw. The denim, rhinestone-studded, Donna Vinci plus-size suit fit her to perfection. The flared skirt with contrasting insets emphasizing her curves, smartly de-emphasizing her expanded waistline while highlighting her sizable ass-ets. Her rhinestone encrusted shoes matched the outfit perfectly and her freshly permed hair was more fly than an airplane. Satisfied that she looked her absolute best, she picked up her purse and headed off to pick up Carla's assistant, Jill.

The irony of this unexpected company for the evening wasn't lost on Passion. It just so happened that she ran into Jill while shopping for her outfit. After casual chitchat, Jill said her car was in the shop and asked if she could catch a ride with Passion to the Paladium. Passion was about to say no until Jill added that after the concert, Shabach would be at the Lees' for a private party. Passion could come along with Jill, who'd been invited.

Even her dislike of Carla wasn't enough to pass up a chance to meet Shabach!

"These guys are hot!" Jill exclaimed, as Blessed Voices, an a cappella singing group from England, blended perfect harmonies. "I'm glad you suggested we come here before heading to the Paladium."

Passion was glad as well. In addition to the male group, one of her favorite gospel artists, Michelle Williams, was also performing before Darius took the stage. Passion planned to stay at the Kingdom Citizens' Celebration until right before Michelle's act was over, then shoot down to the Paladium in time to hear Shabach.

Passion and Jill arrived at the Paladium just in time. Colored flashing lights, fog machines, and a crazy hip-hop beat greeted them. A strong drumbeat announced the imminent arrival of gospel's number two contemporary darling. In the center of the stage was a boxing ring. Suddenly, the hall went black. Two lone searchlights began roving over the audience, settling on a boxer in crimson robe surrounded by his crew. He jostled down the aisle, throwing air punches with huge black boxing gloves . . . Shabach. The intro music to his current hit, "Beat Down for the Devil," filled the auditorium. The crowd went crazy, as fist pumps filled the air.

After the concert, the crush was so crazy that even with special seating and parking, it took more than thirty minutes to get back to Passion's car. By the time they'd navigated New Year's Eve traffic and arrived at the Lees' tony Westside home, it was after one A.M. But the spattering of cars parked in front of their home and the bright lights spilling into the darkness of night told the ladies the after-party was still in full swing.

One of Logos Word's associate ministers' wives greeted them as they stepped inside the Lees' holiday-decorated home. Low instrumental music provided the backdrop for the mingling voices of the thirty or so guests who milled about. Carla and Passion were civil when they greeted each other, and after Passion met Shabach, she walked to the buffet, fixed a modest plate, then found a spot at the dining room table where Dr. Lee was holding court.

"So this minister was out evangelizing the neighborhood when he came across a group of young boys at a basketball court. They were in a circle, surrounding a fine-looking Rottweiler. The minister thought they were trying to hurt the purebred and went over to stop them. 'What are you doing to that dog?' he asked.

"So the biggest kid in the bunch said, 'Nothin'. It's just this dog's been around the neighborhood all week and nobody's claimed him. All of us want him, so we've decided that whoever can tell the biggest lie, can have him.'

"Well, you can imagine the old minister had a problem with that solution. He proceeded to preach a twenty-minute sermon on lying being a sin and the wages of sin being death. 'When I was your age,' he said in closing, 'I *never* told a lie!' There was dead silence as the boys looked from one to the other. Finally the youngest one, about six years old, sighed. 'All right, Mr. Preacher, you win. Y'all give him the dog!'"

A variety of responses followed: laughter, groans,

a combination of both. Passion laughed too, thankful that she was having such a wonderful time. She wasn't with Lavon, but it was okay. She was hanging out with her pastor, whom she greatly admired, meeting terrific people, eating good food, and feeling it wasn't too shabby a way to start the New Year.

She'd just gotten up from the table when she saw him pass through the living room. She could barely believe her eyes. *He has the nerve to come to Dr. Lee's home? While seeing his wife?* Passion was sure she was mistaken, that she hadn't seen Lavon. But she had. He stood near a set of French doors talking to someone, looking distinguished in a black, double-breasted Loriano with an ultrathin pinstripe. Before she could cop an attitude, she decided to go say hello. *It's a new year,* she thought. *I'll let the past go and embrace my future by letting Lavon know he is off my "most wanted" list.*

Jill stopped her en route. "Did you meet Shabach?"

"Uh-huh," Passion answered as she tried to keep moving.

"Hold on, girl. I'm trying to give you the hookup. He's doing a private show next week for some record execs. Want to go?"

"Uh, yeah, Jill, but I'll be right back." Passion turned toward the French doors. Lavon was gone.

Passion walked in the direction she'd last seen him. There was a short hallway near the doors. Without wanting to appear nosy, she ventured a short way down it. There was a study to the left and a bathroom on the right. Both rooms were empty. She shrugged her shoulders. Perhaps this was a conversation best put in an e-mail. She'd had a wonderful evening and wanted to keep this first day of the year on a good note. She decided to see if Jill was ready or could get a ride home.

Just as she passed the French doors, a movement caught her eye. It was dark in the room behind the doors, so at first she thought she'd imagined it. She moved in closer, and shifted to catch the light from the chandelier. There, on a patio beyond the room the French doors framed, was a couple in an intimate embrace. She had suspicions as to who it was, and decided to satisfy her curiosity so she'd know for sure.

A quick peek around showed no one was watching. The party was winding down and most of those remaining were in the dining room. Passion eased open the French door and stepped inside the dark room. The couple on the patio was so engrossed in each other, their audience went virtually ignored. But not for long.

Passion ripped back the patio door in righteous indignation. "Y'all have a lot of nerve," she hissed to the surprised couple, who jumped back from each other the moment the door opened.

"Wait, Passion, we were talking about—" Lavon said.

"Yeah, I saw you *talking*. I should make a scene and expose you right now. The only reason I don't is because of my respect for your husband." She spat the last words at Carla, dripping venom with each syllable. "As for a dog like you," she said, looking at Lavon, "you don't deserve a woman like me."

She looked once more at Carla. "You had everything and it wasn't enough. Hmph. And you're try-ing to lead women on how *they* should live godly? Well . . . we're just going to see about that!"

Two days later, Passion stood in the reception area of *LA Gospel*, a tabloid-style, monthly news-paper filled with mostly positive but occasionally scandalous goings-on in the church community.

"May I help you?" the receptionist asked.

"I need to see one of your writers," Passion an-swered. "I've got a story."

45

Accidents Happen

"It's even worse not knowing," Janeé said gently, handing Princess the pregnancy test kit.

After Christmas in Hintereck, Kelvin and Princess had returned to Hamburg, Germany, with Hans, Janeé, and their two daughters. Princess bonded with Kelvin's half-sisters and became closer to Janeé as well. Princess was glad for the older woman's counsel.

"I'm scared." Princess took the kit but didn't move from the bed, unsure if she could handle the results if they weren't what she wanted.

"I know," Janeé said. "I've been exactly where you are now. But who knows? You may be all freaked out over nothing."

"But my period is never late!"

Janeé nodded and remained quiet. They'd had this conversation more than once. She'd given Princess the box three days ago. It was time to stop wondering and know for sure. But Princess had to come to that conclusion.

Janeé headed for the door. "All right, little sistah . . . Hans and Kelvin will be back in about an hour. And so will the girls from their friend's birthday party. I'll be downstairs."

"Wait!" Princess jumped up and ran to the bathroom. "Don't leave." She closed the door.

Janeé paced the room while she waited, warring with her thoughts. On one hand, she wanted to respect Princess's desire to not tell her mother, and on the other hand, as a mother herself, Janeé believed Tai had a right to know. Then she thought of her own mother, Nancy, and how she had reacted when Janeé got pregnant with Kelvin. It was horrible—one of the reasons Janeé fled first to California, and then to Germany. No, if Tai found out, it would be Princess who told her.

"I can't look," Princess said as she came out of the bathroom. "Will you check it?" Without looking herself, she showed Janeé the stick.

"It's positive."

Princess broke down. Her worst fear had been realized: she was pregnant with Kelvin's baby. "No, this can't be happening," she wailed.

Janeé held Princess, her tears mingling with those of the younger woman.

"I don't want to have it," Princess whispered.

Princess didn't know it but for Janeé, this was a full-circle moment. She had whispered those exact same words when she was Princess's age . . . and pregnant with Princess's father's child.

"I don't," Princess said again, sitting up and angrily wiping away tears. "I don't and I won't. I know it's wrong and I'll probably go straight to hell for it but . . . I just can't do it. I'm not my mom. I can't start having kids now like she did. I'm sorry, I know you had Kelvin young too, but I can't handle a child right now."

"The news is fresh, Princess. I know the thoughts running through your head—fear of how people will react, Kelvin, your parents, friends. How you'll finish school. But don't make a rash decision. Talk it over with Kelvin—"

"I can't tell him!"

"It's his baby too, Princess. He has a right to know."

"But I can't. He'll hate me. He'll break up with me!"

"If he'd break up with you at a time like this, then he's not worth having. He's my son and I said that. I mean it too."

Princess closed her eyes, her face, one of resolve. "I just want to get the abortion. Now. While I'm here in Germany. A couple of my friends have had them; I know it takes a couple days to heal and be okay."

"No, Princess. It takes years to heal, decades, and you're never totally okay. A part of you will always wonder about that child."

Princess opened her eyes. "You've had an abortion?"

"I'm not proud of it but yes . . . when I was about your age."

Princess thought for a moment. "Was it . . . no, I can't ask you that."

And I won't tell you, Janeé thought. *You'll never know how close you and Kelvin's experience resembles mine and your father's. I only hope your ending is different than ours.*

The women listened to the lively sounds of Janeé's daughters as they passed by on the way to their bedrooms. *"Mutter,"* one of them cried. *"Mutter, wo sie sind?"*

"They'll come barging in here soon to find where I am," Janeé said. "Think about everything I've said, Princess. Not just in the last hour, but over the past week. At the end of the day, what you do is your decision. But think long and hard about it. Once done, you can't take it back. And tell Kelvin. He should know."

"Did you tell my father?" Princess asked softly.

"My past is not your present," Janeé said in answer. "And the baby wasn't King's," she lied. But it was a lie she'd own without regret. There was enough bad blood between her and the Brook family, especially between her and Tai. She wasn't going to add King's anger to the mix. She'd lied for more than a decade about not being pregnant with King's baby. It was a burdensome secret to bear alone, but she'd take it to her grave. She just wanted to help Princess not repeat her mistake. "Tell Kelvin," Janeé said once more, and left the room.

"Kelvin, I'm pregnant." Princess whispered the revelation as she and Kelvin lay in bed later that night. "But it's okay," she added quickly. "I'll get an abortion; I don't want to have it."

"Girl, stop playin'. And get on your side of the bed. I'm tryin' not to hit it while I'm in my parents' crib but . . . don't tempt me now. Move over!"

Princess moved over and sat up. "I'm serious, Kelvin. Your mom helped me take the test today."

Kelvin sat up. "What?!"

"It's okay," Princess said. "We don't have to have it. I don't want a baby now and I know you don't. I'm sorry, Kelvin."

Kelvin jumped out of bed. "You're pregnant? For real? I thought you were on the pill," he whispered harshly.

"I was, I mean I am . . . it happened anyway! Janeé said she's heard of it happening before, with people on the pill getting pregnant. I'm sorry," she said again.

A string of expletives rolled from Kelvin's mouth as he paced the room. "Damn, Princess. This is messed up, man. Damn!"

Princess talked through silent tears rolling down her face. "I already feel bad enough, Kelvin," she said. "I said I'd fix it, get rid of it."

After a few more moments, Kelvin walked over, sat on the bed and took Princess in his arms. "It's okay, baby. I'm sorry I cursed at you. But you tripped me out. I wasn't expecting this shit." He lay down with Princess in his arms. "You're right, it'll be okay. Moms knows how to handle it. We'll find out what we need to do and get this taken care of."

"So you want me to have an abortion?" All of a sudden, a part of Princess wanted Kelvin to want the baby.

"Yeah, ain't that what you want?"

"I know you don't want kids right now. You always said you'd leave anybody who got pregnant."

"Baby, we can have plenty of kids. But later, after I get signed."

Ten days later, Kelvin and Princess arrived in Los Angeles. The baggage from the carousel was not the only kind they carried with them to their house. Princess was no longer pregnant. And while a day after the procedure she felt fine physically, Janeé was right—the spirit of the seed that had grown inside her remained.

Soon however, the blur of a busy second semester pushed the holiday heartache behind her. Joni was a great help, totally supportive, with no judgment at all. Janeé hadn't judged her either, although she had suggested Princess keep the child, and offered to raise it if that would help the young couple. Even with the emotional pain, however, Princess didn't regret terminating the pregnancy. As January gave way to February, she could sometimes convince herself she'd never even been pregnant. By March, through the haze of constant marijuana medication, fighting the women off Kelvin, and maintaining her GPA, Princess could almost say to her conscience . . . junior who?

46

No Spring Chicken

"I'm worried about Princess." Tai had waited all day for this now weekly conference call that had started with SOS conference strategizing and now included real talk among friends.

"I am too," Vivian said. "She and Kelvin rarely come around anymore. I know they're busy with school but the last time I saw her it looked like she'd lost weight. And she's little to begin with."

"She'll be all right," Carla encouraged. "Probably going through the same challenges we faced as young women."

"That's what Mama Max says too, says she's been praying and the angels are watching over her. Still . . . I can't stand that she's seeing Kelvin. No disrespect to you, Viv, but he's Janeé's son."

"I thought you forgave her," Vivian gently reminded.

"Forgiving ain't forgetting—trust."

"Kelvin's not a bad man," Vivian continued, "just

full of swagger, and like most nineteen year olds, not ready for a monogamous relationship."

"We always want to grow up so fast." Tai sighed.

"Uh-huh . . . Every generation thinks they're the first ones to go through something."

Carla added, "I know I did. Is she still calling regularly?"

"Yes, she calls . . . we talk. It's almost like it used to be but not quite. Something's going on with her and it's not just her having sex or the pot smoking that she doesn't think I know about. It's something I can't put my finger on but a mama is never wrong."

"Let's add her to our prayer list for the end of the call."

The ladies went on to talk about other things including Carla's marital progress. Stanley had agreed to counseling after finally admitting he'd been molested as a child, and after almost two months, he and Carla were seeing some improvement in their sex life.

"Girl, he let me get on top and I almost died," Carla exclaimed.

"Still no doggy though, huh?" Tai asked bluntly. There was little these first ladies didn't share.

"No, girl. I think that's too close to what his aunt tried to make him do. If she wasn't already dead, I'd kill her. In fact, I wish she'd come back so I could kill her again."

"You don't hear about that much, huh? Women molesting boys."

"Yes, but it happens," Carla responded. The three women were silent for a moment, thinking of how messed up the world sometimes seemed.

"And Lavon?" Vivian asked, after the pause.

"Haven't seen him since January, and we haven't talked in over a month. I'm not going to lie; it's hard. Lavon and I have a connection that no one understands. Shoot, *we* don't even understand it. I know that coming from a married woman this sounds out of order but . . . I really believe that man is my soul mate." Carla's voice went from nostalgic to determined. "But Stan is my husband, and my commitment is to him."

"I've hired another assistant," Vivian said, initiating yet another subject change. "Someone to help Tamika handle the administrative end of things. Maybe the two of them will equal one Millicent."

Millicent Sims was the former administrator for the Sanctity of Sisterhood conferences who was now married and living near San Diego.

"So tell us about this new girl."

"Not a spring chicken exactly, Tai, more like forties or fifties. She hasn't been at our church long but I think she's really hungry for the things of God. I feel pain in her spirit, anger, confusion. . . . She's had some real challenges in life and I think the Lord wants Kingdom Citizens to be a place where she can heal."

"What kind of challenges?" Carla asked.

"I'm not sure. It will take time for her to feel comfortable enough to open up. The biggest one, though, is probably surviving a horrific car crash last year. Now she has scars on the outside to mirror those within. I admire her; she's a survivor."

"Well, we'll be glad to welcome this sister into the fold. What's her name?"

"Mira . . . Mira Monroe."

47

Because It's Fact

The executives at *LA Gospel* sat around the conference table, discussing the May issue.

"We've already sat on the story for three months," one of them argued. "We decided to wait until their Kingdom Keys series had aired. Well, it's aired and it's over. I say we break it now, before summer."

"There's an SOS conference coming up that month so she'll have high visibility then," the writer of the piece added. This writer had a special distaste for mega-church first ladies... thought they benefited equally along with their "gospel-pimping husbands." She'd pushed for the story's release from day one.

"I still don't think we should," the lone dissenter said. "She is an inspiration to women across the country, and an anointed woman of God, no matter her faults. Why do we want to publish this story and bring her down?"

"Because it's news!" one of the execs responded.

"Because it's fact," another said. "The pictures are proof and Ms. Perkins gave a sworn affidavit that her story was true. Any lawsuit filed against us won't hold its weight in court."

"I'm tired of arguing about it," the editor said finally. "We're going to do the story. I want caption suggestions by Thursday."

48

Unrealistic Reality

Stacy watched Bo's expert preparation of stuffed pork chops with a homemade apple butter sauce. Her mouth watered at the thought of how they'd taste and they hadn't even been put in the oven.

If anyone had told her she'd be in this ridiculously unrealistic situation, watching her husband's lover prepare dinner, she would never have believed them. She barely believed it herself.

After the three returned from Big Bear, Stacy sobered to the reality of Darius's request. She'd asked, then begged him to cut ties with Bo. After a month, she gave up. There was no changing his mind. In February, she and Darius married in a quick, civil ceremony at city hall. Not the wedding she expected, but then again, nothing in her intimate life was as she'd planned.

The unlikely trio moved into a gorgeous, million-dollar duplex Cy Taylor found for them: she and Darius on one side, Bo on the other. Relations were understandably strained. As hard as she tried, she was resentful of Bo's presence. Darius played peacemaker, which only infuriated her further. True, he and Bo were discreet, and Darius now slept with her at night. But that still left the day-time hours and their out of town trips for him and Bo to be together. Because of her job, Stacy had only accompanied Darius on a couple trips.

And then two weeks ago . . . things changed. She came home from work, sick as a dog. Feeling she didn't even have strength to make it to the bed-room, she huddled in a fetal position on the couch. Shortly afterward, Bo knocked on the door. She answered it and Bo responded in typical BJ fashion: "You sho' is ugly!"

"Forget you, Little Bo Peep," she'd replied, too ill to be more caustic.

"I'm serious, girl, you look like death warmed over. What's the matter?"

"Isn't it obvious? I'm sick!"

"Lord have mercy."

Bo left her door and returned a short time later with a container of stew, a loaf of French bread, 7 Up, and what he called "pregnancy tea." He led her to the bedroom she shared with Darius, helped her change into a nightgown, and tucked her in bed, all the while tsking and scolding like a mother would her child: "Know you've got that baby growing inside you. . . . Why you trying to starve to death? Have that boy come out looking like ET. He's supposed to be DC, not ET, I thought you knew!"

On and on he went, as he adjusted the pillows around her and gave her the remote. "Don't move," he'd commanded, and then left the room.

He returned in minutes with the tea. Stacy hadn't wanted it but he wouldn't take no for an answer. She was surprised when halfway through the mug, she actually began to feel better.

"What is this?" she asked, when Bo came back up with a tray of food.

"Aunt Gladean's concoction. 'Someden from de islands, gurl.' " He then proceeded to sit on the side of the bed, spoon feed her, and tell her about his life—growing up against the backdrop of culturally rich Queens, New York, with doting Jamaican grandparents, understanding parents, and accepting siblings who loved him unconditionally. He shared the heartache of being homosexual in a condemning society as well as the triumph of realizing, through personal relationship, that God actually loved him. "That's when I got my joy back," he finished. "When I realized that no matter who didn't love me . . . God did."

Stacy had never conversed with an admitted homosexual before, never heard a personal story. She still held her Christian beliefs, that homosexuality was a sin. But she decided to leave the judgment to God. Because Darius had been right. Bo was a good person—kind, caring, funny, who could cook like an Iron Chef on the Food Network. If for nothing more than Bo's chicken and dumplings, vegetable crepes, homemade biscuits, and three-berry pie, she'd find some understanding and cultivate compassion. Interesting that a homosexual had showed her what it looked like.

"Where'd you learn to cook like that?" she asked, rubbing her six months along belly.

"Aunt Glad," Bo said with a fondness in his

voice. "That sistah could cook a shoe and make it taste good." He blanched potatoes in water before coating them in a mixture of flour and spices.

"Why'd you do that?"

"To make them crispy crunchy on the outside and tender on the inside."

Their conversation was interrupted by the beeping of Bo's cell phone.

"Yo, what's up?" Bo said, cocking the phone underneath his chin while he stirred a pot of vegetables. His countenance turned dark as he froze midstir. "What? Aw, hell no. Who told you this? But where could he have heard it? He's just fishing—I wouldn't get too worried. Uh-uh . . . we'll sue his ass. Don't even break a sweat, Bo Jenkins will get on this shit. You don't mess with what's mine. Oh, hell to the no and then hell some mo'. I'll beat his ass until Shabach is just Shh. . . . Hear me? Yeah, whatever . . . bye."

Bo threw the phone down on the counter and paced the kitchen. A colorful array of profanities warred with the smell of baking pork and warming homemade apple butter.

"What is it?" Stacy asked.

"Shabach's trying to destroy Darius, said he's got proof that Darius is gay, and that if he doesn't drop out of this year's Stellar nominations, he's going to out him at the show." Bo grabbed a knife and jabbed at an imaginary Shabach. "I know Jamaican mafia," he said, advancing. "I'll have his ass smoked like Bob Marley ganja. When I'm through there'll be nothing left but ashes!"

Stacy had never seen Bo so angry. He was shaking and at one point she thought she saw tears. "Let's call Darius," she suggested.

"No! We will *not* bother him now. He's doing the photo shoot for *Ebony* and I don't want my baby upset." Bo began pacing again and then stopped suddenly. "That's it! Yes! Okay, Stacy, here's what's not going to happen. Darius will never know that Shoddy Body is trying to out gospel's number one. What is going to happen is our, you and I, turning the tables on one Mr. Shabach Be-atch. You with me?"

"Uh, I don't know, Bo. You and me doing what, exactly?"

"Whatever it takes to shut him up. Everybody's got dirt . . . we just need to get to digging."

Stacy saw Bo's point. "I've got a friend at work who's a whiz on the Internet."

"That's what I'm talking about," Bo said, turning off burners, his beautiful dinner completely forgotten. "Let's start there."

"Let's start after we eat," Stacy corrected. When Bo got ready to object she silenced him effectively with, "Baby's hungry."

Darius's baby, like its father, got whatever it wanted.

49

Bigger Fish

Robin had fully adopted her new persona, Mira Monroe. Unlike her true nature, Mira was quiet, shy even, with a tendency to talk with her head down, and without looking people in the eye. Her body language was that of a meek and humble woman, one who had been through more than her share of life's battles. And though she often wore high-collared shirts or a scarf around them, the burn scars on her neck and the bottom of her chin added to the aura of vulnerability.

Her altered physical appearance made it easier for Robin to fully embrace a different personality. Her nose, cheek, and chin area had been reconstructed, which somehow made her eyes look different, and thanks to several weeks of intravenous feeding, Robin had lost thirty-five pounds. She'd gotten her hair cut into a short, curly, fro-like do and kept the gray that came in during her hospital stay. After years of plucking her eyebrows, and at Beth's suggestion, she'd had permanent black, thick ones tattooed on her face. Beth had been shocked, and even Robin was taken aback at who stared back in the mirror.

Beth, Robin's nurse and primary caretaker for over four months, was Robin's one, lone friend. The day before she was to be released, turned out into the streets with virtually no money and nowhere to go, Beth had offered shelter and income: taking care of a neighbor's aging aunt who lived in Lawndale, a small enclave south of Inglewood. For room, board, and a hundred dollars a week, Robin cooked, cleaned, ran errands, and kept the old woman company. Robin immediately traded off the evenings with a homeless woman she'd met panhandling down the street. After talking with her for a week or so, Robin didn't think the woman was crazy (as if she would know), just down on her luck and a bit too friendly with the vodka bottle. The homeless woman was glad for the roof and cable TV and Robin was glad not to be tied down to "Miss Petunia." She had bigger fish to fry.

Three weeks after being released from the hospital, Robin called Kingdom Citizens' Christian Center and tested her bait: a backslidden Christian desperate to "get right with God." When she told the receptionist she wanted to be a part of a women's fellowship, to volunteer in any way she could, she was immediately transferred to Vivian Montgomery's assistant's line. A few days later, she sailed right past Greg, the bullet-taking, man-handling security guard, and attended a meeting for those wanting to volunteer at Vivian's women empowerment conferences.

That's where she was now, where everything she'd planned was about to fall in place. She had everything she needed except an appointment and . . . unfortunately . . . her Peridol. At the hospital they'd started her back up on the meds as soon as she entered the psych ward but she took them haphazardly, as always. *Those things make me crazy anyway,* she reasoned whenever she forgot a dose.

"Thank you so much, ladies," Vivian said after she'd rechecked the conference handouts, approved the contents for the attendee welcome packets, and outlined the remaining administrative duties. "With the conference less than three weeks away, I feel really good about our progress. Your work is exactly the above-average behavior our theme speaks of. Thank you." She looked at Mira. "Tamika says you've been a great help, Mira. I want to let you know that . . . Mira . . . are you okay?"

Mira could feel her eyes rolling and clamped her hands to try and maintain her sanity. *I should have taken those damn pills!* She was so close to realizing her goal. Then she realized the spasm could work to her advantage.

"I'm fine," she squeezed out of tightening lungs. "Just need some water." *Just get me some H_3O muthafucka!* Had she asked, someone would have gladly informed her that water was H_2O, not three. But she didn't.

"Tamika, get her some water." Vivian reached for Mira's hand and saw tears in the woman's eyes. "Mira, what's wrong?"

"I want to talk about it, but I can't right now.

Can I maybe set a time to talk to you later . . . alone?"

"Why, of course," Vivian answered. "I'll have Tamika set it up when she gets back. In the meantime, let's pray."

Without waiting, Vivian reached for Mira's other hand and began. "Our Father, who art in heaven . . ."

The more Vivian prayed, the more agitated Mira became. She imagined a rash developing where Vivian's hands touched, and her body felt itchy all over. "Deliver us from evil," Vivian continued with quiet force. Mira jerked back her hands. When Vivian looked up in surprise, Mira placed her hands over her eyes.

"Uh, here's the water, Mira," Tamika said, after Vivian had finished the prayer. She cautiously held the glass toward her obviously distressed coworker.

Mira was headed for an all-out psychosis diagnosis. She stood abruptly. "I'm so sorry, I have to go now." She was out the door before either Vivian or Tamika could react.

"You want me to go after her?" Tamika asked.

"No," Vivian said, her eyes narrowing as she focused on the spirit within. "But call her later and set up an appointment for sometime next week . . . Tuesday if possible."

Mira was still on Vivian's mind as she drove home from Kingdom Citizens. She prayed silently, hoping for answers to the afternoon's confusion: Mira's odd behavior. "Something's not right," Vivian mumbled to herself. "Lord, please give me the spirit of discernment, instruct me on how to help her, how to reach her, Lord."

As Vivian turned into her driveway, a picture flashed into her mind. It was an incident that had happened at another time, with another woman. But the incident contained the same type of energy, one of confusion and despair. "Robin Cook," Vivian whispered, as she reached for her briefcase and headed toward her walkway. "Father God, wherever she is, help her too."

50

Time Will Tell

"Is she here?" Vivian asked Tamika as she came into the office.

"She's waiting in the dining room."

"Great, thank you."

When Vivian had found out an afternoon appointment would be difficult for Mira, she'd changed the time to evening, and then decided to make it a dinner meeting. As crowded as her schedule was, it had worked out perfectly. She was starving.

"Oh, I forgot, Lady Vee. There's one phone message you might want to return before your meeting." Tamika handed Vivian the pink slip and Vivian went into her office to make the call.

Robin's eyes narrowed to slits as she sat in the dining room—sat and remembered. It was just over two years ago, in this very room, that she'd been shamed, humiliated, dragged out like a dog headed for the kennel. She was so angry her neck began to twitch as she relived the incident: how she'd finagled a private meeting with Derrick much as she had this one with Vivian, came on to him during dinner, and when Vivian walked in on them, tried to make it seem the other way around—that he'd come on to her. She'd been hoping to make Vivian jealous, cause a rift in their marriage. Things had not gone as planned. *But that's all right, muthafuckas . . . it's almost over now.*

Robin opened her palm and eyed the small, clear vial. It was VX, a tasteless, odorless liquid that could cause death within minutes. She'd heard about it one night while watching a terrorism report on cable TV. Her homeless friend's cousin had helped her obtain it over the Internet. It had cost her a whole month's pay, plus Miss Petunia's gold bracelet and necklace, which she'd stolen and sold at Gold's Pawn Shop. But it was worth it. Vivian Montgomery—the woman who took her man fifteen years ago, dragged him to California, and made Robin come to Los Angeles, steal to survive, and then serve eighteen long, hard months when her crime caught up with her—was about to get hers.

"Hey, Mira," Vivian said cheerfully as she entered the dining room. She leaned down and hugged her. "Don't you look nice."

"Thank you," Mira said softly. "I was waiting on you to get here; but I'm dying for some tea." Mira wanted to put her plan into action without delay.

"That sounds good. Marjorie!"

Marjorie, a long-time kitchen worker and the

same one who'd served Robin when she'd tried to seduce Derrick, came out of the kitchen.

"We'd like some tea," Vivian said. "What kind would you like?" she asked Mira.

"Whatever kind you're having is fine."

"I think I'm in the mood for peppermint. How does that sound?"

Peppermint was strong, it would cover up any semblance of something amiss. "That sounds perfect," Mira said.

Within minutes, Marjorie brought out a tray with a silver teapot, two dainty teacups, a sugar dish, and some homemade rolls. "I know you like sweetener," she said to Vivian. "There's also some regular sugar, and some of that raw stuff that only a crazy person would eat," she said to Mira. "I'll be right back with the butter and jam."

Mira took a packet of sweetener from the sugar dish and stirred it into the hot brew, all the while wondering how she would get the liquid into Vivian's cup.

"Excuse me a moment, Mira. I need to confirm something with Marjorie."

Vivian left the table. Mira breathed a sigh of relief. Remembering the cameras placed throughout the building, she covertly opened the vial, pulled Vivian's cup toward her and hurriedly emptied the contents. She'd just pushed the cup back into place when Vivian stuck her head out the kitchen.

"Come here, Mira," she said, laughing. "I want you to see what Marjorie fixed just for you!"

Trying to hide her chagrin at Vivian delaying the

inevitable, Mira plastered a smile on her face. But her insides churned with gleeful anticipation. *Just c'mon and die, muthafucka.*

As Mira walked into the kitchen, another worker walked out, carrying a tray of butter, jam, and two salad plates. She reached the table, moved the teacups so she could place the items down, and then placed the teacups back in their spots.

"Doesn't that roast look divine?" Vivian said as she and Mira came back to the table. "Marjorie's such an angel. I didn't even think she was listening when I mentioned you liked roast. And just wait until you taste her double-dipped chocolate cake! You'll feel like you've got heaven right here!"

They sat down at the table. Vivian picked up a packet of sweetener and emptied it into her teacup. She stirred it briefly before taking a hearty sip. "This is so good," she said, before quickly taking another. "Just what I needed."

Mira picked up her cup and took a tentative sip. Then realizing the faster she drank hers, the faster Vivian might, she blew on her concoction and as it began to cool, drank quickly.

"This is good," she said, wiping her mouth with the back of her hand.

"There's plenty where that came from." Vivian reached for the teapot and poured more tea into Mira's cup.

As she reached for the sugar packets, Mira watched Vivian furtively. *I wonder how long it's going to take to . . .* Mira dropped the packet in her tea and reached for her throat.

"Mira?" Vivian asked, concerned.

Mira said nothing, simply clawed at her throat as if trying to open up another airway.

Vivian jumped out of her chair and ran around the table. "Mira? What is it?"

Mira tried to speak but could not find breath anywhere. She began wheezing, foam came from her mouth, and her eyes rolled around in her head.

"Marjorie! Call nine-one-one!" Vivian cried. She poured water from a glass onto a napkin and wiped Mira's face. "Mira, hang in there, help is on the way." She loosened the scarf tied around Mira's neck and unbuttoned the first few buttons of her blouse. "Breathe, Mira," she said, before beginning a fervent prayer.

Shortly afterward, paramedics burst through the door. They ran over to Mira and worked frantically to save her. Vivian looked on, horrified.

"What happened here, ma'am?" one of the paramedics asked.

"I don't know. One minute we were sipping tea and the next she grabbed her throat, unable to breathe."

Time seemed to stand still as Vivian, Marjorie, Greg, the kitchen help, and a few other staff members watched the emergency crew work on Mira. After several minutes, they placed her on a stretcher.

Vivian rushed forward to the head paramedic. "Is she going to make it?"

The paramedic shook his head. "No, ma'am. She's dead."

*   *   *

Two days later, Derrick and Vivian were sitting in his offices at KCCC, discussing the tragedy of Mira's death. His phone buzzed.

"It's a Detective Smiley," his assistant said. "Something about the woman who died."

"I'll take it, Lionel. Maybe they've got something," he said to Vivian. Having found no information that would help them notify her next of kin, the church had enlisted the help of law enforcement.

"Yes, Detective," Derrick said, putting the call on speaker.

"Pastor, we were able to find a match for the fingerprints of the deceased, Mira Monroe, you said?"

"Right, Mira Monroe."

"Actually, Pastor, her real name wasn't Mira Monroe. Her real name was Robin . . . Robin Cook."

Vivian gasped and Derrick's eyes widened. "No, there must be some mistake. This is Vivian Montgomery, Detective," Vivian said. "Derrick's wife. See, we know Robin Cook. This woman looked nothing like her."

"According to the files we found on her, Robin Cook was in a serious car accident over six months ago. In addition to the internal injuries, her face sustained multiple fractures that required plastic surgery. We'll still do a DNA, but we're pretty sure the body at the morgue is Robin Cook. Oh, and one last thing. Looks like she overdosed on a lethal amount of VX. That's a nerve gas agent developed for warfare by the British in the fifties. How she got her hands on that is anyone's guess."

The situation was becoming more bizarre by the

moment. "But how could an accident like that happen?" Vivian asked, genuinely perplexed. "She was fine when she came to the church, and we'd only had a cup of tea when she became ill."

"This was no accident," the detective answered. "This chemical weapon works quickly. It would have had to be consumed minutes before it took effect. My guess is she poured the poison into the tea before drinking it. So either she was trying to commit suicide . . . or murder. You owe a thank you to the man upstairs. It's a miracle she died and not you."

Derrick and Vivian sat in silence, too stunned for conversation. Suicide? Murder? Mira Monroe was Robin Cook? It was too much.

Vivian thought back to her conversations with Mira, the discomfort she felt around her, and the day Robin's name flashed in her mind when she'd asked God for revelation. She shared all this with Derrick, who was still too stunned to reply.

After a long moment, Vivian bowed her head. "Thank you God for sparing my life. . . ."

Derrick joined her in prayer and afterward, took her hand in his. "I can't believe I almost lost you," he said, the reality of what had almost happened finally sinking in. "I don't know what I'd do without you, Vivian."

Vivian came around the desk and cuddled into her husband's lap. "All I can say, Pastor Derrick Montgomery, is I hope you don't have to find out for a long, long time."

"I know one thing," Derrick continued after he and Vivian shared a passionate kiss. "Lord knows I'm tired of all this drama in churches. Between

Stacy and Darius's rushed marriage, his feud with Shabach, and now this, an attempted murder right here on the premises? Really, baby, can things get any worse?"

Vivian sighed, snuggling deeper into her husband's arms. "I don't think so, baby. But only time will tell."

51

LA Gospel

Lavon Chapman closed his office door. He'd been deep in the throes of production since six that morning and needed five minutes to take a break and think about nothing. He leaned back in his swivel chair and closed his eyes. Another pair of eyes immediately came to his conscience: satiny brown, wide, and enchanting, shining with playfulness . . . Carla.

Lavon opened his eyes and leaned forward. No matter what he did, it hadn't worked in helping him forget her. After two successful production deals for MLM, including televising the Kingdom Keys series, the network's board offered and he had accepted the executive director position for the network's block of inspirational programming. The promotion not only increased his income but it thankfully also increased his workload. He regularly put in seventy to eighty hours a week, and even that wasn't enough to keep his mind off the woman he loved. But he'd do whatever it took to make her happy . . . including leave her alone. That's what she'd said she wanted, what she needed to try and save her marriage.

He reached over and grabbed the production sheets from the last meeting. So far the inspirational schedule included church services, music videos, live concerts, and a couple religious-themed talk shows. It was all typical religious fare, Lavon thought, something that could be seen any day of the week on TBN or Sundays on BET. Lavon wanted to add something different to the mix, to expand the types of programming aimed at the Christian community. He turned to his computer and opened what he called his "Fire File." They were still being shaped, so he wasn't ready to share them yet. But his show concepts were hot, especially the sitcom idea centered around a young, good-looking pastor and his beauty-shop owning wife. Once his plan of pushing the programming envelope was fully implemented, he was certain MLM Network ratings would shoot to the top.

Working on his dream schedule successfully shifted his mind from Carla to commercial success, his other passion. He turned up the jazz music playing in the background and settled in for another three, four hours of work even though it was already five o'clock.

"My God, Lavon," Tori, his coworker and good friend, said as she entered without knocking.

"Uh, didn't you see the door closed?" Lavon joked. Tori was a top producer, creative and fearless. He liked her.

"You're going to want to lock it and never come out after you see what I have to show you. The proverbial excrement is getting ready to hit the wind blower." She tossed a magazine down on his desk.

Lavon picked it up, ready to see something about a popular gospel artist, actor, embracing Christianity, or famous athlete touting Jesus. He was half right. On the cover of the magazine was a picture of athlete Deion Sanders and family with the caption: STILL PRIME TIME.

The picture in the bottom right corner, however, took his breath away. It was a clear picture of him and Carla—kissing. The caption: A FIRST LADY'S AFFAIR.

"It comes out Saturday," Tori said flatly. She also told him it was being delivered directly to all the mega-churches who, in exchange for their sizable ad purchases, were given free copies for their congregations.

Lavon ripped open the magazine and quickly found the article. His heart beat wildly with each photo image: Carla, Stanley, and family; Carla leading an SOS workshop; Carla preaching in the Logos Word pulpit; Lavon standing with MLM execs and then . . . Lavon twirling Carla around under a streetlight, holding her hand, and kissing her. What had been their love affair, to them so precious and rare in its authenticity, was shown here in a shameful, secretive, horrible way.

"Aw man," he whispered, as he quickly read the article. With every word, his heart sank deeper. The plain facts were ugly: he'd been hired by Stanley Lee to produce a religious program and in the process had had an affair with the minister's wife, who was also a minister. He could hear the Christ-

ian community now: Stone her! Crucify him! Cast
them into the fire! *But I love her!* his heart cried.
And he knew that she loved him—loved, not
lusted. Now it looked like this love would be their
undoing. Both of their lives would be ruined, not
to mention her family. He reached for his phone,
even as he read the last line.

"Give me a minute," he said to Tori in a firm
tone. "I need to call Carla. Then we'll talk."

Carla hesitated for only a moment when she saw
Lavon's number on her cell phone. It was no surprise that he was calling her; she'd thought about
him all week.

"Hello, Lavon."

"Carla. Sit down, baby, I've got news."

Carla's heartbeat immediately picked up. "I'm
already sitting down. What's going on?"

Lavon proceeded to tell her about the article
and pictures in the forthcoming issue of *LA Gospel*.

"Oh my God," Carla whispered when Lavon was
finished. "They can't put that out there, can't do
that to Stanley, my family. Our marriage is finally
getting back on track."

"I'm going over to their offices as soon as I get off
the phone with you. Maybe I can pull in a favor, or
negotiate some type of television time for them in
exchange for pulling the issue."

"Whatever you can do," said Carla, who was now
standing and pacing the room. "Oh God, this is
going to kill Stanley, and the ministry . . . this is
why I stopped, Lavon. So this wouldn't happen.
This is why I walked away from you! Jesus!"

"Baby, Carla, I wish . . ." It was no use saying
what he wished: that it had never happened. More

truthful was that he wished they'd not gotten caught. And deeper still that he wanted to be with Carla, forever, no matter the cost. God worked in mysterious ways. Maybe this was one of them. "I'll call you later."

He stormed out of his office to find Tori lounging on the wall by his door. "Not now," he said, putting a hand up. "I'm on my way to *LA Gospel* to try and stop this madness."

Lavon broke driving rules and speed limits to reach the offices of *LA Gospel* in less than thirty minutes. "Where is she?" he said as soon as he walked in the door.

"Mr. Chapman?" the receptionist answered in surprise.

"Where's Ana," he asked again. Ana Cummings-Black was the editor in chief of *LA Gospel.*

"One moment," the receptionist said as she picked up the phone. A moment later, she told Lavon, "Have a seat. She'll be with you shortly."

Lavon hadn't been able to sit still since Tori entered his office. He'd barely done so even while driving. Instead, he stood with his foot tapping a furious pace until Ana's secretary came around the corner. "Ms. Cummings-Black will see you now."

Ana Cummings-Black was a product of Chicago's south side: strong, savvy, and a woman who could smell game a mile away. Added to this Teflon exterior was a degree with honors from Morgan State University and a membership in good standing with the Alpha Kappa Alpha sorority. In short, Ana Cummings-Black was no joke.

"I've been expecting you," she said as a greeting, coming from behind her desk to shake Lavon's hand.

He was not in the mood for cordialities. "Why?" he asked simply.

"It's news," she answered, equally as simply.

"So a religious publication is following the way of the world now? Just because something is news it gets published, no matter who it hurts?"

"If there'd been no affair, there would have been no story."

It was a point Lavon couldn't argue. "You've got to pull this issue, Ana."

"Can't, distribution has already started."

"Well, you've got to stop it! This isn't, wasn't some cheap affair. I love Carla. And she loves me. The situation is complicated, with facts you don't know . . . that aren't in your so-called tell-all article. But none of that matters." Lavon calmed his tone, tried to adopt one of reason. "This situation has been over since the first of the year. Carla and Stanley were having problems for years but are in counseling now. They're trying to make it work. This article coming out will ruin everything."

"Please, Lavon, sit down." Ana pointed to a chair as she walked behind her desk and took a seat. "This wasn't an easy decision, Lavon. We sat on this story for three months, even though the facts were verified and pictures don't lie. This was a journalistic call, pure and simple. It's news, current news, relevant news, that speaks to vital issues in the Christian community.

"Look at this from my point of view. You have a high profile, popular mega-church, with a charismatic copastor and dedicated female congregants lifting her up as an example of godly living. Add to that her affiliation with the Sanctity of Sisterhood Summits, one of the most popular conferences for women since the Woman Thou Art Loosed conferences. *And* you've got a hotshot producer of the Christian community affiliated with the first network ever to give BET some serious competition. Finally, you've got a credible witness—"

"You must mean Passion Perkins," Lavon spat out the name as if it were poison.

"We don't disclose our sources."

Lavon snorted.

"And undeniable, celluloid proof that these two people are at the very least participating in some inappropriate conduct and at the very most, are smack dab in the midst of adultery. This publication lives and dies on these types of stories.

"As a businessman yourself, I'm sure you understand me when I tell you . . . this isn't personal. It isn't. It's business. And in the end I think the story will work to your benefit."

"Benefit? How in the hell do you think a story like this will benefit me?"

"You know the saying, Lavon, that there's no such thing as bad publicity. It may eventually help your network's ratings."

"You think I'm here because of ratings? You think this is about television? This is my life you're messing with, Ana. This is a woman's home, her family. I think you, as a strong Black woman, would be the last one to tear another Black woman down."

Ana didn't like Lavon's attempt at guilt-tripping her. "Don't try to pull the sistah sympathy card with me, Lavon. This isn't about tearing a Black woman down. It's about reporting news that's appropriate for our publication, even when it's unpleasant."

"Everybody's got dirty laundry, Ana Cummings-Black, even you. And you're getting on the bad side of the wrong person."

"Baby, I grew up on the south side of Chicago. I'm all too familiar with the wrong side!" Ana softened her voice. "You're not going to believe this, but my professional decision does not reflect my personal opinion. I like Pastor Lee, have some of her CDs, and wish her the best. But the story was going to get told, eventually. If we didn't tell it, someone else would. I'm sorry."

Lavon stood and stared down Ana long and hard. "Yes," he said before turning to walk out. "You sure are."

52

Life as I Know It

Four hours later, Lavon walked into an out-of-the-way bistro in Marina Del Rey to meet Carla. Even in such dire circumstances, his heart warmed at the sight of her.

"It's good to see you," he said as he hugged her, taking in her worried expression.

"You too," she whispered.

They sat down and ordered tea and soda, both too nervous to eat. Lavon calmly unfolded the magazine and placed it on the table in front of Carla. Carla picked it up, looked at the picture on the cover, turned to the page Lavon had ear-marked, and read in silence.

"My life as I know it is about to be over," she said matter-of-factly.

"Don't say that, Carla—"

"Look, I'm just being real. I know Stanley; he's a strong, proud man. There's no way he's going to want to preserve our marriage once he finds out about the affair. Especially like this. It's not just the personal anguish but ⬛⬛⬛ ⬛blic humiliation. His status will be jeopard⬛⬛⬛ ⬛is ministry tarnished. Stanley is all about a⬛⬛⬛⬛nces. This is going to devastate him. And i⬛⬛⬛ ⬛y fault.

"That's what's so ⬛⬛⬛⬛ about all this. I made this bed, and I'll lie ⬛⬛⬛⬛ut it's not fair that my family is going to h⬛⬛⬛ ⬛e in it too. Winston is probably young eno⬛⬛⬛ ⬛ot be too affected, but Shay and especially ⬛⬛⬛a—Oh God, it's going to hurt them so much. And I don't know how I can protect them, Lavon. . . . I don't!"

Lavon didn't know what to say. He didn't know how to protect them either, and he told Carla as much. "We'll get through this together, Carla. If you want, I'll be by your side every step of the way."

He went on to tell her about his confrontation with Ana Cummings-Black and the emergency board member meeting at the network he'd attended immediately afterward.

"I told them I'd resign if they wanted," Lavon said. "I don't want my actions to tarnish the network's credibility."

"What'd they say?"

"They are going to take a wait-and-see approach. They love my work, know I'm well connected in the industry. And while I'm over inspirational programming, this is a secular network, and fortunately or unfortunately, scandal and drama happen all the time in this business. Honestly, it doesn't matter if they keep me or not," Lavon continued. "The only reason I took this job was to be close to you. If that can't happen, well, maybe it's time for me to relocate."

Lavon had recently turned down an offer from

a station in North Carolina. With his reputation, he could work almost anywhere.

"I don't want you to leave, Lavon, not now," Carla responded quietly. "I need you. . . ."

They sat silently for a moment, trying to regain their footing in a world turned upside down.

"I'll have to give up my ministry," Carla said.

"Why?" Lavon asked.

"How would it look for an adulterous woman trying to tell other women how to live holy?"

"It would look like every saint: a sinner who falls down but gets back up. Men of God fall all the time, some in public, most in private. Our love doesn't take away from your anointing, Carla. Women love you."

"They do now, but wait until next week. People can turn so quickly." Carla stopped and looked out the window. It struck her as odd, how outside everything appeared normal—cars driving by, people talking, sun shining—when inside her world things looked insane. She leaned back and fumbled with the spoon on the table. "Have you talked to Passion? You know she's the one who did this."

"Of course I know, and no, I haven't. It's best I don't. I'm not the type who'd do well in prison."

Carla smiled sadly. "I can't even be mad at her. She couldn't have taken the pictures if we hadn't been posing."

"We weren't posing."

"You know what I'm saying. And it's not like she didn't warn me. . . ."

"Warn you? Passion warned you about what? Was our relationship the reason she requested that meeting with you?"

Carla sighed and looked out the window. "You know it would be breaking a ministerial confidence to answer that question directly. It's why I never told you what we talked about. But you probably wouldn't be too far off if you drew your own conclusions. I can't blame her for wanting you. . . ."

Lavon leaned back in his chair, his countenance stormy. "I told her I didn't want her, told her I wasn't interested. I never should have given her the time of day."

"But you did. In fact you gave her more than time."

"Yes, I did, and look what it's getting ready to cost me."

Carla chose not to comment. Twenty-twenty hindsight was not productive. She had her hands full dealing with now. "So . . . what are we going to do?"

Lavon took Carla's hand and rubbed it softly. "I'm going to be here for you," he said. "My sole mission, purpose, and goal in life will be to do whatever it takes to help you through this situation, and beyond it.

"My situation is different. Job-wise I'm cool whether MLM fires me or not. As for the affair, the truth is, baby, you'll be the one who gets crucified. You're the minister, married, a mother. It seems like women are doubly hard on each other. They'll just say I'm a man and all men are dogs. That's why my concern is not for myself . . . but you."

Carla picked the magazine off the table, folded it, and put it in her purse. "Waiting isn't going to make it any easier," she said, getting up from the table. "It's time for me to go home, Lavon. It's time to tell Stan."

Telling Dr. Stanley Lee that his wife was an adulterer had just the effect Carla thought it would.

There was no yelling, no screaming. In fact, there was only one question: "Is it true?"

From that moment, it had taken Stanley exactly ten minutes to gather his toiletries and pack a suitcase. Carla tried to reason but Stanley made it clear: he didn't want a discussion, explanation, or debate. Instead, his position was summed up succinctly just before he walked out of the Lee household and effectively out of Carla's life: "I want a divorce."

53

A Little Help

"What's wrong, Mommy?" Onyx asked. Her normally talkative mother was being awfully quiet.

"Nothing, baby," Passion replied.

"Then why are you sitting in the dark?" She climbed on the couch next to her mother. "Hey, I know. Wanna play Uno?"

"No, sweetie."

"War?"

"Uh-uh."

"Sorry?"

Passion hugged her daughter to her. "Mommy doesn't feel like playing a game, baby." *Mommy's too busy dealing with life, and it is not a game.*

"Why are you sad, Mommy?"

"I'm not sad."

"You look sad. C'mon, Mommy, let's put on a happy face!" Onyx placed tiny fingers on the sides of her eyes, pulled them back and made a face.

Passion smiled at her little angel. Whenever Passion was down about something, Onyx's cheery personality could usually bring her up. Tonight was not one of those times. "Come on, Onyx . . . bedtime."

Passion put her daughter to bed and even though it was only eight-thirty, slipped into her nightgown also. The day had lasted forever and she was burdened by the weight of it.

It had begun that morning, just after she'd gotten to work. She'd barely sat down at her desk when the phone rang.

"Good morning, Passion Perkins."

"Okay, girl, are you sitting down?" It was a casual acquaintance from Logos Word who'd gotten her number at an SOS convention.

"Yes," Passion answered.

"Pastor Carla is having an affair!"

So there it is, the news is out. "What?" Passion said, feigning surprise. But of course she wasn't. The writer of the story had called Passion almost a month ago and told her the story would break in the May issue. They'd mailed a copy directly to her house.

"Yes, and guess who with?" The caller didn't wait for an answer. "The man who worked with her and Dr. Lee on the Kingdom Keys series . . . Lavon Chapman! Looks like he was shooting and screwing at the same time!" She howled at her own joke. Passion saw nothing funny.

"You can't always believe everything you read," Passion warned.

"Oh, so you know about this already. You've seen the magazine?"

"Uh, I haven't seen the article but I heard about it."

"I know one thing. I'm going to be at church bright and early, front row center on Sunday morning. I can't wait to hear what Dr. Lee has to say about it. Uh-uh-uh, Pastor Carla creepin'. . . . She always looked the type."

"I've got to go," Passion said.

Fortunately, only one other of Passion's co-workers was familiar with the Logos Word ministry. So after the obligatory discussion with him, and because Passion didn't socialize much with members outside of church services, she was spared from talking about it for the rest of the day.

Passion's telephone rang. *Until now,* she thought sarcastically. She relaxed when she saw it was her mother.

"Hey, Mom."

"I just heard some awful news about your pastor!"

"You've heard already?" Passion was floored that her Pentecostal mother, who barely watched TV, let alone gossiped, had heard the news.

"Why, it's not true, is it?" her mother asked, aghast. "I know that woman of God, wife, and mother did *not* cheat on her husband."

"I don't know, Mom," Passion lied. *Lord, what have I gotten myself into? What have I done?*

"Well, if it is, it's a shame before God. That's what happens to those big-time TV preachers with all that money and fame. They start acting just like the world. No true child of God would act like that. You need to get out of that big church, Passion. Come on over here where we might be few, but we're serious about serving the Lord!"

Passion took a long, deep breath. "How are you doing, Mom?" She tried to change the subject.

"I'll be doing a lot better knowing my grandchild isn't over to some hell-filled church, getting influenced by a Jezebel touting herself as some big preacher."

"The Bible says not to judge, Mom."

"The Bible says not to cheat on your husband, that's what the Bible says."

"Mom, I was in the middle of something when you called. I'll talk to you tomorrow, okay?"

"Okay, Passion. And I'll be praying for y'all over there in that den of sin. You need to come out from among them, Passion."

"Bye, Mom."

Passion hung up the phone, lay back on the bed, and thought about how quickly life could change. Just when she'd felt her life was getting back on track, post Lavon, two bombshells had hit in as many weeks. She hadn't yet digested the news of Robin's death, hadn't come to grips with the fact her former friend was gone.

When Passion first heard the news, she played and replayed in her head the conversation from Robin's lone visit to her house—about Robin being in love with a married man. Passion couldn't fathom that man being Derrick Montgomery, even as she knew he was the main character in many female fantasies. But why else would Robin go to KCCC to commit suicide? Was it to make the Montgomerys feel guilty, or to try and bring scandal to their church? There were so many questions, the answers to which Passion felt she'd never know. A part of her felt guilty, that if she'd been paying more attention to Robin instead of Lavon, her friend might still be alive.

And now this, another scandal, one of her making. She'd gotten what she wanted: for Carla's duplicitous lifestyle to be exposed.

So why didn't it feel good, why was there sadness instead of joy? "I shouldn't have done it," she said to the four walls.

When she'd walked into the *LA Gospel* offices just after the first of the year, she'd never been angrier. Lavon had flaunted his love for another woman—a married woman at that—while throwing Passion's amorous offerings back in her face. She'd gladly poured the story out for the all-too-eager writer, who absorbed every word like a sponge did water.

What she'd done felt good for about a week; then she started having misgivings. She'd called the magazine and told them she wanted to retract her story. But it was too late. Along with the pictures, she'd provided dates, times, locations, and other corroborating information. As if that wasn't enough, she signed an affidavit that what she said was true.

When February and then March went by, Passion breathed easier. She felt her prayers had been answered, and that somehow God had intervened in their printing the story. She even started thinking about Lavon again, about giving their friendship another try. Just when she'd worked up the nerve to call him, she got a call instead. The one from the writer telling her the story would be featured in the May issue.

"Lord, what have I done?" At the very least what she'd contributed to was damaging a family, tarnishing a ministry, and alienating, possibly forever, the man who'd made her happy for the first time in five years.

And what about Dr. Lee? she thought. While she'd always believed exposing Carla was for Dr. Lee's own good, she'd never given much thought to the aftermath of her revelation. Now she did. *I wonder if he's okay.*

"There's only one way to find out." Passion dialed the church number, keyed in the extension for Dr. Lee's office, and left a message she felt would garner a call back.

She was right. Her cell phone rang before eight A.M. the next morning. It was Dr. Lee's assistant. "Passion Perkins?" he asked.

"Yes?"

"Dr. Lee would like to meet with you at ten o'clock. He says it's urgent."

When Carla showed up to the Logos Word offices shortly before ten A.M., she was ushered directly into Dr. Lee's offices.

He joined her shortly thereafter and following perfunctory pleasantries, got straight to the point. "You say you have information on my wife's affair?"

"I'm so sorry for what's happened, Dr. Lee."

"So am I. My marriage vows are irretrievably broken. Ms. Perkins, I'm divorcing my wife. She's the mother of my children, so I won't try to ruin her. Then again, she's done a pretty good job of that already. I just want to be able to get this over and move on as quickly as possible. The information you have might make my negotiations easier."

He fixed a penetrating stare on Passion before asking, "Will you help me?"

Passion was moved by the intense mixture of hurt, anger, pain, and determination she saw on Dr. Lee's face. In that moment she decided how she could feel better. Since she'd been the one to cause his hurt, she could definitely be the one to help fix it.

"Yes, Pastor," she answered in a clear, assured voice. "I will help you."

54

It's a Boy!

"I got it, I got it!" Stacy rushed into Bo's house without knocking. She was so excited she didn't recognize what Bo's flailing arms meant.

"Got what?" Darius asked, coming around the corner.

"Oh," Stacy stopped short. "I didn't realize you were here."

"Well, I am," he said, coming over and rubbing her belly. "Now . . . got what?"

"Nothing," she said, while trying to inconspicuously place the sheet of paper she was holding behind her.

"Let me see nothing," Darius replied. He reached for the paper. At eight months along, Stacy was no match for Darius's quickness. He snatched the paper easily.

"Who's Jo Ann Reubens?" he asked after scanning the paper. He continued reading. "Mental institution . . . son Joseph Reubens . . . Atlanta . . . What's this about?" He looked back and forth between Bo and Stacy. Stacy suddenly became unable to hear and scratch her belly at the same time while Bo became overly interested in the pattern on their hardwood floor.

"Bo, Stacy, what's going on?" Darius asked again.

"We might as well tell him since it's over now," Stacy suggested.

"I guess you're right," Bo agreed.

"You tell him," Stacy suggested.

"It was your idea," Bo said.

"My idea? No, you didn't . . ."

"Will *somebody* tell me what's going on before I die?" Darius said in a raised voice.

"Come on, sit down," Bo said. After they'd all taken a seat in the living room, he continued. "Shabach's been trying to out you, but we've just found some info that will shut his ass up."

"What?" Any mention of his archrival always sent him into a tizzy. That's why Stacy and Bo hadn't wanted him to know anything.

"Calm down now. I said we've got it handled. You all right, Stacy?"

"Ouch, I think so. This boy is really kicking. Ow!"

"Tell me everything."

And they did. Bo and Stacy divulged the events of the past two months: the phone call alerting Bo to Shabach's plans, Stacy and Bo scheming to find dirt on Shabach, and Stacy's victory in doing so.

"Basically, his mama's crazy," Bo said in conclusion. "The woman he refers to in his interviews, and the one who raised him, is actually his godmother. From this paperwork, it looks like his real mom has been institutionalized since he was nine, ten years old."

"Dang, that's hard," Darius said.

"No, what's hard is his ass thinking he was going to expose us. Well, we're getting ready to stop his game with one well-placed phone call. Give me that paper, Stacy."

Bo left the room.

Darius wrapped his arms around Stacy and rubbed her stomach. "Wow, he is kicking," he said after feeling the baby's foot with his hand. "Don't kick your daddy, son," he said to Stacy's stomach.

"I was wondering how you and Bo got so close all of a sudden. But I was just so happy for the cease fire, I didn't want to jinx it by even bringing it up."

"I think I'm going to go lay down," Stacy said. "I feel . . . owww!"

"What's going on, baby?"

"I—I think I'm in labor," she panted.

"You've got another month to go. You can't be in labor."

"I'm in something." Stacy moaned again, even louder.

"That's it. We're going to the hospital."

"What about telling Bo?"

"I'll call Bo on the cell phone. Let's go now!"

"Where is he? Where's my godson?" Four hours after an emergency C-section had been performed to deliver a premature but healthy baby boy, Bo waltzed into the maternity ward. He entered in his typically flamboyant fashion, with a bottle of champagne and a teddy bear almost as big as him. His exaggerated actions suggested he'd already sampled the bubbly.

"May I help you?" the woman at the nurse's station asked.

"Darius Christian Crenshaw Jr. That's who I'm here to see."

"There's nobody—"

"Mother, Stacy Gray; father, Darius Crenshaw. Time's a wastin', sistah, now where they at?"

"And you are?" the nurse asked with raised eyebrows.

"I'm the godfather, Bo Jenkins."

The nurse shuffled through some papers and then directed Bo to Stacy's room.

"Okay, everybody, let's get the party start—Pastor Montgomery, what are you doing here?"

Pastor Montgomery, who had been praying with Stacy, looked up. "Bo Jenkins," he said, rising and extending his hand. "See the lengths I'll go to make sure you hear the Word?"

"Good to see you, Pastor," Bo replied, shaking Derrick's hand. "Keep praying for me."

"Oh, I'm going to do that," Derrick replied. He looked at Bo intently but said nothing further.

"Pastor Derrick was walking out the lobby as we were coming in," Darius explained. "He said he'd come back later to pray with us and . . . here he is."

Bo tried to hide the bottle of champagne under the bear as he sat it down. Instead, the foot of the bear caught the top of the champagne bottle and sent it rolling across the floor, where it knocked up against Pastor Montgomery's foot.

Pastor Montgomery made a big deal of picking up the bottle. "Dom Pérignon . . . the good stuff. But no thank you, Bo. I don't drink."

"I don't drink all that much," Bo said sheepishly,

stifling a belch. "But on special occasions, like childbirths and what have you . . . Speaking of, where's Darius Jr.?"

"Down the hall. He'll have to stay in the incubator for a while. Tanya and Stacy's mother are down there now. Want to see him?" Darius asked.

Bo nodded.

"I'll walk out with you two," Derrick said. "Stacy, congratulations. I'm sure Vivian will be by to see you tomorrow."

Stacy battled droopy eyelids, knowing she'd be asleep in seconds. "Bye, Pastor."

Derrick, Darius, and Bo walked down the hall. When they reached the incubator room, Derrick spoke. "Bo, why don't you go inside and say hello to little Darius. I need to speak with his father a moment."

Bo looked at Darius.

"Go on, I'll be right in," Darius said.

Once Bo had gone inside, Derrick turned to Darius. "I've heard some things," he began without preamble. "And I hadn't said anything before now because, well, because you and Stacy got married and I figured all the rumors would be put to bed. But my spirit is still troubled, Darius. And now that there's a child involved . . ."

"Just what have you heard?" Darius asked defensively.

"I don't want to get into it here, but please, come by my office as soon as you can. It's imperative that we talk right away. Congratulations on the birth of your son, Darius. I mean that."

55

Greetings

Princess smiled as she walked up the steps to her house. It was a perfect May day and her life mirrored the weather. A meeting with her counselors revealed that she'd end the year with a 3.5 GPA. Joni's family had invited her and Kelvin to spend part of the summer at their Hawaiian home. And best of all? Her baby was about to get signed with the Phoenix Suns! It wasn't a done deal yet but they'd been in quiet negotiations for the past several weeks. Only a small group knew about the happening. Princess was very proud to be one of the few.

It had worked out perfectly when her last class got cancelled. She went by "the spot," copped some weed, and was going to order in Chinese food for when Kelvin returned from practice. She had a sexy, new piece of lingerie to show him, and since she knew Joni and Brandon had gone to San Diego, that's how she planned to greet him when he walked in the door.

She was surprised when the strong smell of marijuana greeted her instead. *Brandon and Joni must have just left,* she thought. She started toward the kitchen to get the Chinese food menu, and then decided to use the bathroom first.

Just outside her bedroom door, Princess stopped. She wanted to make sure she heard what she thought she heard, although what she thought she heard was the last thing she expected to hear. But the undeniable sound of creaking springs, grunts, and moans filtered through the bedroom door.

Princess was stunned into immobility. After everything she'd done for him, all they'd been through? She knew he had the occasional fling every now and then, but with athletes, that was to be expected. Those women meant nothing. But to bring one home . . . in their bed?

"Oh, Kelvin, that feels so good. Yeah, do it just like that!"

The command dislodged Princess's feet from the floor where they'd been rooted. She flung open the door and flew into the room. The woman was riding Kelvin, her long weave flowing behind her. That's what Princess used to drag her to the door.

"Come in my house, bitch," she cried as she jumped on top of the naked coed and pummeled her. "Fuck my man!"

The woman was trying to fight back but Princess had a death grip on the weave and was yanking it with all her might.

"Get off me, you crazy whore," the girl cried. "Get—your—ass—"

And then, thanks to Kelvin, the woman was freed.

"Get out," he told her, holding Princess back. "Now!"

"Get your hands off me," Princess said, twisting this way and that to get out of Kelvin's grip.

He held her with little effort. "Calm down, *mami*," he cooed. And then to the girl who was standing there watching them. "Get the fuck out!"

"Yeah, I'll go, I'll go," she said, angrily pulling on her pants and top, sans underwear. "But I will be back. In fact, I'm going to be around for a long time."

"Get your ass out!" Princess screamed hysterically. She renewed her efforts to break free from Kelvin.

"He's yours for the next seven, eight months," Fawn said as she casually walked out the bedroom. "Until I have his baby."

56

God's Love

The SOS crowd buzzed with anticipation. So much had happened to the Los Angeles first ladies set to lead the conference: first the woman who died at Sistah Vivian's church, and then the very public revelation of Pastor Carla's affair, followed by her husband's less public but equally well-known petition for divorce. None of the attendees knew what to expect. Would Pastor Carla show up? Would Sistah Vivian discuss what happened to the woman who died? Was the third conference moderator, Tai Brook, going to reveal some deep dark secret as well? Or were they going to mention nothing of what was on everybody's mind and instead try and focus on the session's ironic theme, Triple A: Anointed, Appointed, and Above Average?

They didn't have to wait long to find out. Sistah Vivian took the stage toward the end of the praise team's enthusiastic opening, full of fire as always. Pastor Carla, Sistah Tai, and other first ladies mounted the podium as well.

"Praise the Lord!" she said, lifting her hands toward heaven. "Oh, I believe you can do better than that. Praise God up in here this evening! He's been too good not to praise Him. He's been too kind not to open your mouth and give a shout of thanksgiving to our God. Hallelujah!"

The praise team resumed singing amid the glorious celebration of saints:

> *"He reigns from heaven above, in wisdom, power, and love*
> *Our God is an awesome God."*

It took several moments for the crowd to quiet. Once they did, Vivian dove right in to what was on everyone's mind.

"Well, my sisters, much has happened since last we met. As you all know, it's been a rough time for your first ladies. We've had some bad days . . . some hills to climb." Vivian continued speaking the words of the popular song and then sang the line, "but God's been good to me!"

The crowd joined her in their declaration to not complain, no matter what. There were tears of sorrow, and of joy, as conference-goers recalled what God had brought them through.

"That's it, that's it, give God praise!" Once again, Vivian waited for the jubilation to diminish. She took a moment to look over the crowd, and began again.

"As this summit approached, the first ladies here"—she pointed to the women on the podium—"and I had many discussions. We talked about what, if anything would be said about the very public events that have taken place. There was even talk about whether or not the summit should still happen. But in the end, we decided that nothing could stop what God had started, and that's why we're here today.

"We want the focus of this summit to be on the theme, on what we are all striving or should be striving to be—anointed, appointed, and above average. However, Pastor Carla pointed out, and leave it to Carla to do so, that the theme is not what's on your minds right now. You're wondering about Robin Cook, the woman who poisoned herself at our church. That's a short story, ladies. Since her death, we learned she suffered from a severe form of psychosis and in her mind imagined enemies around her. As a result, she took her life. So no matter what else you've heard, that's the truth about that. I ask you to keep her family and friends in your prayers.

"And, of course, you're wondering about Pastor Carla Lee. Some of you, and I can see it in your faces, are even wondering what she's doing here, and why she's on the podium with the other first ladies. Pastor Carla has chosen to not participate in the full SOS summit, but she asked to come speak to you tonight. We decided to do it now, this first evening, so we can hopefully move forward with the things God has placed in our hearts.

"And now, I hope you'll hear the heart of our sister. Without further ado, Pastor Carla Lee."

There was a spattering of applause as Carla rose from her seat. Vivian gave her a big hug as they exchanged places, and nodded her support.

"Good evening, ladies," Carla began. "I ask you

for your prayers right now as being here tonight isn't easy. But I knew it was necessary for me to come, to stand before you while I'm in the valley, just like I did when I was on the mountain.

"Sistahs, I'm here tonight to seek your forgiveness. I've sinned and come short of God's glory. I've disrupted a family, tarnished the reputation of a powerful ministry, and cast a dark cloud over a good man, a godly man. For that, I'm truly sorry. And while there is more to this situation than I'm willing to share, I won't stand here and justify my actions. What I did was wrong, being with someone who was not my husband. And now," Carla's voice broke. "And now, I'm reaping the consequences of my actions with Stanley filing for divorce.

"Some of you are wondering . . . is this it for Sistah Carla? Will she step down from the pulpit, from spreading the message about the power of God's love? Honestly, saints, I don't know what the future holds. But I know who holds the future. I'm in the furnace right now, and it's hotter than I've ever experienced. But I want to ask you something."

Carla paused a moment and wiped tears from her eyes. "Would you please be patient with me? You see, I don't think God is through with me yet. I think there's some . . . I think there's some things He's still working on. Some things that need to be cut out, some things that need to be fixed up. But oh, when God gets through with me, sistahs, I believe that I will come forth as pure gold. Hallelujah!

"You know how I know I'll be okay? Because you

might not forgive me . . . but God has already forgiven me. You might not love me . . . but God's love never stopped. You might judge me, but Jesus has already said to me: 'Woman! Where art thine accusers? Go! And sin no more!'"

A round of conservative applause broke out across the auditorium, not the rousing hand claps she usually was afforded, but more than the spattering she'd earlier received. A few "We love you, Sistah Carlas" rang out, and an amen or two could be heard across the room.

Carla went on. "When we first ladies put together these Sanctity of Sisterhood meetings, it was with the thought to lift you up, to help you be empowered, and live the anointed, above average lives you were created to live. But tonight, my dear sisters, it's me who needs lifting, it's me who needs to be empowered, it's me standing in the need of prayer." Carla didn't try and stop the now steady flow of tears. "And I'm just wondering if there's anyone out there who can lift a sistah up, who can love me back up to where I belong. . . ." She stopped, unable to go on.

The room was quiet, except for Carla's sobs. Vivian prepared to rise, to go over and comfort her sister. But the Lord stopped her. She heard the word *no* clearly in her spirit. She sat back . . . watched . . . and waited.

At first nobody moved. And then two ladies stood up together, and with great pomp and circumstance walked out of the hall. A couple more followed them, one murmuring about the Jezebel spirit infiltrating the church.

Then Mother Moseley, who was sitting in the

front row, slowly rose to her feet. "I'll help lift you, Sistah Carla," she said in a loud, firm voice. She waved Carla down from the podium, and met her with a big hug. More voices rang out: "I'll help lift you! We love you, sistah! Keep your head up, Pastor Carla!"

Several more people left the auditorium, but most of the women crowded toward the front, ready to use their love to help lift their fallen sister. Vivian's eyes filled with tears as she witnessed the love of Christ in action, the unconditional love that His Word commanded. She understood why the spirit had held her back. He'd wanted His love to flow from the pews up, not from the pulpit down.

Into this swelling of God's forgiveness came the melodious voice of an a cappella soloist. Her voice was as soothing as a balm in Gilead:

> *"Love lifted me. Love lifted me.*
> *When nothing else could help, Love lifted me."*

Tori dabbed her eyes as she witnessed the powerful scene before her. How grateful she was that the MLM Network's board had decided to keep Lavon as executive director over their inspirational programming division. Because he'd been right, Carla had that "it" factor. She was just what the network was looking for, their first nationally syndicated talk show host.

57

It's a Start

Derrick and Darius sat in silence. For the past hour Darius had painfully, yet truthfully shared with his pastor the reality of who he was—a homosexual who had amazingly and unexpectedly developed a genuine love for a woman. He shared his experience from childhood on in realizing he was gay: how he'd been whipped, shunned, abused, and ridiculed because of his sexual orientation. For the first time, he shared the deep thoughts of suicide that plagued him for years, that even now sometimes whispered into his consciousness. But Bo's love sustained him, and gradually he was learning to accept himself as his lover did. That's why he loved Bo so much. And that's what he told his pastor.

Derrick listened quietly, asking few questions. When he was confident Darius had emptied his heart, he spoke. "Darius, I want to thank you for manning up and being honest with me. When the member came forward voicing his concern with

what he believed was a dangerous situation, both
for the church and your child, I wasn't sure how to
handle it. I prayed on it for a long time before ap-
proaching you in the hospital. But since there was
a child involved, I felt that I would be less than
your pastor to turn a blind eye when I felt I could
help steer you on to a more honest path."

"Are you sure it wasn't one of Shabach's people?" Darius asked. "He's been trying to out me for
years."

"No," Derrick said. "It was someone in our ministry, someone, I might add, who loves you very
much. He didn't come to me with judgment, but
with real concern for the future of our ministry,
and your participation in it. And he was right.
With your growing celebrity, especially with the
VH-One nomination, and our getting ready to
broadcast on the MLM Network, we had to have
this conversation. I can't have something hidden
that can blindside me and this ministry. You see
what just happened at Logos Word. I think they'll
recover, but they're already experiencing financial
difficulties with the sudden drop in membership
and the cancelled subscriptions to their outreach
ministry network."

Darius took a deep breath. "Well, I might as well
drop the real bomb then."

"Your being gay isn't the real bomb?"

"No, this is—I'm married to both Stacy and Bo."

Derrick did not move for a full minute. Neither
did Darius.

"You're kidding me, right?" the pastor asked finally.

Darius went on to explain the set of circumstances that led to his bigamist situation. "This situation is so messed up," Darius moaned, tears in his eyes. "But I don't know what to do, how to fix it."

Derrick chose his words carefully. "My professional position," he began slowly, "is that homosexuality is wrong. It is so stated in the Bible, and it is the position of the Christian community at large, that it is a sin."

Darius hung his head.

"But my personal position," Derrick went on, "is that I don't have a hell to put you in and even if I did, I honestly don't feel in my spirit that God is going to cast you in to the lake of fire because of something you didn't choose."

Darius's eyes brightened. He could not believe that this Christian minister, this man of God, actually thought Darius could go to heaven. "Then . . . you're not condemning me?" he asked in a whisper.

"I'm going to share something with you. You know my favorite uncle I lost recently, Charles Montgomery?"

Darius nodded.

"Aside from my father, he was the finest man I've ever met—smart, funny, wise beyond this earth—and he loved God with every fiber of his being. It was his example in my early life that led me fully onto the Christian path. I wanted to be just like him. I didn't find out he was gay until I was in my twenties.

"When I decided to go into ministry, he was my staunchest supporter, heard all of my early sermons, paid some of my expenses. And earlier this year, as I watched them lower his body into the ground, I felt with every fiber of my being that I'd see him again on the other side . . . in heaven. I think you'll be there too."

"But why don't you preach this, Pastor? Gay men and women are dying because of the church's rejection. Churches are full of homosexuals. We lead praise and worship across the country every Sunday, we give our tithes, but we can't come out. We can't publicly be who we really are. And this has gone on for years.

"As Christians, we won't talk about the famous homosexual men and women who worship openly but are forced to love privately, in a closet, on the down low . . . all because we want to stand next to our straight brothers and sisters and praise God."

Darius wiped away tears, and waited for Derrick to speak. "You're right," the pastor said after a long pause. "It's a conversation long overdue. And while I can't tell you I'll come out next Sunday and proclaim Homosexual Day at Kingdom Citizens I will bring this topic up at the next Total Truth Association meeting. I promise you I'll do that. And I can't say how you'll be accepted by our members if you come out, but if that's what you decide to do, you'll have me and my wife's support.

"Right now, you've got a bigger issue to deal with. You're married to two people. You've got a child with one of them. Now if you asked my opinion—and you didn't—I'd encourage you to stay with Stacy, raise your son, and let Bo be free to find love elsewhere."

"I'm going to be in my son's life no matter what happens," Darius said firmly.

"I can't tell you what to do; I can only give you my opinion. And I've done that. Now you've got to pray, search your heart, and do what you feel is right. But you've got to do something, Darius. I won't toss you out because you're gay, but I won't let you stay if you continue living this double life with Bo and Stacy."

"I'll handle it, Pastor," Darius said, rising. "And, Pastor? Thank you. Thank you for loving me, and accepting me for who I am."

The two men hugged—one glad that he'd been able to show love and acceptance, even when it was uncomfortable; the other glad that he was receiving it, even if only privately. For both of them, it was a start.

58

Staying Alive

Darius sat in front of the duplex, warring with his decision. He'd gone back and forth a zillion times, and had taken a long walk on the beach to further delay the inevitable—choosing. But he didn't want to put it off any longer, didn't want to go to bed with the matter unresolved.

Darius thought of Bo and smiled. Memories from years of togetherness played like a film across his mind: trips, parties, amazing home-cooked meals, devilish fights, raucous fun. Bo helped him be more of who he really was. He was his best friend, an ardent lover, and his number-one fan.

And then he thought of Stacy, and the son they'd just brought home. His heart flooded with love for them both. He'd never expected to truly love a female, in fact had believed it impossible. Most would consider him bisexual, but in thirty-plus years, Stacy was the one and only woman to whom he'd ever been attracted. He'd never been able to sustain an erection with Gwen, his ex-wife, which is why she'd left him. He'd been as shocked as anyone when arousal happened, and continued to happen with Stacy.

Each of his spouses brought something totally different, yet completely wonderful to his life. Which is why choosing between them was so difficult: Bo, arguably the love of his life, or Stacy, his more socially acceptable wife and the mother of his young son. Darius had been unaware one could love so deeply, so quickly, but that's what had happened when he saw Darius, Jr.: love at first sight.

That was it, go with the deepest love. In that instant, his answer became crystal clear. Darius took a deep, long breath and got out of the car.

As he walked up to his future, the trepidation faded away and was replaced by an indescribable joy. Somehow, in that instant, he knew everything would be all right. He took out his key and slowly placed it in the lock. Before he could open the door all the way, he looked up and stared into the eyes of his tomorrow, of the person with whom he hoped to spend the rest of his life. He smiled and received a smile in return. He came in and closed the door behind him.

"Hey you," he said softly.

"Hey, yourself." Bo walked up and kissed him gently. "Come this way. I just made the most amazing Chilean sea bass with a bouillabaisse sauce to die for. I know you're going to love it."

Darius's smile was bittersweet as he followed Bo into the kitchen. His news would probably make his lover the happiest person on the planet. On the other hand, things were going to get ugly when he broke the news to Stacy, that he was legally married to Bo and that his and her marriage would be annulled.

"Baby, I've got news," he said to Bo after he'd sampled the mouth-watering bouillabaisse sauce. "Can we sit down for a moment?"

They did, and Darius shared with Bo his earlier conversation with Derrick. Bo was pleasantly surprised to hear Derrick's personal views on homosexuality. His mood changed abruptly, however, when he learned of the pastor's ultimatum: Bo or Stacy.

Abject fear showed in Bo's eyes, but he remained silent. For a moment, so did Darius. "I'm staying with you," he said finally.

Bo burst into tears. "I'm so glad I didn't have to choose the Armani suit," he said.

"What?" Darius pulled back, confused by Bo's statement.

"After I killed you . . . that's the suit I would have chosen for your burial." Bo went on in mock seriousness. "Stacy, it wouldn't have mattered what she wore, in fact I would have cut her up so tough hers would have probably been closed casket. But you . . . definitely the navy blue Armani."

Darius pulled Bo into a loving embrace. "You nut . . . that's why I love you."

It was a little after nine in the morning when Darius put his key into his and Stacy's side of the duplex.

Stacy was sitting in the living room, feeding Darius Jr. "That's the first night you've spent over there

since we've been married. He usually gets days . . .
I get nights."

Darius stood by the door, momentarily second-
guessing his decision. The vision in front of him
was picture-perfect: Stacy looking tired yet radiant
in a white, satin robe, their tiny, six-pound baby
suckling at her breast. Future photographs of the
three of them flashed into his mind: Darius graduating from kindergarten, playing baseball, visiting
Disneyland, being swung between his mom and
dad.

But all too soon the vision faded. Those picture-
perfect imaginings were a pipe dream. They'd
never come true. They couldn't come true. Husband to a wife, a female wife, was not who he was.

"There's something I have to tell you, Stacy. I
wish I didn't have to tell you now, like this, especially with our son so young. . . ."

Stacy's heart leapt into her throat. This did not
sound good. "What about our son, Darius?"

"Not about him . . . about us, really. And no
matter what happens with us, I will always be there
for my son."

"What is it, Darius?" Stacy asked firmly.

Darius nibbled his bottom lip for a moment, his
hands clammy from the sudden nervousness he
felt. There was no way to say it except to say it. "We
have to annul our marriage."

Stacy laughed. "You can't be serious. I know you
love Darius Jr. too much to even think about leaving me. Leaving me would mean not seeing your
son again so I *know* you're not thinking some crazy
shit like that."

Darius took a deep breath, trying to calm himself. This was already hard enough without making a scene. "I'll always have deep feelings for you," he continued. "I'm hoping we can remain good friends as we raise our son together."

"Hmph. That's up to you." Stacy placed Darius Jr. up on her shoulder and began to burp him. "As long as you're here, we'll raise him together. You leave me . . . I'll raise him alone."

"Our marriage isn't legal," Darius said, choosing not to argue visitation rights at the moment.

"What is it? Did Bo hit that booty especially good last night? Jiggle part of your brain loose?"

"Bo and I are married."

Stacy laughed. "Whatever."

"In November, in Canada," Darius continued in a low, civil tone. "It was an official marriage ceremony recognized by Canadian law. The matching rings we wear are our wedding bands."

Stacy rose from the couch and placed Darius Jr. in a basinet. She turned back to Darius, crossed her arms, and remained silent.

Darius went on, telling Stacy about his conversation with Derrick and the reason for finally telling the truth about the situation. "I was confused, didn't know what to do. I was already married when you told me you were pregnant and I wanted to do the right thing, wanted to—*will*—raise my son. . . . I never meant to hurt you, Stacy."

"Hurt me? Hurt me? You son of a—" Stacy picked up a vase of fresh flowers and flung it at Darius's head. The vase clipped his shoulder and shattered against the wall behind him. Books, pillows, and a candy jar followed, before Stacy advanced with fists flailing.

"Stop, stop it, Stacy," Darius said, working to control her violent thrashing.

Stacy was hysterical, a madwoman. She wanted to hurt Darius as bad as she was hurting right now. At six weeks, her C-section incision had barely healed. Now here came Darius making another incision—in her heart.

"I want you out, out! You'll never see your son again!" she screamed. She raced over to the sofa table and began throwing picture after picture against the wall: pictures of her and Darius. Once she'd emptied the table of photos, she went for the DVD cabinet, X-Box, basically anything that wasn't tied down, and wasn't too heavy to lift.

"You think you're going to dump me like yesterday's garbage, nucka? Well . . . think again!" Dozens of CDs rolled out of their cases as the CD rack came crashing to the floor.

A banging from outside joined the interior cacophony. "Open up this door. Leave Darius alone, Stacy. Open up this door or I swear I'll break it in!" Bo yelled.

"Oh, you want some of this?" Stacy screamed back. She ran for the door.

Darius intercepted her in a tackle that would have made any NFL coach proud.

"Owwwww!" Stacy screamed, clutching her stomach as she fell to the ground. Soon, Darius Jr. joined in, his cries an octave higher than hers.

"Go home, Bo!" Darius yelled over the incessant wailing of mother and babe.

"Not without you!" Bo screamed back.

"Get away from my door, punk!" Stacy shouted.

Darius Jr. cried louder.

"The baby," Darius said softly, trying to break through Stacy's hysteria. "We need to get the baby." He was afraid to let her go, afraid she'd go straight for the door and Bo, who was still standing on the other side, banging furiously.

"Bo, if you don't leave that door, I'm divorcing you too!" Darius screamed, totally exasperated.

Bo stopped knocking.

Stacy stopped wailing.

Darius Jr.'s cries turned to a whimper.

"Let me up," Stacy said in an exhausted tone. He did, and Stacy stumbled over to pick up their son. "If you walk out that door," she said, breathing heavily, "don't come back. Not for your clothes, not for your furniture, anything you own in this house. If you walk out that door . . . you're walking out our lives for good, me and Darius Jr."

"Our marriage is over, Stacy. But we can be friends. We can be good parents. I don't hate you. I love you. I just love Bo more."

"You disgust me," Stacy spat out. "Choosing a dick over your own flesh and blood. You and Bo deserve each other. Just remember, God don't like ugly. You're going to rot in hell."

Darius left the living room and returned minutes later with a suitcase. "Good-bye, Stacy."

Stacy followed him to the door, talking to his son. "There goes your faggot daddy, Darius Jr. He's never going to see you again!" She screamed at Darius's retreating back, as he walked next door to his home with Bo. "You want it to be over? Fine, it's over. And I'm going to tell everybody why you left!"

"You won't have to," Darius said as he spun around angrily. "I'm going to tell them for you."

Right then, Darius decided he would come out, admit his homosexuality. It was the twenty-first century. He was sick of hiding. He was tired of going the way of so many popular gospel artists, living one way in public and another in private. He was tired of being another Black Christian male on the down low. He was tired of living a lie.

"I'm going public," Darius said, as he opened the door and took the glass of wine Bo immediately offered. "I'm going to tell the truth, and I have to trust that the church loves me enough. And if the church doesn't, that the fans love me enough. And if the fans don't . . . that God loves me enough." Darius downed the glass of wine and took Bo in his arms. "And then I have to trust . . . that His Love will be enough to keep me alive."

59

No Place like Home

Princess bit her fingernails nervously as she watched the once familiar sights on Kansas City's Interstate 35 roll past her. She'd told no one she was coming home, and since she also hadn't called in almost a month, didn't know what kind of reception she'd get. It had only been six months since she'd come home for Thanksgiving, almost a year since she'd first set out for UCLA and her new life. Tears filled Princess's eyes as she mourned for the excited, innocent girl who'd boarded the plane bound for LA, full of hopes and dreams about college life. That girl was long gone, and belatedly Princess realized that although she wanted to, she couldn't go back and get her.

The news that Fawn carried Kelvin's baby put Princess in bed for a week. To his too-little, too-late credit, Kelvin moved out of the condo. Unfortunately, if rumors were accurate, he'd moved in with the mother-to-be of his child. Princess relived the pain of her abortion every time she thought of them together.

Finals, and the thought of failing the semester after months of hard work, was the only thing that pulled her out of her depression, that and her friend Joni, who became a one-woman cheerleading squad and at times a drill sergeant.

"You are *not* going to die over this," she'd voiced emphatically, forcing Princess to eat, and after six days of nonstop use, taking away the drugs that Princess used to hide the truth. "You can't smoke the pain away, but you can smoke your GPA away." Joni had pranced around the room, chanting the statement until Princess, laughing for the first time since Fawn's baby news, finally got out of bed. Burying her head in studies had gotten her through the remaining weeks. It was also the excuse she used for not calling home. After finals, she felt it was easier to go home than call home. So that's what she'd done.

Princess felt her heart pounding as the cab turned the corner and she noticed her grandmother, Mama Max's, car in the driveway, along with another car with Chicago tags. *Michael.* Her older brother, home from his final year at Northwestern University. For some unknown reason, she teared up again. She and Michael had been close once, but the distance between them had grown this past year. A part of her was filled with trepidation, but the bigger part was glad he too was home. She felt she could use a big brother right about now.

"Hey everybody, it's Princess!" Tabitha yelled

when she saw Princess gathering her suitcases from the taxi. She ran outside and picked one up for her sister. Her twin brother, Timothy, was right behind her. Tai met her at the door and gave her a big hug. "It's so good to see you, Princess. I missed you!"

Princess almost lost it right there. "You too, Mama," she replied, a bit too cheerfully. She broke the embrace and walked into the living room. There her father, King; her grandfather, the Reverend Doctor Pastor Bishop Overseer Mister Stanley Obadiah Meshach Brook Jr.; Mama Max, and Michael gathered. They all rushed to hug her, breaking the hold she had on her tears.

"What are y'all doing here?" she asked. Knowing how the Spirit talked to her grandmother, she asked her sincerely, "Did God tell you I was coming home?"

"Oh, the Lord tells me everything about you," Mama Max answered.

Princess's look turned serious.

"Oh, girl, I'm just playing with you. After more than half a century in the pulpit, your grandpa here is fixin' to announce his retirement."

"Oh, okay," Princess said with relief. There were some things she definitely did *not* want God discussing with her grandmother.

"You need to get that weave tightened," Michael said, teasing her as he'd done since they were children. "You're trying to look like Beyoncé and instead you're looking like one of Bebe's kids."

"Forget you, Michael," she said with a hollow laugh.

"Yeah, Michael, please," Mama Max added. "With those padlocks or deadbolts or whatever that is on your head. . . ."

"Dreadlocks, Ma," Michael deadpanned.

"Yeah, well, you got the dread right."

Princess wanted to open her mouth and join in the teasing. But she could feel an avalanche of tears threatening to escape, a torrent no amount of time away from home could explain. She grabbed a carry-on and hurried toward the staircase. "I need to, uh, get something," she said, before running upstairs.

Tai looked at Mama Max. King looked at Tai. The twins looked at each other and shrugged in typical fifteen-year-old fashion, and Michael looked toward the stairs. "What was that about?" he asked the room.

"She's probably overwhelmed," Tai said. "I'll go check on her."

Tai opened the door to find a near hysterical Princess sobbing into a pillow. "Baby, baby, what's wrong?" she asked, taking Princess into her arms. *Oh, Lord. Is she pregnant?* "I'm here, Princess," Tai continued reassuringly. "No matter what you're facing, we'll get through it together."

For several minutes, Princess couldn't talk for crying. It was as if all the hurt, pain, rejection, betrayal, and heartache of the past year were spilling out of her heart.

"Me and Kelvin broke up, Mama," she said between sobs. "He got another girl pregnant!"

Well, thank God it's not you, is what Tai thought. "Princess, I'm sorry," is what she said.

"But it hurts so bad, Mama. I gave him everything, did anything he asked me. So many things I shouldn't have, so many things I'm ashamed of."

Tai wasn't sure she wanted to know what those things were. Still she asked, "Do you want to talk about it?"

Yes! Princess screamed inside. She wanted to tell her mother about the drugs, about the wild sex, and especially about the abortion. She wanted to bare her soul and cleanse her conscience. But she was too embarrassed and ashamed. She felt used and degraded, and didn't think her mother would understand. In fact, she thought her mother would reject her outright if she ever learned how far from her home training she'd strayed.

Princess shook her head no. "Mama, is there any sin God won't forgive?"

Tai searched her daughter's face for the words left unspoken. "No, baby," she said finally. "There is nothing you can do to stop God from loving you."

"But I turned my back on Him, I stopped loving *Him.* I haven't been to church in a really long time. I even started thinking there might not be a God."

Tai's eyes misted over at that revelation. What had happened to her baby, she wondered. What had the world done to so shake her daughter's faith?

She placed her hands on her daughter's shoulders. "You may have rejected God, but He never rejected you."

"But you don't know, Mama, what all I've done."

"What, the drinking, getting high, promiscuous sex, stuff like that?"

Princess's eyes widened as Tai ran down four of the five items on Princess's list of shame. "How'd you know?"

"Believe it or not, I was your age once. And I had friends your age. There's nothing new under the sun, Princess. Every generation feels they're the first to experience growing up. But we all go through it. Yes, the culture changes: the music, politics, fashion, slang. But the basics, the trials, tribulations, and even victories that help us grow into ourselves? They're basically the same."

"Mama, I . . ."

"What is it, Princess?"

The tears started anew as Princess struggled with whether or not to tell Tai about the terminated pregnancy. In the end, she felt that God might forgive her for that action, but that Tai never would. In time she might tell her mother about the abortion, but not now.

"I love you," she said instead.

"I love you too, Princess."

They sat cuddled in each other's arms for a long time, until Princess ran out of tears.

"You were right, Mama," she said finally, her voice barely above a whisper. "About grown folk's pleasure coming with grown folk's pain. I wish I'd listened to you. Some things would not have happened, and I wouldn't hurt so much."

"Earth has no sorrow that heaven can't heal. Put Christ back in your life, Princess. I promise you'll get your joy back; you'll have even more than before."

"But when, Mama . . . how?"

Tai looked at Princess with every ounce of a mother's love shining in her eyes. "We'll do it together, baby. One prayer, one praise, one day at a time."

Although small, Princess offered her first genuine smile of the day. It would take time, but maybe this wasn't the end, maybe things could get better. That's what Tai said, and now Princess was ready to give her mother credit for knowing a little bit more about life than she thought she did.

"Mama," she said, hugging her close again, "thanks for coming to check on me. It's good to be home."

60

Someone's Passion

The flickering candlelight danced across the stark, white linen, which showed off the porcelain and silver to perfection. Crystal goblets came together and clinked softly, a perfect complement to the sounds of light jazz in the restaurant's background ambiance. The brilliant colors of a July sunset streaked across the room.

"To you," Stanley said, hoisting his glass of sparkling water toward Passion.

Passion acknowledged the toast but asked, "To me?"

"Of course. Because of the evidence in my case, evidence you'd gathered, Carla conceded to everything I asked for in the divorce."

"You know, Dr.—"

"Stanley, remember?"

"Right." Passion took a nervous sip of her sparkling water. "Stanley, I don't feel good about what I did. I know that what Pastor Carla did was also wrong, but two wrongs don't make a right."

Stanley set down his goblet and leaned back in his chair. "You know what I think, Passion? I think that in a peculiar sort of way, things are working out just as they're supposed to. What the devil meant for evil, God just might work out for good."

"How so?"

"I've been observing you through this entire process, Passion—how invaluable you've been to me these past few months, how supportive. Your unwavering commitment to the ministry even while it's in turmoil, even your desire to not speak badly about my ex-wife. These are commendable traits, virtuous traits."

"Oh, I'm a long way from Proverbs thirty-one," Passion countered.

"Not too far," Stanley said in a husky voice.

Passion was taken aback, and became preoccupied with eating her dinner to cover up her confusion. Was her pastor flirting? Was *the* Dr. Stanley Lee coming on to her? True, she'd been a sounding board for him ever since their second meeting, where she turned over copies of the pictures she'd taken and shared all she knew about Lavon and Carla's affair. They'd exchanged numbers and after the first few times, Passion began looking forward to receiving Pastor's calls, even though they often came late at night, after his long workday, and she had to be at work early the next morning.

When he'd become angry and depressed at the reality of Carla's betrayal, ashamed at the public airing of the disgrace, and then alarmed at the sudden drop in church membership, Passion switched from sounding board to counselor, offering encouragement, compassion, and the assured belief that "this too will pass." She reminded Stanley that he was God's man, an eloquent, intelligent minister, excellent father, and that he had been a loving and faithful husband. Each compliment had been a gust of wind under his slacking sails. The calls had gone from once to several times a week.

But Passion had remained reserved. This was her pastor and, although he'd filed for divorce, still a married man. She hadn't exposed Carla's affair to take her husband. So during this time her position, in her mind, had been that of trusted confidante to her pastor, fueled, she believed, by the unique yet pivotal role she'd played in his breakup. And even if she were interested (and who wouldn't be?), Stanley was still a married man. After swallowing her food, taking a sip of water, and wiping her mouth with her napkin, she'd recovered enough to say as much to Stanley.

He smiled. "Yes, technically I'm still married for another four months. I'd never ask you to do anything inappropriate. But surely you know that I find you attractive, and without sounding arrogant, I think you do me as well."

Passion's cheeks warmed at Stanley's words. "I find you extremely attractive," she admitted. She was rescued from saying anything further by the waiter bringing dessert menus.

"I'm not much for the single life," Stanley continued, after they'd decided to split a hot fudge sundae. "I like the idea of having a woman by my side, a woman in the home. Over the past week or so, I've begun to believe you might be that woman."

Inside, Passion was excited, confused, and scared

at the same time. Of all the things she thought would happen as a result of her actions, this wasn't it. In fact, when she took the pictures to *LA Gospel,* she hadn't thought one second past her anger. It wasn't until weeks passed that she began to fully process what she'd done, and to regret it. Still, could her happiness be built on top of someone else's sadness? Passion didn't know.

"Don't you think you might be rushing things? You've only been separated a few months, and y'all were married ten years. All due respect, Stanley, but I don't want to be anybody's rebound romance."

Stanley gazed at Passion, stroking his chin thoughtfully. "Not far," he repeated, referring to her being a close virtuous woman match.

Passion looked away from Stanley's soulful gaze. His overt flirtations were disconcerting. She thought back to the times when she imagined her husband. She thought he'd be someone godly and strong, someone like her pastor. But she never thought he would actually *be* Stanley. The one and only Dr. Stanley Lee, pastor of the renowned Logos Word Interdenominational Church. It was almost too much for her to wrap her brain around.

Stanley wisely switched the topic to safer subjects. Their dessert was enjoyed amid discussion of his children, Passion's daughter, the ever-changing political climate, and the realization that they both loved football. By the time Stanley walked Passion to her car in the parking lot, they'd resumed the comfortable camaraderie they usually enjoyed.

"How'd you get the name Passion?" Stanley asked suddenly, as if the thought had never crossed his mind before.

"My grandfather," Passion replied. "I guess I used to kick a lot when my mother was pregnant with me. Her father told her that I had spunk, fire, passion. A few months later, that's what she named me." Passion smiled fondly at the memory of her grandfather. "When I was little, he used to call me 'his little passion.'"

"Hmm," Stanley said, with a light touch on Passion's arm that sent shivers down to her toes. "Do you think you could become this preacher's passion?"

Her answer was swallowed up by his lips pressing against hers. Before she could censor her actions, her tongue probed against Stanley's closed lips as she wrapped her arms around him. Stanley gently broke the kiss and pulled back to look in Passion's half-moon eyes. "Hmm, Ms. Passion Perkins," he said with a smile, "I definitely think you can."

Six Months Later

Only four persons stood in attendance: Stanley, Passion, a witness, and the Antiguan marriage officer. The January wedding was simple and low-key, just as they wanted. Later, when their children, families, and church members had fully acclimated to their union, they'd hold a large reception and shout their wedded joy from the rooftops. For now, the only ones who needed to hear it were the two of them.

"I'm nervous, Stanley," Passion admitted, when after a romantic dinner and walk on the beach, they retired to their suite.

"Me too," Stanley agreed. He'd shared bits of his sexual dysfunction with Passion. She'd shared the five years she'd been celibate, and was secretly thankful she hadn't had sex with Lavon. The nervousness these formerly married-with-children adults displayed added to the night's charm.

"Let's just cuddle and see where it leads," Passion suggested. She went into the bathroom and changed into a silky, midnight blue negligee with matching robe. When she came out, Stanley had stripped down to his boxers, and was covered in a robe as well.

They climbed to the center of the king-sized bed, which was positioned to face the ocean. The sound of splashing waves could be heard through the open patio.

"That sounds nice," Passion said, wrapping her arms around Stanley.

"That feels nice," Stanley replied, wrapping his arms around her.

The newlyweds cuddled, nuzzled, and nibbled away their discomfort. After a while, Stanley kissed Passion's ears, eyes, and each cheek, finally claiming her mouth in a titillating kiss. His hand rubbed her arm, and then pinched her nipples through the satiny fabric. Passion moaned, squirming, as her furry jewel felt instant heat. She reached for his manhood, surprised yet delighted at the thick length of him. Sensitive to his conservative nature, she curbed the urge to talk dirty or do what she really wanted, lavish her oral praises along the length of his shaft.

Instead, she spread her legs in silent invitation. Stanley placed a hand inside her top and massaged her naked breast. With his other, he rubbed her love box on the outside of her nightgown. Passion's pussy screamed for more direct attention. She lifted her nightgown and raised it over her head. He stripped as well and entered her in one quick, firm thrust.

Moments later, Passion listened to the soft, even sound of her husband's snoring, interspersed with the sound of the ocean. The crashing waves beat a sensual, rhythmic melody against the shore, one that was soon mirrored by Passion's fingers in her cat. She ground herself against her fingers, trying to find the release Stanley had left wanting.

Finally, she gave up the attempt, and sought comfort by cuddling spoon-style against Stanley's strong, broad back.

"I love you," she whispered, with a kiss to his neck. "This will get better, I'm sure of it." *But I might have to explore some alternate ways to climax until you lose your inhibitions. Maybe I'll get a vibrator.* This would have been a guilty thought when she was single, but being married, it now felt okay. After all, the marriage bed was undefiled. *That's it! That's what I'll do—get a big rubber penis to help me release, while I stay faithful to my husband.* Passion smiled at her ingenious solution, even as she snuggled closer to Stanley. *I'll just think of it as my special friend.*

She giggled aloud at her last thought before falling asleep. *Maybe I'll name it "Denzel."*

Lutishia Lovely dishes up a sexy new series
following the hot tempers and tantalizing
temptations of a family whose restaurant is *the*
place for a tasty meal . . .

All Up In My Business

Coming in March 2011 from Dafina Books

Here's an excerpt from *All Up In My Business* . . .

"The way to a man's heart is through his stomach."
—*Amanda Long, grandmother of Taste Of Soul*
restaurant board member Candace Livingston

Adam Livingston loved the taste of her thighs.
Tender on the inside and crispy on the outside,
nobody could fry chicken better than Candace, his
wife. Even now—after living and working together
for more than three decades—his mouth still
watered at the thought of this juicy, dark meat.
Whether the succulent morsels on his dinner plate,
or those he hovered over when between the sheets,
Candace knew how to please him. Unfortunately,
the way she sexed and handled a bird aside, Adam
knew that Candace in the kitchen wasn't necessarily a good thing. His wife rarely cooked these days,
preferring to either eat at one of their restaurants
or have their on-call personal chef whip up an intimate lunch or dinner with guests. Now, when Candace graced the kitchen with her presence, it

usually meant a conversation was coming regarding something he'd rather not discuss with her—namely her extravagant spending sprees, plastic surgery, or the ongoing competition between their sons.

Technically, money wasn't a problem. The restaurant his parents had opened in Atlanta fifty years ago had grown into a soul food empire—with ten highly successful restaurants in seven Southern states. Additionally, the barbeque sauce his grandfather had created, which was used to slather on their most popular menu item, baby back ribs, had been sold in grocery stores nationwide for the past five years. Still, Candace could spend money faster than Usain Bolt ran the one-hundred-yard dash. Just last year she'd renovated their kitchen to the tune of fifty thousand dollars, had their backyard relandscaped to resemble the scenic islands they'd visited on their thirtieth wedding anniversary, and had one of the guest bedrooms converted to a closet to handle her almost daily jaunts to Nordstrom, Bloomingdale's, and Saks. These renovations had increased the value of their mansion, and had made Candace happy. So Adam hadn't complained . . . too much.

When it came to plastic surgery, Adam thought his wife had had enough. She'd always been beautiful in his eyes, ever since he saw her walking across the Clark Atlanta campus back in the seventies. She'd looked like a Fashion Fair model to him that day, her dark caramel skin enhanced by the beige mini she wore along with similarly colored thigh-high boots. Her long thick hair had moved with the sway of her hips as she'd casually chatted with a friend. A couple of days later, when he saw her in the cafeteria, he'd immediately gone over and introduced himself. She was even finer up close than she'd been from a distance, and after taking one look into the almond-shaped brown eyes that sat above a wide but nicely shaped nose and luscious lips, Adam had gotten the distinct impression that he was looking at the mother of his children. This feeling proved prophetic—Candace became pregnant during her junior year, when Adam was a senior. They'd married that summer and welcomed their oldest, Malcolm LeMarcus, the following December.

Even after having their second son, Toussaint LeVon, Candace stayed slim. Into her forties, when she finally gained thirty pounds that didn't shed easily, Adam still thought she was fine. She was five foot seven and to him, the extra weight hardly showed. Candace hadn't seemed that bothered by it either, until her sister-in-law, his twin brother's wife, Dianne, had commented on Candace being "fat" during a family get together, and had suggested liposuction as a quick way to take the weight off in time for their cruise to the Fuji Islands. Candace had been so pleased with the results that a tummy tuck soon followed, and breast implants followed that. Any brothah would be pleased to squeeze a set of firm titties, even if he'd had to pay for them, and Adam was no exception. But a couple of weeks ago, when Candace started complaining about her wide nose, Adam had shut her down immediately. "You're becoming addicted to this shit," he warned. "If you don't stop cutting on the body God gave you, you're going to become as obsessed as Michael Jackson was, may he rest in peace. You look fine, Can. Give it a rest." So he hoped she'd gotten the message because he didn't intend to pay the highly skilled and equally expensive cut and paste doctor another dime.

That left the topic of him and Candace's sons. The mid-year company meeting was in two weeks, right after Juneteenth, so most likely, Candace wanted to butter him up regarding some plan in the works—probably another of Toussaint's outlandish ideas. Adam loved his youngest son but he swore that boy didn't have a fearful bone in his body. Where Malcolm was more like Adam, in looks and demeanor, Toussaint was definitely his mother's child. Like her, he was brilliant, but he'd also inherited her traits of impulsiveness and flamboyance. Toussaint had run an idea by him some months ago, an idea that Adam had nipped in the bud as quickly as he had Candace's nose job suggestion. The ecomony was too unstable to do anything new now, he'd explained. Adam wasn't sure how the other players would feel about contructing more Taste of Soul locations across the country, but hoped that he and Candace's vote would be the same—no f'ing way. The more Adam thought about it, however, the more he thought this might be exactly why he smelled chicken frying. *Damn, I have too much on my mind to argue with Candace about this right now.*

One thing on his mind was the email he'd just received on his Smartphone, from the woman who'd been trying to seduce him for the past two years. He'd met Joyce Witherspoon in the clubhouse after a golf outing, and exchanged business cards because she'd told Adam of her plans to start an event planning business, and her desire to contract Taste of Soul as one of the catering partners. Her emails had slowly gone from strictly business to potential pleasure, even as she launched the successful, high-profile business that kept the Taste of Soul catering arm busy, Adam was flattered, and Joyce was attractive, but he had told the sistah that he was happily married. Joyce's response had been quick, and witty. "You're married, but are you flexible?" Even after assuring her there was no room in his bed for a third party, she'd continued her erotic banter in various phone calls and emails. Adam reread Joyce's detailed description of what she wanted to do to him with her mouth, and then pushed delete. He had always been faithful, but could no longer ignore the fact that Joyce's constant flirtations and rapt adoration were wearing him down. *I've got to do something about this . . . and soon.* Adam picked up the *Atlanta Journal Constitution* and pulled out the sports section, determined to swap thoughts of Joyce's mouth with those of his wife's thighs . . . the ones he'd be eating at the dinner table soon, and in the bedroom later.

Candace Long-Livingston poured melted butter into the baking pan, and then sparsely coated each buttermilk biscuit with the warm liquid before spacing the dough out evenly in the bottom of the pan. She loved cooking, especially now since she didn't do it often. It was a love she'd inherited from the grandmother who'd help support a family of four by cooking for an affluent family in their hometown of Birmingham, Alabama. "The way to a man's heart is through his stomach," Amanda Long would tell Candace as she whipped up a slap-your-mama pound cake or an oh-no-you-didn't peach cobbler. Candace smiled at the memory of those kitchen counseling sessions. Adam may have thought it was her small waist and big booty that had captured his heart, but Candace knew it was those candied yams and collard greens she'd fixed while they were dating. But somewhere between the birth of their first son and the opening of their second restaurant, the thrill had gone. She'd worked long, arduous hours at the Buckhead location, the same tony suburb where they lived, and while it had been a labor of love, her joy for fixing food had been replaced by repulsion. There'd been days when she'd thought that if she fried, smothered or baked another anything . . . she'd lose her mind.

Tonight she cooked with love, purpose . . . and guilt. Love for the fact that when it came to cooking, she knew she could "throw down." Adam loved food, and her fried chicken was his favorite. Purpose because she thought Toussaint's latest idea was a stroke of genius, that the timing for said idea was perfect, that Adam would surely be against it and that if anybody could change his mind she could by using various types of thighs. And guilt? Guilt because after months of harmless flirting with Q, the personal trainer she'd hired to help tone the very thighs her husband admired, they'd taken their relationship to another level. During her last two sessions—sit-ups, squats and running on the treadmill weren't the only reasons

she'd sweated. And while Candace knew she
should stop the madness, should never even have
started down this road, she honestly didn't know if
she could heed the red light and make a U-turn
back into monogamy. There was no doubt that
Candace loved Adam. But thugalicious cocoa cutie
Quintin Bright, who was younger than Toussaint,
had turned a sistah out for the second time in as
many weeks—with sixty minutes of working out
followed by nine inches of love.

Oh—my—goodness!
Did a "what goes around comes around"
just go down???

And speaking of comings and goings . . .
What's up with Cy and Hope Taylor,
her cousin Frieda,
Stacy and Darius . . . Darius and Bo?
They're all back, as are
Millicent, Carla, Lavon, the Brooks, and
Montgomerys, in . . .

Heaven Right Here

Enjoy the following excerpt!

1

Babies Are Blessings

Stacy Gray, Hope Taylor, and Frieda Moore sat enjoying the warm breeze coming off the Pacific Ocean. Eighteen-month-old Darius Crenshaw Jr. sat cooing and clapping in his high chair, obviously enjoying the warm November weather as well. It was the first time in months the ladies had hung out together, and for all three the good food and great conversation was just what the doctor ordered.

"I don't care about what she did, I *love Conversations with Carla*. That sistah keeps it real!" Frieda jabbed a fry in the air for emphasis.

"I like her too," Hope said. "I'm just saying it's amazing how someone who fell so low could rise again so quickly."

"I'm with Frieda," Stacy added, taking a napkin and wiping mashed potato from her son's face. "She did wrong and she was punished—lost her husband, her ministry, dignity, respect. No one on the outside looking in will ever truly know how much her present success cost her."

No one knew, but many speculated on the price Minister Carla Lee had paid for the very public scandal she endured a year and a half ago. A personal affair with a church associate had become very public via *LA Gospel,* a Los Angeles-based magazine targeting the Black church community. Her husband had promptly divorced her and married the woman who revealed Carla's secret, Passion Perkins, now Passion Lee. Carla's base of Christian women supporters, which once numbered in the hundreds of thousands, dropped to four figures, and several Christian bookstores pulled her DVDs. But now, less than six months after her television show debuted, Carla was attracting a following that promised to eclipse that of her former popularity, one that included women of every race, religion, and socioeconomic status. Her Dr. Phil-style directness, Oprah-like warmth, combined with religious sensibilities and southern charm, had sent her ratings, and those of the MLM Network, sky high.

"Did you see the girl on there the other day?" Frieda asked. "The sixteen-year-old who already had two kids? I wasn't expecting Carla to get with girlfriend like she did but telling that little sistah to put a closed sign on the punanny was real talk!"

"She said that?" Hope exclaimed.

"Pu-nan-ny, on national TV. That's why women love her."

"What did the girl do?"

"Started crying, and then promised Carla she'd put her stuff on lock."

"What I liked," Stacy interjected, "is that Carla agreed to be her personal mentor, that she cared enough to get involved with her guest like that."

Stacy and Frieda kept talking, but Hope didn't hear. She tried to not let the talk of babies affect her, but it did. She and Cy had been trying for almost two years to get pregnant. She'd gone to several doctors and got mixed diagnoses: one said she was fine, another that her uterus was tilted, and a third, something about low-producing ovaries. Her first lady, Vivian Montgomery, had told her she just needed to relax and stop *trying* to get pregnant. But Hope wasn't getting any younger, and she and Cy wanted at least two children, if not more.

"I know one thing," Stacy was saying when Hope finally began to listen again. "If Darius thinks he's going to force me to have my son stay in that den of sin he and Bo call home, he better think again."

"But he the daddy, girl," Frieda reasoned. "Let that boy get to know his father and his *uncle*," she said with a wink, referring to Darius's lover, Bo Jenkins.

"You can't keep the boy away from his father," Hope agreed. "A child needs both parents."

"Yeah, well his *father* should have thought about that before he chose Bo over me."

Time had not dimmed Stacy's resentment of the way Darius chose to end his bigamous ways: remain married to his male lover and have his and Stacy's marriage annulled. It hadn't helped matters that his subsequent coming out didn't receive the backlash she hoped it would. Granted, it generated all types of controversy in religious circles and he wasn't getting as many requests to play in churches, but his concerts were selling out and his attempt to cross over into R & B was proving successful.

"Having a child is a blessing, Stacy," Hope said softly. "Don't miss out on the joy of it by holding on to anger. I'd do anything to have a baby right now. . . ."

Just then they were interrupted by a well-dressed man who stopped at their table. "Stacy Gray?" he asked.

"I'm Stacy," she replied.

"This is for you." He handed her a large envelope. "You've been served," he said brusquely, and quickly walked away.

"What the . . ." Stacy didn't even finish the sentence, but put down her drink and tore open the envelope. Her eyes scanned the papers quickly. "Oh my God, I don't believe this. I don't believe the man had this kind of nerve. He's out his mutha—"

"Calm down, Stacy," Hope interrupted, putting her hand on a woman who was about to go postal. "What is it?"

"It's Darius, acting like the asshole he is," Stacy responded, her eyes welling with tears. "That fool is taking me to court. He's suing me for full custody of my child!"

Don't miss Lutishia Lovely's
Sex in the Sanctuary
and
Love Like Hallelujah

Available now wherever books are sold!

From *Sex in the Sanctuary*

Mr. Snakeskin Boots

It squeezed her booty without apology. But that was only part of the beauty of a St. John suit. The other was its flawless design—its intricate stitching—its wrinkle-free fabric. The way it hugged every inch of her curved, firm body. She was a perfect St. John size six. Thirty-eight years and two children, still a perfect St. John size six and she was proud of it.

Vivian Elise Stanford Montgomery stepped back and briefly inspected her image in the mirror. She moved to the dresser and, pushing aside the two-carat-diamond studs, decided on the round ruby dangles with matching choker. The black onyx jewel setting provided a fitting backdrop to the precious stones and complemented the black piping around the jacket as if they had been designed specifically for the occasion.

The ruby and the black and the herringbone all worked to complement Vivian's unblemished, coffee-colored complexion. Well, coffee with a wee bit of cream. She'd been pretty her whole life, although she didn't always think so. It took Sistah Lillie and Brothah Benson's son Titus to convince her she was really pretty, worth a Snickers candy bar and the faux-pearl ring he got out of his Cracker Jack box, but that's another story. To this day she still wasn't sure whether Titus really thought she was pretty or if he just wanted her to play hide-and-go-get-it behind Brother Armstrong's toolshed, but again, that's another story. She could remember being in the Sunbeams and having the mothers of the church comment, "Ooh, ain't she a pretty little Black thang?"

Her shoulder-length black hair framed her face softly in a trendy flip style, a style that accented the Asian slant of her wide, brown eyes. Sitting at the vanity, she finished her make-up, adding just a hint of blush and a subtle layer of ruby red lipstick to her full, well-defined lips.

Vivian opened the set of double doors to her dressing room and grabbed a snazzy pair of Manolo Blahnik pumps, black with a patch of ruby and black herringbone fabric encased between the leather toe and heel. She slid into them effortlessly while eyeing the matching bag on the lower shelf. She glanced briefly at her watch, and amidst the dazzle of diamonds that caught the light from every direction was the message that she'd better hurry.

Crossing to the dresser, Vivian splashed on a generous amount of Spikenard, a present from her best friend Tai's most recent visit to the Holy Land. With one last glance in the full-length mirror, rather a stop-pivot-turn, stop-head-back-pivot-turn again, Vivian exited the spacious master bedroom and entered the hallway.

"Derrick! Elisia! Let's go!" She never stopped walking as she knocked on each child's door and headed for the stairway. She knew that Anastacia, the housekeeper and children's nanny, would have them dressed and ready to go. "We're down here, Mama!" yelled Elisia, all satin and lace. Derrick was sitting on the settee in the foyer, already looking like a deacon at the ripe old age of seven. Why did he insist on dressing like that? Because it made him look like his father, that was why, and his father was his hero.

His father, Dr. Derrick Anthony Montgomery, was many people's hero. Senior pastor of Los Angeles's latest soul-saving sensation, Kingdom Citizens' Christian Center, he was a preacher's son, preacher's preacher, scholar, teacher, much-sought-after conference speaker, and one of the finest brothers this side of glory. Vivian smiled as this last thought popped into her head. But how could she help it as she looked at her husband's spitting image, albeit thirty years younger, in front of her?

You know how people say when you meet your husband you'll know? Well, Vivian had that very experience when she laid eyes on D-2's daddy fifteen years ago. Lord! Where had the time gone? And why did the moment seem like yesterday?

It was back in her home state of Kansas at the Kewana Valley District's annual Baptist Convention. Vivian hadn't wanted to go. The only reason she, a twenty-one-year-old communications graduate on her way to becoming the first Black Barbara Walters, had agreed to revisit her old religious stomping grounds was because her best friend's husband was being installed as the new and youngest assistant moderator of the district, and her friend thought Vivian's attending would add a bit of "celebrity" to the affair.

Her best friend was Twyla "Tai" Nicole Brook. Vivian and Tai (so named because her goddaughter and namesake couldn't say Twyla; it always came out "tie-la," so they eventually settled on Aunt Tai, and the name stuck) had been friends since the ninth grade. That's when Vivian's father, Victor L. Stanford, had made a sizeable contribution to Kewana Valley District's Higher Learning Scholarship Fund, and in doing so had become even more important than his propensity for eloquent speech and impenetrable loyalty already afforded him. Her father had been invited to join the district's board, and shortly thereafter invited to a board meeting, family included, in the Florida Keys. Vivian dreaded the trip because she thought she'd have to endure a week of "old fogies" and was delighted when she met fourteen-year-old, auburn-haired, freckle-faced Twyla in the lobby of the posh Hilton Keys Hotel. They had run off to their rooms, donned modest two-piece swimsuits, headed to the beach, and shared lifetime secrets, dreams, and aspirations that only thirteen- and fourteen-year-old girls could share. They were fast friends from that very day, and even a hundred-mile distance—for that was how far they lived from each other at the time—could not separate them. They wrote each other every week and talked on the phone almost every day from the ninth grade through Vivian's first couple of years of college.

Just before her senior year in high school, Tai informed Vivian that she was getting married. Vivian was not surprised. Tai's singular goal after graduating was to become a wife and mother, and she had talked nonstop about King Wesley Brook from the moment she met him. She surmised after their first kiss that he would be her husband, and after their first unofficial date a short time later, a surreptitious meeting in the church parking lot during a midnight revival, said he would be the father of her children. She was right on both counts and became Mrs. King Wesley Brook shortly after her nineteenth birthday and six months before their first child, Michael Wesley Brook, was introduced to the world.

Tai had asked Vivian to deliver a motivational speech at the Saturday Night Youth Extravaganza. Vivian went to the Friday night services to gauge the type of crowd attending the meeting. She wasn't sure whether to be more spiritual, religious, or political. It was a fine line during this time, the '80s, and with her ever-increasing personal relationship with God and widening social and political views as a news correspondent, she was always walking that line.

She tried to sneak in after the devotional (which she found boring) and before the offering (where she wanted to be sure and give back to God). She excuse me'd down to the center of the pew three rows from the back and had just opened her program when the lady to the left tapped her and nodded toward an usher who was motioning for her to follow him. She looked around and saw Tai's widened eyes, which said "come *on*, girl," so she dutifully excuse me'd back down the row, avoiding a few angry eyes but not missing the "umph"s and "tsk"s of a few sisters before bowing her head and following Mr. Black-Suit-White-Shirt-Pinstriped-Tie down to the second row.

She barely had a chance to squeeze Tai's arm, giving her a little pinch, when she saw him. He came in with the pastors and others designated to participate in the evening's program. She was staring without knowing it and, even after she knew it, couldn't stop. She checked him out from the top of his s-curled, collar-length hair to the soles of his buffed and polished snakeskin boots. Snakeskin boots! Who was this brother?

"Who's Mr. Snakeskin Boots?" she hissed at Tai. Tai just smiled and rolled her eyes while rocking to the choir's fiery rendition of "Jesus Is a Rock." Vivian tried to regain her composure, but snakeskin boots had cooked her collards. He was wearing a dark navy, double-breasted suit that emphasized his broad shoulders which narrowed down—*can we say "vee"*—into a highly huggable waist and then fanned out, oh-so-slightly, to reveal a perfectly shaped, hard butt . . . Jesus! What was she thinking? And in the middle of church service, no less. Right in between "rock in a weary land" and "shelter in the time of storm." *Pull yourself together, girl!*

She tried to divert her eyes as he sat down and even joined Tai in a rock, clap, rock, clap as the choir bumped it up an octave. She threw in an "amen," raised her arms, and closed her eyes, trying to capture the image of Jesus as a rock. But all she could see was curly hair and snakeskin boots, and it was making her hot! She opened her eyes just in time to see Snakeskin staring at her intently. She closed her eyes again and tried to start singing, but since she didn't know the words, it just looked as if she were singing in tongues, and they didn't play that at the Baptist Convention in 1985! When she stole another peek Snakeskin was smiling broadly, as if he knew she'd been thinking of him.

Vivian was thankful when a lady two rows behind her got happy and started jumping up and screaming, "My Rock, my Rock!" That brought other members of the audience to their feet, and before she knew it Tai was on her feet, thankfully blocking Vivian's view of Snakeskin. About this time Tai's husband, King Wesley Brook, mounted the podium along with his father, the Reverend Doctor Pastor Bishop Overseer Mister Stanley Obadiah Meshach Brook Jr., Vivian's father, and a group of other board members. The song had reached a feverish pitch, and the choir was rocking, literally. Just before delivering the song's final verse, they paused. The choir, director with hand in midair, pianist, organist, drummer, lead singer—everybody stopped. It seemed everyone in the audience was frozen too, holding their breath, all except for the "happy" woman two rows back whose "My Rock!" had toned down to a quiet "Rock" between sobs as she was furiously fanned by two ushers in white. Oh, it was on now! The Holy Spirit was moving, people were remembering how Jesus had been their Rock, and there was shouting and crying and dancing going on all around. All that time the choir remained frozen, as did Vivian, but she for a totally different reason. Slowly the lead singer, a Karen Clark-like soprano-alto, sang the final line. She hit every note on the musical scale as she brought the song to its dramatic conclusion. Adding several syllables to each word, she belted out, "Jesus is my Rock."

The drummer started a roll on the snares, the guitarist held on to a string, the note reverberating in the air, the pianist and organist seemed to be in a competition as to who could hit the most keys in the shortest amount of time, and the lead singer had gone on a journey to find notes that heretofore had not been hit. The song never really ended. It just faded away. The lead singer started her own personal praise as she walked back to the choir loft, the musicians were in their own player praise, and the audience added their adorations to the Lord.

Vivian had sat there quiet and still, a small smile playing on her face as she felt the power of God. She stayed that way a long time, through the shouting and the clapping and the praise pause and the player praise. She opened her eyes when she heard the voice of a man that reminded her of her father's soothing tremor, but the voice was raspier, lighter. She cocked her head as she opened her eyes and stared into those of Snakeskin Boots himself, Derrick Anthony Montgomery.

"Are you ready to go?"
Vivian jumped, shaken from her walk down me-

mory lane. She was sitting in the living room, waiting for her husband to come down. And here he was in front of her, still melting her just like he did fifteen years ago when she watched him deliver his eloquent tribute to King Brook at the Kewana Valley District's Baptist Convention.

"Yes, I'm ready," she responded as she grabbed her purse and, rising from the couch, kissed him lightly on the mouth. They headed to the garage and the iridescent, pearl white Jaguar waiting there. They all settled in as Derrick hit the garage door opener, started the car, and drove down the long, winding driveway.

"King called," Derrick began after a brief silence.

"When?"

"Just now."

"Must have been important," Vivian pondered aloud. "He knows how busy Sunday mornings are. What did he want?"

Derrick's brow creased slightly as he tried to figure that out himself. "I don't know. I told him I'd call him later today, between services maybe."

Vivian leaned back and looked out the window. It was a beautiful Sunday in Los Angeles with clear blue skies, fluffy white cumulous clouds, and picture-perfect palm trees lining the streets. Her mind drifted to the conversation she and Tai had had a couple days ago. Tai had seemed unusually quiet and reserved, and when Vivian asked her if everything was okay, Tai had said she was just tired. Since they had four, Vivian had assumed it was the children. Now she was wondering if it was the kids, or something else?

From *Love Like Hallelujah*

I

Remember to Forget

Cy moved with calm precision, feeling perfectly at home among Victoria's Secret's wispy feminine apparel. Not the most traditional gift to give his soon-to-be wife, but Cy couldn't think of anything he'd rather see her in than a silky negligee, except her bare skin. He knew her body would show off to perfection the diamond necklace he'd just purchased at Tiffany's, and he wanted a delicious piece of lingerie to complement the eight-carat teardrop. He couldn't help but smile as he fingered the delicate fabrics of silk, satin, and lace, unmindful of the not-so-covert glances female shoppers slid his way. It hardly mattered. His fiancée, Hope Serenity Jones, had captured Cy's attention from the moment she'd appeared at the back entrance of Mount Zion Progressive Baptist Church, a piece of sanctified eye candy wrapped in a shimmering gold designer suit.

Female admirers ogled Cy as he continued his deliberate perusal. He stopped at a hanging negligee, red and pink flowers against a satiny white background. The top had thin spaghetti straps that held up a transparent gown hitting midthigh. The thong had an intricately designed rose vine for the string, a trail he would happily follow once it was on Hope, first with his fingers, then with his tongue. . . .

A perky, twenty-something salesclerk came over with a knowing smile. "Are roses your favorite flower?" she asked, flirting.

"They could become my favorite," Cy countered easily, "if worn on the right person."

"That's a very popular design," the salesperson offered, encouraging the purchase.

"I'll take it," Cy said as he casually handed the lingerie to her.

"Will this be all?" she asked, unconsciously moving closer to the live Adonis who had walked into the store and (blessings abound!) into her area.

"No, but I'll keep shopping on my own," Cy murmured as he eyed something on the other side of the store. The salesperson followed without thought. "I'll let you know if I need any help," Cy said with emphasis.

"No problem. I'm here if you need me." The salesclerk turned around, a look of regret barely concealed behind her cheery smile. Cy was oblivious to the wistful stares his six-foot-two frame elicited from the saleswoman and other shoppers. His naturally curly jet-black hair may have been hidden under a Lakers cap, but his raw sexuality was in plain sight. He had no idea that his sparkling white smile lit up the room like the noonday sun or that the dimple that flashed at the side of his grin was like a finger beckoning women closer.

Cy picked up a bra and panty set that had Hope's name written all over it. It was a soft, lacy, yellow number. The panty was designed like a pair of shorts—very short shorts—and Cy reacted physically as he thought of Hope's bubble booty filling them out. He quickly added this set to the black and beige more traditional sets he'd selected earlier.

While making his way to the perfume counter, another outfit caught his eye—the perfect backdrop for the diamond pendant. It was a lavender-colored sheer nightgown with matching floor-length jacket. The beauty was in its simplicity, and he smiled again as he thought of how Hope would look wearing this purple paradise. He held it up and closed his eyes, mentally picturing her ebony splendor wrapped luxuriously inside the soft material rubbing against her silken skin as he kissed her sweet lips.

Cy felt the presence of someone behind him. Figuring it was the attentive saleswoman, he turned to apologize for taking so long to make his decisions, and for the growing pile of lingerie she'd collected on his behalf. The smile died on his lips, however, as did the clever banter he'd thought to deliver as he completed the turn and stared into the eyes of the person he'd most like to remember to forget . . . Millicent Sims.

Or so he thought, initially. The woman could have been Millicent's twin sister; that's how much alike they looked. But after the initial shock subsided, Cy realized it wasn't she. The eyes were similar, but this woman's nose and lips were larger. Her face was a bit fuller, the cheekbones less prominent. One thing was definitely the same, though; the woman looked at him as if he were a chicken nugget and she the dipping sauce. He quickly excused himself and went around her, making a beeline for the cash register. A close encounter of the Millicent kind had cooled his shopping frenzy.

Moments later, he closed the rear door of his newly purchased BMW SUV. It had been hard to get him out of his Azure, but looking back it hadn't made sense for a Bentley to be his main driving vehicle. As the salesman had promised, Cy found the BMW to be a perfect ride for jetting around the city. He fired up the engine, hit the CD button, and zoomed out of the parking lot. The sounds of Luther Vandross's greatest hits, redone to perfection in snazzy jazz styles as a tribute to his memory, oozed out of the stereo. Cy bobbed his head as Mindi Abair got ridiculous with her alto sax version of "Stop to Love." As he crossed lanes and merged onto the 405 Interstate, his thoughts drifted back to Millicent. His heart had nearly stopped when he thought he saw her; it had been a while since she'd crossed his mind. He wondered how she was doing, where she was. Even after "the incident," he wished her well.

The incident. It had been a while since he'd thought about that too. But seeing Millicent's near twin in Victoria's Secret had brought the memories back with a vengeance. That crazy Sunday when, out of the blue, and in the middle of a regu-

where he saw the note as soon as he turned the corner:

> *Hey, Baby, tried to reach you on your cell. I'm with Frieda. Hollah.*
> *Love you, Hope*

He set down the packages, pulled the cell phone from his briefcase, and noted a couple of missed calls. Belatedly, he remembered how poor the cell phone reception was in some of the mall stores. Smiling, he hid Hope's honeymoon package in the closet and decided to fix a protein drink before calling his baby. Yes, Hope was the woman he wanted to be thinking about, the one he wanted on his mind. He hoped Millicent was happy, but she was his past. The woman occupying number one on his speed dial was his future.